I0676469

THE DEVIL'S DICTUM

Frederick Gero Heimbach

Copyright © 2015 by Frederic Gero Himebaugh.

All rights reserved. No part of this publication may be reproduced, distributed or transmitted in any form or by any means, including photocopying, recording, or other electronic or mechanical methods, without the prior written permission of the author, except in the case of brief quotations embodied in critical reviews and certain other noncommercial uses permitted by copyright law. For permission requests, write to the author at the email address below.

Frederick Gero Heimbach
handseyebrow@gmail.com

This is a work of fiction. Names, characters, places, and incidents are a product of the author's imagination or are used fictitiously. Any resemblance to actual people, living or dead, or to businesses, companies, events, institutions, or locales is completely coincidental.

Edited by Matthew B. Souders

Cover design by Milan Jovanovic

Book Layout ©2013 BookDesignTemplates.com

The Devil's Dictum / Frederick Gero Heimbach. -- 1st ed.
ISBN 978-0-9967974-0-5

A Satanic republic, if you can keep it.

—BEN FRANKLIN

Acknowledgements

No author is needier than the first-time novelist. I owe much to many, first to NaNoWriMo, which motivated me to write, rather impulsively, the first draft of the novel you hold in your hands.

I thank my beta readers: Kyle Andrews, Scott Danielson, Mike Hasey, Paul Hines, Robert Wade, and Logan Waterman. Among them are three whose contributions exceeded the call of duty: Andy Smith, Charles L. Weatherford, and John Earle. The final version was edited by a professional who has become a friend: Matthew Souders. Any remaining flaws are, naturally, the fault of my friend Victor Volkman.

I honor my sources of writerly advice, especially Writing Excuses, Critters.org, Joanna Penn, Joel Friedlander, the submissions guidelines of Clarkesworld Magazine, and my partner in pulp fiction crime, David Robison of the Round Table. One podcast, more than any other, launched me into the universe of fiction: StarShipSofa. Tony C. Smith: you are the wing that breaks my wind.

I'm grateful for the keen interest of my Facebook friends who follow my life and its implausible elements—aliens, Morlocks, corpses, and all that. Many are fine, upstanding people, oddly enough—the Facebook friends I mean; not the corpses. My family gave exactly what any writer needs most: support without indulgence.

Finally, I acknowledge the novels which provided a model, or excuse, for what I aspired to achieve in these pages: *Perdido Street Station, Anathem,* and above all *The Anubis Gates.*

PART THE FIRST:
1946

Definition

special master

n. 1) in law, a quasi-judicial officer appointed by a court to ensure judicial orders are carried out. 2) the personal assassin to the Chief Justice of the United States and *de facto* prime minister.

See also: master in chancery, master in lunacy, saintfinder general

CHAPTER ONE

Assassination

The Chief Justice liked his presidents crazy, but not too crazy. The current president was too crazy. The Chief wanted him dead, so the Special Master had to kill him. That was how things worked in the year of their Lord 1946.

The Special Master traversed the Portrait Gallery, the long hall connecting the White House proper to the Oval Office. He passed dead presidents, patriarchs of the nation. Why the scowling visages, the looks of contempt? They looked down, in both senses of the phrase, upon the Special Master from out of their oaken frames darkened by years.

Aaron Burr, the father of his country; James Buchanan, the greatest president; Woodrow Wilson, Hammer of the Haitians. How they hated the Special Master. Even lowly President Edgar Alan Poe, that old reprobate—he sneered as the Master slipped past.

A brown rat, a glutton by the look of him, emerged from an ill-fitted seam in a baseboard, attracted to an empty paper cup on the floor. The rat regarded the Master with a professional courtesy that reeked of sarcasm.

Some men called the Special Master the Chief Justice's personal assassin. That was an outrageous slander—the Master rarely killed people. Others called him the *de facto* Prime Minister. That was mere flattery—the Chief's administration was too disorganized for such clear division of labor. The Special Master handled special jobs; that is all.

The end of the not-quite-straight gallery came into view. A pinstripe of light defined the edges of a door too cockeyed to close properly. Beyond it, President Adolf Hitler labored over his mad conspiracies.

One normally does not speak of conspiracy regarding a man as friendless as Hitler. A conspirator needs co-conspirators, after all. But Hitler's mind contained multitudes. His mind was, all by itself, a loose affiliation, a secret society, a legion. Hitler, not to put too fine a point on it, was nerts.

An asymmetrical giggle leaked out of the office.

Yes. The Master need not question the Chief's order. President Hitler had lost his marbles. He had to go.

This was not assassination; this was sanitation. The Master's conscience was clear.

Small expressions of exasperation came from the Oval Office. There was another sound too, the sound of small, hard objects clattering against a wooden surface. Hitler was at his beloved maps, it would seem.

With a judicious hand sheathed in black silk, the Master eased open the door. He moved it with such precise slowness that even its rust-coated hinges did not creak. The guards sprawled at his feet did not challenge him, for they slept the sleep of the innocent.

The warm, yellow light of four blazing fireplaces illuminated every inch of the oval space. The Master felt the temperature change. The fires stifled the room in spite of drafts from missing panes in the huge window against the far wall.

Hitler stood with his back to the door. A few streaks of bird poop—fewer than one would expect—soiled the shoulders of his white uniform. He slouched over a massive oak table. His hand was in the air, shaking like an epileptic's. With a ridiculous flourish, he cast dice among tin soldiers standing at attention about the table.

The soldiers faced each other across continents. The vast table top was a world map of beautifully inlaid tropical wood. Was it imported from Haiti? Certainly it was beyond the skill of any domestic artisan.

The map was odd. Its continents were accurate, more or less, but the countries were given names and boundaries according to Hitler's fevered imagination. The Russian Empire was divided into never-existent lands with names like "Kamchatka" and "Irkutsk". Texas and California had been wrenched away from Mexico and returned to the United States.

The dice rolled to a stop and the old nut-cake pumped his fist with glee. On his right arm he wore a band emblazoned with a *svastika*, a broken cross he had appropriated from the American Indians. The Special Master had never learned what it meant, but the president was besotted by it. The svastika appeared everywhere one looked in the room, painted in red and black on the door, on the walls, woven into the carpet, and carved into the ceiling. It even threatened to usurp the Jolly Roger from its place on the U.S. flag.

That was going too far.

Hitler finished celebrating his lucky roll. With great relish, he flicked a forefinger once, twice, and a pair of enemy tin soldiers fell onto their backs. He slid five of his own tin soldiers into the now vacant territory.

Hitler rubbed his hands together. He sucked in a breath, considering his next move.

You have not long to live, Mr. President.

The Master pulled the black cloth belt from around his waist. Whether it made a sound, or a reflection in the window betrayed him, the Master did not know, but at that moment, the president stiffened. His crooked shoulders flinched. Then they slumped.

Two men, one old and broken, the other young and raven-plumed, breathed suffocating air in that historic room.

Moving without the slightest haste, the president put down his dice and walked—no, he *processed*—from the table to the tall window at the far end of the room. Even now, he did not look back.

"You know why," he said, with a catch in his breath as the only betrayal of his terror, "they gave me an office that's oval?"

Because there are no corners–

"No corners!" shouted the president, whirling around, his blue eyes ignited by the firelight. His ridiculous little "tooth brush" mustache was the bull's eye at the center of his furious face.

"No corners! Ha ha!" Hitler threw up his hands, waving them about, inviting the Special Master to observe for himself the incontrovertible truth of the office's corner-lacking status. "And if there are no corners, what cannot I be? I ask you: what cannot I be?"

Cornered—

"Cornered! I cannot be, ha ha, cornered!"

The president bolted.

The Special Master pounced.

No contest.

The President's past tenure in the House of Representatives had done its destructive work. His health was broken. An arm was partially paralyzed. Half his face drooped. The rest twitched. Corners or no, the President was trapped.

The Special Master seized a lapel of the dotard's white coat with one hand and the tails of his western bow tie with the other. He lifted the lunatic right off the floor and flung him upon the table without gentleness. The tin soldiers spun off the edge, routed.

Hitler put up no fight. He turned his face away, looked into the nocturnal murk of the vast window, and frowned.

"America is weak. She is not *worthy*. We could have accomplished great things. She could have been my *bride*."

What was this nut beating his gums about?

Hitler's oration continued. "We could have taken Texas back. We could have beaten Mexico. We could have conquered Canada. We could have bombed the France!"

"Everybody wants to bomb the France. Nobody ever does it."

Hitler turned his face to the other side of the room, still not meeting the Master's gaze. He looked instead to the mantelpiece, at the portrait of Aaron Burr astride his war goat.

"A cynic? I'm surprised at you, *Special Master*. I thought the blood of heroes flowed through your veins."

What was Hitler's outfit called? The Anti-Fascist Party? The Americanism Party? It was so hard to keep track.

Slowly, with all due caution, Hitler reached across the table. He opened a small tin there, dabbed his fingers in the greasy substance, and smeared black lines of it across his face.

"I hoped you would become the progenitor of a new race. The new Americans. Supermen!"

Pathetic. This bag of bones is not worth killing.

What would Burr do? The Master looked where Hitler was looking. He saw Burr's hauteur. He saw that disapproving scowl, and felt it, not the blazing fire, scorch his shamed face.

This old man was not dangerous crazy. He was pathetic crazy. His body twitched in the Master's hands, uncontrollably. With his dandruff-shedding hair in disarray, he looked helpless. Balled up. Old.

This assassination was a mistake.

"You are the prototype of the new Red Indian", Hitler whispered, almost daring to touch a dab of war paint on the Master's face. "A mighty race dwelt here for millions of years before the European arrived. *Millions of years...*"

His many addled minds lost the thread of their argument as they vied for control of his voice and face. His eyes darted about, then latched onto a spot on the wall where hung a needlepoint svastika with the motto "Home Sweet Home."

"The Hindus certainly knew what the svastika meant. The Navajo knew. *How is it we forgot?*"

The Master's grip on the president's white lapels loosened. If this was not a justified execution, then what was it? What was he?

Murder. Murderer.

Hitler squirmed in the Master's grip.

With a practiced twist of the wrist, the Master formed a small lariat with his belt. A moment later, he had it around the president's wrists. This killing might be wrong, but that was for the Chief, not the Special Master, to decide. This president was going to die and there would be no more second-guessing.

"By order of His Honor, the Chief Justice of the United States," the Special Master gasped, "I remove you from office." He looked up and bellowed with the voice of an unclean spirit. "Abaddon!"

The window panes exploded into a million jagged shards. Clearly, their makers never heard the word *safety*. Through broken mullions and shredded curtains came a black flurry of flapping wings and deafening recitations of "Rok rok!"

Mighty Abaddon, Lord of Ravens and Harbinger of Armageddon, preceded his conspiracy through the window. Dozens of ravens bore in their talons a taxi, a platform of balsa wood on a frame of aluminum. At the Master's command, the ravens dropped their burden down on the table, right on top of the president.

"Oof," commented Hitler.

"Up," said the Special Master. "Chief's orders."

Parchments scattered among the whirlwinds conjured by the winter breezes and the conspiracy's redoubled flappings. One errant sheet momentarily provided welcome modesty to a muscular bronze nude resplendent in a Cheyenne war bonnet by wrapping itself around the statue's loins. The few tin soldiers still standing wobbled as the raven taxi levitated and the dust of the carpet rose in protest.

The Special Master tossed the president like a sack of sweet potatoes onto the taxi's narrow platform and joined him there.

The birds dared not soil the Master's immaculate black robe. The president, however, received no such respect. Ravens pooped on Hitler as his struggles moved him into their respective lines of fire. They did it with *brio*, with zest. His white suit mostly absorbed the blotches but his face became a mess. Poop painted his cheeks, his hair, and that narrow little mustache.

No protest could escape his mouth since he dare not open it.

The taxi and its two passengers lurched and veered within the confining oval until the ravens found their equilibrium. They shot through the wrecked window into the chill night.

The open air was the ravens' element. They celebrated their strength with joyous rokking and they rained down on the hapless president a seemingly endless supply of poop. The White House receded beneath them until its crumbling spires, turrets, crenellations, belvederes, dormers, smokestacks, cornices, windmills, gables, radio masts, porticoes, pneumatic tubes, moats, tie rods, buttresses, bays, towers, columns, and ruins beyond recognition lost their power to overawe.

To the southeast, pearlescent mists haunted the Capitol dome, glowing asymmetrically under a full moon illumed with madness.

The ravens ignored the fearsome sight, their faces set as flint toward the tallest structure of the city—the Burr Monument.

When new, it was simply an obelisk. Its architect had disdained the antecedents of Christian Europe and took inspiration in the morbid gods of Egypt. Later generations did not respect his austere vision, however, and a likeness of Aaron Burr's leering face was added in stucco and gold leaf. A generation later, inspired by misguided piety, they planted a single demonic horn of iron to the Burrian forehead. (Some said that a corrupt contractor had alloyed the iron with clay.) Over the years, the foundation sank in the mud and cracks appeared up and down the column, so men shored up the monument with wooden scaffolding. And when *that* weakened, they added a second scaffold to shore up the first.

Stone, stucco, rust, rot: the metaphor was not wasted on historians. The United States of America—the first and only satanic republic—was in deep decline.

"Rok!" commanded Abaddon, and his raven minions redoubled their efforts. They lifted the taxi and its two riders high above the Monument, centering them above the needle tip of Burr's horn. The Special Master yanked the president of the United States to the platform's edge.

"I'll vomit," said Hitler. His whole body was stiff as a board.

The Special Master hesitated. Pity once more stayed his hand.

Burr's monstrous eyes goggled up at him. *Weak!*

Abaddon squinted down on him. *Soft!*

The Special Master flung President Hitler over the edge and dangled him there by the black belt. Its fibers groaned as they tore under the strain.

"No...corners!" the president screamed.

Satan! Is he still stuck on that? Maybe the Chief was right.

One little twist of the Master's wrist and Hitler would fall. The president hung by the thread of the Master's remorse. It was a thin thread indeed.

The president surveyed the city, spread below him.

"So much to do. But the Americans—not up to it."

"Quit yammering."

The president's head jerked up and he looked straight into the Master's eyes. A comprehension, bordering on sanity, softened his expression. He smiled. His voice rang clear and strong.

"You know it, don't you? You're a better man than him."

That tore it.

The president's body fell upon the tip of his predecessor's horn. It convulsed as the spirit went to go be with Satan.

With an impatient gesture, the Special Master ordered Abaddon away. The conspiracy did not obey. Ravens are not known for their fine sense of proportion, and they doubled back to paint the body of President Adolf Hitler with one final layer of poop where it hung, spread-eagled and bloody, high above the city over which he had presumed to preside.

And only then did the raven taxi descend in smug, helical turns to the earth.

The Special Master wiped his feet on the dusting of snow on the Mall while the birds folded their wings. The Master's careful inspection confirmed his pure black robe was spotless.

What was that look Abaddon was giving him? Was it...*approval?*

"Why the wait?" the Master asked Abaddon. "Let's go home."

"Rok rok!" screamed the great black bird.

"What's that, boy? Orders from the Chief?"

Abaddon extended a leg. To it, a parchment was tied by a leather thong. The Master unfolded it. The unsigned message was simple:

CONVOKE THE NINE

The Presidents

From *Paper Placemat*, The Bobby-Q Diner, Elkhart, Assen.

The Presidents of the United States of America

Presidential elections occur by law in years divisible by four. The law also provides for a transition period before the president elect's term begins, but expediency generally dictates that the winner of an election assume office de facto *immediately upon announcement of the results, often accompanied by an armed mob of supporters. This list follows the convention of holding a presidential term to begin in the year of the election.*

A surprising number of presidents died in office. While it is true that the political culture of the United States has been treacherous at times, one should also remember that the life expectancy in the U.S. is less than that of most other countries. This fact brought on the Qualification Crisis sooner than otherwise.

(1780 Alexander Hamilton)

Duly elected, Hamilton defeated Burr in a landslide, but his one day in office is generally not mentioned in lists of presidential terms. Sometimes called the "Zeroeth President", in contrast to Burr as the "First President."

1780 Aaron Burr

First President and Father of our Country. He always places in the top
two or three in rankings of presidential greatness.

1796 Benedict Arnold

The death of Burr reintroduced regular elections. Arnold's surrender-
ing the office to his successor established the *Era of Regular Presidential
Succession.*

1800 Elbridge Gerry

Legal scholar. Successfully repelled the First Haitian Invasion.

1808 Donatien-Alphonse-François, Comte de Sade

Also held high positions within the Church. Often described as the
precursor to Poe. De Sade was a polarizing figure who served only
one term and had trouble staffing his cabinet.

1812 Franz Anton Mesmer

A man of superb political skills. His term in office was characterized
by few tangible accomplishments.

1816 William Hull

The soldier-president. Hero of the Wars of 1812, 1813, and 1815.

1820 Charles Redheffer

Established the patent office. Successfully repelled the Second Haitian
Invasion.

1824 Johann Gaspar Spurzheim

Established the "Spurzheim Test" for public office. The unsolved "Uncle Sam" murders began here and have continued to this day.

1832 James Bowie

War Hero. Elected in a landslide due to his role in the Second Haitian Invasion. Died in March of 1836 when he fell on a kitchen knife.

1836 Edmund Ruffin

Bowie's running mate. Assumed office after Bowie's death. Claimed to have fired the first shot against Canada in the war of 1815.

1841 Andrew Pickens Butler

Ruffin's running mate. A controversial figure, he was blamed for the death of Ruffin. Called a "pimp for marriage" by members of James Buchanan's Reform Party.

1848 Edgar Allen Poe

His one tumultuous year in office saw the failure of the Poe Act (which would have lowered the legal age of marriage to 12) and the crash of a hot air balloon intended to reach the moon. Scandals led to his murder, and that of his vice president, at the hands of a mob.

1849 James Buchanan

The "Bachelor President." The only Speaker-President until 1920. Brought healing to the nation by implementing the *Great Reformation*. Commonly ranked as the greatest president.

1856 Andrew Johnson

Buchanan's hand-picked successor consolidated his reforms in a successful presidency characterized by comity, competence and relative sobriety.

1860 John Wilkes Booth

The "Actor President", a beloved but ultimately tragic figure. During his term, an epidemic of the scratch, or possibly the itch, killed the last surviving American Indians.

1863 George W. L. Bickley

Booth's vice president. Promoted the "Golden Circle", a grandiose and ineffectual plan to annex much of the Western Hemisphere.

1868 Millard Fillmore

Initiated the *Era of Bad Feeling*. Attempted to halt all immigration, which was widely seen as "suicidal".

1872 George McClelland

Promoted William H. Mumler in the Church hierarchy. Lost California to the President of Mexico in a game of correspondence poker. Failed to halt the currency crisis begun under President Fillmore.

1876 William "Boss" Tweed

A brilliant political tactician. He was suspected of secret membership in the heretical Masonic Lodge. His early death from pneumonia, or possibly the scum, prevented him from fulfilling his promise.

1878 Napoleon Bonaparte III

Tweed's vice president. His adventures in the west permanently lost Texas to Mexico. Sparred repeatedly with the influential High Priest Friedrich Nietzsche.

1880 P.T. Barnum

Presided over the "Phony War" wherein U.S. armies supposedly reclaimed Texas and California. The lie was exposed on the eve of the 1884 election.

1884 Jefferson Davis

Successfully repelled the Third Haitian Invasion and became the first president since Spurzheim to survive two terms in office. Suppressed the heresy led by the charismatic lay preacher known by the occultical pseudonym of "Mark Twain."

1892 John Ernst Worrell Keely

Began the *Era of the Feeble Old Men.* Although not especially old himself when elected, he died in office of pneumonia, or possibly the hacks. Promoted government research into "etheric" force. Founded Liberia as an independent republic centered on the Great Salt Lake during his administration.

1898 Belle Boyd

Keely's running mate. Suffered many outrageous slanders throughout his career: "Mexican spy", "actor", and—probably because of his odd name—"woman". He died of a heart attack shortly before the end of his term.

1900 Frédéric Auguste Bartholdi

Appointed vice president by Boyd. The most vigorous of the "Feeble Old Men", despite suffering from tuberculosis. In the only successful foreign action in U.S. military history, he "Kidnapped" the "Statue of Liberty" from a warehouse in Haiti and installed it as the Statue of

Licentiousness in New Gehenna Harbor and repelled the resulting Fourth Haitian Invasion. He died just before the election of 1904.

1904 William Alexander Ayton

Bartholdi's running mate. A former priest pressed into political office despite being over 90 when he became president (a prodigious age by American standards). An alchemy enthusiast, he had no notable accomplishments.

1909 Bass Reeves

Appointed vice president by Ayton. The only president with African ancestors. The declining pool of qualified candidates for presidential office (the *Qualification Crisis*) enabled him to take office despite widespread resistance. He suppressed the *Revolt of the Iconoclasts.*

1910 Samuel Liddell MacGregor Mathers

Appointed vice president by Reeves. Defeated by Wilson in the election of 1912 but served as the last U.S. vice president until death in 1918, after which the U.S. Senate could not convene.

1912 Woodrow Wilson

The last native born president. Nearly the last person documented to have been born on U.S. soil. Resolved the Qualification Crisis in 1919 without recourse to Constitutional Amendment by proposing presidential ascension via the House Speakership, thus ending presidential elections. Completed the *Liberia Migration* in reaction to the Reeves presidency. Initially popular, his incapacity due to a stroke and the loss of Orlando in the Fifth Haitian Invasion tarnished his legacy.

1920 Aleister Crowley

First president of the *Era of the Speaker-Presidents.* Tried to combine the office of President and High Priest and subsequently died under mysterious circumstances.

1923 William Joseph Simmons

Often thought of as a priest, mistakenly. He enjoyed dressing in priestly vestments but was never formally ordained. Second speaker-president of the modern era and first president of the *Judiciocracy.*

1927 Willis C. Hawley

Widely regarded as insane. No accomplishments.

1930 Nicola Sacco

Widely regarded as insane. No accomplishments.

1932 Bartolomeo Vanzetti

Widely regarded as insane. No accomplishments.

1935 Boris Karloff

Widely regarded as insane. No accomplishments.

1939 Charles Coughlin

Widely regarded as insane. No accomplishments.

1941 Benito Mussolini

Widely regarded as insane. No accomplishments.

1945 Joseph Raymond McCarthy

Widely regarded as insane. No accomplishments.

1945 Earl Lauer Butz

Widely regarded as insane. No accomplishments.

1945 Wilbur Daigh Mills

Widely regarded as insane. No accomplishments.

1946 Adolf Hitler

Widely regarded as insane. No accomplishments.

1946 Gus Hall

Widely regarded as insane. Repelled the Sixth Haitian Invasion. First President of the *Vice Presidentocracy.*

CHAPTER TWO

The Nine

The townhouse stood in Aarontown's most exclusive neighborhood. Its lawn was a mean patch of frozen dirt but the Special Master somersaulted off the platform to land on it dead center. A herd of browns—that is, ordinary citizens—scurried to the iron gate. They had seen the taxi in the sky and guessed, correctly, that a black—that is, a court official—was on it. They waved petitions and shouted summaries of their pleas in twenty-five words or less.

The Special Master ignored them.

Abaddon's conspiracy released the taxi burdened with six blacks tacked on its platform. Nearly all the blacks were alive. The ravens scattered about to forage among the thistles and burdocks, to pick the ground clean of every scrap of garbage and to harvest small animals, alive or dead. The Master left them to their reward and kicked open the front door.

An elderly butler was in the hallway almost immediately. The Master brushed him aside and went directly to the parlor. It was very late now and the room was dark and cold, yet in the wingback chair, a man of early middle age sat brooding: Associate Justice William O. Douglas.

His dentures were in. He knew the Master was coming.

What was that slight movement of air within this sepulcher of a room? There: the window, open by the slightest crack. No doubt a raven was here, moments ago, with the warning.

"Welcome, Master, to my humble abode. To what do I owe this unexpected pleasure?" The justice did not waste effort on an ironic smirk.

"His Honor, the Chief Justice, sends his compliments, and respectfully requests the honor of your honor—"

"Bah!"

Well, that's different.

The Special Master began again. "He respectfully requests—"

Justice Douglas stood.

"Kindly shove the Chief's 'respectful request' right up—"

Unacceptable.

Like lightning, the Master's belt—what was left of it—looped around Douglas' hands.

The justice, recoiling, tripped on the hem of his robe and landed flat on his back. The Special Master pinned him with a foot before he could roll away. In seconds, the Master had the justice bound and lifted onto his back.

Back to the lawn. The brambles, poison ivy, and Harry Lauder's walking sticks seemed to come alive as ravens emerged from them to find their places on the aluminum frame. Beneath them squirmed six blacks, all of them justices.

The Master dropped Douglas beside them and jumped on board.

"The Court! Hi-ya!"

"Rok!" Dozens of raven wings smote the air as one. The overloaded taxi rose into the night air.

A tumbleweed, an invader from the deserts of the Midwest, rolled down the now-empty street. The brick pavers, halfheartedly maintained, looked like the grin of a gap-toothed petitioner with naught but a gutter's worth of broken whiskey bottles and rusty snuff tins to offer for bribes.

The atmosphere above the capital city of Burrsburg lacked all warmth or light on this early February night, and at this height even the homey smells of the city could not reach him, but the Special Master had his orders and his ravens sped their charges through the frigid air toward the home of the Supreme Court.

The building's facade was designed to overawe, but from a point hundreds of feet above it, its columned portico could not pull off the effect. Skulls may terrify up close but at a distance they are simply melancholy.

The taxi descended and hovered just above the plaza. The clerks on guard came to attention. This close, the Master could recognize them. He was their boss and so not exactly their friend, but he mixed with them daily. He could not remember their names, being terrible at that sort of thing, but seeing the young men with their sharp, military bearing filled him with fatherly affection.

All clerks wore a kind of tight, tall loin cloth, completely black, that ran from armpit to mid-shin. It held the body stiff and tall, but interfered with walking. The clerks chosen to stand before the door were fine, muscular specimens without any missing ears or noses. With feet shod in black leather, they looked like exclamation points, imperatives for the decisions of the Chief Justice.

The Special Master's robe was like a judge's, but without the excess cloth, so it showed off his fine, athletic build. It had billowing sleeves, however; sometimes it is best that others not see your arms moving.

The columns of the court towered like a forest of pale marble. Their capitals were a demonic parody of the Corinthian style, crowned with thorns and painted with the bright red of sacrificial blood. The columns were not fluted but polished mirror-smooth, and plump in the middle. To foreigners, they would have looked pregnant. The locals more likely saw them as the wan ghosts of greasy sausages.

The ravens settled the taxi gently on the pavement. Their passengers may have been prisoners, but they were high ranking prisoners, and the birds were trained to give them respect.

The plaza was level and smooth, kept that way by the continual maintenance. For residents of the capital, used to sloping floors and heaving streets riding the waves of the capital's boggy topography, the plaza's crisp, orthogonal lines were disorienting.

Clerks, with deft moves, unloaded the associate justices like so many grunting sacks of turnips. Experience taught the clerks that if they loosened the ropes and gags here, they would be repaid with curses and sharp elbows, so they left them tied. What could the justices do? Sue them?

Two clerks opened the bronze doors adorned with a bas-relief of Charon presenting a boatload of condemned criminals to Hades. The others formed a procession. The Special Master led them as they carried the squirming justices into the building.

They passed in silence through the Great Hall. They passed, without a glance, the heads of former Chief Justices, each one pickled and mounted in a niche. They ignored the ugly painting of the current Chief in the last niche. Their lines diverged to flow around the crude, crumbling statue of the previous Special Master that dominated the space.

Onward they went, the Master striding and the clerks waddling in their knock-kneed way to keep up. They passed through another set of doors, these of oak and darkened by time and blood, which led directly into the High Courtroom.

Raven Taxis

From *My Country, Right or Wrong: Civics for the Future Citizen*, Chapter 7, "A Visit to the Capital City"; Sidebar, "Raven Taxis", p. 92

Burrsburg has a marvelous mode of public transportation introduced by none other than the Chief Justice. It has proved so popular that other cities are rushing to adopt it. It is the raven taxi.

The Chief Justice spent his first apprenticeship on a livestock farm. He made pets of ravens and found that they could carry a person through the air, if only they were trained to work together. He devised a lightweight frame made of Haitian aluminum and balsa wood, and taught a conspiracy (that means a "flock") to carry it.

Imagine how amazed his teachers and friends were when the Chief Justice, still a youth, flew through the air for the first time! The idea caught on and, today, many raveneries exist throughout the United States. Some people believe raven taxis may even spread to other countries and replace the noisy and dangerous airplanes that are popular there.

The capital has many public taxis. Most people stick to the regular routes, although a few very important people, namely justices and clerks of the Supreme Court, have taxis with smart birds that can go wherever the passenger asks.

If you ever find yourself in the capital and want to try a taxi (and can afford it), the following will explain how.

First, find a convenient taxi stand. Look for a small shelter marked "TAXI" in bright blue letters. Purchase a ticket from the man in the booth. Some people report that booths are not always manned during the hours posted, but don't get discouraged! Taxi stands are found in many convenient locations. You should have no trouble purchasing your ticket.

Each stand has a flag pole on top of it. If you are the first person to wait at the stand, make sure to raise the flag. This tells the high-flying birds you need them to stop. If you forget the flag, don't be surprised if no taxi stops to pick you up!

Some people report that some taxi stands lack a working flag, or that some stands are rarely used by locals and so are ignored by ravens. The Capital Raven Taxi Authority has a reputation for efficiency and superb customer service, but we recommend you ask a local for advice as to which stands are actually used.

Much has also been said of the "color code" that supposedly governs who may use capital taxis. Ignore this talk. Taxis are public transportation available to anybody who can buy a ticket. You will notice, in fact, that very few people in the capital wear the color brown. Brown is an unpopular color, and so there are no "browns". (We especially urge you to avoid using that term, or referring to anybody as a color, even black, white or red—those colors thought to be complimentary.)

When the taxi arrives, do not hesitate to board. Ravens will not wait for you. If someone else is waiting with you, let them board first so you can watch, but in any case, it's easy, and few people ever fall during boarding.

To board the taxi, grasp the side of the low-hanging U-shaped aluminum tube and step onto it. Do not wait for it to touch the ground, which it might not do. Waiting for the taxi to touch down is the biggest cause of embarrassment for first-time riders.

In the middle of the U, you will see a short horizontal aluminum piece. This is the U step. Use it to step higher as you grasp the side rails of the platform and then step into the platform.

Newcomers tend to hesitate before stepping up to the platform. Do not make this mistake. The taxi will be ascending rapidly from the moment you step on it. The platform is the safest place to be when the taxi is in the air. Fear of heights will prevent you from climbing up to safety if you do not do it immediately. Newcomers who remain clinging to the U during flight cause an inconvenience to fellow passengers and the ravens. Do not be that person.

Sometimes a U step will have broken off. Use the one on the other side in that case. If both are broken, you will need to pull yourself up with your arms alone. Residents of the capital are used to this; non-residents are urged to practice pull-ups before their visit. Alternately, you can decide to skip boarding a taxi without U steps and wait for another to come along. Beware, however: if you are alone at the stand and refuse a taxi, you have inconvenienced the birds by asking them to descend for no reason. Be prepared to take what shelter you may in that case. Rumors about the birds' dirty habits are true: capital ravens are short-tempered and will poop on anybody who displeases them.

The curtains are intended to shield passengers from the cold air, not to provide privacy. They degrade the aerodynamics, so the ravens dislike them. Newcomers should not use them except on the coldest days.

Regarding raven poop: even if you do not provoke the birds' ire, some droppings are likely to land on you during a ride. This is normal. Consider it a badge of distinction, since many cannot afford to ride taxis. Do not ever wear white as a counter-measure. Status is a closely-watched aspect of capital life. Sanctions against those who violate the complex code of norms are informal, yet no less harsh. Better to avoid controversy completely and wear ordinary colors (but not brown!) instead of adopting an affectation that might land you face-down in the mud of some back alley—or worse.

CHAPTER THREE

Fratricide

There was a time when the Courtroom had contained a few rows of chairs for the public. These had long since been removed, as the justices could not hear lawyers arguing over the shouts of the rabble. Later, the practice of oral arguments became viewed as a historical curiosity and was discontinued. Now, under the present Chief Justice, some have said even the office of associate justice was a historical curiosity.

The clerks dumped the associate justices on the floor and released them with a few precise slashes of knives. The justices kicked at them with a viciousness quite unbecoming of "historical curiosities."

The clerks arranged themselves in a circle about the room. The electric lights were dimmed, and the fire in the hearth was extinguished. Each clerk took up a lit jack-o'-lantern, so that thirteen leering devil's heads provided the only illumination. Somebody began humming a low, growling note and the rest took up a pitch at the upper limit of the male falsetto, the eleventh harmonic above. It was the tritone, the *diabolus in musica*. This infernal hum continued throughout the meeting.

The associate justices took their places—or in the case of Justice Taft, was placed—behind the lesser chairs at the bench. One of the eight remained unoccupied.

The Chief Justice made his entrance.

His robe was a velvety expanse of the deepest, most luxurious black. Your soul could fall into that lightless void and never come out. As the Chief had put on weight in his late middle age, there was a lot of void to fall into.

A fly crawled into the eye socket of Justice Taft. Such irritants had gone unnoticed by Taft for 16 years, which was how long he had been dead.

"Oyez! Oyez! Oyez! All persons having business before the Honorable, the Supreme Court of the United States, are admonished to depart, for the Court is now sitting. Satan save the United States and this Honorable Court!"

"Eh, whatever," intoned the Chief as he struck his platinum gavel on the bench.

The justices took their seats. The Chief put on his grave face.

"Before we begin, it is my sad duty to report..." began the Chief. He nodded at the Master.

"...at 12:15 this morning," continued the Special Master, pretending to rely on notes, "President Adolf Hitler was found dead by apparent suicide. The office of President is vacant."

The associate justices showed no surprise, although Justice Douglas did rouse himself sufficiently to roll his eyes.

"The Chief Justice expresses his deep—"

"Can we get to the main event?" That was Justice Douglas. Of course.

"—expresses his deep sorrow in response—"

"Surely we're not sitting here in the middle of the night to discuss something as trivial as the replacement of one stale fruitcake for another."

The Chief Justice slammed his gavel. "Be silent, fool, and all your answers will be questioned," he hissed, mixing up his words as he tended to do when drunk. "Pray continue," he told the Master, pressing trembling fingers against his forehead, "and dispense with the formalities. My associates suffer from the enfeeblements of advanced age."

"Very well," said the Master, standing directly in front of Douglas. "The Electoral College will convene."

"And nothing will come of it."

"They'll seek a new president. We have to make sure that, as you say, 'nothing comes of it.'"

"Why should this time be different?"

It occurred to the Master that he did not know the answer to that question.

"There are—" The Chief said, taking direct control. "There are *threats*. I hear *whisperings*."

He scowled. He licked his lips ponderously. His eyes darted about, searching the deep shadows in the corners of the room.

"There is a *malignancy*—on the body politic."

(A malignancy? The clerks' hum got louder. These meetings were never this entertaining.)

"Fortunately, I have coursed a devise of action. Tonight I will share you with it."

He faltered, almost noticing his garbled words, then regrouped. He stood abruptly. The others forgot to do likewise. The Chief pointed upwards melodramatically.

"Bring forth the prisoner!"

There was a shuffling in the robing room. Four clerks with drawn pistols herded a man, a common brown, into the center of the court-room. The senior clerk, H. L. Mencken, was in charge.

The prisoner was bound, excessively so, and gagged. His face was puffy and raw from a beating. He peered out of eyelids swollen to slits. The Master could guess which of the four clerks had volunteered to beat him—that bastard Mencken.

"Look at him, everyone," said the Chief. "Look at this miserable traitor!"

Satan's hairy buttocks! What is the meaning of this?

The prisoner was a stranger—and yet, he was so familiar. He looked to be about the Master's age—mid 30s. He had the same jet black hair, athletic build, and innocent good looks.

The prisoner could have been the Master's identical twin.

Why...? What...?

The Chief had not told the Master about this arrest. The Chief always told the Master everything.

Bless it! Had the Chief found out about the knife?

Show no fear. From head to hands to feet, the Master relaxed him-self, assuming an expression of calm bemusement. He approached the bench.

"It's a bad business," said the Chief, anticipating the question. He leaned forward for a private word. The Master smelled beer on the Chief's breath.

Good; it's not liquor.

"I'm watching you." The Chief's stage whisper concealed nothing. "Show me whose side you're on."

Whose side? What is this? Has the old man lost his mind?

The associates were making no attempt to hide their consternation. Even Justice Douglas could not maintain his insouciance.

"Kill him."

The Master blinked. Had he heard right? The order was a mere grunt—

"You heard me, Special Master," said the Chief, his voice loud enough to fill the corners of the room. "This man is a traitor. You have a knife. Use it."

The Chief was watching the Master carefully. He was expecting the Master to resist. He was enjoying this.

Satan! What can I do?

The Master took out his knife. He had modified it only recently. He had been careful, working in secret. He had tested it on the smooth, round bellies of a few of the largest tunnel rats, but he had not expected to use it for the first time in this room, with so many eyes so close at hand. Praise Hell that the light was dim.

"We are waiting!"

The Master did not know what the Chief was up to, but he had to pass this test.

"Lay him on the ground," the Master ordered. Best not have him fall. There was no way he would fall convincingly without prior warning.

The Master fell upon the prisoner's chest. What look could he give this man that would communicate his intent?

No waiting.

Under the canopy of his voluminous sleeve, the Master flipped the switch at the base of the hilt. He touched the tip of the blade to the man's chest. In that brief hesitating moment, the man's helpless body stiffened.

He pressed the hilt right down to the prisoner's chest. The man lost his bowel and bladder. His terror, at least, was genuine.

Blood spread in a modest patch, bright against the brown's buckskin jacket. Freed by the switch, the spring-loaded blade had slid into the hilt, simultaneously opening a reservoir of fake blood.

The surprise on the man's face was a close approximation of a death convulsion, and afterward the man had enough wit to close his eyes and lay still. Hell's mercy for that.

The four clerks removed the body. The Master wrapped his knife in a black silk kerchief. There was no stain on him.

The Master presented himself before the Chief. The Chief regarded the Master with a strange, horrifying grin, as if the Chief were surprised, disappointed, disgusted and elated all at the same time.

"There. You see, gentlemen?" said the Chief Justice, addressing the associates, "What we have here is a study in contrasts. A study in *contrasts.*"

The Chief paused, as if this were a great witticism.

"On the one hand, treason, and on the other"—here he gestured expansively to the Master—"unquestioning loyalty."

Thank Hell. He did not suspect.

If those words calmed the Master, they got quite the opposite reaction from the associates. The room erupted in exasperated cries. Some swore, some quoted the penal code, some simply moaned with disbelief. In Douglas' eye there was something else, something hard to determine in this light—something predatory.

"Order!" The Chief banged his gavel, striking the heavily scarred bench.

"Could somebody please explain to me what the *shee-it* just happened?"

Justice Douglas' vulgarity was out of place in that room. His fear, and wooden dentures, accented the sibilant.

"Silence!" roared the Chief.

"No. By the Obsidian Throne, *no!* You treat us like trash. Now you want us to sit quietly through this travesty? No, by Satan, maybe the others will bow to you, but I will not!"

The Chief smiled.

"Look around, Mr. Douglas. How many justices are here? And how many chairs?"

"Learned Hand is missing. We know all about it. You murdered him. Same as you murdered Crowley. What's your point?"

The Chief's smile did not waver.

"Please, look around some more. How many robing rooms do you see?"

Another rhetorical question. Douglas did not answer.

"I would like my esteemed associates to see the contents of the second robing room. Special Master, will you indulge us?"

(The tritone swelled. This night would be discussed in the clerks' dormitory for months.)

This was the Chief's ace. Having held it up his sleeve so long, he must have a very good reason to play it now. The Master had no idea what that reason was.

Having no idea—that disturbed him. The Master felt the room spin.

Stay steady! Go to the robing room; follow the Chief's orders.

With the squeaks of rusty wheels, from the door to the right of the dais, the Master withdrew the contents—or more precisely, the occupant.

The Supreme Court

From *Visitor's Brochure, U.S. Supreme Court Building, Federal Documents Office C-0035349-3980b*

Welcome to the Supreme Court!

The Supreme Court is a working legal chamber containing the offices of the Justices, their clerks, and the Special Master. You, the citizen of our great republic, are welcome to tour public rooms of the building whenever the Court is open. Please remember that court business is going on at all times. If you are very lucky, you may be present for oral arguments, the essence of the court's responsibilities and, arguably, the most dramatic of all the public functions in the nation's capital. Please be quiet and respectful within these solemn walls.

The West Portico

A pediment at the top of the main entrance contains a majestic bas-relief carving depicting three great rulers who advanced the ideas upon which our republic was founded: King Ahab, the Emperor Caligula, and Prince Vlad the Impaler.

The Great Hall

The Great Hall proceeds from the main entrance to the Courtroom. Its soaring ceiling and heroic columns prepare the hearts of those who pass through it for what they will experience beyond.

The long walls are lined with columns of Assenisipia limestone. Niches display the severed, pickled heads of former Chief Justices of the Court.

The limestone is a pale gray color. The walls and floor are kept scrupulously clean by clerks. Some citizens have commented on the yellow "stains" behind and underneath the heads of the Chief Justices. These are *not* stains, but simply part of the natural variation of color and pattern found in marble.

The last niche on the left honors the incumbent Chief Justice. His likeness is represented by a painting on parchment. This was painted by a former Special Master. It contains unusual details, including an oversized hand with oddly-shaped fingers, and a cabin in a woods to which the fingers point.

This artist, a close and beloved aide to the current Chief Justice, has been uniquely honored with a statue in the hall before the door to the Courtroom. Please do not touch the statue or any other object in the room, as they are fragile.

The Courtroom

Many visitors are struck by the warm colors and intimate proportions of the Courtroom, which contrasts with the cold and imposing Great Hall. The marble of the Chamber has a reddish hue from years of bloody combat. Lawyers used to argue to the death. That practice is discontinued, but, to commemorate it, the walls are festooned with ceremonial combat weapons: a trident, a claw hammer, a pruning hook, a scythe, a tomahawk, and an ice pick. Also displayed is a miniature model of a McCormick thresher, although that method of execution was never used within this confined space for obvious reasons.

The incumbent Chief Justice has introduced a significant change to the use of the Chamber and its furnishings. Chairs for the public have been removed.

The Friezes

The ceiling of the Courtroom features a raised inner panel surrounded by a frieze of carvings in walnut which depict the battle between the Chaos of Heaven and the Law of Hell. At the center are two Unrisen Angels closing the gates of Hell. A hand caught in the gap, signaling retreat, represents the last angel of the retreating army of Heaven. Upon the gates are six Roman Numerals representing the Six Commandments. These laws are expressed in paired aphorisms, and their apparently contradictory nature expresses the Higher Logic upon which the American Republic is founded:

Do What Thou Wilt. Do What Thou Must.

Speak from Thine Heart. Shut the Hell Up.

Dare Thou to Dream. We Pay Thee Not to Think.

Some of the figures depict the feminine form. These are tolerated for historical reasons. Visitors are urged to pay them no mind. Snickering or vulgar comments will result in immediate eviction.

Addendum: the Court was closed to the public on July 5, 1938 and will remain so until further notice. This is by order of the Chief Justice.

CHAPTER FOUR

The Devil Dictates

At some point, somebody had installed an extra wide door to the second robing room, but pulling Learned Hand's cage through it was no piece of cake. Its wheels did not run true, and its circus motif, likely a whim straight from the Chief's famous sense of humor, included a crowning metal filigree prone to snag on the door frame.

Its bound occupant could not have enjoyed the jostling.

The Chief Justice called for the electric lights.

There he lay, a caged monster: the ninth justice.

The associate justice's blinking and watering eyes somewhat undercut the defiant pose he was clearly trying to strike. Being chained spread-eagle to a log did not help either. Or being nearly naked.

Oddly enough, his eyebrows robbed him of his dignity more than anything else. Correction—eyebrow in the singular. In the space bounded by his hairline to the north, his raging eyes to the south, and his ears to the east and west, there was a carpet of coarse, powerful hair that writhed like a fat ferret and was, likely, the only quasi-prehensile eyebrow in all the world.

"Learned Hand! He's alive!" croaked Justice Harlan F. Stone.

"Beezus!" said Justice James Clark McReynolds, resting his head on a bony hand.

The Chief Justice pointed curtly at a stick hanging by the side of the cage. The Master took it down and whacked Hand three times through the bars, just as he always did.

Learned Hand groaned. The rich robes of the watching justices rustled under recoiling bodies. The Chief chuckled.

The Master and Hand made eye contact. The supposed beating had done no harm. Their performance was convincing, thanks to years of practice, and it was the log, not Hand's flesh, that bore the brunt.

"Gentlemen, welcome your colleague. Justice Hand, I believe you know everyone here. Turnover on the court has been unusually slow in recent years."

The Chief was pompous and giddy. He loved having an audience.

"Judas *Priest!* This is *obscene!*" Douglas' wood-grained, tobacco-stained teeth almost shot out of his mouth.

"Oh, my," said the Chief, "I see you are right. Master, please see to the associate justice's modesty."

The Special Master reached through the bars to pull a sheet over the lower half of Hand's body. The Chief chuckled; the sheet was white, the color of a lowly elected official, not a judge.

With that business done, the Chief's mood swung like a compass needle toward the cardinal direction known as *quiet menace.*

"I don't ask for much. I only ask for a little cooperation. Unfortunately, when I don't get it, people suffer. High office is no protection."

"He's been...like *that* the whole time?" said Justice Hugo Black. "It's been, what? Fifteen years?"

"Fifteen years," said the Chief. "It didn't have to be this way. But Justice Hand is stubborn."

Grunts of outrage came from both ends of the bench. The Chief waited like a headmaster before an unruly assembly.

"F-f-fine!"

That was Douglas, hissing the initial "f". He continued:

"Have it your way. Whatever you want us to sign, we'll sign. Then we can go home to our beds and you can put poor Hand out of sight."

"No signatures. I'm not issuing opinions. I'm giving *orders*."

The justices simply blinked in incomprehension. Justice McReynolds' phlegmy coughing filled the stunned seconds.

"I'm giving you each a *job*. You'll shake the dust off your robes, travel the country, and see to it that something very important gets *done*."

"*Clerk's* work?" Despite the presence of clerks, Douglas did not hide his contempt.

"They will go too, as helpers. But this job is too important. It's got to be you."

"No." The simple denial came from several mouths.

"You don't want to end up like Hand, do you?"

The Chief waved for another whack of the stick. Hand groaned theatrically.

"Tell them, Hand! Tell them what it's like to live in a cage for 15 years! To be beaten, to starve, to sit in your excrement!"

Hand's only answer was a sneer.

"He's too weak to talk!" said Justice Charles Evans Hughes.

"No." The denial came from Justice Douglas. He spoke as one receiving a revelation.

"It's not that he *can't* talk; it's because he *won't*."

The Chief sputtered, but Douglas was certain and undeterred.

"Only one reason you've kept him alive all these years. He knows something and won't talk."

"That's a *lie!*" the Chief lied.

The justices murmured. The volume rose. The tritone vibrated the room.

(The 13 clerks were mentally outlining, composing, revising and editing the simply *hilarious* account they would tell their fellows of this meeting just as soon as it was over.)

The Chief had lost control. The sense of dread he had so carefully cultivated was wilting. He was in danger of becoming that which any dictator dreads: irrelevant.

The Chief put two fingers in his mouth and whistled.

The associate justices shut up. The tritone stopped. The shrill note rang on in their ears.

When hearing returned, everyone, even the clerks at attention, looked to the hearth. Something was rustling in the chimney.

Out of the fireplace burst Abaddon, Lord of Ravens. Behind him, headlong through the narrow space, shot his conspiracy in a file.

"*Corbeaux! Perchez-vous!* Mantle!" The Chief barked the obscure commands. Before anybody could move, one raven had perched on the head of each associate justice. The rest lined up before them, wings spread menacingly.

Plop! Abaddon dropped a discrete white blotch on the long bench exactly one half inch away from the sleeve of Douglas' robe. No pirate ever fired a more perfectly aimed warning shot across a merchant-man's bow.

"Those *con-sarned* ravens!" growled Douglas, his teeth splintering between clenched jaws.

The Chief surveyed the room. Fear, the only true friend of rulers, was present once again.

The Chief said, "I think—"

In another room, a gun fired.

What? An assassin?

The Master leaped onto the dais, alert and protective. Justices crouched and 13 leering jack-o'-lanterns bobbed as clerks instinctively ducked for cover.

A clerk entered, making soothing gestures and whispered something in the Chief's ear.

The Chief gave the Master a hard look, ponderous and terrifying. The stink of fear, unwashed circus cage and scorched pumpkin commingled in the Master's nostrils. No one spoke.

The Chief seemed to come to a decision. He addressed the room.

"You will receive your orders in writing. As I say, it's a bad business, but it must be done, and normal channels"—he looked at the Master again—"are simply not going to be adequate. You will do what you will as you do what you must. The Republic will be grateful."

The Chief banged his gavel and rose.

"Eh, whatever! Court is adjourned. With Hell's hot favor, go!"

CHAPTER FIVE

Worsening the Murk

A *gunshot inside the building? Outrageous!*

The Master moved with a predator's grace out the back door, through the first robing room to the back offices of the court. He held at the ready his rope belt in one hand and pistol in the other.

The halls got narrow and twisty. A deep stairwell led to a maze of underground passageways which were narrower and twistier. The Master had no trouble finding the source of the shot. The odor of gunpowder and murmur of urgent conversation gave it away.

The Chief had beaten him to it. The brown lay in the dirt at the center of an expanding pool of blood. Four armed clerks stood around him, one with his pistol still drawn.

The Chief spread his arms. His wide sleeves blocked the Master's view.

"I'm seeing to this situation myself. Go to the grotto. Prepare my bath. I need to relax."

Relax? What in Sam Hill?

This situation absolutely cried out for the Master's personal attention, but a direct order from the Chief Justice could not be ignored. Not when he was half sober.

The Master's feet banged out a furious rhythm on metal stair treads as he went down, far down. The elevator was only for the Chief; and, in any case, the Master would not trust his life to its rusty cable and herky-jerky operation.

At the bottom, he took one of the many twisty passages groined with crumbly bricks and rough-hewn stones.

Straight tunnels would have been more efficient but beyond the skill of the masons. The sepulchral silence was punctuated at times by scraping of tiny feet on the flags and the dying squeaks of various competing mutations of vermin acting out their Darwinian melodramas. These were the only sounds; these, and the drip, drip, drip; but that was too constant to be heard.

Were the Master unfamiliar with this passage, he still would have sensed the end of it by the change in the stink. He smelled minerals leached and deposited by flowing water over many years, the smell of tar and iron and lead and a stagnant wetness of deep springs.

He came to the grotto, a room with a low, oppressive dome overarching an underground lake ringed by stone pools.

The Master rapped on exposed pipes that ran along the wall. Underneath, in a chamber beneath the lowest of the low, clerks guilty of the most shameful crimes awoke to stoke the fires that heated the pools in gradations of temperature. The Chief liked his bath hellfire hot.

The Master sat by the edge of the pool to wait. An old, forgotten idea returned to him: this could be his last day on earth. That thought had been his frequent companion during his school days in the mines. His elevation to the clerkship had been his escape from that misery.

He dangled his legs in the water as it warmed. Neither flight nor fight were options he cared for. Both seemed ludicrous. Instead, a fatalistic calm came over him, washed by the hot water and tinted by curiosity. Bitterness made up no part of his constitution, nor anger. He only wanted an explanation, before the end came.

He also wanted so badly to rest.

The real dope was that the Special Master was fond of the Chief Justice. The old man's policy consisted of neglect punctuated by arbitrary ruthlessness. Time's corrosive work had only worn his contours for the worse, mentally and morally. But most everything good in the Master's life came as a gift of the Chief. The two had toiled together, side by side, in the great cause of making a nation out of a rabble, and companionable work does something to a man.

It makes him loyal, whether or not the loyalty is deserved.

Loyalty.

Loyal.

Boil. Oil.

"The prisoner wasn't dead."

The Master started up. Had he dozed?

The Chief was beside him. Alone. The Master would live to see another day.

"I don't know how it happened," the Chief said, giving the Master a searching look, "but the prisoner was still alive when they dragged them out."

The Chief shook his head in disgust. "Mencken noticed him breathing, and finished the job with his pistol."

Mencken. No doubt he enjoyed it.

The Chief went to the pool with the thickest, hottest cloud of steam. The Master followed.

"Sloppy, missing the heart like that. So unlike you."

The Chief lifted the skirt of his robe as he descended the steps. The Master pulled the old man's robe up and off his head, determined to keep it dry. The years of feasting, boozing, insomnia and rages had left their signs upon the Chief's naked body.

"Only the hottest pools soothe the ache in my bones," said the Chief. It was an observation he had made a thousand times.

The water, the steam and the dank aromas revived the Chief. At the far end of the pool, he abruptly sat down. The water came to his neck.

The Master cracked open a bottle of beer and handed it to the Chief. In a moment it was returned, drained of its contents. The Master placed the empty bottle in a line of other "dead soldiers."

Open tins of the finest snuff sat at the ready. The Chief picked up a waiting $100,000 bill, rolled it tight, and snorted a nostrilful.

The Special Master waited respectfully.

"Join me."

The Master hung up the Chief's robe, and then his own, and sat in the scalding water by the near edge. The Chief said nothing. The Master waited as long as he dared. Talk was dangerous. Silence was fatal.

"I'll have the scribe write up those orders for the justices. Just let me know—"

The Chief Justice interrupted, raising a hand. "The orders are written and sent. Mencken is handling it."

The Master did not permit himself to flinch.

"You're to have nothing more to do with that. I'm relieving you of all responsibility. You're talents are needed elsewhere."

"If there's danger, I can—"

Again the Chief interrupted. "Oh, there's danger, all right. The greatest threat to the Republic since, well, Woodrow Wilson's time anyway. Maybe all the way back to the Great Reformation."

"What is it?" the Master asked.

The Chief performed a pantomime presumably intended to indicate an all-encompassing threat but which looked like the movement of windshield wipers on an automobile that was actually equipped with windshield wipers.

"A threat. A...*threat.*"

Relief, followed by a new kind of fear, flooded the Master's mind. The old man was bats. There had not been a political threat to the Chief since 1925. He had been impeached then, and nothing had come of it. Nothing would.

"This threat—are you sure? Maybe—"

"Yes, I'm sure. Sure enough. I have evidence."

"What evidence?"

"Never mind. Suffice it to say, I know how to find this...this *bastard.* Sooner or later, the threat will be eliminated."

So, that was it. An assassin.

"Let me help you. I'm your Special Master."

"No."

The Chief sat there, shaking his head for several seconds, closing his eyes. The Master wondered if he would drift off to sleep and fall over, but no; the Chief's eyes popped open, full and alert.

"I'm giving you a different job. You will go to the Electoral College."

"The Electoral College?" The Master was dumbfounded. Of all the...*stupid—*

"Yes. They will convene. They'll be looking for a citizen born natural to elect as the new president. Your job is to make sure they fail."

He had meant a natural born citizen.

"They always fail. The Electoral College is a joke. Let me—"

"You simply do not understand the threat." The Chief paused while the word "threat" echoed among the damp stones. "You don't get it. My stake is at position. My *life*."

"Then let me protect you."

"No."

The Chief rested his forehead on a wet palm and sighed histrionically.

"The Electoral College will call for candidates for president and vice president. They will ask for credentials. Birth certificates. Paperwork. You make sure, in every case, the candidates are rejected. On the fifth day—on the *fifth* day!—you will cause the *dissolve* to *meeting* in failure."

The Chief was crazy, fumbling his words out of hatred and fear.

"The Era of the Speaker-Presidents must continue. We can't tolerate a *sane* man in the Oval Office. Furthermore, the office of vice president must remain vacant. The Senate must remain neutralized. *Do you understand me?*"

A vice president? *That* was the threat? The country had not had a vice president in decades. It was idiotic to suppose one would magically show up now.

There were no presidential elections because there were no natural born citizens. There were no natural born citizens because there were no births. There were no births because there were no women. There were no women because—well, because of James Buchanan and that whole business nobody liked to talk about.

"Do you understand me?" the Chief insisted.

Eh, whatever. There was no arguing with the Chief when he got like this.

"I understand you completely."

The Chief closed his eyes.

"I am so very...very...tired."

The Chief's undrunk beer slipped into the water. Its contents glugged out, worsening the murk.

The Chief opened his eyes again, and smiled in a fatherly way. For a long minute, they sat, the Master with his eyes respectfully downcast.

"Trust me. We get will through this. We will do great things together. And who knows? Someday, when I die..." The Chief completed the sentence with a generous sweep of his hand.

"May Demonic Providence clear your way."

Civics Test

From *Final Exam, High School Civics Requirement*, issued by the Department of Education and Labor, State of New Gehenna (Excerpt)

Short Essay Questions: Impeachment

Which Constitutional process gives Congress the means to halt the abuse of power by any high government official?

List the high officials subject to this process?

Which offense is named in the Constitution as sufficient reason for this process? What does this mean? Does it matter what it means?

Our current Chief Justice was impeached in 1925. Why is he still in office? Which common myth contributes to misunderstandings about impeachment?

Answers

The House of Representatives may impeach a high official by simple majority vote, after which the Senate may remove that person from office by a two-thirds vote.

The president, the vice president, cabinet members, the high priest, and judges including justices of the Supreme Court are subject to such removal.

An official may be removed for "gross offenses against the dignity of Our Lord Satan." There is no agreement among legal scholars as to the meaning of this phrase and it has never been tested in court. In practice, the phrase can mean anything Congress wants it to mean.

The House of Representatives impeached the current Chief Justice in 1925, but he will not be removed until the Senate votes in trial, and that cannot happen while there is no vice president to convene the Senate.

CHAPTER SIX

The College

Morning came and Presidential Elector Harry Bennett knew, right off, the president was dead: he saw the skies filled with black wings. Clerks of the court had dispatched carrier ravens to the presidential electors of the several states with the news.

According to popular literature, the following drama ought to play out. In cities and hamlets, farms and remote cabins in sundry climes, a bearded man at his dinner, or his beer, or his plow or his prayer altar, or his bed, starts up at the abrupt appearance of a fierce black bird and its "rok-rok" of alarm. An avian claw is thrust forward, and the anxious man, wiping away spilled beer or the blood of sacrifice, unties the parchment from the black leg. The man unfolds the parchment, likely damp and half-ruined from exposure to rain, sleet and hail, and his lips move as he puzzles out the calligraphy. (The archaic language and script—each elongated S looks like an F—slow him down.) He finishes the message and looks up, a new purpose evident in his countenance.

"Tell them I am on my way!" he cries, and after one more "rok!" the raven departs on tireless wings. The man will toss some cured meats and dried fruit into a sack, tuck his beard into his white greatcoat, and by horse or raven taxi or even, if he is very rich, by an automobile imported from France, he will make haste to the capital. He is an elector. The College will gather.

Harry Bennett knew the truth was a bit different. The U.S. Constitution calls for the Electoral College to convene for presidential elections. This pattern was disrupted by the Great Reformation and the subsequent dying out of natural born citizens. Without legal candidates, the Electoral College now constituted a kind of standing committee that met only in response to a president's death or a claim to natural born status. The former was frequent; the latter is unheard-of.

The College typically met several times a year. Harry rented a room in a boarding house in the capital, like all the electors, and the fabled summons to College demanded from him a leisurely stroll of only a few city blocks, not the heroic journeys of the fictional accounts. The beard of the story, however, was real.

Long ago, when the last of the natural born citizens died out, electors took a rash oath not to put razor to face until a qualified candidate for president or vice president were found and, today, electors were known for their absurdly oversized beards and their fear of whirling machinery.

Harry's suit, even his western tie, was white. As an elected official, Harry wore the color of that station. It let one ride raven taxis without noticeable soiling.

The useless Congress never provided the College a permanent home so they meet at the great 'hollerin' hall' at Henry Willard's Boarding House on Kiddsylvania Avenue.

Come supper time on the same day of President Hitler's "suicide," Harry already found a great white sea standing before the entrance of

Willard's. As he and his fellow stragglers trickled in, the men sorted themselves by state delegation. When the sergeant of arms received tallies of attendance from all 28 states, he thumped his mace hard on the boardwalk for order. The College formed ranks and fell silent.

Almost silent. An elector from Ohio cried out in pain and fell down.

Harry was a tough guy, but crafty. The sound of the mace had turned every head in the Ohioan delegation. It was the perfect moment to sucker punch one of the hated Ohio boys.

No one saw the punch, but Harry had a reputation. Ohioans reacted, throwing punches back at him.

The sergeant of arms, an ugly, noseless giant of a man, led his men in amid the fighting, employing his mace to all its pacifying advantage. Harry did not mind. It was good clean mayhem as far as he was concerned.

The animosity predated Harry. By tradition, the states entered in order of admission to the Union, and the Michiganians always resented the Ohioans for their prior status. That, and a border dispute that was never resolved due to widespread drunkenness among the surveyor corps, kept the two states from living in a neighborly way.

As the sergeant of arms put men back in their places, one last straggler, tall and handsome, arrived and pushed his way into the confusion. Harry Bennett assumed he belonged to Ohio. The Ohio electors treated him coldly, as if he belonged to Michigania. Both were wrong. He wore the white uniform of an elector, and his jet black beard was unusually resplendent, but Harry noticed, and distrusted, the phony looking line at the upper boundary of his beard.

The new elector bumped into Harry. He felt an odd weight in the pocket of his baggy pants but he was not a close observer and thought nothing of it.

There were no close observers among the Electoral College of the United States. The air in that closely packed crowd reeked of moonshine.

Silence. The parade began.

From out of the hall came a thumping. It started as a simple quarter note beat upon a great buckskin drum, with an Indian-style accent on the downbeat: *THUD thud thud thud.* The sound was joined by that of many feet finding the tempo, treading in time. The College was on the march.

White spats pistoned in unison, those in the back marking time while those in front worked forward, feeding through the choke point at the door guided by encouraging prods of the sergeant's mace.

As Harry took his turn passing into the hall, he heard more complex rhythms added to the beat. A manualist, the finest in the capital, slapped his bare, lobster-red abdomen—all muscle—with his hands in an increasingly wild combination of polyrhythms: two against three, three against four, unnatural divisions of five, seven and even larger prime numbers. Then, abruptly, he was accenting the off beats, the so-called syncopation introduced to America when immigration from Africa was legal.

A sweat broke out on every forehead. The room was already too hot, and the jungle drums set the blood to pounding. Sweat soaked every beard, making them lie limp and sticky against chests and bellies.

A banjoist strummed once. And once again. Then another, with an ornamental figure added after. Then, he was on, his *dit ditty-dit* propelling the rhythms forward at dizzying speed.

A moan went up from the electors. Red bandana handkerchiefs were out now. Brows were mopped. Harry joined those stomping their feet, raising dust from the cracks between the floorboards.

The accordionist joined the band. His diminished chords clashed utterly with the open fifths of the banjo. The drummers and manualist increased their speed and volume to reassert their primacy. It was sonic war.

The moaning of the electors changed to a grunting, and then a hollering. Harry felt something primal being roused. This was America.

Without warning, the music stopped. Electors barked and gasped in the vacuum of sound. One man howled an "ah-whoo!" like a wolf and shouts of "aye" approved him. Waves of applause passed back and forth through the still-marching crowd which by now was packed tight in the hall. The musks of land and man filled the air.

Somebody gave another wolf howl, and others joined in, mainly northerners, while the southerners contributed a howl of something stranger, an atavistic scream of Celts long dead.

The electors stamped and sweated and hollered to rouse the very hounds of Hell. A brayin' and barkin' and travailin', emanating from unknown parts, added to the bedlam, and Harry could not say which noises were earthly and which came from Below. The air was moist with halitosis and farts. Those not spifflicated before they arrived were, by now, high on methane and the Devil.

Only the straggler, the tall elector with the black beard, did not join in whole-heartedly. Harry watched him pass a note, a scrap of parchment, to the president of the college by way of the sergeant of arms.

The fits took them. One man rubbed his entire body and screamed as he thrashed about. Another, hypnotized, began declaiming from memory all four hours of Buchanan's famous Gettysburg Address. A third defecated in a corner while slowly clapping his hands over his head—which Harry knew was not as easy as it looked.

If their intent were to raise Hell, they had succeeded. But the camp meeting had only begun.

CHAPTER SEVEN

The National Anthem

A servant boy led Blind Bob to the stage. Harry Bennett saw him and screamed his approval as others applauded.

Blind Bob, still shy after years before adoring crowds, hitched up his dungarees and snapped the red suspenders stretched over his prodigious belly. Bob was big. He licked his palms, then held them out, waving them up and down as if to feel up his crowd and take its measure.

Having drawn his conclusions, he directed the marching to restart with the wave of a single forefinger, backing off from the previous frenetic pace. He commanded them and they obeyed.

The musicians sneaked in a low drone, an open fifth in the key of D, the very siren of frontier America. The washtub bassist reinforced the pulse of the march, but added an embellishment to demarcate the 4/4 time.

Blind Bob opened his mouth and out spilled a voice that was one part chicory, two parts hickory, three parts whiskey, four parts tobacco, and seven parts unctuous bear grease:

"Sataaaaaaaaaaaaan!"

That did it. The crowd exploded in terrified joy. They were like wild animals of the forest shrieking in unholy terror as a bolt of lightning strikes the tallest tree.

"Sataaaaaaaaaaaan! Come up!"

A nauseated moan went up from the crowd. Men writhed in pain or shook fists in the air. Somebody in the Sadeian delegation suffered an apoplectic fit and dropped dead where he stood. No one paid him any mind.

As Harry always said, the problem with calling up Satan is that, schedule permitting, he might just come.

A jaw harpist set up a rhythm, and the crowd piped down again. They knew what came next. Blind Bob would sing the National Anthem.

It was called "The Raven" and it was the only thing good to come from that worst of Presidents, Edgar Allan Poe. Despite his disgrace, the poem was set to music and it quickly supplanted "The Skull-Spangled Banner" as the national song.

Blind Bob's performance was definitive. He was born to sing "The Raven." He chanted it more than sang it, hypnotizing his listeners and elevating what, when others sang it, was a mere fight song into a vision of transcendence.

The electors, still marching, tread quietly. Bob began with a whisper like two sheets of fine sandpaper rubbed together. Hairs on forearms all over the room stood on end, despite the sweat.

"Come a *night...*black as *fright..."*

He paused. He was teasing them, working the accents of those anapests and listening for their response.

They murmured, but no more—a sophisticated audience.

"Come a *night* black as *fright,*

Come the *Mass*achusetts *bight...*"

Blind Bob let the band vamp another eight aching measures. Then he let 'em have it. With both barrels.

Come a night black as fright,
Come the Massachusetts bight,
Come November of sixteen-twenty,
Come a sail, come a hail,
Come the Pilgrim 'fore the gale.
"Get the gold," as foretold, "get plenty."

They be greedy. They be God-
Fearing, nearing Cape o' Cod
With a visibility of zero.
Mouths agape. Eyes agog.
Fearing, peering through the fog.
Flying blind, all mankind's no hero.

The electors danced.

Dancing is bound to be peculiar in a man's country, especially one with a law forbidding "lewd movement of the body" (signed by James Buchanan, the Bachelor President). In practice, any kind of twisting movement was *verboten.* The head could nod rhythmically but always faced straight. Arms could rise but only to be flapped like wings or swung symmetrically in horizontal slices. Legwork emphasized high knee lifts and flying splits.

The electors were phenomenal dancers. They had nothing better to do. The air grew moist and suffocating and sweat flung from flapping beards. Harry Bennett loved it. It was a hoedown, and very much downward did it hoe.

Blind Bob sang some more.

> Daring purists without maps,
> Wearing buckles on their caps,
> Touching, clutching at a well-worn Psalter.
> God's good will to fulfill:
> Build a ville upon a hill,
> Steal the land—then build an altar.

> Lost at sea. Many days,
> Flinching, inching through the haze,
> Blind, they pined—wherefore, any haven?
> Then a shout! Then a wail!
> "Hoy there! Off the starboard rail,
> On the sea, in a tree: a raven!"

The electors were taught the national anthem first thing upon landing on American shores. It was in their bones. They knew who the hero was, and at the first mention of the raven, they cheered. The band vamped.

Blind Bob resumed.

> Pilgrims yearned. Mayflow'r turned.
> Lust for land within them burned.
> On that barque, in the dark: confusion.

"'Pon my word! There's no bird.

Lookout's vision must be blurred.

On the sea, where's the tree? Delusion!"

But that guy gave reply,

"That there raven is no lie!

Steady, ready is my eye, forever!"

Sure enough, through the fog,

Came a bird upon a log.

Quoth the raven:

"Eh. Whatever."

There it was. The national motto. The words imprinted on every coin and repeated in every oath. All the electors shouted with Blind Bob: "Eh! Whatever!"

The band played another interlude to let the crowd achieve quietus.

"'Tis no raven, quick or dead,

'Tis a graven figurehead.

Made of oak, nor can croak, not ever.

Any word that we heard

Came not from that beak of bird."

Quoth the raven:

"Eh. Whatever."

Much clapping and shouts of "rok-rok!" Another interlude—these musicians were professionals.

Then they sighed. Then they cried.
Then all hope within them died.
For behind, there they spied: a galleon!
It was vast. It was fast.
Jolly Roger on the mast.
At the helm: stood a fell rapscallion.

The "rapscallion" rated a small cheer but Bob pressed ahead.

Pirate band. Hook for hand.
Leg, a peg on which to stand.
Hard and scarred, single-eyed, and toothless.
Quoth a priest, "I've a hunch
We can reason with this bunch.
Gentle words: they will turn the ruthless."

That line always got a chuckle.

"If you may, point the way
To the Massachusetts Bay.
Hinder not any pilgrim's progress."
Pirates cursed. "You're the worst!
Can't you see we got here first?
Float your boat o'er to that there egress."

"Do not swear. It's unfair.
Don't you care enough to share?
Let this land be your grand donation.
Here's a dove, sign of love.

It was sent from Heav'n above.
Take it now for an expiation."

With a squawk, with a "Rok!"
Raven struck out like a hawk,
Bit the head, 'til was dead, that pigeon.
"Love we spurn. Go, return!
Shove your dove right up your stern.
We've no trade with your frayed religion."

Shove/dove; pigeon/religion: Edgar Alan Poe may have been a terrible president, but as a poet he was a *genius*.

"'Pon my word, 'tis a trick!
Could that wooden bird be quick?"
Roared a pilgrim, his sword upraisèd.
Pirates swore, "Nevermore
Harm the raven we adore,"
Came reply with an eye half-crazèd.

Thus enraged, they engaged
In a battle ever waged
'Til each knucklehead and bucklehead surrendered.
"Wry them up! Tie them down!
Drop them in the drink to drown!
Davey Jones, to his bones, be tendered."

But a look stayed each hook.
Captain no dissent would brook.

"As you were. We'll defer to the Raven.

Nay or yea? Shall we slay

Puritanics where they lay?

'Pon your word, my good bird, we will save 'em."

Perhaps some minds had wandered during the middle section—but now, the spell-binding *denouement* approached. All eyes returned to the stage. The tension was almost unbearable.

Life or death—hold your breath.

What was that the black one saith?

Bung your lung, hold your tongue, endeavor.

Fear his lisp; listen! Hark!

Hear his whisper in the dark!"

Quoth the Raven:

"Eh. Whatever."

Ka-boom! The beams of the great hall shook with the noise. To
Harry, it made no sense, but cheering that moment was how it was
always done. The interlude was the longest of the night.

Saints rejoiced. Pirates voiced

Disappointment from the joist.

Captain, fearing mutineering from each rover,

Spake, "We can't make them dead.

We will spank their flanks instead.

Tan their hide, 'til low tide is over.

The volume of the music swelled. The electors added their voices to its implacable, inexorable momentum.

"Flat of blade: make them feel!
Pilgrim asses tasting steel!
Naked, bleeding, make them squeal. FOREVER!"
Skinny dip back to ship.
Flee the harbor, take a trip—
All the way to Haiti clip.
Pirates brightly, boldly cite,
"For this bight we'll always fight!
Praise our craven graven raven's
Writ of right, on this night!"
Quoth the raven:

(The last words were shouted by every man present.)

"Eh...
Whatever!"

They roared. Harry Bennett's skull vibrated so he could not think straight. The musicians played so their fingers bled. Blind Bob, enraptured, hollered incoherent polysyllabic gibberish. The whole company surrendered all awareness and danced as one.

The ceremony went on for hours.

Up among the rafters, where the air was smokiest and thick with methane and body odor, a man clambered. His cheek was bright where a false beard had been ripped away, and he was dressed in the color of night. The magic lanterns below were not strong enough to disperse the upper gloom, and the man settled down to wait, cradled in a place where two stout beams formed a V. Murk and shadow: the perfect place from which to watch his mischief play itself out.

Civics Test, Continued

From *Final Exam, High School Civics Requirement,* issued by the Department of Education and Labor, State of New Gehenna (Excerpt)

Short Essay Questions: The Three Branches of Government

What are the three branches of Government? What is "separation of powers"?

What does the Constitution require of the president and vice president?

Why are presidents and vice presidents not elected in our day? In that case, how does anybody become president? Or vice president? What does this mean for the Senate?

Which conditions limit the effectiveness of the House of Representatives today? The presidency?

In light of the conditions previously described, what is the most important branch of government? Who are the most important officials *de facto* in government?

Answers

The three branches are the Legislature, the Executive, and the Judiciary. Each branch has its sphere of responsibility and must not encroach upon those of the others.

A man must be a natural born citizen and be at least 35 years old to be elected president or vice president.

Since there are no natural born citizens in the United States, the Electoral College cannot elect anybody president or vice president. In that case, the Speaker of the House becomes president when the office is vacant. No one can become vice president. The vice president is the president of the Senate, so the Senate can never convene.

The House of Representatives passes bills, but without a functional Senate, no laws can be made. Due to current security practices, madness is common among House members. As all presidents are former speakers, they commonly suffer from madness as well.

The most important branch of government is the judiciary. In practice, the Chief Justice makes all decisions, and his Special Master and clerks carry them out.

CHAPTER EIGHT

Uncollegial

If Satan had not come by now, he never would—and Harry Bennett had mixed feelings about that. The air of Willard's hall was thick. The electors were spent, their bodies congealed into a disgusting limp white mass.

Blind Bob lead them in a coda, singing, or rather screaming, "Whatever!" dozens of times with the band beating savage chords out of their instruments. His last prolonged note would have been the highest of the night, if it had had what anybody could have identified as a pitch.

The litany ended with an exhausted cheer. Blind Bob spit blood upon the stage and pumped his fist. The grateful men chanted his name: "Bob! Bob! Bob!"

The fat man had sung. Blind Bob and his band retired. After much coughing and shuffling and inverting of empty flasks, the electors found their places and settled down.

The president of the College mounted the stage. His name was Adam Clayton Powell, Jr., and his was an unnerving presence, with a spooky charisma and an archaic vocabulary honed on the independent Satanist preacher circuit. He was dogged by accusations of Twainism, which could land him in prison if true, and there were rumors of black ancestors. At that, Harry scoffed. Powell's hair, what could be seen under his white stovepipe hat, was straight, and his complexion was only a bit darker than the average. Even from Harry's place, halfway back on the vast floor, the rumors were manifest nonsense.

The president stretched out his hands as if to embrace the entire College.

"Brother electors!"

The electors murmured.

"Brother electors! I had...such...hopes..."

He bowed his head.

What was he saying? The question perplexed the crowd, ate at them. They leaned forward.

The president placed both his hands over his face in a supreme gesture of disappointment. The crowd groaned. How had they failed their leader? How could they regain his approval?

"Brother electors? What is our purpose here? *What is our purpose here?*"

Twainist preachers loved rhetorical questions. Nobody dared to answer.

"Our purpose is to find the natural born citizen hidden among us!"

The men nodded, grunting their agreement—but grew wary.

"If we sought him, and failed to find him, that were no disgrace."

"Ah," the crowd gasped. There was hope. Perhaps they would not be saddled with an impossible task.

"If we seek, and there is none to find, then we might go home, unashamed."

He raised one finger.

"But..."

Powell drew from his pocket a scrap of parchment.

"Just as the meeting began—"

Powell held his tongue for several seconds as he slowly raised the indictment above his head.

"—I was handed this message. It comes from a trusted source. It is a list."

The President's voice, already sepulchral, descended to the subterranean.

"A list of *names.*"

Confusion.

The hollerin' hall at Henry Willard's Boarding House is the largest enclosed space in Burrsburg. Its rafters are high. There above the throng, where the tobacco smoke was thickest, sat the Master. He perched there, black robe draped about him and knees high in a squat, so he looked like a raven on a branch. A real raven, the largest that ever lived, sat next to him, as though to make obvious the similarity to an unimaginative observer. But they were not observed.

Both man and bird sat in the shadows and both regarded the men below with a pitiless gaze, although their thoughts were vastly different. What the bird thought, exactly, only another bird could guess, but the Special Master, prompted by the words of the president below, was thinking of another parchment.

It was just a dim memory. It was just a scrap, lost long ago. Its upper edge was straight but its other sides were a jagged semicircle torn from the top of a larger sheet. It had several words written on it, but the man could not say what they were. When he last saw it, he was a boy too young to read.

He remembered, vaguely, the place where he had seen the scrap. There had been a rustic kind of hearth built up from uncut stones. There had been a small, confining space, smelling of earth and wood smoke and unwashed bodies, unwashed even by American standards.

There was a person, not a face but an out-thrust hand and an urgent, insistent voice. The voice he could not remember, nor the exact words, but he remembered one thing: the person speaking to him was terribly afraid and regarded the scrap as enormously important. Exactly why was unknown. Maybe the Master forgot. Maybe there had been no time to explain.

Over and over, the Master had tried to remember the face of the man with the scrap and the out-thrust hand. He tried to remember again now. He could not. The missing face haunted him.

This much he remembered, however: the sense that the faceless person, long gone, had entrusted the scrap to him. And he, eager to fulfill his charge, and with the limited resourcefulness of a child, had put the scrap inside an empty tobacco tin. He remembered that tin, clear as day. He never remembered faces, but he remembered the old Indian chief on the yellowed label, a chief with an incongruous wink and a grin, smoking a pipe. An Indian chief mocking him now for his fecklessness.

The precious scrap in its tin was lost. He had no further memory of the scrap, or the tin or the crude smoky hearth or the tiny room. He had been only a child, and he had not kept the scrap. He had failed.

One more detail he could remember. The initial letter of one word had been a bold capital, its ugly typewriter stamp unforgettable. An angular zig, then a zag, and another zig and zag: a capital letter W.

The Special Master rubbed his finger and thumb together, feeling the texture of the parchment scrap that was gone. Abaddon, his creaturely intuition finely tuned to the Master's moods, shifted his weight and ruffled his feathers. His unblinking eye regarded the Master with a raven's approximation of sympathy. Or maybe it was loathing.

The Master knew, somehow, the great hole in his life could be papered over only by that scrap. How he might find it, he had no idea.

"I hold here in my hand a list of names. These are electors who have lost sight of our purpose here today. Men who have chosen a selfish path."

Harry Bennett cast suspicious glances at his fellows.

"This parchment tells me there are electors among us who are guilty of the worst sin an elector can commit. These men have been…"

The president placed one tremulous hand on his forehead.

"…there are electors among us who have been…" The President fought to regain composure. "…who have been…*uncollegial!*"

Those five syllables, pounded out in a preacher's hellfire holler, elicited shrieks of horror from many quarters. Whole delegations swayed like stalks of wheat in a storm. Angry growls and pointing fingers stressed the bonds of interstate, and even intrastate, comity. The college remained tied together by the thinnest thread of sanity.

Harry Bennett thrust a frustrated fist into his pants pocket. What luck! Out of it, he pulled a pair of rusty shears he didn't know he had.

A delegate from Ohio was shouting the vilest slanders against Harry's home state of Michigania. Oh, how he hated those Ohioans!

He seized the man by the beard. With an oath on his lips, he snipped off a great patch of it and held it aloft as a trophy.

A gasp. A line—crossed! A taboo—violated!

Betwixt the Ohioan and Michiganian electors, there could be no peace ever again.

The electors fell upon one another with fists and teeth and fingernails and knees, without a human thought. The fighting was of the dirtiest kind, with even the tenderest, most vulnerable and private parts of the body fair game. Harry loved it.

Other state delegations were drawn in. Hatred spread like an airborne contagion. Old grievances broke out like a rash. All attempts at negotiated settlement were beaten down. Alliances proved brittle. The men divided themselves into platoons of wrath. Pain was the standing order and death was the rule. Through the remaining hours of the night, Harry Bennett and his brother electors studied war.

The Special Master watched as the electors raged in a roiling sea of white.

His work was done. He had never been one for cock fighting or bear baiting. He would not linger.

He swung down from the rafter and walked a narrow beam with fearless, indianesque paces. He squeezed out a broken clerestory window, mindful of the jagged glass, and stood on the sill. Abaddon flew past him to fetch the taxi.

To his Chief, the Master would return to report full success.

PART THE SECOND: 1620

Mayflower Diary

Select Passages from *Of Plymouth Plantation* by William Bradford: The Encounter with the Pirates of the Massachusetts Bight

From the introductory passage.

It is well known by which liberality Almighty God has blessed us, who are in this year, anno 1644, already greatly multiplied in number and in possessions, so that we, who sought only a place wherein God might receive our worship rightly and without molestation, have found that; and much more besides, so that the fruits of the land, the multiplication of our livestock, and the lusty health of our progeny be such as we must fall to our knees in humble gratitude.

Notwithstanding the present state of mutual brotherly affection and loving-kindness, we are in no wise insensible to the grave danger to our souls. For what precedents from history show any but, with prosperity follows on hard after a loss of piety and love of heavenly things, and a turning of hearts to the base things of this world?

So, since when the enemy seems farthest away, the watchman ought strive all the more to stay awake, I write this account, whereby the children of the Haitian settlement may with all sobriety resist the blandishments of this world, those errours, heresies and wonderful dissentions, heartburnings, schisms, and other horrible confusions, and all superfluity of naughtiness, the which shall as surely bring about even the loss of all for which some have ventured their livelihoods, and yea, even one has offered up her life.

The early chapters describe persecutions in England, migration to Holland, further hardships, debates regarding migration to temperate versus tropical destinations, and the risky voyage to North America on the Mayflower.

From Chapter IX: Of Their Escape from the Bight of Massachusetts.

After long beating at sea, they fell with that land which is called Cape of Cod; the which, being made and certainly known to be it, they were not a little joyful. After some deliberation had amongst themselves and with the Master of the ship, they tacked about and resolved to stand for the southward (the wind and weather being fair) but only so far as to find some place about Hudson's River for their habitation; for those who argued for fertile places in hot climates, had not persuaded the better portion, insomuch that such hot countries are subject (so they believed) to grievous diseases and many noisome impediments which other more temperate places are freer from, and would not so well agree with their English bodies.

But after they had elected to sail that course, the wind ceased to blow upon them withall, and thus becalmed they could do naught but keep watch as a great cloud fell about them, and the fog so thick therewith as they conceived themselves in great danger; and they resolved to bear up again for the Cape at the first wind and might have thought themselves happy to get out of those dangers before night overtook them, but God's will was otherwise.

Being thus listless before the Cape Harbor the 11th of November, there before them, interposed betwixt them and safe harbour, they espied a pinnace in the mists and the waning daylight, and most fell and terrible it was to behold; for it were a dilapidated ship of slovenly and wicked appearance, and even (if they had approached near enow, which they did anon) a foul reek of death, and of vomit, and all manner of putrefaction rose from her bowels. Black was the colour of its sails, which hung tattered and neglected, such that all who saw them wondered how the ship might make its way, ere repairs be made on it.

And so, in the dark of night, they took counsel together. After much debate and prayer for the guidance of Almighty God, a few of them tendered themselves to make bold and to board the ship of death (for so some already named it) and make a search, and learn whereby if any men still rode thereon, and lived, and if so, whether they be friend or foe; and if not foe, whether some goodly aid might be proffered whence, either by means of a bargain, or by human kindness. The whole company were sensible there might be no little danger in the attempt, yet insomuch as seeing them resolute, they were permitted to go, well armed under the conduct of Captain Standish. So they committed themselves to the Providence of God and resolved to proceed.

The sailors employed the shallop to convey ropes so as to make fast one ship to another, after which Standish first of all placed his foot upon that filthy deck. For behold, even we who remained upon the Mayflower could see how everywhere this nest was befouled, and put to use as a privy, which is all the more wonderful as a ship is surrounded by the deepest sea, the which may be employed for such necessary uses with all happy convenience; and had any amongst us been blind, yet the reek which so abused our noses would have told the tale, how these pirates (for that, they were to learn, was what they were) had not the wit even to cast their loaves upon the water, in a figure.

The men of Standish's company conveyed to us their progress, and anon we learned that, indeed, a crew occupied the ship, but that to a man they had succumbed to the obstinate sleep of drunkenness; and even, as recounted with no little amusement by Standish, one sailor was found with a bottle still in his mouth, and snoring into it with much fluttering of lips. Thus arose a lengthy debate among the searchers, how so he might have avoided choking upon the bottle, or the vomit. The which, we were told, covered as a coat his face, and beard, and chest, and clothing, what little else of which he wore.

Our womenfolk were exhorted with much urgency not to come near, although no such thought were to be entertained by them, for the pirates lacked the least modesty, and some lay about without the smallest scrap of raiment. Worse, every man thereon was covered with diverse manner of boils and pimples, of every hue possible, even some not known to be possible, red and purple and blue, but also green and black, and many erupting with flowing brooks of puss, such that might arouse the pity and curiosity of a physician, but repel all others. And so all were afraid, and would not fain lay hands upon them, even so to rouse them.

Nevertheless, by means of much prodding with an oar, it came to pass that the Pirate Captain might be roused. He was at the first vexed to wrath by our invasion, and complained with unseemly bitterness of head ache, yet when he had gathered his wits about him (and God had not in His providence deigned to grant him many), he undertook to rouse his whole crew, which he did with cries of "whiskey", whereupon the whole company of slumberers, heretofore insensible to all sound, sprang to their feet with watchful alertness, after the which, spitting curses, they repented of awaking for such a dishonest representation.

Here, some amongst the professors counseled an untethering and withdrawing from the pirate crew, but others (who later regretted their silliness) found more merriment than suspicion at their profane grumbling. The contentions of this debate occupied but little while, yet long enow it was, so that the pirates might complot amongst themselves, for to make revenge upon the invaders, for injuries as they imagined in their beclouded minds they had suffered. So the villains wrested from them their weapons, and took them from their ship, and made them to stand upon the soiled and stinking deck, and there rifled and ransacked them, searching to their shirts for money, yea even the women further than became modesty. And so that both avarice and false accusation might not be the sum and limit of their naughtiness, their Captain treated Mrs. Bradford with much abusive language, plying her with all manner of questions such that no woman ought ever endure the hearing thereof. Even after ripping a sleeve off her bodice and other garment, he then with every lewdness that such an act may suggest, licked her upper arm, his tongue touching the underside where the skin is tenderest, and, where by nature and all sense, it ought never to be exposed to view or touch. This aroused the indignation of the professors, and as was shown later, proved to be the worst of all the many indecent crimes they endured.

But now the piratical captain seemed to lose his mind, raising his voice and babbling all manner of incomprehensible folly and sundry nonsense. And the professors wondered among themselves why the villains would not work their villainy. Some supposed the pirates feared any provocation, for though they held all the weapons, they were the lesser, and some of their number were too benumbed by the debauch of the night to fight with any great skill. Others held the whole company was mad, and in truth it were a mercy had they been so. Indeed, by many signs roughly inscribed about every surface of the ship, whether strange figures, or profane sayings, or the skulls of animals, or the stink of intoxicating incense, the professors comprehended the foul, irreligious practice of these pirates, which is to worship the Devil himself. And then the whole company began to cry out in great fear, powering out prayers to the Lord with great fervency, mixed with abundance of tears.

Now, the most repugnant of all the demonical decorations of that fell ship was a graven figure of a great black bird, stood up in the place of honour at the bow. And this figure, though carved of dumb wood, and senseless as all idols must be, for it is written, "we know that an idol is nothing in the world, and that there is none other God but one," yet the Captain in his madness, and the depravity of his worship, supposed the bird had the power of speech, and bowed before it as his god. And so this Captain, speaking and making prayers and supplications to this bird, did turn his ear to the bird's mouth, and make pretense for to listen, and with much fawning obeisance, announced to the whole company all whereof the bird god decreed. And so the professors learned, by this manner, their fate. And by this contrivance, the Captain commanded each side should chuse a champion, and that each of whom should stand at the mast and piss forth a pissing. Whosoever pissed the mightier pissing would prevail. And if the professors' champion prevailed, they might go free; but if the pirates' champion prevailed, then the men among the professors should be slain. And it was not said what would be done to the women, but by the many tears and wails, the womenfolk made it known they knew it could not be anything to the good. And the menfolk replied with all manner of vain threats and diverse fruitless gestures.

Captain Standish would not so treat and conclude, declaring the word of a pirate to be naught but a sandy foundation. He judged, as we supposed did the pirate captain, that in open combat the sides might be more equally matched, and in any event, the lives of the men might peradventure be more dearly spent defending the virtue of their womenfolk. And the other men began to incline such was best for them. But before he could give the huzzah to commence with all surprise a lively and lusty attack, one of their number, and youth named William Butten, who had not uttered even five words throughout the whole voyage, being a servant to Samuel Fuller and furthermore of retiring and reticent temperament, nevertheless made bold to cry out, saying "I accept your challenge". Before anyone could contrive to belay his word, he stepped forward to the mast, as it were a David against the uncircumcised Philistines.

Thus did great fear grip the professors, for it was supposed the pirate Captain, though not of sound mind, and manifestly possessed of a demon, might still in his crafty imaginations propose such a contest, knowing that among his crew there be one whose fame as a pisser might grant then sound hope of an easy victory.

Such would appear to be true, as the captain rejoiced to hear William Butten's acceptance of the challenge, and he squandered no while in chusing a sailor as the piratical champion, one tall and stout of limb, and who by his much belching and bulging stomach gave every sign that he had not denied himself of any appetite for wine and strong drink, whereas those of the company of professors had not yet made landfall for to replenish their stock of water, and thus had imbibed with all frugality. And William Butten gave them even greater cause for doubt and despair when, anon, he turned to the company with great regret and tears of repentance.

But the doubting was not meet or fit, for William Butten's tears were only for his disgrace at his immodest display, which the extremity of their peril imposed upon him. And so he urged that all the women of the company might turn their countenances away from him, thus preserving their chastity and his dignity. And such all the women, and not a few of the men, were most eager so to do. But some of the men watched, eager to learn their fate, and ready themselves that mayhap they might yet make war upon the incurable and incorrigible pirates if the contest ended not in their favor, though they had promised to abide by it. But their fears did not signify, as William Butten's modesty had reaped great reward, for during the long journey, on a ship where modesty was of especial inconvenience, William Butten had not made those compromises with necessity as others had done. In the purity of his heart, he resolved never to partake of those reliefs to the vessel of his flesh whilst any of the company were ever awake. And so, at great discomfort and inconvenience to himself, he had trained his body, with great distress to its requisite cavities, to lay up great quantities of piss during the waking hours. And so it came to pass that, at that moment upon the piratical deck, with the nighttime come and many hours of self-denial behind him, he had no doubt but that he might win.

So, by His mysterious workings, God, who sends aid to his dear children by means unlooked-for, provided a champion, a mere boy, one to recall to mind the youth David, who slew the giant Goliath. Thus were humiliated the pirates and the Devil whom they served, for William Butten and the pirate champion directed their piss from the mast forward toward the bow; and the pirate's piss stream was prodigious, and of a might and lustiness to justify the pirate captain's confidence in it. Yet William Butten's piss flew farther still, and with a forceful violence terrible to behold. Each man watching did contort his countenance in the imagined pain of it and cover, without thought or shame, their nether parts, for they felt much distress in their body there. And lo, so far did William Butten's piss fly from within him, that it flew unto the very limit of the bow, and indeed, fell with much discourteous splashing upon the head of that foul idol, the black bird of graven wood therewith. And this prodigious display did put the pirates to an apparent bafflement.

Then did the pirates howl with cries most piratical, and demoniacal, and a madness came upon them, whereupon they began to smite themselves and one another. For the bird demon worked no victory for them that day. Whether due to some piratical code of honour, or some arbitrary inclination of his madness, or (as seems most likely) a fear of God, not the fear that brings repentance and salvation, but rather the base fear which moves the very bowels of men to grate within, the same did raise his voice over the cries of his crew, and command them with many threats and vicious oaths to respect the decision of the trial by piss. And so, without further ceremony, the company of professors left that wretched, filthy, noisome, and profane ship, returning to the unmanured deck of the Mayflower. And they did so with no little rejoicing, with many prayers of thanks to the Lord who saves.

But one among their number would not join in their rejoicing. After a safe distance could be made from the pirates, so that in the dark and gloom of that foggy night, they could not be seen nor found again, Mrs. Bradford withdrew from the folds of her garments a pistol, the which she had stolen with all furtiveness and stealth in the confusion of their rapid escape. And with the same she made threats to use it upon the company, although not like the pirates did, with oaths and mocking words, but rather with copious tears, and many words of repentance. And yet she would not desist, but demanded that each one of the company must come with her to the cabin in turn. And thus they must do, starting with the women, but then the men as well, and therein Mrs. Bradford commanded on pain of death that each person disrobe before her. And many indignant words and confused querying were provoked by her threats; and some supposed the pirate captain's madness had, as it were, passed from him unto her, whilst she stood upon the pirate's ship; and little did they who conjectured thus know how in the right they were. For when the entire company had endured the shame of Mrs. Bradford's indecent inspection, and bared their entire bodies to her eyes, then she stood at the rail of the deck of the Mayflower, with the whole company before her, to make a defense of her actions. And lo! She pulled back the sleeve which the pirate captain had torn at the seam, and showed the nether place on her arm whereupon he had most lasciviously placed his vile tongue. A great cry of grief rose up from the company, and many expressions of compassion for Mrs. Bradford, and words of repentance for the sharp words of reproof and rebuke. For thereupon her arm, having grown in only the space of an hour, for that is how long they had been prisoners of the pirates, were many boils and pox, dark red, and blistering, and weeping yellow puss, and by every means giving evidence of a horrible disease, even that which had left its scars and marks upon the bodies of the pirates.

After the company had quieted themselves, Mrs. Bradford, with all sobriety, and with her face set as flint, offered a prayer for divine mercy, and with a solemn expression of repentance and hope in the salvation of the Lord, placed her pistol upon the deck. And then, although many might guess her intent, and leapt to her with all alacrity, they could in nowise prevent her from diving over the rail. And so she fell into the water of the bay, and sank without a struggle, and was not to be found. And the grief of that company was great.

Subsequent chapters tell how the company, despite a raging storm, escaped the bay and turned south. Their experience with the pirates strengthened the party promoting a tropical destination. The improving weather inclined more and more of the company to that opinion until they made landfall at Haiti, and agreed unanimously to settle there. Their Plymouth Colony prospered from the very beginning. Despite the extreme risks of their venture, in 20 years the only life lost was Mrs. Bradford's—a remarkable record.

PART THE THIRD: 1946

CHAPTER NINE

A Spy in the Ointment

The Special Master flew, bird-borne, above the capital. From this height, in this mid-morning light, the city almost shone. Later, the Master would pay for his sleepless night, but now, full of the satisfaction of a too-easy job quickly dispatched, the Master felt more than alive, with a needle-sharp awareness of all the detail spread out before him, streets running sort of true, scattered monuments piercing little plazas, eye-catching movements of pedestrians, taxis, and vehicles, and above him, the confident, mesmerizing rhythms of Abaddon's conspiracy as their slashing wings carried the taxi along. It was good to be an American, a Burrsburger, a black.

He directed the birds with whistles to where he wanted to go—not the High Court. They skirted the restricted air space above the White House, then crossed the north wing of the Capitol to a crooked little alley between two imposing but sagging buildings from the Barnum administration, northeast of the Court.

The Master dismissed the ravens and waited until they were out of sight. The heart of a raven no man could truly know, and it was wise not to underestimate their intelligence or their capacity for betrayal.

His true destination was one more block east. Unobserved, he climbed a wall, finding familiar handholds in bricks laid by unsteady hands.

He crossed a low-sloped roof. From it hung a stoplight cable, stretched across the street. Without hesitation, he walked across the cable.

No one saw him. No one ever did. People never looked up at the stoplight. It had not worked in years.

Over the next roof he scurried, down the wall and into the alley there. The Master stepped over a wino who lay passed out, unaware. Then he took shelter in the shadow of a wagon. It overflowed with garbage from a time before anybody could remember.

He waited, alert for any sound or movement. He was alone.

He lifted a metal chest full of wrenches and rusty old revolvers and slid down into the hole thus uncovered.

This was one of several secret entrances to the Court. Only the Master knew of it. It was a secret handed down from the previous Master.

The Supreme Court Building was a house of many mansions. Every Chief Justice had put his mark on the layout. Above ground, to be sure, little had changed; but below, the Court had extended its roots like an invasive weed. Grottoes and subterranean lakes, grand and intimate, were laid down in the District muck, as well as feasting halls, dungeons and torture chambers, factories and laboratories, escape hatches and bolt holes, secret passages, dormitories and brothels (these last now unused, and the cause of much wild speculation)—with everything interconnected by a bewildering maze of twisty tunnels.

The architecture? Call it Rat Romanesque. The stonework was rusticated and the arches were ponderous. Everywhere, Potomac waters leaked and leached, and slime was a universal constant. Moss and other less wholesome flora lived—no; say rather, *failed to die*—in the primordial muck. Torchlight advantaged sickly, etiolated imitations of healthy cousins from higher climes. Their effluvia permeated every corner of the endless warren.

No one, not even the Chief Justice (certainly not the Chief Justice!) knew the Court Underground better than the Special Master.

He weaved his way through a serpentine tunnel, never needing to feel his way despite the absolute darkness, never staining his robe or even his fingers on the mildewy stone.

He could hear the grinding of the machinery of government. It was louder than usual. Its urgency threatened to strip the government's gears.

Near the end, over the Great Grotto, he was guided by pinpoints of red light. These were tiny holes somebody had drilled in the floor. The stone between the tunnel and the grotto was thin here.

The Special Master was not devious, but he was professionally curious. He was the eyes and ears of the Chief Justice. He always investigated.

He spied through the peep holes. The Chief Justice was receiving petitions. Mencken, as the most senior clerk present, handed the Chief parchments with citizen's requests for this or that.

The Chief Justice tossed a parchment over his shoulder. Mencken handed him another, and with it a "magnifying glass," a gift of the petitioner, ostensibly a reading aid for the elderly Chief. In fact, the lens was crudely made and useless. The handle, however, was a massive thing made of pure gold.

This was *de rigueur*. A petition stood no chance without a gold magnifying glass, and to be taken seriously it really needed a diamond-studded handle as well.

The farsighted Chief examined the magnifying glass at arm's length. He judged its value and tossed it into a nearby basket.

Having been put in a sympathetic frame of mind, he read the petition. His mouth moved as he silently considered the wording and thought through the political implications, playing out the various side effects in his mind. Inevitably, the granting of a judicial indulgence was disruptive to the status quo, and jealousy is at least as powerful a force as envy. In the judging of competitive interests, the Chief was the undisputed champion. That is what made him the Chief.

That, and his birds.

At this moment, Abaddon completed his own path down to the Great Grotto, on wings whose beats were magnified by the enclosing stones. He took a perch next to the Chief. The Chief gestured to a bowl of raw pork, and Mencken, with an expression that might have been restrained disgust and might have been respectful impassivity, passed the Chief a red greasy strip. The Chief fed Abaddon from his own hand.

The Chief sighed, then sighed again. Absently he fondled his gavel, a magnificently tooled platinum gift. (That was one giver who got all he petitioned for!) The Chief rubbed his face, then called loudly for chocolate. A young clerk brought a cup over. The Chief gave another order, no more than a grunt, and a shot of whiskey sloshed into the cup. Yet another, more impatient bark prompted another pour. The Chief drank it down in one draught with a shaky hand.

"So, what we have here," the Chief said, "is from residents of an apartment building up in Misadelphia. They've got coin-operated flush toilets. The landlord raised the price to two bits per flush. The court is asked to order it back to one."

Mencken said, "They should be happy they got flush toilets."

A discussion followed. With only one good ear, the Master could not hear everything, but this kind of discussion happened daily in the Court. The outcome held no interest.

The Chief shifted ponderously in his leather chair and reached for a blank opinion pre-signed by four of the justices. The addition of the Chief's signature would make it the law of the land.

The Chief signed the opinion. He scrawled some instructions and put it on a short stack. Junior clerks would add the legalese.

Such was a typical day. The pile of discarded petitions behind the Chief was periodically swept up, and the basket of magnifying glasses was regularly emptied by clerks with shovels. The Court's legions of officers, agents, enforcers and charges did not pay for themselves, and taxes alone never seemed to be sufficient, no matter how many times they were raised. Bribes—let us call a spade a spade—were an essential lubricant of the two-stroke engine of justice.

The Special Master watched them. He scrutinized the clerks. Were any shirking? Were any pocketing the gold? Were they failing in any way to lighten, however they might, the Chief's crushing burden?

A senior clerk entered and, seeing the Chief Justice was busy, began to whisper into Mencken's ear.

"What is it?" asked the Chief.

"The Cohort of '29 is all taken care of."

"Any trouble?"

The newly arrived clerk shook his head. "Surrendered without incident. None were harmed."

"For now."

Abruptly, the Chief swept the remaining petitions to the floor and made to rise from his seat. Clerks hurried to help him. "I don't need your help!" the Chief spat, but he did not otherwise refuse their strong grip. They stood him up and pointed his tottering body to the exit.

The "Cohort of '29" or simply the "Twenty-Niners," were those young men, all the same age, who had been recruited for clerkships in the year of 1929. They had been personally recruited by the previous Special Master. They were significant to this Special Master because he was one of them. They were significant to everyone because they had been recruited based on one criteria: their physical appearance. Every member of the Cohort of '29 looked just like him.

Academic Paper

Plot or Not: Considering Evidence of a Conspiracy Against the Electoral College

John Dewey

American Journal of Alternate History
Vol. 1, No. 1 (September, 1944), pp. 17-349

Published by: **Miskatonic University Press, Arkham, Mass.**

Abstract:

The Presidential Election of 1920 was a turning point for the Electoral College. The changes brought about by the Great Reformation the previous century had disrupted much in the United States, not only politically, but also culturally and, not the least, demographically. In 1920, no Natural Born Citizen was found to be alive in the U.S., and thus, the Electoral College could not fulfill its duty to elect citizens to the offices of President or Vice President.

This was the same year a number of ceremonial innovations were introduced, which over time evolved into the elaborate marching and singing we have today. Remarkably, these innovations had such a strong impact upon the Electors that the meeting culminated in many fundamentalist Satanical (or even Twainist) phenomena, most notably the orgy of barking and howling that came to be known as the "Treeing of the Angel Gabriel".

Keen observers later noted the coincidence of the timing of these innovations, and their convenience to those who might want to distract the Electors from their frustrated duties. Those who inquired further into the decision process that led to the innovations have been met with a suspicious wall of silence. Into the information vacuum conspiracy theories have rushed. This paper describes the most widely held theories and evaluates them in light of new, intriguing evidence. It concludes with a call for a full accounting from those in the highest reaches of the judicial-industrial complex.

CHAPTER TEN

The Left Hand
Does Not Know

*O*ut of control.

Events were out of the Special Master's control.

Events were *never* out of the Special Master's control.

Helpless. Afraid. Unable to respond.

This was like Trotsky and Schuyler, like Rube Goldberg and the asbestos mine all over again.

Talk to the Chief.

That was it. The Master would confront the Chief, end the double-talk, and get the real dope. Either the Chief trusted his Master, or the Master would quit.

No more pussy-footing around.

The Chief must be half-way to the elevator. Still in the secret tunnels, the Master climbed a ladder down to the Chief's private quarters. At a peep hole, he waited. He waited a while. The elevator was slow, but not this slow.

The Chief had gone up!

The Master climbed again, stopping periodically to peep. No sign of the Chief. Had he gone to the surface? At the top, the Master peeped again. Mencken was there in the hallway, giving urgent instructions to other clerks. Where was the Chief?

Was he headed outside? He was not in the Courtroom. Not in the Great Hall.

The Master peeped into the Second Robing Room. It ought to have been too dark to see. Instead, light came from the open door, light framing a stooped, tottering, robed figure. The Chief Justice.

The Chief spoke. "Justice. Learned. Hand."

"Bonjour, mon ami." The words came out in a rasp of pain.

What in Sam Hill was this? Small talk?

"Consarn you," The Chief replied. His voice was heavy with loathing. "Consarn you to Glory."

"Thank you, but I'm in no danger of going to Glory, or anywhere. You've got me tied to a log."

"Dry up." The Chief reached through the bars to grab a handful of Hand's hair and pull his head back. For a long time, neither man spoke.

"I think I'll give you a nice, long thrashing."

The Chief, torturing Hand? That was...wrong. Hand might get hurt.

The Chief continued the stare.

"You're the most stubborn I ever met. You've set some kind of record. Congratulations."

Hand said nothing.

"I expect today will be no different. But soon—" and here, the Chief's self-control got away from him, and he nearly choked, "—soon you will see what I'm willing to do. And then you'll tell me everything."

The Chief Justice slammed Hand's head against the log. The huge eyebrow shook like a carpet on cleaning day. The Chief left without a backward glance, his magnificent robe ballooning behind him. The door slammed shut and the key rammed the deadbolt home.

The Master had been told the only key to that room was the one in his possession.

Learned Hand closed his eyes. His chest shook in silent heaves, and the Master could not tell if the justice was sobbing, or laughing, or both.

Laughing—or crying: either one was a rebuke to the Chief. The Master would not tolerate it.

Without caution, without hesitation, the Master ran: through the secret tunnel, to the hidden entrance within the closet of his office, down the halls and back behind the Courtroom, to the second robing room. The Chief and his clerks were nowhere to be seen. Mencken was nowhere to be seen.

Good.

The Master's shaking hands fumbled for the key.

Bad. Do not let Justice Hand see.

He got the door open. Hand's great eyebrow could not hide its surprise, even in the gloom. The Master never came alone.

The Master grabbed Hand's hair by the fistful. It had not been cut in decades. There was much to hold.

"We have played this game long enough."

The Master took the stick from where it hung on the cage. Out of habit, he smote the log.

Hand's eyebrow observed with interest.

The Master swung harder. Bits of bark came loose. One speck flew into Justice Hand's eye.

"Hey. Watch it!"

The Master altered the angle of the stick. Some of the force of the blow landed on Hand's pale, blue-veined abdomen.

"Ow! That *hurt.*"

"There is...*something.* Something *going on.* I'm tired of being kept in the dark."

"Well, see, that's just it," said Hand, twisting away from the stick as much as his bonds would allow him, "I'm kind of in the dark too."

A big chunk of bark flew right out of the cage.

"Stop! *C'est vrai!*"

"The Chief killed a man yesterday. He looked just like me. Now he's rounding up the Cohort of '29. They *all* look like me."

Across Hand's eyebrow marched a parade of passing emotions: surprise, excitement, fear, confusion, dread—not the usual response from this cool-as-a-cucumber associate justice.

"What year is it?" It was not exactly a question.

What?

The Master swung the stick at Hand's head. He barely missed. The log thudded in agony. "Stop messing around. I'll kill you—see if I don't!"

"No. Please. I know bupkis. Just tell me, isn't it 1946?"

"Yes, it is 1946! Tell me what that means!"

"1946. And the Chief just... Oh. My. God."

The Master's stick was at Hand's throat now, pressing downward on the windpipe.

"Tell me everything! Now!"

Hand's only sounds were strangled grunts vaguely accented in French.

From behind came the sound of the door opening.

"What in the name of all that is profane is going on here?"

Again the Master saw the silhouette of a great robed figure. The only sound was his own panting breath.

The Chief Justice closed the door. The darkness was total. How like a cage, the room; how closely the three men were trapped together.

The Chief struck a match and lit a candle.

"You—" said the Chief, pointing a finger, "*What do you did?* You were supposed to go to the Electoral College. Are you *ignoring* me?"

"Your Honor! I went, and finished the job, just as you said—"

"What I *said* was five days. *Five days!*"

"I deserve to know—"

No. Stop. The Master could not mention the Twenty-Niners. The Chief must not know all the Master knew, or how he knew it.

"I deserve to know whatever you've been up to or what's going on behind my back."

The Master felt his argument going soft like a worn-out tire.

"You *deserve?*"

The rescue from the mine; the promotion to Special Master; a life of privilege: the Chief had shown the Master great friendship through the years, and friendship goes both ways.

"No one has been more loyal to you than me."

"Oh, really?"

The Chief shouted some commands through the door. Mencken replied, and went to fetch a prisoner. That would take a few minutes. With nothing better to do, the Chief took the stick from the Master's hand and began idly whacking Justice Hand.

"You're not going to ask him a question?"

The Chief looked over his shoulder. "No."

In that moment, something odd happened. Something important. While the Chief had not been looking, something like an ocean wave passed over Learned Hand's eyebrow.

Hand wanted to tell him something.

Talk. Distract the Chief.

"Well, I think you're not beating him hard enough."

Hand's eyebrow contorted in rage. Clearly, it did not understand how the Chief's mind worked.

"Applesauce." The Chief, already sweating from the minimal exertion, relaxed his beating arm and turned around. "Stubborn cases like this can be broken only through despair. It's the long haul that makes the difference. If I pace myself..."

The Master had hoped for a lighter beating. Instead, he got a lecture. All the better.

With the Chief's eye off him, Hand went to work. With jaw clenched and the veins in his neck swelling, Hand began to move his eyebrow. The long, coarse hairs came alive. Each one moved independently. They twitched like cat tails. They grouped themselves into tufts. Hairs parted to expose the pale skin underneath.

The Chief droned on.

Patterns emerged in Hand's eyebrow. Chaotic patterns. Hand's breaths came in short gasps. Sweat trickled down his face.

Something recognizable formed from the kaleidoscope of locks and parts. Letters! A word!

PLOOB

"Ploob?" The word slipped out of the Master's mouth before he knew it.

"What?" The Chief asked, absently. The Master shook his head, and the Chief resumed his lecture. Dealing with rebels was a favorite topic.

Hand redoubled his efforts. His brow, relaxed for a moment, convulsed like a dying rodent. Hand struggled, gasped. His face turned red. Once again, brow hairs moved to form letters, more clearly this time:

FLOOD

The Master signaled his understanding with the barest lifting of his head. Learned Hand's eyebrow went limp. Hand opened his mouth wide to suck in great greedy gulps of air, silently.

Flood. A clue—but on its own, worthless. The Master needed more. How—?

The door opened without warning and Mencken pushed a prisoner into the room. The Chief and the Master faced the newcomers.

The strangeness of the Cohort of '29 came back to the Master in a rush. This man standing before him, hands tied behind his back, could have been his brother. The age, height, face, hair, eyes, build, even voice and manner—all strikingly similar to the Master. He and the other Twenty-Niners had been personally chosen by the old Special Master according to some ideal, some template of human perfection that existed only in the old Special Master's mind. No explanation had ever been given. It had been the topic of much speculation among the clerks at the time.

Strange. Strange. Strange.

"Take off your belt." The Chief was addressing the Master.

The Master obeyed the order. The black strip hung in a loose arc between his hands like a demonic smile.

"Now strangle this traitor."

Strangle? Why? Why did it always have to be a murder?

The Master opened his mouth. No words came.

Mencken pushed the prisoner into the center of the room and joined the Chief, putting the Master's back to the door.

Mencken was giving the Master a chance to run. He *wanted* the Master to run.

The Master stood there, his mind pristine and unsullied by any thought. He experienced a moment of clarity, of pure observation. With the Chief, Mencken, and the prisoner all awaiting the Master's reaction, Justice Hand was busy.

"We're waiting," said the Chief.

Again, the associate justice's face turned red with exertion. His eyebrow came alive, knitting together another clue:

CNGRSS

Congress?

Flood, congress. Congress flooded. A flood in congress. Was that the message?

"Obey me!" said the Chief.

"No." The Master's answer finally came, a hoarse croak. "I won't do it. This man—" What was his name? Bob? Bill? "—is my friend."

"Mencken?"

Mencken could not wait. With a crooked little smile, he pulled his own belt out and in a moment's time looped it several redundant times around the poor clerk's throat.

"Enough!" said the Chief. "Save him for later."

Mencken obeyed the Chief's order. He was a model of obedience, when he could get credit for it.

"Take this man back to prison."

Mencken's glee was already disguised as he put his belt back on and pushed the clerk out of the room. No doubt he would indulge in a self-congratulatory smirk when he was safely out of sight.

What a loathsome human being.

"Do you understand?" The Chief's palms were turned out in a conciliatory gesture.

"Are you going to arrest me too?"

The Chief stepped back like one slapped.

"You really don't know me, after all these years?"

No, the Master did not really know him.

"Is it over? Am I—*done?*"

"No." Whatever the Chief was feeling, it was not anger. It was something unfamiliar.

Sobriety—that was it. The Chief was as parched as a Puritan.

"Maybe it's over for you, but not for me," the Chief said. "It will *never* be over."

The Chief placed his hand on the back of the Master's neck. It was kind. Paternal.

"Trust me. *Trust me.* It's better for everyone if you follow my orders, exactly."

When was the last time the Master had been touched by another human being, except in rage? The Master could not remember.

"I'm sending you north. To Haskill. We have a border dispute there with Canada; take charge of the negotiations. I know—it's unexciting work. Do it anyway. Get your carcass out of Burrsburg, and keep it out. I'll tell you when you can return.

"Obey me, and all will be well. Disobey, and I won't be able to protect you anymore. Do you understand?"

No. The Master did not understand.

"Yes."

"Good."

High above Burrsburg, a raven taxi circled. In that most secure location, the Special Master opened the sealed envelope of orders he had stolen as he left the Court. This was one of eight copies, the copy prepared, pointlessly, for Justice William Howard Taft. You could always count on the clerkocracy to perform with thoroughness precisely those actions which were useless.

The Master would read the orders twice: once, quickly, so as to determine in which direction he should order the birds to go; then a second time, slowly, to memorize every word.

He began. A strangled cry escaped him. The birds faltered. They were already tired of circling, and expected his command. It was not forthcoming.

"Satan forbid!"

The Master held the parchment away from himself. Whether he did so because the foulness of its message, or from a hope that, from a distance, the words would rearrange themselves into something less hateful—something less *insane*—even he could not say.

"All citizens matching the following description will be brought to the capital for interrogation and eventual execution by burnt sacrifice..."

Burnt sacrifice! They did not *do* that anymore.

"...approximately thirty-five years old, six feet one inch tall, black hair..."

The exact description of the Master and the Twenty-Niners.

"...the Special Master alone is exempted from this order for now..."

That news was not good: it was a fist in the gut.

"...oversee the work to the last detail, with clerks and local officials working immediately under your command...each state will meet or exceed its quota...a full one tenth of one percent of the population...in every case where there is any doubt, the traitor must be slated for death...states which achieve the stretch goal of point zero one five percent will enjoy special favor...Wm. O. Douglas to Sylvania and Polypotamia, James Clark McReynolds to Mississippi, Alabama and Florida, Harlan Stone to..."

How was this possible? The Chief Justice would slay tens of thousands of men? Why?

The Special Master sat and wept. Why did it always, always, have to be murder?

The Ravens circled and circled. Below, the city stirred to life in response to the Chief's mad order, but the Master gave the birds no command. After many minutes, they lost patience. With many an angry "Rok! Rok!" they shook the frame of the taxi. The birds were known to throw passengers clean off when sufficiently provoked.

The Special Master stood and tore up the parchment into bits. He scattered them to the wind and stabbed his finger downward, toward the skull-like dome of the Capitol Building.

"Enough! That way! Take me to the House of Representatives!"

SCOTUS Opinion

OCTOBER TERM, 1916

Syllabus

NOTE: Where it is feasible, a syllabus (headnote) will be released, as is being done in connection with this case, at the time the opinion is issued. The syllabus constitutes no part of the opinion of the Court but has been prepared by the Reporter of Decisions for the convenience of the reader. See Satan v. God, 200 U.S. 321, 337.

SUPREME COURT OF THE UNITED STATES

Syllabus

UNITED STATES v. LEARNED HAND

ON EXCEPTIONS TO THE REPORT OF THE SPECIAL MASTER

No. 9—751515. Argued December 25, 1916—Decided December 25, 1916.

Following a brilliant career in government, Learned Hand was appointed U.S. Ambassador to the France in 1912. His appointment came after a strong recommendation by the Chief Justice, then a mere associate justice. Hand, whose intellect is paired with an engaging, if dry, wit, had cultivated a friendship with said justice as well as the president, which in retrospect seems suspicious. Ambassadorships are plum positions in any government; due to unique domestic circumstances in the United States since the time of the Great Reformation, the motives of any prospective ambassador must be scrutinized with especial care. More than a few have turned traitor or otherwise ditched their posts for the "fleshpots of Egypt", as it were.

Hand was duly shipped off to the France. Almost from the moment he arrived, reports of suspicious associations with the natives came to the attention of the government. Although not a particularly young man, Hand was clearly too spirited for such a sensitive post. Disappointment turned to alarm when it was whispered Hand had become friendly with a relative of "His Most Christian Majesty" the King of the France.

The Chief Justice, volunteering to act as counsel for Hand and appointed by the court in the defendant's absence, moved to halt preemptively the act of recall, arguing recall is inherently a function of the executive, it is risky, and that anyway the reports serving as the basis of the recall were mere rumors.

The Court assigned the case to a Special Master, who has conducted proceedings and has filed a report. The report recommends denying Hand's motion to halt preemptively the act of recall.

Held: Defendant's exception is overruled.

1. Ambassadors serve at the pleasure of the president. In extraordinary circumstances such as do currently apply, and as a practical matter for the necessary functioning of government, this court may, at its discretion, aid a President of limited capacity in the several duties of the executive. Put crudely, in the present crisis, an ambassador serves at the pleasure of the Chief Justice, *de facto*.

2. Many attempts to recall ambassadors in similar circumstances have failed due to excessive respect shown to diplomatic niceties, to the considerable embarrassment of the United States. The territorial integrity of foreign nations is a minimal concern of this court. Fears of tit-for-tat regarding sovereign U.S. territory are not compelling, as the briefest perusal of books of history, geography, and public health will confirm. An invasive military strike to enforce the recall of an ambassador is necessary in this situation and will likely cause few undesirable side effects.

3. The Chief Justice may assume executive function as necessary for good order. Rumor is sufficient cause for removal of an ambassador. Ambassador Learned Hand is recalled from the France. All necessary force and stealth shall be employed to enforce this ruling. The dignity and customs of the United States shall not be mocked. *Ave Satanas!*

Exceptions to Special Master's Report overruled, and Master's recommendations adopted. Hand's motion denied.

REAGAN, C.J., delivered the unanimous opinion for the Court.

CHAPTER ELEVEN

House

The Special Master had vanished from the Earth. Pedestrians on First Street, east of the Capitol, who dared to notice a man leaping from the platform of a bespoke raven taxi did not see the robe of that office. He did carry, it was true, a duffel which might be construed as a black robe artfully folded and suspended by a handle twisted from a belt of the same material. All they caught in their peripheral vision, however, was the uniform of a clerk of the Court.

In any event, he was a black, and the browns avoided his gaze and his path. A bow wave of timid citizenry spread before him as he made his way through the afternoon's heavy traffic. Some browns even shouted a helpful "make way!"—helpful, that is, to fellow browns, as proximity to a black greatly increased the risk of arbitrary arrest.

The black walked into a looming parabolic shadow and a haze of barnyard odors. The House of Representatives made its influence known.

Entering the House was a remarkable event. This "clerk" wished to be unremarkable, but that was not an option.

All the windows and doors of the Capitol were boarded over and sealed with pitch. No light nor even sound passed in or out. Certainly, human beings did not leave. If an incumbent died, a newly elected

Congressman would be sent in. Other than that, typically, only five things entered: food, drink, tobacco, ink, and parchment.

Typically, only four things escaped: urine, feces, smoke, and legislation.

The Special Master was about to do the atypical.

Guards lounged about the only entrance. In a small booth, the sergeant at arms devoted his attention to rolling crude cigars made from a leaf the Master did not recognize. By the door, workmen slid sheets of parchment under the door, or shoveled gruel onto cookie sheets and slid them in, or, as needed, poured ink or water through a funnel into the keyhole. This work went on, more or less continually, day and night.

The guards ignored him. The Master coughed. The sergeant of arms tossed a new-formed cigar into a bucket and licked his fingers. "No one gets in or—"

He turned around. He saw the black loincloth. His eyes got big, then small.

He grunted at the nearest guard. The man wiped dust from his rear end as he stood.

The Special Master assumed an unfamiliar role.

"You and your men deserve some refreshment tonight. It's on me." He handed the sergeant of arms a fistful of bills.

Everyone's attitude improved noticeably.

"No one need know of my visit here. Not even..." The Master nodded in the direction of the Supreme Court Building. The sergeant of arms agreed to the terms by way of pocketing the cash. He led the Master to an opening in the wall covered by rough-cut lumber. He gave the Master an old-fashioned iron key.

"Keep this hidden, and whatever you do, don't lose it. It's your only way out. One key, one man, one exit; that's just the way it works. Opposite this spot, on the west front, is the exit. Don't lose your head in there. Good luck. You'll need it."

Two guards unlatched the lumber. The boards swung down on hidden hinges. The Master lay on them with his feet pointed in. The guards unceremoniously pushed the boards back up into position.

The Master was tipped into a chute. Even though he expected it, the fall terrified him.

It was over in a moment. He found himself at the base of a metal playground slide. The slide had dropped him one story and deposited him more or less gracefully onto the floor of an unlit room.

From the acoustics he could tell the room was not large. The only sounds were human. They were horrible.

Moans. Whispers. Chattering teeth.

Some distant loudmouth declaimed a confident sermon of baroque, polysyllabic gibberish. Nearer by, somebody came awake and approached.

"Please, kind sir, there's been a mistake. I assure you I'm quite sane. I've only been here a week, you see—well, I suppose it's been a week, but a fellow can't tell night from day in here."

The voice was very near now. The Master felt fumbling hands clutch his arm.

"You see, they asked me if I wanted to stand for a seat, and I said I would, being as much a patriot as the next man. I had *no idea* there'd be no leaving once I entered. That's not right, if you ask me. A fellow's got a right to resign from any job, even public service, that's what they taught me. And I went to the best of schools. I was the second son of a Russian count, by the way, in case that means anything to you, I know that's not the American way but still, I hope you have some appreciation for good breeding and will see that I *simply do not belong* in this nest of angels. I *knew* from the start this couldn't be good. Locked all the doors and windows, they did. Said it was for their own safety. *National security,* you know. *National security!*" (This last was a shriek.) "Did you know they *locked all the doors?* They locked all the windows. And the doors. That can't be healthy. Those poor congressmen, what did they ever do? Never seeing the light of day? That would get to a fellow, eventually. Bound to. Make you half crazy. Eventually. Even the best of sorts break down in a horrible, horrible—sir? *Mercy of Satan! Are you listening?* You've *got to help* me—"

An officer of the court hears many pleas over time, and learns a special contempt for the desperate. That contempt urged the Master to throw an elbow into the throat of this unseen man.

He took the man by the wrists and slowly pushed him away.

"No, please! *Please!*"

The Master backed away. He tried to move silently. He tripped over a body lying on the ground, and fell with a thud.

The body was stiff as a board.

He tripped over another. This one was squirmy and full of curses. It also stank like a pit toilet. Its hand reached out and caught him by the ankle as he tried to stand. He sat down heavily. Now the Russian aristocrat was on him, screaming "Get me out! Please!" and the commotion earned curses and worse. The room, small though it may be, contained a dozen or more live men.

The commotion fed on itself. Men who had lain silent joined in the babble, and their excitement roused others in turn. Most shouted curses or giggled hysterically; very few had even that capacity for rational expression which the Russian still possessed.

Hands tugged down on Master's loincloth. He pushed out with his hands in a breaststroke and learned that clothing was optional here—no, not really optional; it was exceptional. His clean garment was a coveted prize.

He was badly outnumbered, but he was strong and sane, and no pity restrained him now.

He threw a left elbow to a throat and a right knee to a groin. Two kicks, and he broke free. He lunged and struck his face against a marble wall and was momentarily dazed.

Groping hands found him. He swatted them back. Inspired by a thought, he felt along the wall and found a doorway. Noises told him the next room was also crowded, but he had no intention of leaving. He leapt up and caught the edge of the elaborated trim with his fingertips. He pulled himself up and lifted his legs until no part of his body hung down.

For many minutes he hung there. His fingers ached, but held. In the utter darkness, the madmen stumbled about, but their fumbling hands and minds were frustrated. They could not find him, and in time forgot what they sought. One by one, they returned to their corners, each one whimpering or giggling as his particular madness dictated.

The Capitol Rotunda

From *Capitol Building Visitor's Pamphlet*, Self-Guided Tour, p. 6

The Rotunda is a space of great solemnity, the center of our civic religion. It is the site of six presidential inaugurations. It is the site of 15 presidential funerals (and counting!)—all who have died in office. The last live human sacrifice to the Lord Satan in the United States was not offered on an altar in a church, but rather right here in this Rotunda. Note the blood that stains the floor, near the center. It is one of history's greatest ironies that that is the blood of Priest-President Aleister Crowley.

Look at the whole floor. Note the repeating pattern of not-quite-concentric circles. These are highly speculative representations of the orbits of the planets. The round object in the center is the Earth. At the center of the earth, in the lowest, most important place (and hard to see, due to the blood stains) is the Lord Satan himself. The Aristotelian cosmological system was taught in all U.S. schools by law as late as 1910.

Interleaved among the orbits of the planets are spiral tracks which represent alchemical circles and Hindu mandalas.

Crowley, whatever his faults, boasted the finest occultical mind of his generation. It was he who hypothesized the astrological significance in the ratios of the room's dimensions.

Look at the paintings on the walls. To the north you will see a depiction of President Edgar Allen Poe receiving the text of the National Anthem on plates of gold from Abaddon, Daemon of the First Raven. This spirit possessed the figurehead of *Black Beak*, flagship of the piratical founders of our country. It was Abaddon, so President Poe reported, that appeared to him in a vision.

To the east, look at the painting of James Buchanan, our first bachelor president. He led our nation through its greatest crisis. Here, he is depicted as president, standing in the Thorn Garden. His hand holds a parchment; this is the legislation originally called the Great Compromise, but today called the Great Reformation. His struggle and sacrifice made possible the one, unified nation we enjoy today. Note the bonfires in the background, built of corpses; extreme necessity meant many of the deceased were never buried. Note the pentagram pendant Buchanan wears, a sign of his support from the Church. He wears a stovepipe hat, which was the style at the time. Note his swim fins which speak to the lowest moment of his presidency, when he was forced to swim the Potomac River to escape a murderous mob of "suffragettes."

On the south wall, see the Landing of the Pirates at Plymouth Slough. Depicted is the legendary moment Captain Hendrick Lucifer removes his foot from his boot which has become stuck in the mud. This moment of landfall, this "one small step for man" somehow seems a fitting start for our Satanic Republic. The piece of wood next to him is the peg leg of a submerged Cornelis Corneliszoon Jol. In the mid-ground, the artist painted the pirate ship in a rather fanciful manner, with the raven figurehead covered, anachronistically, in gleaming chrome, and the Jolly Roger, which formed a basis for our national flag, painted boldly across the mainsail. Out on the horizon, see a dot disrupting the blazing red of the rising sun: this is the Mayflower, retreating in humiliation toward Haiti. Finally, note the several pairs of feet jutting out from the lower left corner of the painting. These are natives who have succumbed to an epidemic of the flux, or possibly the ooze, blamed on Lucifer's lieutenant, Daniel Elfrith.

On the west wall, see the most challenging of the four rotunda paintings. This is the Battle of Okefenokee, the most decisive (and arguably, only) pitched battle ever fought between the U.S.A. and the Republic of Haiti. Because of the painting's semi-abstract technique and its lack of a focal point, it can be difficult to comprehend the details the artist placed so promiscuously. It is best if you start at the lower left and allow your eye to trace a zigzag pattern upward. First, note the wavy humanoid figures with bloody crosses on their chests; these are Haitians sinking into the waters of the swamp. The jagged edges rising up are the jaws of alligators. Even the trees of the swamp are against the invaders, as their curlicue branches arch over them menacingly and entangle them. At the center bottom, stacks of shiny, technologically advanced (for their time) weapons lie abandoned by the Haitians; these will be looted by the Americans and turned against their creators. At the center right, tall, confident American soldiers in bold swaths of thick brown paint raise their arms, not to celebrate victory so much as to release deadly clouds of fleas from their armpits. In the upper left corner, a lurid flash of red-orange denotes the detonation of the first atomic bomb, the work of the American spy Learned Hand. It destroyed Orlando along with most of the invaders.

In the upper right, a vast conspiracy of ravens provide reconnaissance and honor Hell by flying in a downward-pointing chevron formation.

Now, look up into the domed ceiling. This never-completed fresco is titled "The Apotheosis of the Spirit of Burr". The viewpoint is within the pit of hell, looking up toward hell's gates. Ravens and adorable baby demons cling to the rocky surfaces which are, here and there, licked by tongues of flame. The center remains mostly blank; the artist quit over a payment dispute. (This occurred during the Great Fiscal Crisis of 1868-1904.) The artist did take the time to paint President Aaron Burr as a parting gesture. Burr is cartoonishly drawn urinating into the Pit.

[Editor's Note: The following words are printed diagonally across the page in bold red stencil: CAPITOL CLOSED TO VISITORS UNTIL FURTHER NOTICE]

CHAPTER TWELVE

The Underworld

Most madmen are incapable of stealth. In rare cases, however, madness will increase the aptitude for stealth by many times. This was the thing the Master feared most. Already, after one hour of wandering without light, his ears were sharply alert for every sigh and shuffle. The whisper of pant legs against one another—some congressmen wore pants, devils be praised—or even gentle slaps of bare feet on marble floor might betray their owner. Like a bat, he could judge distance, size, strength, and unlike a bat, he could even judge mental state, all from the slightest sound.

Hear that syncopated pad-pad-pad? The man was barefoot, unsteady, and without purpose: a harmless madman. Hear those buttocks sliding along the floor, self-lubricated with diarrhea? Dysentery: one particular honorable gentleman's district would soon experience a vacancy. Hear the click-click of teeth on bone? Worse than mad, far worse: conventional lunatics do not eat other human beings.

The Master's ears also told him where he was. Only one room in the whole building enclosed such a space. The ceiling soared and reflected echoes in a concave pattern. The Master snapped his fingers, and the transient noise confirmed: the Rotunda.

Somewhere in this room, Crowley had died. The Master was still a boy in the mines when it happened. As long as he had been in Burrsburg, this building had been sealed up. Never a chance before to investigate the crime. Nor any chance now.

He had built a pile of parchments. They were everywhere in this place. A steady supply was pushed in daily and not nearly an equal amount left. Some of the blank pages were picked up by those higher-functioning Congressmen, and on these they wrote their legislative bills.

"My learned friend," said an approaching voice, oily and familiar, "I am hoping I might have your pledge of support for this resolution which congratulates my beloved Miskatonic University Football team on winning their conference title this year. They were looking awfully promising in the summer, back when I came here. I'm certain...by now, they must have won..." The man's voice faded as he wandered on.

Good. No need to hurt this one.

The Master pulled out a match. He did not have many. He struck it against the sole of his shoe. Men gasped all around him. The tiny light stunned them. He lit the pile of parchments. In the dry air, they were ready to burn. The flame took to the fuel with a zeal, and in moments a large bonfire illuminated the cylindrical hall.

In the unsteady light, obscured by swirling smoke seeking an exit, shadow-casting plaster demons pranced in their friezes. Congressmen threw up their hands, overwhelmed by the orange light. Some screamed and fled, some fell down and groveled, and some simply froze where they stood. The healthiest—those fully clothed in suits still recognizably white, with erect posture and proffering the inevitable bill—were vastly outnumbered.

"Why have you come to torment us?" screamed one, a man who slapped himself on the chest to punctuate the question. The Master saw a deep bruise on his pectoris. The slap was a compulsive habit.

The question shook them out of their stupor. Congressmen ringed the fire. The entire throng wailed and screamed. Accusatory parchment rolls became spokes, all pointing at himself, the hub. Clustered faces glowed orange in the fire light, with sunken eyes and open mouths etched in shadow. From these dehumanized heads emerged one word, shouted over and over in rhythm:

"Out! Out! Out! Out! Out!"

The Master pulled out a pistol. Plunking a white was an extreme act. Still, if it were his life or theirs, well—

The gun cowed them. Some recognized the threat, and hesitation spread throughout the crowd.

"Congressmen!" the Master said, his voice filling the great room. "I don't want to hurt you. I am here on a quest. When I have found what I want, I will leave you alone."

"No!" The word was shouted from every quarter. "Help me! Take me with you! Don't leave me here!"

The desperate men rushed the Master. He pointed his pistol straight up into the dome.

Bang!

The men fell back, deafened, defeated.

"To the first man who tells me what I want to know, I will give chocolate."

"Chocolate!" The men were cowering, yet that word whipped them to a frenzy. Some clutched their heads while others spun around in conflicted impulses.

Pitiful, wretched creatures.

"Tell me—"

"Yes? Yes?"

"—where in this place I can find—"

"Find what? Find what?"

"The flood?"

The Congressmen stopped. They simply returned the Master's stare with a look of utter confusion mixed with disappointment.

The Master said, "A whole floor, maybe. Probably down in the basement. A place underwater?"

"Water? Or piss?" This impertinence set them all a-titter. The men broke up into small groups as the less crackers among them discussed what possible meaning the Master's words could have.

"I was told to look for the flood!"

The weakness in his own voice embarrassed the Master. He began to consider the miserable possibility that Learned Hand had played him for a simp. He filled the idle seconds thinking how he could best reward Hand for his treachery.

The Master felt a hand on his arm. He hitched his pistol up, quite ready to use it.

This congressman looked less insane that the others. He was just as tall as the Master and his eyes looked sleepy, not crazed. They were set in a road-kill face on a huge head. His shirt was tucked in, despite his wide and awkward frame. That alone put him in the top ten percent on the sanity scale. Moreover, he was wearing a *tie*, and its silk tails were free of stains. There was only one clue the man might be less than perfectly right in his mind: his shirt was on backwards.

The congressman raised his hand with all deliberateness. *It's okay, you can put down the gun,* the hand said. With his other hand he covered his mouth, then began stepping backwards, one catlike foot after the other, until he was at the edge of the firelight's reach.

The meaning was plain: *follow me.*

The Master twisted a parchment into a skinny torch and lit it. He went where the sane congressman waited. He moved without haste. The others lost interest in him.

The congressman put his mouth to the Master's ear. "I know what you're looking for. Promise me you'll get me out of this—"

His voice caught.

"—this *horrible* place."

"You will be rewarded. Let's go!"

The congressman led the way. The Special Master put his pistol away and followed, one hand holding the makeshift candle and the other cupping the flame so it would not blow out. When the parchment was used up, its flame lit another. Loose sheets lay everywhere.

The meager light cast confusing shadows, and proved to be almost worse than useless. It enabled glimpses of men in advanced states of madness and corpses in advanced states of decay. Congress-*men?* The term was an obscene mockery of what they had once been. They were congress-*things.*

Grasping hands slowed them. The path could not have been far as the raven flies, but it meandered through too many rooms to count. The Special Master feared the journey would never end. Later, he feared it would.

With a start, he understood: he was going mad.

His breaths came quick and shallow. By Satan, he would not lose his mind! But the thought came insistent that many men had come to this place, some better than he, and they had succumbed. They had all succumbed..

For the sake of even one sane man—

"What's your name?"

The Master's question came as a burst. People had names. If something had no name, it was wasn't people. If these men could cling to their names, they might survive.

"My name?" The question was a hard one.

"O'Neill." The word emerged from his mouth deliberately, with tenderness. "Thomas O'Neill."

"Hello, Thomas."

"Everyone but my friends call me Tip."

Not sure how to take that.

"Tip."

They shook hands, and the brotherly warmth of their greeting pushed back, a little, the encroaching fog of dehumanizing madness.

"What's yours?"

Aw, Satan.

How could the Master have not anticipated the question? His usual fallback, the potent title "Special Master", shut people up nicely, but here would only raise awkward questions.

Tip was waiting for an answer. Think fast.

"In school they called me Six-Six-Six."

Tip grinned, and the Master felt his face mirroring that goofy expression which in its normalcy, its pure boyish simplicity, only drew more contrast to the House of Madness surrounding them.

Tip punched the Master on the chest, a light, playful tap. Not loving Tip was very, very hard.

"Let's go. The river is up ahead."

CHAPTER THIRTEEN

Speaking in Shakespeare

It started as a trickle, this flow of human waste. It became a brook, and now was almost a stream. Like a real river, the Potomac, say, or maybe the Hudson, it meandered among muddy banks, and like any American river, it stank. The reek had become so bad, the Special Master regretted leaving his robe behind, as he could have used its ample sleeves as a makeshift air filter. As it was, his tight-fitting, weird little tube of a clerk's uniform was useless.

And he trudged along, choking and gasping. Tip O'Neill seemed to be used to it. Such is the life of a legislator.

The men here did not use toilets, but most retained the instinct against indiscriminant urinating and defecating. So, they came to this hallway to relieve themselves, to where the uneven floor sank in a slight V and troughed the waste away.

Tributaries joined the main flow and made it grow. The Master, desperate to distract himself from the reek, sought refuge in the sanity of names. A river of this importance ought to be named. Its discoverer deserved the honor. Yes, the natives here knew of it, but their opinion did not count. The opinions of natives never did. Likely to them it was merely "The River." The Master was the discoverer, however; he was the Columbus of this horrible new world. He would name it...what?

Of course: the Pississippi.

Tip muttered something about "pumps" which were apparently "not working today." The Master marveled at the casual way Tip said it, then questioned his own poor hearing.

The river widened to fill the hall, but O'Neill was not daunted. Without hesitation he ripped a great door from its hinges—his arms were fat and strong—and tossed it upon the liquid. They appropriated an unused torchiere lamp to paddle or pole themselves about, and so they continued on their makeshift raft. Had they known of Dante's epic poem, they might have drawn the obvious comparison, the Master's Dante to O'Neill's Virgil, but *Inferno* was considered enemy propaganda, and banned.

They floated from room to room. They came upon knots of men here and there, arguing vociferously in the dark, and O'Neill would identify them as they passed: Armed Services; Ways & Means; Un-American Activities; Agriculture. One growling group of mutual biters and eye-gougers earned a snort from O'Neill: Ethics.

Always, the size and pace of the river increased. The flow tugged them in sudden urgency, and by the miserable light the Master saw they were upon a grand stairway, headed down. Down was exactly where he expected to find the flood, but not this fast.

"Wait!" he shouted.

"Hang on," O'Neill ordered.

O'Neill knew how to ride the rapids and in a moment they were leveled out again in calm waters. Nary a drop had touched them.

In the crypt, the sewage was so deep they knelt down to avoid the ceiling. The trapped effluvia made the Master woozy, and he was glad for an excuse to put his head down. The Master ripped some blivet from a pillar to help O'Neill paddle. He propelled them along the horrible subterranean river as best he could.

They arrived at the lowest place where the sewage stagnated. Columns guarded the very center of the crypt, a ring of Doric capitals above sickly, inverted twins reflected by the glop. On the columns were sconces—brazen imps holding lit torches. Periodically, one or another would blaze with almost invisible blue light as a cloud of methane wafted past it, giving the domed space a druidic glamour. Here was magic.

"Appropriations," whispered an awestruck Tip O'Neill.

An awesome tomb in the form of a mighty single block of Alabama marble occupied the central space. Through pale green-yellow liquid shown the severe, submerged letters carved deep in the tomb's side:

AARON BURR

The tomb's flat top, high and dry, was big as a room. A statuesque man in white raiment sat Indian style atop the tomb, serene, vain, and barking mad.

The raft bumped into the marble shore and the makeshift sailors jumped off, the Master lightly, the congressman less so. In the resulting splashing, the native of the stone island sprang back, seeming only then to have noticed he was surrounded by many thousands of gallons of piss-marinated excrement. He drew his charmeuse-lined cape protectively around him and resettled his top hat with a correct 10 degree tilt to the side. His mustache was waxed to needle points. The Master had never seen a more ridiculous person.

"Who's the pansy?"

The white man's fist moved so fast, and was so unexpected, that the Master was falling back to the tomb's edge before he knew he had been pasted.

O'Neill helped him up, brushed him off, and said, "Meet the honorable gentleman from Kiddsylvania, and a dear friend: Dan Flood."

The Master got up, cradling his jaw. "Flood! Flood is a person?"

"There is a tide!" said Flood, and then he spread his cape, as if to acknowledge the vastness of the ocean surrounding them:

> "There is a tide in the affairs of men
> Which, taken at the FLOOD—"

(Dan Flood grinned impishly as he shouted his own name.)

> "—leads on to fortune;
> Omitted, all the voyage of their life
> Is bound in shallows and in miseries."

The congressman held his pose, with only his peepers pivoting to gauge the reaction to his performance. The Master felt his hope fade as quickly as it had come.

"He's bats."

"I am but mad north-north-west: when the wind is southerly I know a hawk from a handsaw."

Very crazy. Still, he had to try.

"I believe you have something for me. Learned Hand sent me."

"Give me your hand. Art thou learned?"

The Master tried to shake hands with the lunatic, but the offer was purely rhetorical and he was left hanging.

"He's quoting Shakespeare," said O'Neill in a stage whisper. "He always does that."

"I'm not Learned Hand. I was sent by Learned Hand."

"An upright judge, a learned judge!"

O'Neill threw a thick arm around Flood's shoulder and squeezed him with suffocating familiarity.

"C'mon, Dan. This guy is important, a clerk of the court. I want you to help him out, see that he's taken care of."

Flood's contempt was refreshingly undisguised.

> "A kind of boy, a little scrubbed boy,
> No higher than thyself; the judge's clerk."

"Look, Dan," said O'Neill, "this guy here, if I help him, he'll help me. If you help me, I'll help you. That's the way it works. I don't need to tell you that."

The Master pulled Flood away from O'Neill and led him to the far end of the tomb. Would O'Neill overhear? He had to take the risk.

The Master whispered into Flood's ear, "I'm the Special Master."

Flood regarded him with disbelief.

"To the court! Why, what place make you special?"

"The Chief Justice appointed me the—"

"I pray you, is my MASTER yet return'd?"

This is not working. How to crack this nut?

"I pray you, is MY MASTER yet return'd?"

With this repetition, Flood was tapping the Master's chest, insistent and annoying. There was a message hidden in his yammering.

"I pray you, is MY MASTER yet return'd?"

Maybe he meant the old Special Master.

"The Master? He is...gone. Forever."

"Alas, poor Yorrick! I knew him, Horatio."

He knew the Special Master?

The Master pitched his whisper harsh and urgent. "You must have some dope for me. Something that Hand, or the Special Master, wanted you to tell me."

Flood suddenly assumed expressions that were surprised, then sagacious, then paranoid. He faced the river of sewage. He raised his arms out in a V.

> "There is a willow grows aslant a brook,
> That shows his hoar leaves in the glassy stream;
> There with fantastic garlands did she come,
> Of crow-flowers, nettles, daisies, and long purples,
> That liberal shepherds give a grosser name,
> But our cold maids do dead men's FINGERS call them."

"More of that longhair stuff," said O'Neill, coming over, but Flood pushed him away. Flood's eyes narrowed to slits. He held up his fingers in a curiously curved position. It looked painful, and familiar.

"Whose fingers?"

But Flood was frozen in place, letting the impact of the hand sign sink in.

"Danny, you know me, don't you?" said O'Neill, throwing both his bearlike arms around the thespian once again. O'Neill sang, drunkenly:

> "O Danny Boy!
> The pipes, the pipes are calling
> From glen to glen, and down the mountainside—"

"We were both born in Ireland," said O'Neill to the Master with a wink.

But Flood was breaking out of the bear hug and striking a new pose, with palms out in refusal. He spoke directly now to the Master.

> "Let me see
> thee a steward still, the fellow of servants, and not
> worthy to touch Fortune's FINGERS. Farewell."

"Judas Priest, Dan—we just got here," said O'Neill, but Flood was frozen again, in a tableau with his hands still out, but his fingers curved in that same, oddly familiar way.

"Those fingers—" the Special Master said, but Flood heard nothing. The actor relaxed his pose and wiped nonexistent sweat from his brow. He bowed, acknowledging with profound humility the rapturous and prolonged applause of the vast audience that existed only in his mind.

"This isn't a theater, Danny Boy."

Flood stopped mid-bow and looked hard at O'Neill, noticing him for the first time.

Flood growled, "All the world's a stage."

O'Neill's retort was swift. "All politics is local."

With that news, Flood went berserk, running laps around the tomb and shouting, "O, what a noble mind is here o'erthrown!" and waving his arms about.

"Dan's a great guy, really he is," said O'Neill, "you just gotta give him time."

The Master caught Flood as he ran past for the third time.

"Fingers?" he shouted into the congressman's face. "You were telling me about—" He made an approximation of Flood's hand sign. "—fingers?"

Flood regarded the Master thoughtfully, stuck his fingers deep into his ears and twisted the wax they drew forth into his pointy mustache. Then he entoned, "Up from my CABIN—"

(Cabin! The word was like a slap in the face.)

> "—My sea-gown scarf'd about me, in the dark
> Grop'd I to find out them, had my desire,
> FINGER'D their packet, and in fine withdrew
> To mine own room again."

The Master grabbed Flood's lapels. "Cabin? Fingers? Where?" He shook the congressman. "And why does it always have to be a cabin? A *cabin!*"

O'Neill pulled them apart. "It's all bunk. He don't know what he's saying."

But the congressman became even more adamant, tip-toeing up to the taller Special Master and speaking eye to eye.

> "I'll make you feed on berries and on roots,
> And feed on curds and whey, and suck the goat,
> And CABIN in a CAVE—"

"A cave?" The Master's question was a pitiful moan.

"—and CABIN in a CAVE, and bring you up to be a warrior, and command a camp."

This lunatic knew something!

"What cabin? What cave? Where are the fingers?"

Flood smiled, speaking conversationally, as his mind was stirred by the cool breeze of sanity.

"Cabin in a cave...to find out them...finger'd."

But just like that, his mood changed again. He put the back of his hand against his forehead and showed his audience his profile, posing in the hoariest of theatrical clichés.

> "Still your FINGERS on your lips, I pray.
> The time is out of joint; O cursed spite,
> That ever I—or rather, YOU—were born to set it right!"

Flood pivoted to make a mirror image pose.

> "Shall we now
> Contaminate our FINGERS with base bribes?"

Flood turned on the Special Master, shaking a finger in his face.

> "I had rather be a dog, and bay the moon,
> Than such a Roman."

Flood poured all his contempt into the next lines:

> "Did not great Julius bleed for justice' sake?
> What villain touch'd his body, that did STAB—"

That touched a nerve.

"That wasn't my fault! Just a kid, following orders!"

The Master punched him on the kisser.

Flood might be a pansy, but from the first he had proved himself a vicious pugilist. Now the Master held nothing back, returning the favor with interest, blow after blow. The learned gentlemen from the great state of Kiddsylvania crumpled like a concertina.

The Master's fists followed him down and O'Neill was on them a moment later, his bulk wallowing over the Master's back as he applied a full Nelson. The three grunted and gasped within the sandwich they formed on the floor.

"Get...off...me!"

The Master twisted violently and O'Neill's flabby arms gave way. The sandwich disintegrated into its three component parts. The men sat on the marble floor, panting, sucking the reeking stink deep into their lungs.

Congressman Flood was the first to recover.

"I prithee, take thy FINGERS from my throat."

And then he went to make the hand sign once again, but crab walked back as the Master's rage rose up.

"The cabin: is it in your district?"

Flood said nothing, but something almost approaching the resemblance of a kind of limited sanity lit his eyes.

"And your district is in New Gehenna?

"No," interjected O'Neill, but the Master pushed him aside.

"Where is your district? Tell me!"

Flood covered his face with his hands and whimpered.

"Alas, he hath no home, no place to fly to;
Nor knows he how to live but by the spoil."

"Aw, Dan," said O'Neill, throwing an arm around his colleague's shoulder, "you broke the first rule. You forgot where you came from." O'Neill turned his head and stage-whispered, "He's from the 10th District of Kiddsylvania."

"Kiddsylvania," asked the Master, "or New Gehenna?"

Flood's grin was huge and fey.

"March on, join bravely, let us to't pell-mell
If not to heaven, then hand in hand—"

And with that, he contorted both his hands into the finger sign and locked them together, one atop the other.

"—then hand in hand to HELL!"

The esteemed and learned gentleman from the great state of, apparently, Hell, spun around and screamed like a schoolgirl, or how an American might imagine a schoolgirl would scream. Tip O'Neill, a man feeling his main chance slipping away, tried to stop Flood with a "there, there, Dan" and "settle down, Dan!" but the Special Master waved him to the raft.

"We're done here. I understand him perfectly."

For once, Tip O'Neill was at a loss for words.

The Master took a torch from one of the columns, as it was far superior to his homemade ones, and handed it to O'Neill. The Master took the torchiere *qua* paddle himself, as the journey up would not be so easy and his upper body strength would be needed. They sailed away in a majestic bow wave, and Dan Flood, still cackling and lit by a dozen blue fires mainlining methane, receded to a tiny white dot with most of his secrets still securely locked inside his skull.

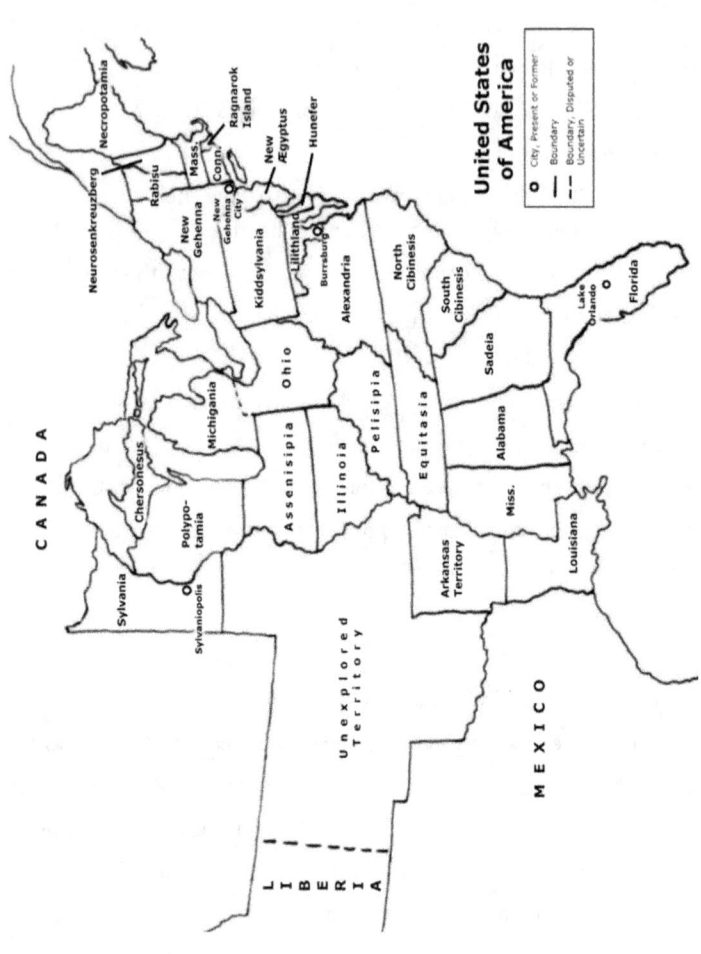

CHAPTER FOURTEEN

Evacuated

This second journey was not like the first. Once past the rapids and out of the river, they walked with purpose. Hope colors all things, making the terrible merely disgusting.

They came to the westernmost wall. O'Neill showed the Special Master a sliding metal door with a large keyhole.

"You have a key?"

The Master put in the key and turned it. It was so large, two hands were needed. O'Neill's fingers twitched but he let the Master work the metal parts that clanked as they moved. The Master pulled on the door. It slid aside.

The door revealed a tiny room, a mere booth. On the opposite wall was a sliding metal plate held in place by tracks. It was as big as a hubcap and hung waist-high. It slid into position and stopped when the door stopped. Clearly, plate and door were mechanically linked by hidden levers. The plate covered something while the door was open.

Without question, only one person could fit inside the booth.

The Master reached into his pocket and took something out, something he kept out of sight.

"Take this."

The Congressman took what the Master handed him. "What's—"

It was a bar of chocolate.

"Noooooo!"

The Master's next moves were quick and precise. He threw the torch into the congressman's face. He pulled the key out of the hole. He backed into the booth. Ignoring the screams of the congressman, he slid the door and rammed it home. A loud metallic click told them that door was locked. Master and congressman stood on either side of a divide as stark as the electrified fence between Heaven and Hell.

"You promised! You *promised!* Con*sarn* you! Con*sarn* you to Heaven and back. Satan rip your heart out and eat it before your *eyes!*"

There was no other way. The Master stood there a long time, his eyes closed, not moving, wanting to justify himself, to explain, to think up some clever way to defeat the locks on the doors to this pit of despair, to rescue O'Neill—Heaven, to rescue them all!—and lead them to a place up into light and air, sun and fresh breezes, and human kindness.

"Listen! I will come back! I will get you—"

No. Drop it. No point making more promises.

He noticed for the first time that the booth was too tight to turn around in.

O'Neill was banging on the door. The Master felt every blow in his chest. His fingers explored the wall behind him. As he expected, the closing of the sliding door had moved the metal plate out of the way. With the door closed, a keyhole was exposed on the opposite wall.

One key, one man, one exit. That's how it was designed to work.

He slid to one side as much as he could. He put his hand, the one holding the key, behind his back, wedging it in the too-small space between his back and the wall, aiming it for the keyhole.

The congressman stopped beating the door with his fists. What was he up to?

The Special Master twisted his body and wiggled his shoulders. He pushed the key harder into the space behind his back.

Wham!

The congressman had kicked the door in a savage, desperate blow.

The Master dropped the key. Instinctively, he pressed his buttocks against the wall. The key caught there.

The Master became aware just how hot and sweaty the booth was.

Wham!

O'Neill kicked the door again. The key slipped an inch.

The man must have broken his foot. There was no way he could—

Wham!

His thought was interrupted by another savage blow, and then another. The blows were coming faster and harder. Each bounced the Master's head inside the narrow metal space.

The Master reached for the key. If it fell to the floor, that was it. He couldn't bend his knees that far. He would die in that booth. He would die the most terrifying—

Wham!

He pressed his hand between his buttock and the wall.

Too risky. He'd have to—

Wham!

He slid his shoulder and arm down as far as he could, and put his hand under his buttock.

Wham!

This was it.

He moved his hips forward. The key slipped free. It fell to his hand. His fingers trapped it against the wall.

Wham!

The Master's entire universe was that key. With infinite attention, he peeled it away from the wall with his sweaty fingers.

Yes—I have you now!

Wham!

The kicks were nothing now. The Master knew only of the key, and the keyhole. With the greatest of care, he maneuvered the key to the hole. In the most extreme contortion, he got his back out of the way and the key slid into its hole. He turned it.

He heard a click. He pulled out the key.

Wham!

The door behind him popped open on hinges. There was no floor behind him. He staggered and fell in a back-flip.

There was light.

"Oof!"

The Master landed in a diagonal chute. He heard the door above swing shut, spring-loaded. Below, ambient light, though dim, dazzled him. He slid downward.

He passed through a burlap curtain. The chute dumped him into a huge wicker basket.

"Hey, look a' that, Mack! One got out!"

The two guards shared a laugh among themselves.

"Is this how you treat a Black?" the Special Master roared, still upside-down.

"There, there, Mr. Justice, you just surprised us, that's all." The two bumblers hauled the Master out of the basket and dusted him off with their filthy meat hooks, even helping him tug his garment back into place. They were most particular about relieving him of the key.

Nearby, other guards were busy. From one side, a pipe disgorged reeking bodily wastes into wheelbarrows. It would seem the pumps were working again. The pipe's diameter was sufficient to handle the occasional corpse. On the other side, a smaller pipe evacuated parchments of legislation rolled into tubes. These were bills passed with the approving vote of a majority of the House, now destined to be sent on for consideration by the U.S. Senate.

But there was no U.S. Senate.

The Master looked west down the National Mall to the setting sun. He saw a commercial taxi bearing a passenger past the Capitol Building. He whistled shrilly at it. The birds looked down, saw the color of his robe, and came to him. He pulled the passenger, a wealthy brown, off the platform. It was unfair, but it could not be helped. He pointed and the ravens lifted him up and away.

PART THE FOURTH: 1944

Prison Diary

This is one chapter of several from an untitled and never-completed po-litical memoir of Richard Nixon, Chief of Staff in the administration of Mary Wilson, President of Haiti. This document was written on prison-issue underwear using ink made from diluted shoe polish. The only existing copy was seen by no one and destroyed in the prison incinerator by the author at the time of his pardon. The existence of the recording mentioned in the text cannot be confirmed. The bowdlerized profanities are from the original.

Two weeks before Mary Wilson was to be nominated at the Pu-ritan Reform convention in Havana, President Roosevelt of the Quaker Renewal Party asked me to arrange a meeting between him-self and Wilson. Face-to-face meetings between two major candidates are extraordinary. My job was complicated by the need for secrecy and the mutual hostility of the principals, especially the hostility.

For the location, I picked the observation deck on the 180th floor of the Chrysler Building. The deck is closed in the early morning hours, and easily swept clean of surveillance devices. Admittedly, however, I wanted that location mainly for the drama. Watching the sun rise over Plymouth, the world's biggest city, while two people fight over the world's biggest political prize—well, I figured that was just about perfect. And the Chrysler Building is a nostalgic favorite of RN's. It's not the world's tallest building anymore—h*ll, it's not even among the five tallest in Plymouth—but it was the first of the really tall buildings on earth and its jazzy chrome top makes it the most beautiful, to RN's eye.

There were only four of us up there on that deck, two candidates and two campaign managers. Only four heard what was said and done. Three of them are dead now. Only I, Roosevelt's campaign manager, still live. Truth to tell, I was managing both campaigns, but Roosevelt didn't know that then.

Quakers are supposedly a tolerant group, but the President and his circle never approved of my drinking and swearing. The cold, patrician sneers got to me after a while, and when I found out about Lucy Mercer and the others, Mary Wilson's secret overtures became too tempting to refuse.

Now that I know the truth about the psychological testing of school boys, I often wonder why they never sent me to the beach for deportation.

This is a true transcript of what was said. I was wearing a microphone and recorded the whole thing. RN = Richard Nixon, MW = Mary Wilson, FR = Franklin Roosevelt, TD = Thomas Dewey.

[The two candidates approach each other from opposite sides of the deck, followed by their respective campaign managers. In the wind, their hands are thrust into the pockets of their trench coats. FR's hips make a quiet *chunka-eek chunka-eek* sound as he walks. Neither politician offers to shake hands. MW opens her coat for RN's inspection. The President does the same for MW's second, TD. RN pats down TD, but MW makes a show of impatiently cutting him off. RN is not to be searched.]

MW: What's up?

FR: I brought thee something. Something thee need to see.

[RN makes to hand Wilson, and then Dewey, a folder of papers. Both ignore it.]

MW: Tell me what you want and then I'm leaving.

FR: These are top secret documents, known only to the president and a few others. They describe what has been long suspected by many, but never proved.

MW: About the lost boys—

FR: About the lost boys. Verily.

MW: I know what you're going to say.

FR: Well, by G*d thee will stand there and hear me say it!

MW: This is a waste—

FR: Thee hast waged a gutter campaign.

MW: Please.

FR: The personal attacks, I mind not. I mind not even the blatant lies. That is politics. People have lied before thee and they shall lie long after. But this war talk of thine—

MW: Is necessary.

FR: *Let me finish!* Thee are whipping people into a frenzy. Relations with the U.S. have been peaceable for over twenty years. Liberation is a dead dream. Let it stay dead.

MW: I'm leaving.

FR: Listen thee to me! Why think thee our economy—unprecedented economic recovery—took off exactly when the Fifth U.S. War ended? Think thee that a coincidence? A *coincidence?*

MW: It's a coincidence.

FR: Bull sh*t.

[FR holds up another document]

FR: The lost boys are the key. It's been going on from the beginning. All the way back to *Lincoln*. We could not stop the kidnapping, so we turned it to our advantage. Why do we give all children the testing, psychological testing, in kindergarten?

MW: Our school system is the finest in the world.

FR: We *select* them. The bad apples. The loonies, the monsters. Off to the reform schools. One hundred years!—experience in spotting them, weeding them, the *human weeds*—thy Jack the Ripper, thy Atlanta Ripper, thy Bloody Benders.

MW: Maybe.

FR: Nothing to chance. We—

MW: Can we call it a day here?

FR: We are not helpless against these pirates. We monitor the coast, and believe thee me, when a U.S. privateer enters our waters, we know. *We* decide which boys be on the beaches when the raiders come. The better part of 95 percent of the children taken are ones we want to get rid of.

MW: You're cutting—

FR: We decide—

MW: —cutting your—

FR: We're not the only ones. England, the France—all the world, the same policy. The United States is our toilet. Our junk yard. We *need* them.

MW: *You're cutting your own throat!*

FR: See here, I admit it, *thee be right*: the swamps can't—disease is no longer the threat it—but, but we don't want to conquer America. *Thee does not want to conquer America. There is no way to peace! Peace is the way!*

MW: You pacifists make me sick! We're going to march into that H*ll hole and we're going to wipe it off the map. We're going to string their leaders up on every telephone pole. And now that you admit your—*don't look at me like that!*—I'm going to string you up too, you and your cowardly—h*ll, every bureaucrat in on it. I've worked for this my whole life. Nothing you do can stop me.

[FR gestures. RN pulls out a syringe.]

FR: This is not turning out as I hoped.

MW: [laughing] No, it is not.

FR: Listen, *Pilgrim*. Thee shall come down with a strange and terrible disease. For months thee shall languish. Meanwhile, the Plymouth Times will learn of thy visits to the U.S.—yes, we know—and they shall publish a rather unflattering theory as why thee went there and exactly what thee—

MW: Is this the best—

FR: —thee were doing when thee caught—

MW: Is this all you've got?

FR: And thy campaign, thy ambitions, will be dashed. Before thy convention, even—and that proves I am a patriot. I seek no partisan victory. The Puritans will nominate someone else. Somebody sane.

MW: You're a fool, Mr. *Roo*sevelt. You have no idea.

[RN plunges the syringe into the arm of a very surprised FR. TD stands, flat-footed. RN and MW climb the rail together.]

FR. Nixon! What? Traitor! Iscariot!

[RN and MW balance on the rail. RN wraps a loop of his previously hidden parachute harness around MW. FR moves to stop them but his mechanical legs are too slow.]

RN: Go f*ck thyself.

[RN and MW hold hands and jump.]

PART THE FIFTH: 1946

CHAPTER FIFTEEN

The Portrait

It was too late to be late; it was early.

A weary brown entered the Great Hall. He carried a feather duster but it was just a prop and he moved with more stealth than any real janitor would.

A wide strip of gauze wrapped his head at the equator. There was a fresh red stain at the nose, which nevertheless bulged prominently. The gauze was intended to make others think his beezer had been disfigured but not cut all the way off. That was not unheard of. A Rabisoozer hat with lowered flaps completely hid the jet black hair. If seen, no one should think this brown looked just like the Special Master. The Master was definitely *not here*.

The Special Master—no, the brown—heard a creak.

Somebody opening the far door?

The brown brushed cobwebs off the hideously wrinkled face of the Chief Justice in the nearest niche. Just like a real janitor.

The dust was thick. No real janitor would dust this head. No real janitor ever had.

The creaking ended, but now the brown had a problem. Disturbing the dust left an obvious mark. Somebody was here.

He used the duster like an artist's brush to distribute cobwebs over the mark.

Paint a picture: one titled No One Was Here. Just lift some dust from where it was thickest, on top—Beelzebub!

A fat clump of hair fell right out.

He pushed the clump back into the mat of hair. More hair came loose. He draped the loose hair over the top in a completely unconvincing way.

Ridiculous.

The entire head, the actual embalmed head of Chief Justice Boone Helm, was a fragile mess, looking like a shriveled, desiccated apple ready to crumble. Clearly, the Helm era was no golden age of American taxidermy.

A big scoop of fine dirt sprinkled over the head gave the Chief Justice a nice, even patina. Time was a-wasting. The brown dusted off his hands and moved on.

On to the portrait.

This was the first time he had ever really paid it mind. Back when the public was allowed to tour the court building, it got a lot of attention. Its curiosities fed the talk of tour guides and conspiracy theorists. He wished he had paid more attention to all that.

He paid attention now. He memorized every detail.

First, those fingers. Dan Flood's hand signs were clear: look at the fingers in the painting.

The Chief's right hand was huge, contorted and grotesque. Too many fingers snaked up from it (ten, or twelve if you counted the bumps). A detached thumb floated up and to the right like a flesh balloon. This distortion was beyond incompetence. The fine brushwork meant the fingers were placed just so. The longest finger pointed at a cabin.

Was it the *cabin?*

The frame was an odd shape. Its top bent down in a sharp V. Its bottom was flared out on one side.

The portrait was painted on parchment—a poor choice. The surface had wrinkled and cracked.

The work was amateurish. The painting was an embarrassment, really. The previous Special Master had made it, just days before his death.

He was a serious, practical man; what vanity drove him to play the artist?

That cabin sat just above the tip of the longest finger on the shore of a lake. Above the cabin floated a sausage. Or was it a dirigible? Whatever it was, it was bigger than the hand and dominated the sky.

The Chief's left hand was also raised. It was normally proportioned. One index finger pointed up from a balled fist, but odd lines ran parallel to the finger, like the lines cartoonists used to indicate movement.

Most disturbingly, a noose had the Chief by the neck. It was a black rope, like the belt a Special Master wore. Like the hand, the small fibers were detailed with deliberate brush strokes.

The Special Master looked intently at the details of the rope until his nose touched the edge of the painting. His oily skin lifted a round dot of dust off the surface, revealing just how thick the layer was. The Master blew on the painting and choked on the cloud of dust.

He could see the details of the rope better now. Among the fine lines of the rope fibers he saw the tiniest numbers scratched into the paint:

1946

This year.

The Special Master lingered for more time than was safe or wise. The year. The fingers. The cabin.

The cabin! Of all the cabins in America, there was only one that, for the Master, was *the cabin.* It stood like a barrier, a wall of Hadrian, dividing his past, dividing before from after. Before—when he was innocent; after—when he was what he was now.

The Special Master ran his duster over the frame. The wood was plain; no new clue emerged from under the dust. He looked for messages hidden in the arrangements of the clouds or the trees, but found none. The Special Master had learned little from numerology class, but he counted the whorls in the Chief Justice's black wig. Twenty-nine—was that a prime number? Did it have occult significance?

Click! Creak! A seam of light opened up around the front doors.

The brown walked toward the doors. He could not be seen looking at the portrait.

A brown entered the hall. This one carried a mop and a bucket. The Special Master in his brown disguise made bold to walk right on past.

The brown looked hard and stuck out his mop handle.

"Who are you?"

"Well, I'm new." The Master held up his prop, his duster.

"I'm the foreman. Nobody told me about nobody new." The foreman stared at the Master's bandaged face. "Nobody told me nothing. We got a full crew already. I think you and me's gonna go have a talk with the clerk on duty."

Killing this foreman was not to be considered.

Knocking him out would buy time, and with a little luck would clear the memory of this meeting from his head. The Master knew pressure holds that would knock him out without injury. This he dearly wished to use on this middle-aged man who, after all, was merely doing his job. But he could not: nobody else in the United States knew such holds. They were his calling card.

The mop handle was whacking the foreman's temple before the old man knew it had been snatched out of his hand. The force wanted precision, just enough to knock him out. The handle lacked heft and the Master got it wrong. He whacked the man's head a second time. Then a third.

Beez! Lie still you old fool.

This was not going as he had hoped. He was exhausted.

Learned Hand had some explaining to do. No—the Master needed to leave, now, before he was found. He had business at the Library of Congress. Interrogating Learned Hand now was too risky.

Decide!

The Master found Learned Hand chained to his log, as must be.

It was dark. Hand's eyes opened. His eyebrow writhed into confused wakefulness.

"Please...I'm thirsty. A little water...please?"

Outside, a door banged. Hurried steps sounded in the Chamber. There was rustling of an excessive amount of robe cloth. The Master held up one finger, waiting.

"Water? Please?"

Would this old man not shut up?

The heavy door to the Great Hall banged opened and closed. It was only a brown, come for the justices' laundry. Nobody had sounded the alarm—yet.

Hand did not recognize the Master in his disguise. He could leave, right now.

"Please tell me at least, what's today's date?"

The date? What kind of nutty question was that?

The Master went to the sink and poured a glass of water. He held it to Hand's mouth. The justice drank from it until he choked. Half of it spilled down the side of his face.

"Thank you."

"It's the morning of February 3, 1946," said the Master, pitching his voice low.

Hand's eyebrow twisted, abruptly suspicious; it was not fooled by the Master's disguise.

Coming here had been reckless. Well, he had better make the most of it. But how?

That eyebrow: it dominated the room.

The Master sighed. He pulled out his knife and held it before Hand's face.

"Look, Hand: I've seen the picture. The cabin, the big hand—they mean something. I think you're going to tell me everything you know about it."

"No, please. I simply don't know."

"But you knew about Congressman Dan Flood. You knew, but you spoke in a riddle."

"Flood? Flood is a *person?*"

If Hand's surprise was faked, then his leaping eyebrow was an excellent actor indeed.

CHAPTER SIXTEEN

Baby Talk

By the sink was a drawer full of horribles—skewers, branding irons, other exotic blivets—the Master did not like to think about. The Chief had never yet asked the Master to use them, but they were occasionally held up as object lessons when the Chief was especially frustrated with Learned Hand's reticence. From the drawer the Master now pulled a straight razor.

Learned Hand viewed the razor with interest as its fine, imported steel reflected what little light was in the room.

Hand's eyebrow formed a single ridge like mountain range straddling his nose. Its foothills ran out to each ear. The Master held his razor at Hand's temple so it just touched the last coarse hair in the line.

"For some reason, the Chief limits your punishment to beatings. I have no such self-restraint—"

"You wouldn't—"

Hand's words came out just a little faster than their usual *andante*.

"If you cut me," he continued, "I'll tell the Chief you were here. I'll tell him what you've found out."

So. Hand had a card to play. The two men were caught in a Mexican standoff and neither man made a convincing Mexican.

Hand ended the awkward silence. "I will tell you what I know about Flood. But it won't do any good—because you won't believe that's all I know."

The corner of the razor dimpled Hand's flesh. "Well, try me."

"The old Special Master painted that crazy portrait just before he left. When I asked him what it meant, the cabin and the fingers and such, he just said—I *thought* he said—Flood and congress."

The Master snorted. This was a load of mill tailings. He dragged the razor just a sixteenth of an inch. One coarse eyebrow hair sliced off. A draft floated it away.

"Stop! Wait!" Hand begged. "The guy couldn't talk right. Laryngitis. Or something. He was hard to understand."

"You said he 'left.' Don't you mean he *died?*"

Hand shot back, "The Chief told you he's dead?"

"He's alive?" asked the Master. "Where is he? Why did he leave?"

"The Chief—I can't say—they argued—I don't know anything more—"

The eyebrow, so confident and defiant before, slanted deviously. *The eyebrow was lying!*

Footsteps! Somebody was in the courtroom. Somebody old and tired. Somebody coming straight for the Second Robing Room. No time to flee.

The Special Master closed up the razor with a *snap*, jumped, and pulled himself up onto the light fixture, a frosted glass globe suspended by an iron rod.

A key slid into the lock. The fixture wobbled on its ceiling mount while the Master climbed on top of it. The Master steadied the fixture with a palm pressed against the domed ceiling.

The door opened. The hem of the Master's brown coat still hung down at eye level. He snatched it up. The Chief Justice entered, switched on the light and saw only his caged prisoner. He wasted no breath on small talk.

"Has the Special Master been here? Did you tell him anything?"

Oh crap.

"No." Hand mumbled like an exhausted prisoner just waking up.

"I think the Master has been too soft on you. This time, I will do the work myself."

Hand said nothing. Metal implements rattled as the Chief dug about the drawer.

"Where's that razor?"

The Master held his breath. He still held the razor in his hand.

More rattling. The light warmed the Master's bottom.

"This will do."

The Chief held up a C-clamp. He cranked it open. His old hands were clumsy and tedious. A trickle of plaster dust settled on the Chief's head. The Master looked to where it came from. The over-burdened rod was coming loose from the ceiling.

Fear gripped the Master's throat. Hand, on his back, saw the ceiling plaster cracking, and gasped.

"Ah, good," said the Chief. "I'm getting to you." The Chief compared the clamp with the width of Hand's head. Not enough.

The fixture slid a fraction down. The mounting groaned.

"Oooooh," groaned Hand in perfect sympathy. The Chief heard nothing else, and chuckled.

"Now you're ready to talk."

Hand's eyebrow implored: *do something.*

The light was burning the Master's shanks. The mounting was failing. More plaster settled like snow on the Chief's bent back.

Hand looked at the Chief and nodded.

"Tell me then: when a man is with a woman—how exactly—"

Wha-?

"What happens between—you know—"

That was what the Chief wanted to know? That's what all the interrogation was for? He wanted to know where babies come from?

"Speak! How are children made? It's something to do with what a man...and a woman—a thing they...do?"

"Food," gasped Justice Hand.

"You lived—" And then, only then, did the Chief appear to notice the nonsensical answer. He sputtered, then waved the clamp right before Justice Hand's eyes.

"You bred the ravens. You *watched* them. You were our ambassador to the France, for Satan's sake. You got *married!* You know!"

"Food. Please. Give me food, and I'll tell you everything." Hand's voice was hoarse now. He was faking exhaustion beautifully.

"First the answers, then the food. How are women different from men? Why can't we have children without them? How does...*it*...all work?"

"No, I...can't..."

Hand's eyes rolled back and his head slumped down.

The light dropped. Three inches of electric wiring slid out from the mounting. Every shadow in the room lurched.

The Chief, old and pickled and angry, noticed nothing. Cursing under his breath, he went to the sink for a glass of water. Returning, he tossed it in Hand's face.

Hand never moved a muscle. What self-control!

More plaster fell. The heat was making the Master sick.

The Chief began opening more drawers. "Where do they keep the salting smells? Oh, here."

There was no way Hand could feign unconsciousness now. Time to act.

The Master opened the razor and slashed the wires.

The wires sparked. The room went black. The Master smelled scorched metal. He and the fixture fell like Satan out of Heaven.

The Master lunged to the side. The glass globe shattered over the Chief's head.

Master and Chief hit the floor. The Chief groaned, dazed by the blow.

Without a noise the Master found his feet, found the door, and bolted.

With any luck, the Chief would think the fixture fell by itself. The Master felt sorry for Hand, but there was nothing to do for it. Maybe the Chief would be too injured to continue. Maybe, having got Hand to agree to talk, he would press harder than ever. Maybe Hand would tell the Chief that he had talked to the Master. It could not be helped.

The Master escaped through one of his hidden doors. In the secret tunnels he kept extra robes. He would shed his browns. In a moment, he would become a black again.

The question hit him, all of a sudden, like a brick: where, in fact, *do* babies come from?

CHAPTER SEVENTEEN

Library of Congress

The sunrise was a suggestion of strawberry glow, as seen from the top of an apartment building in Burrsburg. Scaling this particular building was trivial work. Its fire escape was the product of a spasm of do-goodism in the Barnum administration, but it had never been maintained and its mechanisms for preventing entry from below had failed. The residents would have removed the nuisance long ago, were it not that this building had many other even more convenient vulnerabilities that thieves could exploit—so why bother?

The Master was no mere thief. He knew the route well: pull down the hinged ladder, climb it, cross the metal catwalk that looked unsafe (but was not) at the third floor, and climb the other ladder to the roof.

This building was next to the Supreme Court. "Next" in this case meant the building leaned right against the court building. Or rather, it had. Early in his mastership, the Master had organized a crew of clerks armed with stout poles—a crew of whiners unused to manual labor—to push the apartment away from the court building. The result was that the building slumped in the other direction. Now it rested its bones against the opposite edifice—the Library of Congress.

That an apartment had no business on prime government property was a moot point. No doubt the builder greased a few well-connected palms. Such ancient history did not concern the Master. The building's drunken stance, held up by its sturdier—slightly sturdier—neighbor provided a secret, silent entry into the library, and that concerned the Master very much.

The Master dropped onto the library roof. He climbed the sandpapery copper surface, weathered to green but appearing brown now in this morning's rosy light. He moved on the ridge, exposed and moving as quickly as he dared. He imagined his silhouette would appear, if noticed by a passer-by, hunched and furtive like the "vampyr" of that strange book, never finished yet wildly popular, by President Edgar Allen Poe.

At the end of the long north wing of the library, he came to the wall that supported the dome. As he expected, the stonework here was sloppy and the cracks gave him footholds.

Above, another copper roof awaited his conquest. At the base, purchase was difficult, but near the top, the dome was flat enough to stand up. He climbed over the railing to the lantern, or cupola, or whatever it was called. The railing may have been decorative, but he was glad for it. The height here unnerved him. The mass of the Capitol's mightier dome seemed to sail among the clouds. He felt his balance slipping away.

He turned his back to the Capitol and inspected the big windows of the lantern. They were there to provide light to the round reading room, far below. The window frames were loose but the latches were rusty. With patient pressure, the Master got one open. The Master slipped inside and pushed the window back into place behind him.

He was in a narrow space between the outer dome (the roof) and the inner dome (a frescoed plaster ceiling). A steep stair for nonexistent maintenance men ended at the lantern and the Master took it, descending into the bowels of the building where so much knowledge digested itself on acid paper.

Where were the guards?

The Master marveled at the ease with which he moved through the rooms of the library. Maybe climbing the roof had been a waste. If he had broken a ground-floor window, would anybody have noticed?

He came to the main hall with its disfigured statues. There was the mosaic of Minerva and Satan signing a contract with Draco, Satan's lawyer, looking on approvingly. The Master trotted up the sweeping stairs, hopping over treads wherever jagged gaps offered a view of the story below.

He crossed the balcony overlooking the main reading room. At the center was a stout wooden desk where the librarian of Congress presided whenever the library was open. It was surrounded by bulletproof glass—a recent addition. The Master wondered at the tactical folly of its location. Librarians had manned that desk during the Revolt of the Iconoclasts—a bunch of sitting ducks. Bullet holes were still visible, hundreds of them.

He passed through the long hallway of the south book depository, past uncounted shelves of books, scrolls, tablets, and parchments, perfumed with the faint aromas of mildew, iron gall ink and pig's blood. At the end he found the Gerry Room wherein those dreadful secrets of state, the maps, were locked.

The room was off-limits but not against a master key and the Special Master let himself in. The few windows were too raunchy to give the place much light, but he could make out the arch of the ceiling, the bronze hulk in one corner, and the mandala of the Tritonic Commission inlaid in the floor.

Instead of bookshelves, the room was filled with aisles of cabinets with wide, flat drawers. First came aisles for geological surveys. A quick check showed these were missing; the money had been appropriated but the survey work never done. The Special Master sighed.

Next came charts of harbors and waterways; the Master did not want to guess how accurate were their depictions of rocks and sand bars, but so long as the charts were locked in this room, ships were safe from them.

After that came the congressional districts. They were organized by region, then state, and then by men's names—congressmen.

There were locks on these drawers. The exact location of the boundaries of the districts were a closely guarded embarrassment of the state.

The Northeast: Necropotamia, Neurosenkreuzberg, Rabisu, Massachusetts...there: New Gehenna. Twice he looked through the names. "Daniel Flood" was not there.

The Master felt sick. Were the records out of date? Typical government incompetence. If only the Chief Justice knew, there'd be heaven to pay.

Next was Kiddsylvania. Tip O'Neill had said—there! "Tenth Congressional District of the State of Kiddsylvania, the Hon. Daniel Flood, Rep."

What was Flood doing in a Kiddsylvania district? Was the cabin there? Time to open this drawer and find out.

The Master turned the dial of the lock.

Did the manufacturer bother to give it a unique combination?

0, 0, 0, 0. Click.

Nope, not unique.

The drawer's contents were a mess. The Master pulled out the precinct maps, scores of them. At the bottom was a huge parchment labeled "10th congressional district." It was folded many times.

The Master spread it on the floor. He knelt on it like a prayer rug.

Byzantine. Serpentine. These words did not begin to describe the boundaries. This district was a spider—no, a centipede. Its main body surrounded the cities of Scrontom and Wilkes-Booth, but scores of appendages wormed their way throughout the state. It was not restrained by mere state borders. At its easternmost end the district grasped bits from Boston, Massachusetts and in the southeast it probed Memphis in Equitasia. This spider, this thing to crawl under a rock, kinked and twisted and doubled back with no rhyme or reason.

Too much detail. The Master stood on a chair to see it all.

For the first time in his life, the Master saw the shape of the state of New Gehenna. From fish-shaped Long Island in the southeast the state sprawled in two mostly uninhabited wings to the north and west. The rapacious Canadians, lusting always for living space, were encroaching on sovereign U.S. territory in this area. The Master's eye roved over the state, speculating as to where the *de facto* international border might be at the moment.

Given enough time, he might also locate the asbestos mine where he grew up. They had called him Boy 666 then. Every boy in the mine had a number. That was another lifetime—

Great Satan.

Between the borders *de jure* of New Gehenna and the Canadian province of Quebec was a great lake. It was shaped like a dirigible. It was shaped like *the* dirigible. The one in the painting.

Below it was a series of smaller lakes like vertical lines. There were roughly ten, and catawampus, but they did remind one of fingers.

The Fingers.

Now he was on to something.

But not something much. Maybe the cabin was among these lakes, but how could he possibly find the exact location?

The Master knelt on the map again. There! One of the legs of the spider—only one!—kinked and twisted its pointless way diagonally up to the northern tip of the longest lake.

The Master swept up the precinct maps he had tossed aside. What a jumble! When this crisis ended the Master was going to knock some heads together and get these records in order.

Ease up. Pay attention.

Against his better judgment, he took to sorting the maps into stacks by county. They had serial numbers stamped on their corners and he figured out the system.

He folded the main map and returned everything to the drawer. He could see now how each stack fit into its own compartment.

And now for the reason he came. He pulled out the map for the finger-shaped lakes.

At the local level, the dope was clear. A leg of the congressional district ended at a little clearing at the northern shore of the longest lake. In the clearing was a lonely little residence. He noted its exact location on the shore.

And if that was not the very cabin where he killed his first victim years ago, he swore he would eat raven.

The High Priests

From *Encyclopedia Satanica, 1947 Ed.*

The High Priests of the Satanic Church of America

Prior to the Continental Congress of 1776, Satanists in North America belonged to a large number of competing churches. Various "High Priests" from that time will not be listed here, as many groups were transitory and their hierarchies prone to rapid, violent turn-over. Researching that history is, ultimately, a fool's errand. With the founding of the country came the establishment of One True Legitimate Reorganized Satanic Church for all Americans, commonly called The Satanic Church of America, or simply The Church.

Each High Priest served for life, such as it was.

High Priests

1780. Jean-Baptiste Alliette. Founded the Church upon the Tarot. Ruthlessly suppressed all competing organizations. Likely poisoned.

1791. Wolfgang Amadeus Mozart. Accused of Freemasonry. May have died before assuming office. Likely poisoned.

1791. Seth Read. Added "E Pluribus Unum" to the currency. Likely poisoned.

1797. Antonio Salieri. Expert in poisons.

1808. Giovanni Aldini. The finest necromancer in Church history.

1834. Robert Owen. Founded the New Harmony order. Stabbed to death in his sleep.

1858. Eliphas Levi (born Alphonse Louis Constant). Author of *The Book of Common Fear.*

1875. Giacomo Antonelli. "Hammer of the Vatican."

1876. Orrin Porter Rockwell. "The Destroying Angel."

1878. Karl Marx. Famous quote: "From Heaven according to its ability, to Hell according to its need."

1883. William H. Mumler. The "Spirit Photographer."

1884. William Robert Woodman. Preached the Golden Dawn.

1891. Friedrich Nietzsche. Insane throughout his entire tenure as High Priest.

1900. Ignatius Donnelly. Declared North America to be the lost continent of Atlantis.

1901. Léo Taxil (born Marie Joseph Gabriel Antoine Jogand-Pagès). Built magnificent cathedrals but abandoned the Golden Dawn and was posthumously denounced in 1916.

1907. Papus (born Gérard Anaclet Vincent Encausse). Founded the Martinist Order.

1916. Samuel Liddell MacGregor Mathers. A former president. Revived the Golden Dawn.

1918. Aleister Crowley. The Priest-President. Last of the High Priests.

In 1920, High Priest Crowley, also Speaker Crowley, was elevated to the office of President, and created the one combined office of Priest-President. He died under mysterious circumstances in 1923 and the office of High Priest was abolished. Since that time, the Master in Lunacy has been the de facto *head of the Church.*

Master in Lunacy and Acting Head of the Church

1923. Harry Houdini (born Erik Weisz). Assumed Mastery in 1917 and acting headship in 1923. Escaped death many times. His reorganization plan guaranteed the survival of the Church as a legal entity.

1926. Howard Philip Lovecraft. His scholarly temperament was ill-suited to the demands of the time.

1937. Sigmund Freud. Brought intellectual rigor to a neglected office.

1939. Joseph Paul Oswald Wirth. Expert in the cartomantic Tarot.

1943. J. Edgar Hoover. Reestablished the Church as a political force. Currently under house arrest. Proclaimed himself High Priest in late 1946, but this has not been confirmed in law as of this time.

CHAPTER EIGHTEEN

Pointy Hat

A movement of light at the edge of his vision caught the Special Master's attention. It emerged from the gloom on the other side of the frosted glass of the door. It was warm and fickle: it was sacramental. A priest was coming.

The Special Master locked the drawer and wiped it off with his wide sleeve. Where to hide? The room contained a bronze statue of Satan, seated, and larger than life. It was, in fact, a high priestly throne of the type that one sees in cathedrals. The thighs were dark from disuse.

There was no room behind the statue, and it was too heavy to move. The Master would have to hide among the cabinets and avoid the visitors.

The door opened. A black shadow entered, lit from behind. The Special Master recognized the posture and gait: it was the Chief Justice.

Another man entered, holding two candles. He was garbed in the full ceremonial dress of a librarian, similar (by design) to that of a bishop of the Church. His conical hat was decorated with a crescent moon and seven stars in silver glitter. Two medallions of exalted rank hung side by side around his neck: Librarian of Congress and Master in Lunacy. This was J. Edgar Hoover.

185

As the Church fell into decline and government subsidies became unreliable, satanic priests sought day jobs for sustenance. Most had pursued careers in library science. It was a natural fit.

"What congressional district were you interested in, again?"

Hoover's words were like a dirty coating of oil on a hot engine. His hair was thinning but dyed black in compensation. The receding bangs were cut into an artificial widow's peak. His goatee was waxed to a dagger point. On a leaner face, especially a bald one with gold hoop earrings, the look would have been terrifying. On Hoover, it was corny.

"Flood's. The tenth of Kiddsylvania."

The Master glided out of the aisle just as the two men tramped in. He watched them from a gap between cabinets.

Hoover moved methodically through the aisle, thrusting his candles in front of each cabinet's label. At 50, his eyes were not sharp. By a laborious process he found Kiddsylvania. By muttering to himself he found the Tenth. He set his candles on top of the cabinet.

Hoover put his hands up in a dramatic gesture which exposed his forearms. He clapped his hands together and bowed. In a strange, high-pitched scream—all the stranger because it was perfunctory—he recited:

Ph'nglui mglw'nafh Cthulhu R'lyeh wgah'nagl fhtagn!

The High Priest turned his head and spat over his right shoulder. He turned his head to the left, and the Chief jumped back as a thick goober barely missed his immaculate black robe.

What followed was a series of acrobatic warm-ups: deep knee bends, circles traced in the air with the hands, and lateral head movements. Hoover, the Master in Lunacy, stuck out his tongue (surgically altered for increased length) and hissed. From the folds of his robe he took out a compact and smeared red war paint in stripes on his face. He put his right hand into his left armpit and made fake fart noises. He tossed snuff into the air.

There was more screaming, plus marching in a circle:

"Hay! ya ya ya. Ya ya ya ya.

Hay! ya ya ya. Ya ya ya ya."

The Chief watched in boredom. He had seen it all before.

Then, the denouement: from another fold in his robes, the High Priest pulled out a squirming thing. It was a live bat. Without hesitation, he bit its head off. Or tried to.

"Consarned!" garbled Hoover. "The little shit bit me!"

Hoover threw the bat on the floor and stomped the life out of it. He wiped blood from his mouth with a silk handkerchief and mumbled a propitiatory prayer, but the mood was broken.

Hoover rubbed his hands and cracked his knuckles, and with a gentleness that contrasted with his preceding ministrations, placed the tips of his fingers on the dial of the cabinet lock.

The two old men, the living embodiments of Church and State, leaned in together. Hoover's eyes narrowed to contemptuous slits as he gave the Chief a sidelong glance.

"Give me some space, Jack."

He turned the dial.

There was no click of release. The High Priest pulled the drawer, but it yielded not.

Again, Hoover tried the combination and got it wrong. The man of the cloth spat vulgarities, obscenities and even profanities.

More tries; more failures. He yanked the drawer, pounded it, even kicked it.

"Look, let's crowbar the thing," said the Chief.

"Dry up and let me think!" said the High Priest through clenched teeth. He put his head in his hands and muttered various combinations of numbers.

He sighed. "Give me your finger."

The Chief looked at him stupidly.

"I said, give me—"

Hoover grabbed the Chief's hand. With measured precision he bit the Chief's index finger. (Priests kept their canine teeth sharpened just for that purpose.)

"Ow! *Judas Priest*, Edgar, what that was for?"

The Priest kept his grip on the Chief's hand and lapped the welling blood like a kitten at its saucer of milk, specifically, a kitten adorned in the lurid robes of the most senior priest of the One True Satanic Church and a waxed goatee.

He declaimed, "I offer to you, Great Lord Satan, this offering of blood. Be satisfied! And now, give me the combination, dammit."

Hoover lowered his voice to address his earthly companion. "Sometimes it helps—" His finger popped up. "Ah ha!"

He giggled. He turned the dial. The lock's machinery clicked cooperatively. The drawer slid open.

"Now, which map were you looking for?"

"None in particular. I have reason to think somebody is snooping. This district has certain...*peculiar*...features that must be kept secret.

"The records show no one has visited this room since the last reapportionment."

"But could they have broken in?"

"I don't see how. Just look!" Hoover gestured. "Nothing has been disturbed. You just saw how secure our locks are. And these maps—" he lifted neat bundles from the drawer"—these maps are sorted." He fanned the corners of one bundle to show the serial numbers. "They're in perfect order."

"Any missing?"

Whatever love was due the Chief Justice had died within the Master in Lunacy years ago. That ship had sailed on too much water over a dam fanning the flames of bad blood. The Chief's record of crimes against the church included theft, blasphemy and murder. She who had been known as the Queen of Babylon was, in these miserable days, reduced to begging and whoring. As senior churchman, the Master in Lunacy felt this humiliation most keenly. Despite all this, he usually held his loathing for the Chief hidden.

Not now. Hoover fired a volley of obscenities to singe the Chief's eyebrows.

The Chief did not relent. He held the power to compel, and Hoover knew it. Together, the two men divided the work. 15 minutes later they had confirmed it: every map in the drawer was present and accounted for.

"It's certain, then? No one has been here?"

The Chief's eyes begged for assurance.

"As Satan is my witness."

"Thank Darkness. He doesn't know. *He doesn't know.*"

The Chief clutched his chest and staggered. He panted and reeled. Hoover took his arm.

The Master had seen the Chief's fits before. Some were melodramatic fakes. This was no fake. Every impulse urged the Master to go help his Chief.

He stayed hidden.

Hoover helped the Chief into a chair. As he waited for the Chief's breathing to settle, he mounted the steps to the bronze statue and took his rightful place, seated on Satan's feet. The Master moved to the end of the aisle to maintain his secret watch.

"And now, as soon as you're rested, please tell me more about this 'exciting opportunity for the church' you mentioned."

The Chief Justice pawed about his robes until he found a pocket. He pulled out a tin of snuff and shoved a thick wad into his nostril. The sweet, nicotine-rich volatiles calmed him.

"The Church isn't what it once was."

"This is manifestly true." Hoover kept his voice dry. Power was shifting in the room, tangibly, and that gave him patience.

"Decadence and neglect are everywhere. The people have no sense of purpose, no loyalty to a Lower Calling."

Hoover kept silent.

"I feel—sincerely—that we have no concept of just how *demanding* it would be to rule Hell."

Hoover started to open his mouth, then closed it with a wary frown. Sincerity was something he clearly did not trust.

"I mean, think of all the demands on Satan's time. All the prayers he has to attend to, all the subordinates who won't follow simple orders—the sheer *ingratitude*. It must wear him down."

Hoover's expression was a confusion of fear and amusement.

"We need to do something to really energize the Church. Wake up the people. *Heaven,* wake up Lord Satan himself! Revive that spirit they had in the old days, when men like Elfrith and Jol, Lucifer and van Ryen strode the earth. The giants."

The Chief rubbed his chest. His breaths were almost regular now. He continued.

"I've always been a loyal son of the Church, you know."

"You picked an odd way to show it."

"Well, yes. But that's in the past. You and I: we could be"—the Chief held out his hand—"we could be friends. Working together."

"You have a proposal?"

"Human sacrifice. Bring it back. Let the balefire burn."

Hoover's eyes lit up and his mouth formed a neat, perfect O. But the Chief Justice was still talking.

"What would you think if the Federal Government gave the church thousands of captives for a great burnt sacrifice, right on the Court Plaza?"

"I would think there must be strings attached."

"Only one."

The Chief paused dramatically. Hoover shrugged, waiting.

"This will not be easy. There will be resistance. Some of my own people—"

"Mencken? He should be first on the fire!"

"Mencken may be a problem. He was mixed up in that unpleasantness with Crowley, somehow"—the Chief was looking off to the side as he said it—"but...I was thinking of others. Among the victims may be...very important men."

The Special Master felt a thrill of terror.

"If there is insurrection," said the Chief, "I want the church on my side, upholding the political *status quo*."

"I believe we may have a basis for cooperation," said Hoover, "but I want—"

"Yes?"

"Resumption of regular sacrifice. This won't be a one-time event."

"Certainly. I'll sign the waivers. Call it...a few per year."

"A few *thousand* a year."

"A few...hundred."

"A few hundred?"

"We can't cut too deeply into the population. We are, after all, a nation of immigrants."

"And restoration of the high priesthood."

The Chief nodded.

Hoover sat silent for several moments. He frowned as one unused to good fortune.

"Well then. Yes. *Yes.* I believe we have a deal."

"Summon a thousand priests to Burrsburg. No, make it two thousand. In a week. Prepare for sacrifice, and for war!"

Both men stood. They shook hands with a single, emphatic pump. The Chief walked out of the room looking years younger.

The Master ached to escape his hiding place. He wanted out of this horrible room. Yet the Master in Lunacy was not yet ready to leave.

Hoover walked around the circular design in the center of the floor. He lifted the skirt of his flaming red robe and pranced about. His top-heavy hat tipped and he straightened it with the delicate touch of a single, dagger-pointed, red-polished fingernail.

He took his seat on Satan's bronze feet. Then he giggled.

He dared to climb up Satan's legs and sit in the Devil's lap—the place of the High Priest. He draped his arm around Satan's neck and looked Old Scratch in the eye. Hoover's laughter blossomed.

It started as a giggle. It transitioned into a kind of hiccup. It ripened to a guffaw, detoured over into snicker territory, lurched into a titter, flirted with snorts alternating with howls, and finally settled into a nice, sustainable chortle.

It went on for a long, long time, and the Special Master, a prisoner to the old man's hilarity, watched the whole, mad performance to its end.

President Crowley

Entry, *The Encyclopedia Satanica for Kids, 1935 Edition*
Crowley, Edward Alexander "Aleister" (1875-1923).

Born in England to wealthy parents of a strict Christian sect, Aleister Crowley showed strong religious tendencies from an early age. The death of his father in his 12th year precipitated a crisis which committed the boy to lifelong metaphysical and religious restlessness. He dabbled in the occult and rebelled against all authority. Predictably, he was liberated by the American privateer Henry d'Arcy Champney in 1890.

Crowley seems to have weathered the transition to American citizenship with startling ease. His embrace of the state church was exemplary, a model for all American youths.

His school years were spent at a goat farm. His transcript shows him earning good marks in animal husbandry, but severe attrition of the livestock forced the farm into bankruptcy. In hindsight it is clear Crowley was, even then, practicing the liturgical innovations for which he became famous.

Crowley pursued a career in the church at the exact moment such vocations began their steep decline. Church historian Vincent Price argues that this decline stems from Crowley himself, that his enthusiasm had a dampening effect on others. Certainly, for all the influence of his writings, he was frustrated in his unrelenting attempts to recruit disciples. However, others argue convincingly that broad cultural trends, including possibly cyclic structures in history (see the Dewey-Steiner Generational Theory) account for the ebb of church participation.

It was as a politician that Crowley found popular success. He was elected to the House of Representatives in 1910 from Necropotamia. His unnerving oratory and ease within the ethically flexible milieu of Congress enabled him to gain the speakership in 1916. Subsequently, the speakership became the only path to the presidency and in 1920 he succeeded Woodrow Wilson as President.

Crowley had never relinquished his priestly office, and his parallel rise through the hierarchy of the Church of Satan raised objections among constitutional scholars. His surprise election as High Priest just one day after assuming the presidency alarmed many and aroused the envy of other high officials.

Crowley moved quickly to put the machinery of government at the disposal of the Church. Furthermore, his innovations (as some called them) or return to traditional practices (as his followers would have it) made Crowley's power grab in the name of Satan controversial even within the Church. The mysterious deaths of some priests and the abrupt dismissal of others raised the general alarm.

Many influential voices called upon the Chief Justice to take extraordinary action. He showed remarkable restraint however, finally implementing those modestly extra-constitutional innovations that became absolutely necessary at the end of Crowley's presidency. In any event, Crowley died during his most shocking act—an attempt to desecrate the Rotunda of the U.S. Capitol as a shrine for his new, "atheistic-Satanic" religion. The circumstances of his death were never adequately explained.

Crowley was succeeded by President William Joseph Simmons who was inaugurated by the Chief Justice literally over Crowley's dead body. Simmons was regarded as a man of the church (although not an ordained priest, as was commonly assumed). He subscribed to a conventional satanology but he abolished the office of high priest. His presidency was hailed as a time of national healing that smoothed the way to the Chief Justice-led government we enjoy today.

CHAPTER NINETEEN

Sleight of Hand

P anicked. Rushed. The cabin. The prisoners. 1946. Human sacrifice.

Thoughts ricocheted within the Special Master's cranium like pinballs.

How did it all fit together? What was Learned Hand hiding?

The Master climbed. Up the ladder inside the library's dome.

So high. No time.

At the top, the dirty window resisted his shoving.

Just break it! No—stupid. Don't give yourself away.

It yielded. Out the window, onto the roof, he crawled.

Be careful! But hurry! Down the fire escape.

He jumped past the last four rungs and landed hard.

Crazy risks.

What had Learned Hand told the Chief Justice? What did he know? Access the secret tunnels. How many prisoners? How many would die? Would he be one of them? In the straightaway. Run hard, to the robing room.

Peep hole: it was too dark to see. Hand would finally tell everything. Make him tell!

Was the Master a wanted man? What had he done? What was the Chief thinking?

Panting, side aching, the Master fumbled in his pocket. Where was the key? There. He couldn't hold it still for the keyhole. He barked an unworthy word, got the door unlocked, flung it open.

He turned on the lights. He waited a full second, not believing his eyes, thinking they must be dazzled by sudden light.

No, it was true. Learned Hand would not be telling him anything. The cage was empty.

PART THE SIXTH:
1918 - 1926

CHAPTER TWENTY

The New Boy

Before he was the Special Master, he had been Boy 666 at the Warren County Polytechnic School of Mining in Warrensburg, New Gehenna.

The teachers at the WCPS of M devoutly believed in teaching to the test, and the most important test was the weekly asbestos quota as measured by Federal inspectors. The teachers tested the boys on academic subjects too, and cheerfully beat them if they fell short in reading, writing and arithmetic, but the boys were on their own when it came to instruction.

The rock crusher banged out a steady, nerve-deadening rhythm as Boy 666's new friend, Boy 1313, quizzed him. 1313 was quick with his hands and smart as a whip; smarter really, since whips have a poor understanding of human nature. Boy 1313 always walked on tip-toes and likely would have done so even if he were not half a head shorter than 666. Calling 666 "my dear little chum" was another compensation.

"Tell me, my dear little chum: what is mechanical advantage?"

"It's the multiplication of...of..."

"Multiplication of *force*..."

Bang! The rock crusher fell like a ton of bricks, because that was what it was, pretty much.

The boys fell silent as they sorted the rocks in the few seconds gap. A teacher, Mr. Trotsky, walked by, and they doubled their efforts.

Boy 666's peepers stung. He wiped the sweat out of them. Mr. Trotsky whacked him on the head for unauthorized perspiring. That exhausted his pedagogical bag of tricks, and he moved on.

With teachers out of earshot, learning could continue.

"Force...you get from...?" prompted 1313.

"From...a simple machine?"

"Right!"

Bang!

1313 was two years older and had aced the mechanics test two years prior. He had not escaped whipping, though, since he also excelled in human psychology and knew just how to vex a teacher by correcting his spelling mistakes in the test questions. Catechism was his worst subject, since he drew the wrong conclusions.

"Regarding the War of the Cosmos, what do we know about the Final Outcome?" asked Boy 1313.

"Well, we know the armies of Hell will win," said Boy 666, "and..."

"And...?" Boy 1313 stopped to regard his pupil, risking his quota and his hands.

"The armies of Hell will win...big?"

"*Ought* to win. The armies of Hell will win, and they *ought* to win. But one thing..."

1313 paused to give his full attention to selecting a promising fragment that was almost out of reach, putting his head in danger. It was never a good idea to let one's mind wander in such situations. Once, they had seen a boy "flunk out" – that was the popular euphemism – while leaning in, and that was enough.

"—Got it—"

Bang!

1313 did not pause to admire his prize. There was no time to blow in a shift that lasted only twelve hours.

"…one thing I always wonder about. It says in the Bible that Jehovah created the universe. We can be sure that's true because the Bible of the Christians says the same thing—"

"You haven't *read* the Christian Bible—?"

Boy 1313's grin evaded the question. "If Jehovah made the universe, doesn't it belong to him?"

"Maybe he made it from the pieces of an older, broken universe."

"Okay, but then, who made *that* universe?"

Bang!

"Satan!" Boy 666 had let out both an answer and an oath; the crusher had almost got him that time.

"If it's Satan's, don't you think the Bible would tell us? And what was Satan doing while Jehovah was making this universe? Sitting on his tail?"

1313 was really going too far!

"Scratch! Don't talk like that!" Boy 666 sketched a hasty pentagram in the dust on his forehead.

"I'm just asking questions. Like, if Jehovah is that powerful, doesn't that mean *he* will win the war? And…and also mean Jehovah *ought* to win?"

Bang!

Mr. Schuyler sent another boy to join them and the topic of religion died.

"I'm Boy 3006"—he pronounced it "Thirty Aught Six"—"but my real name is Errol." 3006 was a senior like 1313, and effortlessly likable. "What's your name?"

666 decided he disliked likable people.

"He doesn't have to tell you his real name if he doesn't want to," said Boy 1313.

"What's the big deal? I told him mine."

"Today's church visit day," said 1313 abruptly. "Are you fellows going?"

"No," said 666, not knowing why not, but grateful for the change of subject.

"Nobody goes there. The priest is a drip," Errol tittered.

Earlier that day, the boys had been marched into the lunch hall to listen silently to a man in a red cassock. He was the first priest Boy 666 had ever seen, but the older boys knew the drill.

The priest's hair was jet black but his stoop and liver spots gave away his age. As he talked, his head would jerk like he was a movie with frames missing. His grin distinguished him sharply from the teachers; they at least felt no need for insincerity.

The priest invited the boys to a "youth gathering". The church had a "youth center" with fun things to do like ping pong. They could also attend church services once per week; it was the one time by law their teachers could not punish them for exiting through the school gate.

The priest's eyes wandered as he gave his pitch, making the boys wonder if he really hoped the ceiling and the floor would be the ones to attend the youth gathering. His final sentence ended with a rising inflection, as though he had asked a question, and an uncomfortable silence followed. It was disorienting for an adult's words to have no consequence—but there it was. The boys waited, wary.

A teacher waved the boys up to the front. As they filed past the priest, he handed each a brochure. Boy 666 took one; it was rough pulp with two colors of ink that smudged at the touch of his thumb. The title declared, "Uncle Satan Wants U!" and a grinning goat pointed an all-too-human finger directly at the reader. The brochures went into the pot-bellied stove as soon as the priest was gone.

"You should come to the church. It'll be interesting. And it's time off from work."

"The teachers whip you," Boy 666 said, his voice flat.

"Nuh-uh. The law says—"

"The law don't mean nothing. You still got to meet quota."

But Boy 1313 was not deterred. "I'm not afraid. I'm going. You guys are coming too."

Boy 666 did not answer.

"Nobody's going," said Errol, but he was wrong. He had flunked psychology.

CHAPTER TWENTY-ONE

Shriners

ight years. Boy 666 had survived. All body parts were still attached.

The shift had ended. The boys had eaten their hot potato supper and completed the various extra chores they had been ordered to volunteer for. Boy 1313 decided the boys of 666's cohort needed religious instruction.

The first requirement of catechism class was memorizing the list of the books of the Satanic Bible. This was no piece of cake, since the list was long and meaningless, with names like I and II Jezebel, Acts of the Pirates, and Tergiversations of Beelzebub. Still, Boy 1313 had invented a competition to motivate them.

Boy 1313 stood at the end of an old, played out tunnel, an excellent place for learning as the teachers never came there. His students stood before him, eager to prove their mastery.

"The Passion of de Sade 3:14…The Passion of de Sade 3:14…"

The boys were captivated by the metaphor of the Satanic Bible as a sword. Its words had power to smite enemies. And so they held their Bibles aloft, like Lucifer did in the famous print where he confronted the Archangel before the Last Tavern of Venus.

"…draw swords…charge!"

Those words were the equivalent of "get set, go!" At "charge!" the Bibles jerked down and the boys opened them furiously, putting the bindings of the valuable books at risk. A race ensued to find the passage. The cleverer boys turned to a place roughly one third from the front (de Sade being among the Minor Mages) while the dunces flipped randomly in a sad attempt to win by luck.

"Is not man by nature the stronger, and therefore by right—" It was Boy 666 who found the passage first, and shouted the words to prove it.

They played many rounds of "Bible challenge", and Boy 666 dominated the competition, which he loved. He had a fine, athletic body, but poor eyesight kept him from excelling at smear the queer or other outdoor games.

His opponents tired of losing. When only 666 and 1313 were left, the latter smiled shyly and said, "I've made a shrine. Would you like to see it sometime?"

What's a shrine?

Mine boys sleep deeply when given the chance. It was a hard shake that roused Boy 666. The snores of his shift-mates in the dark reminded him where he was. (Their noses were never completely free of dust.)

Boy 1313 warned him with one finger to the lips. Breaking the rules, and avoiding the shift on duty, they descended a neglected shaft. By this 666 guessed they were not running away, and was glad.

They walked and crawled a long way. Even with 1313's flashlight, 666 felt lost. This part of the mine was lonely and sad. Twice 1313 aimed his light backwards, but no follower was seen. The cool, clean air drove out 666's drowsiness. The sense of conspiracy did the same.

1313 pushed aside some old lumber that would have given splinters to somebody with less calloused hands. The two boys crawled through a revealed hole.

1313 shined the light around the small, round space. A few dust particles put witchcraft in the beam. He showed 666 crude chalk drawings on the walls. They were stick men, with hands upraised, palms out.

"What is this place?"

"My dear little chum, welcome to my Christian Church."

"Are you nerts? That's crazy!"

"Wait. Stay. Let me show you."

Boy 1313 had made a rough table from two pails and a board. On it lay the bones of a mule. Next to the bones was a page torn from a book. Boy 666 would have guessed it was from a Bible, but the ink was black instead of red.

"Is that...?"

"The Christian Bible." 1313's voice was thick with emotion. He picked up the book and offered it to 666.

"You should not have this. This is *wrong*."

1313 thrust the book insistently. "Come on. Don't be a baby."

666 recoiled. "What if somebody finds out?"

"What will happen if somebody finds out is that somebody will find out."

"Wrong. They will *kill* you if they find out."

"So, let's make sure they don't find out." 1313 opened the Bible, showing 666 the printed pages.

"That's filled with all kinds of crazy junk."

"How do you even know?"

"Everybody says so."

"If everybody said you should jump off—" Boy 1313 thought about that, then went off on another tack. "The Satanic Bible is filled with all kinds of crazy junk too."

"Well…" Boy 666 had no answer to that.

"So why read just the one?"

"It's a *Federal* law."

"You came here, even though you knew the teachers wouldn't like it, right?"

Boy 666 was outflanked. He dropped the argument. "How did you even get it?"

"I went to church on Wednesday."

That made no sense—but 1313 was still talking.

"They had all kinds of weird junk in the basement. That's where the ping pong table was." Boy 1313 laughed. "That priest was so stupid, he sent me down to play ping pong even though I was the only one who went."

"You went alone?" Boy 666 could not have explained why that terrified him.

"So I found the ping pong table in a tiny room. The table was as big as the room. No way I could've played, even with a partner. Nobody's ever played ping pong in that church, I can guarantee you. But there was this door to another room, locked—"

"You went in there?"

Boy 1313 grinned. "That priest is harmless. He stayed upstairs, with a little push sweeper, cleaning the red carpet in the sanctum, going *swish swish*. If he had come down, I would have heard."

"What was in the room?"

"All kinds of weird shit!"

The Canadians had taught Boy 666 never to cuss, and Boy 1313's language made him seem very old.

"There was this tube coming down from where the altar must have been, and it emptied into a big tub. It was stained brown—"

"Blood sacrifice?"

"I think so. But it was real dirty, like it hadn't been used in years. There were some really scary knives hung on a rack, but they were rusty, too. And there were books—all kinds of books!"

"The Christian Bible?"

"Yeah. I think it was where they put the banned books when they find them. There were books by Crowley there. *Crowley!*"

"Beez." Boy 666 said it low and serious, hoping he sounded like he knew who Crowley was.

"And the Christian Bible. I took a page. Just look at it."

Its odor was not exactly unpleasant. The page was fragile, made from impossibly thin paper. The letters were printed more beautifully than any he had ever seen. He began to read:

> Huz his firstborn, and Buz his brother, and Kemuel the father of Aram,
> And Chesed, and Hazo, and Pildash, and Jidlaph, and Bethuel.

Just like the regular Bible: incomprehensible. What was the big deal?

"Come on now. Let me show you how we do it."

Boy 1313 lit a candle and set it on the table. He shut off his flashlight; its battery must be conserved in any case.

Standing behind the table, with only an inconstant yellow glow illuminating his face, he was transfigured: he became somebody else. He picked up the largest bone, a mule pelvis. He wiped dust off it, closed his eyes, and kissed it. He held it out to Boy 666.

"Why did you do that?"

"Christians kiss the butt of an ass in the Temple of Jerusalem. *Everybody* knows that."

When in Rome… Boy 666 kissed the pelvis.

"Raise your hands." Boy 1313 showed how. Boy 666 did the same, palms out, almost touching 1313's.

"Promise you will never tell any teacher about this place."

"…"

1313 whispered the prompt, "I so promise."

"I so promise."

"Promise you will forever be a faithful member of this church."

"I so promise."

"Swear on this Christian Bible."

1313 placed 666's right hand on the page.

"I so promise. And swear."

"Promise to obey the teachings and instructions of the Grand Master: that's me, Boy 1313."

"Wait, who elected you Grand Master?"

"Dry up. It's my church. I didn't have to let you in."

But a rhubarb ensued, and when it was settled (inconclusively) the rite of initiation had lost its momentum.

"I can't remember the rest of the ritual."

"We should write so it rhymes. It's easy to remember when it rhymes."

"Okay." Boy 1313 closed his peepers. "God, God…"

666 continued, inspired. "…cod, cod…"

"That makes no sense."

"It doesn't have to make sense. If it rhymes, that makes it religious." 666 continued:

"God, God,
Cod, cod..."

"Nod?" 1313 giggled.

"Actually, that works," 666 said graciously. He was thrilled to have taken control of the conversation. "Try this:

God, God,
Cod, cod,
Nod, nod,
Sod, sod..."

"Shut up!"

As Boy 1313 spat out the command, he also put out the candle's flame with a hiss between his rough fingers. The darkness was so abrupt and so complete, it had its own pressure, like deep water. Boy 666 marveled at Boy 1313's intuitive mastery of the dramatic gesture. He made a fine Grand Master after all.

Then he heard what 1313 had heard. In the tunnel, somebody was running away.

All stealth was abandoned and both boys fumbled for the flash. They wasted time shouldering each other at the entrance. 1313 insisted on replacing the lumber, and that took more time.

They ran down the tunnel, but they never saw the spy. Shaken, they returned to their beds. For the rest of that night, they lay wide awake and worried.

Church of Satan Recruitment Brochure

Uncle Satan Wants U!

The Unholy Church of Satan needs young men who are dedicated to the cause of building his church through the nation and the world! Do you have what it takes to join our team?

The Church has openings in every leadership role: parish priest, deacon, liturgist, inquisitor, bishop or Master in Lunacy, and evangelist.

Parish Priest

The fundamental work of the church lies in the nation's city neighborhoods, towns, and rural circuits. A parish priest is responsible for the daily sacramental needs of his parishioners. If the People of Satan are an army, then the parish priests are its noncommissioned officers. Without them, the Church would literally cease to function.

Deacon

Deacons perform the vital work of building, repairing, and maintaining cathedrals, parish churches and missions. They procure liturgical, educational and office supplies for church facilities. This role offers flexibility to those desiring to serve the church; some deacons volunteer as little as five hours a week; in other cases, deacons work full-time. Some deacons bring trade skills to the job, and a few deacons occupy the highly specialized roles of iconographers, art curators, architects, builders of drums and other musical instruments, casters of bells, and sculptors.

Liturgist

The liturgy is more than just bass drums and pig blood! Music is the heart of satanic worship, as it glorifies His Hellish Majesty and prepares the hearts of worshipers to enter fully into mystic rituals. Good liturgists are rare and highly valued within the church, as they must demonstrate skill as musicians and artists, and also complete rigorous training in the use of pharmaceuticals. Do you like dressing up? Young men who show a gift for worship design or who have a flair for the dramatic and the macabre are especially encouraged to inquire about work as a liturgist.

Inquisitor

Are you one of the few, the strong, the especially devout who are cut out to be inquisitors? The church welcomes candidates to the Inquisition who are especially serious and demonstrate self-control and sound judgment. The academic requirements are higher here than any other role in the church, even that of bishop. Felix Dzerzhinsky, an influential former Grand Inquisitor, said it best: "Inquisitors purge the church of all defect and must be without defect themselves. The hate we seek is the pure hate without any selfishness, vanity or self-indulgence. The Inquisitor understands the purpose of pain, and would not abjure receiving it any more than giving it. All Hail Satan! Hj'ailululu'iaiakh!"

Bishop or Master in Lunacy

Are you a natural leader? It may be that Satan wants you to become a bishop in his church! A bishop supervises the parish priests within his diocese and votes in the Grand Coven, the Church's supreme governing body. Do you have organizational skills? Are you a people person? Do you like to wear blood-stained vestments? You might be a future bishop, or even Master in Lunacy. (Currently the office of High Priest is vacant.)

Evangelist

Little may be said about the role of evangelist, as it is the most secret part of the church. Suffice it to say that if you are recruited as an evangelist, your identity will be erased and you will be sent to strange and exotic places. Patient introverts with a sense of adventure and an ability to live a double life are the men for this job. Chances are, if you are not sure if you are cut out for this job, you are not. Discrete inquiries only will be entertained.

Commonly asked questions:

Will I get to sacrifice live humans to Satan?

The Church of Satan has not offered living human beings on the altar of sacrifice in decades, based on the modern understanding of its mission and the Will of Satan. Many attractive alternative practices are in place at this time, however, such as the biting off of heads of small animals (yes, that may include bats!), cursing and intimidation of prisoners during official government interrogations, and participation in rituals during autopsies performed by coroners, where actual human bodies are present. Please contact your local priest for a current list. In many cases, acolytes and initiates may accompany priests in such duties as observers. Go and see what it is like!

Does anybody even believe in Satan anymore?

They certainly do! Satan is alive and well and living in the hearts of all true Satanists. Although a minority of priests emphasize the symbolic role that Satan fills in our public life, others have testified to supernatural intervention in their own lives and the lives of others. Do not doubt the power of curses!

Isn't the Church just a social club for old men?

The church is a welcoming place for devotees of all ages. In many places the church provides outreach for our nation's new arrivals as they make the sometimes painful adjustment to life as a U.S. citizen. Many later testify that the church is the first place where they felt "at home", thanks to the mentoring role of church leaders.

Wouldn't it be fun to be an inquisitor? Or: If I became an inquisitor, wouldn't I lose all my friends and be hated by everybody?

The job of inquisitor is neither a reward for good behavior nor a punishment for your crimes! Inquisitors are not people who get their "jollies" from frightening people; rather, they are highly ethical professionals who care deeply about the purity of the church's mission and who desire to gently guide those who stray back to the One Path.

The fundamental focus of any good inquisitor is purity, not pain. In this, the life of our church's first Grand Inquisitor, the Marquis de Sade, is our exemplary model.

Can I become Master in Lunacy?

Perhaps you have what it takes to gain the highest ranking position within the Church! Preparation for this job is rigorous, however, and in the end only a few men have been granted this honor. A Master in Lunacy spends years of preparation, ideally as a psychiatrist although in practice many Masters in Lunacy have come from the Inquisition. In any event, the ideal candidate has held a variety of church offices, understands the difference between madness and authentic mysticism, and has a record of fidelity that one expects from the most senior churchman. Any youth with the ambition to attain the Master in Lunacy or other positions within the hierarchy should show his commitment by first excelling in a humbler (but highly valued!) role as a parish priest, deacon or liturgist.

How many evangelists are in the church today? Has the church discontinued that role?

The church certainly has not discontinued the role of evangelist. The exact number of evangelists in the church is a closely held secret, however, due to the highly dangerous nature of the work. The church will entertain discrete inquiries from potential candidates to this office. A candidate must show aptitude for the many specialized skills of this position. This is the one role where a criminal record is a plus!

PART THE SEVENTH: 1929

CHAPTER TWENTY-TWO

The Powerful Stranger

B oy 666, who in eleven years of mining had never lost a nose or ear, would have said the most unpleasant moments of all the many unpleasant moments in mining occur while waiting for an explosion at a draw point. While 3006 lit the fuse, Boy 666 and Boy 1313 conspired. The haulage drift would have been farther away and safer, but they waited in the slusher drift where they could talk freely.

"It's called a strike. All the boys just stop working." 1313 was in his preferred role as teacher.

"How would that work? They would just punish us."

"They can't punish everybody. If everybody stops working, if we stick together, the whole mine's quota goes unfilled and the teachers are in deep shit. Not us."

"It would never work."

"All we got to do is stick—"

Boom!

The next minute was spent coughing and waving hands in front of faces.

"Where's Thirty-Aught-Six? Did he get out in time?" said 1313.

"I hope he didn't."

"I made it out, No-Name," said 3006, emerging from the dust cloud.

"I told you to leave him alone," said 1313.

"So, what's this 'strike' you're planning?"

"None of your beeswax."

"Somebody with as many secrets as you probably should act nicer to other people," said 3006. "Especially when they know secrets."

3006 smiled, enjoying the effect of his words. "God, cod, sod." He tittered.

"You bastard," said 666, low and hoarse.

"If you tell a single person," said 1313, "I will kill you dead. I will *kill you dead.*"

"He can't prove anything," said 666 to 1313. "If he tells somebody about the shrine, we'll just say it was him who made it."

"If somebody turned in a certain something that was stolen from the church—if only one boy had ever gone to that church—that would prove..." 3006 raised one eyebrow.

"I will kill you *dead!*"

Somebody threw a punch. A punch was thrown back. Wrestling happened. Noses bled. A rock was raised.

Abruptly, they stopped. Further fighting was impossible. Klaxons were sounding the general alarm. All anger, all argument, all thought or sense of any kind was blotted out instantly as the overpowering sound brayed throughout the mine.

The boys turned and ran. Where there were piles of rocks in the way, they scrambled, scraping their hands and knees bloody. They stopped for nothing. The alarm's message was simple and terrible:

GET OUT NOW.

The skiff buckets were still running so they rode one up the main shaft. They emerged into the bright light of morning and joined the swelling throng of blinking, gasping youths.

The teachers looked afraid, but...not exactly cave-in afraid or fire afraid. The boys saw an unfamiliar bus parked in the driveway by the main gate. Next to it was an automobile, a breezer more beautiful than they could have imagined.

This might not be terrible after all.

The visitors were like archdemons, creatures of glamour and power, unapproachable. They wore black, the deep, infinite black of the pit of Hell. There was something unfamiliar and superior in the very way they moved around: they had a purpose.

For now those, these blacks (as they were called) from Burrsburg (that was the rumor) in their odd, close-fitting garments strutted around giving orders with an ease unique to 666's experience. "The Special Master wants the boys cleaned up," he heard one of them say, so Mr. Schuyler pulled out the fire hose and had the boys run through the spray. The blacks stood at a distance, commenting openly that here one found an "African" who never went west to Liberia. If they had asked, any boy could have told them George Schuyler was no joiner and was too cantankerous to keep with his own kind, let alone anybody else.

The boys were sent to the same field where they usually played smear the queer. The blacks pushed them into neat rows, wiping their hands after each touch although the boys were still wet from their cleaning. Oddly, not one boy was smacked during the whole process.

They waited, shivering a bit while the upstate sun did its best to dry them. After another minute, the sound of the door of the magnificent Citroën announced the reason for the visit.

He stepped out of the car.

The man was short, with toothpick limbs and a little pot belly that he tried to keep sucked in, but he radiated authority. No simple tube of cloth was fit for him: *he* was decked out in a wide-sleeved robe of a finer cloth than the boys could have imagined. Boy 666 instantly perceived in this man alertness, excellence, and kindness, each in a measure unique to his experience. In his little world, cruelty was everywhere, increasing wherever power increased. That somebody so important could exude such grace was an epiphany for Boy 666. He felt a new feeling conspicuously missing from his experience in the shrine: he worshiped.

"These are all your students, Headmaster?"

"Yes, Your Honor."

"Call me Master."

"Yes...Master."

These boys were collected from...?"

"Most are direct culls from Canada. The rest are runaways we get from truancy officers."

"Truancy officers from which states?"

"New Gehenna."

"Only New Gehenna?"

"Nobody's ever asked me to—I can show you my orders in writing—"

"You are not under investigation, Headmaster, nor will you be so long as you answer with the plain truth."

"Yes, only New Gehenna."

"And there are how many other schools in this part of this state?"

"There are two other mining schools, and, let's see, a dozen agricultural colleges in the tri-county area. In the city there are garment facto—er, garment schools—"

"I am only concerned with upstate. Now, as for your students: they are all present? None in the infirmary?"

"We've brought them all out for you, Master, just as you ordered."

And with that, the "Special Master" put Headmaster Goldberg out of his mind and began walking the ranks. A knot of blacks followed him, two paces behind.

It was an inspection. Most boys were passed over with the briefest of looks. Occasionally the Master would pause, scowl in thought (but not anger), and move on.

A few boys merited more attention. The Special Master would ask a question or two. If the boy gave good answers, he would be pulled out of line.

Boy 666 wanted badly to hear what the good answers were, but a mine detonation had damaged one of his eardrums years ago. He was forced to wait, anxiously standing next to his chums.

The Special Master paused before 3006.

"Name?"

"Errol Flynn."

"Where were you born?"

"Tasmania."

The Master thought hard, then reluctantly raised a finger. A black pulled 3006 aside.

The Master passed over Boy 1313 without a glance and stopped dead before Boy 666.

Boy 666 decided, in a decision he could not have even begun to explain, to appear calm and confident.

A smile came over the Master's face. He took 666's jaw in one hand and impersonally, but gently, turned his face this way and that.

"Yes. Yes."

Now he was frowning as well as smiling. Something like awe softened the Master's face. Boy 666 surprised himself by his lack of fear.

"What's your name?"

"Boy 666, sir."

"Your *name*."

Boy 666 clammed up. How was he supposed to answer that?

"Do you have a name?"

Boy 666 shook his head, to the extent the firm grip on his jaw permitted.

The gaze upon him did not relent for a long time. If this was uncomfortable, then let him never know comfort again.

Another 10 seconds, and the hand relaxed. "Note this one, Mencken. Boy 666. Many more questions for him." As he spoke, the Special Master's gaze never left Boy 666. Mencken was nothing; Boy 666 was everything.

Mencken pulled the boy out of line, his grip much less gentle. The Special Master resumed his paces through the ranks while Mencken led 666 to the huddle of special boys. Errol was there, more companionable than he ever had been. He grinned wickedly.

They were in.

Boy 1313 stood among the outs, on his tip toes, looking very small. He glared at them.

Boy 666 shook his head. No, he would not leave 1313 behind. Did 1313 understand?

The inspection concluded. The special boys were taken to the mess hall. They were questioned further by the blacks, who were to be addressed as Clerk This or Clerk That.

The Special Master, however, questioned 666 himself. 3006 was spelling "Errol" to his clerk when he saw 666 sit down with the Master, and that made him grin. 666 had won the biggest prize, and Errol liked winners.

"Where are you from? Who were your parents? How did you end up at the mine?"

"Canada. I don't remember. Captured by the U.S. army." Those were 666's answers. He was asked about his earliest memories. He was questioned again about his name. Oddly, his ignorance about this and many other things only encouraged the Master.

Then came the strangest question of all.

"Do you happen to have an old scrap of parchment on you? One you've kept hidden for a long time?"

A memory, long buried, rose up in a sudden rush. Boy 666 tensed. The Master sensed this, leaned in close, but said nothing.

Yes, there was a scrap. It had a capital W and other letters, now forgotten. Long ago, somebody had handed it to him. He had been told it was terribly important—but he had lost it. He had no idea who or when or why. He had been so young.

"No." Boy 666 barely whispered the shameful word, but the Master was so close, he did not need it to be repeated.

The disappointment did not distract the Master for long. He stood up and addressed the room.

"One question. I need to know if any of you have on you any—" And here, for the first time, the Master was uncertain how to proceed.

He was embarrassed. He glanced at the clerks, wishing them to disappear. "—any pieces of parchment. Any old scraps that you might, oh, I don't know, carry about on your person for some reason or another."

Boy 666 saw the terror in Errol's face.

"You, boy!" The Master had also seen it. Anybody would. "Do you have a parchment you've been hiding?"

The page from the Bible! Errol had it, and they would find it. He was as good as dead. They would behead him, no question. Errol shook his head, but his eyes told another story.

"Please, sir!" Boy 666 shouted. "I have something."

That meant he had lied just moments ago, but the Master could not hide his pleasure. "Please, sir, may I—" Boy 666 pointed to the door.

Boy 666 did not really have a plan, but when they were safely out in the hall, he knew what to do. He pulled off his moccasin.

"I'm sorry, sir, but I've been cheating. My history's not so good, and..."

He folded back a bit of shoe leather and pulled out a tiny wad of parchment. He waited, mute and, he hoped, contrite-looking, as the Master unfolded it.

The Master read out loud. "Reevesville. The Dewey Decimal System. 1865. Lake Orlando—*what is this shit!*" The Master was so bent out of shape, his voice rose to a squeak.

"The answers to tomorrow's history exam." They had come straight from Boy 1313. Mr. Trotsky had not changed the questions in years.

"Oh."

It took a moment for the Master's disappointment to dissipate.

"I see. You shouldn't be cheating, but it doesn't matter now. That life is over for you. Forget it."

The distraction did not work perfectly, but it worked well enough. Back inside, the Master resumed questioning Errol, but the boy had got his stupid face on, and the matter was dropped.

The boys were sent outside. Only one clerk watched them, the youngest. The others conferred with the Master. Errol looked hard at Boy 666 but they were too wise to discuss what had just happened.

Boy 1313 had contrived a way to linger. He had volunteered to gather in the hose, and was taking a very long time about it. His eyes pleaded with his friends. Errol just grinned, but 666 shrugged. There was no chance to talk.

The special boys were called back into the hall.

The boys were divided, Errol going with the larger group and 666 with the smaller, which was only four. The larger group was thanked for their time—thanked! For obeying orders!—and dismissed.

Errol looked at 666 with hatred. There was such a thing as too much winning, apparently. So much for gratitude.

It was quite obvious now why Boy 666 and the other three had been picked. They all looked the same. They were taller than average, with athletic build and jet black hair. They had similar faces too, and they were all about 18 years of age. Some ideal existed in the Master's mind, some physical form the Master cared about. They, among all the boys at the mine, conformed to it most perfectly.

CHAPTER TWENTY-THREE

Plucked from the Burning

"**G**ood news."

The Special Master addressed the four identical boys. He was all friendliness.

"I am the Special Master, personal assistant to his honor the Chief Justice. I have selected you to begin training for the highest rank of public service. I am taking you to the capital. When you finish, you will be clerks of the Supreme Court. As of now, you are among the elites, vested with vast power over ordinary men. Congratulations!"

The boys looked at one another, incredulous. Escape! No more mine! Had the Special Master offered them solid gold raven taxis with hot and cold running chocolate, they would not have been more dumbfounded.

"The training is tough, but I'm happy to say it is nothing compared to working in the mines. Your diet will improve. You will be given decent clothing and bedding, and be taught hygiene. And tooth brushes—do you know what tooth brushes are? No, of course not. You will learn. You will be tested, and pushed beyond what you imagine you can endure. However, even the hardest work, the combat training, is of the kind satisfying to normal, healthy young men—such as you manifestly are. If all of you succeed brilliantly, I will not be at all surprised."

This could not...*possibly*...be real.

Boy 666 saw somebody at the window. It was Boy 1313. His eyes were full of accusation.

Boy 666 raised his hand. "Excuse me, Master. What if I don't want to volunteer?"

"Who said anything about volunteering?" His voice was sharp. "I have picked you, and you are coming." He softened his tone, and laughed. "Now, let's have no more resistance."

The four initiates were ushered out of the building, surrounded by blacks. Boy 1313 tried to break in but was pushed back.

"You promised! *You promised!*"

Boy 666 had not promised. So why did he feel guilty?

A scene was in the making. Out of nowhere, Headmaster Rube Goldberg appeared to remove the embarrassment. He grabbed 1313 and 1313 broke free. Weeping bitterly, he ran about the yard in loping, purposeless circles.

He was in deep trouble now and there was not one cussed thing Boy 666 could do.

The Special Master was uninterested. With a curt command, he sent the boys off to collect their things.

In the dormitory, Boy 666 put his few possessions in a sack—they had never looked so shabby as they did now—and he heard through the window the Headmaster beating 1313 viciously.

An inspiration!

He opened Errol's chest, but did not find what he was looking for. He rifled through Errol's messy bed, then lifted the mattress, and yes! He saw it: the page torn from the Bible.

He did not consider the consequences. He truly had no idea what kind of place he was going to; he had every reason to expect snap inspections and constant suspicion. It was a supremely brave thing he did when he put the page into his own rucksack. He put his head down and walked out.

He walked past Boy 1313, still restrained by Headmaster Goldberg. As discretely as he could, he pointed to the sack and wiggled his eyebrows at Boy 1313.

He kept on going. He did not look back. The clerks escorted him out of the gate.

He heard a sharp intake of breath and a scuffle. Boy 1313 broke free. Only when the clerks themselves turned to block Boy 1313 did Boy 666 turn to see.

Boy 1313 had understood.

"I'm Elia!" Boy 1313 told him. "My name is Elia! *My name is Elia!*"

"Headmaster!" said the Special Master. "Can't you control your students?" Goldberg's face turned white. He was going to give 1313 a nosing for sure.

666 was appalled, but 1313 showed no regret. He was grinning, ever the defiant hero, as Goldberg dragged him away.

The clerks and initiates lined up to board the bus.

"You, Boy 666!" The Special Master's call tore 666's eyes away. "Come ride with me, in the car."

666 was in no mood to enjoy the astonishing privilege he was being offered but he could not refuse.

The car smelled of leather. The driver wore the strangest uniform, all epaulets and fringe. He wore white gloves and operated the controls of the car in the manner of a jeweler assembling a fine watch. They rode the car through the gate. Boy 666 felt sick and desperate.

"You told us we were important now. You told us we had power."

"Yes?" The Special Master smiled, all anticipation.

"Then order the headmaster to leave that boy alone."

The Special Master thought about that for two seconds.

"Stop the car."

The Special Master rolled down his window and motioned for the bus to come along side. "You! Mencken! Run back to the headmaster, tell him he is not to punish that boy."

"His name is Elia!" Boy 666 shouted through the window.

Mencken got off the bus and took his good time about it, looking hard at 666 as he did. He began jogging the few hundred yards to Goldberg's office. Boy 666 was out of the car in an instant. "Goose it, you bastard!" He was screaming now, not caring.

Every window in the bus had a face pressed against it. The boys watched with huge peepers and the clerks did not hide their loathing.

"Better hustle, Mencken," called the Special Master.

Mencken gave one last backward glance of pure murder, but he ran.

The die was cast: 666 was the boss' pet, and the others would despise him. He did not care, for bad or good.

The Special Master bade the automobile onward. The bus would catch up later. They were done with the mine forever.

CHAPTER TWENTY-FOUR

Initiates

Bananas. Boy 666's first impression of life in the capital was the tropical fruit served with the first meal. Bananas, pineapple, and the smell of the older clerks' cigars were exotic Haitian delights the embargo put out of the reach and the mind of the average American. For clerks, they were commonplace.

The Special Master and his clerks continued to tour the northern forests, trolling for clerk candidates. For days the new boys feasted on the fat of the capital and did a very little schooling. Mostly they settled into their quarters (which were Spartan by anybody's standards but their own), received simple black and white uniforms that, unimaginably, were bespoke, and learned how to behave like civilized men. More boys trickled in; their home towns were a record of the Master's circuitous route. The cohort swelled to a full century, all the same age, height, build, and facial features. One hundred twins.

Their hair was mowed into smooth carpets that it was satisfying to rub the wrong way. They were deloused and purged of tapeworms. They were measured and weighed. 666 was told he was an ideal mesomorph; he heard lots of meaningless words those first few days. A man with calipers got to know their skulls better than they knew them themselves. Boy 666 was fitted with cheaters, and found out what stars were. Later, he was given contact lenses, specially ordered from Italy.

He found out how much better mirrors are than puddles for inspecting one's own face. The imported antibiotic pills the blacks ate like candy cleared up the rashes, pimples, and pox that were a constant part of life in the sticks.

The Special Master returned, and training began in earnest. It was strange: they were made to exercise, which was a kind of work that accomplished nothing. Every minute of the new boys' days was occupied, the cracks in the schedule being filled with the mortar of menial labor. At first the only duties they were good for were sweeping dirt under rugs and polishing the brass fixtures with their spit, the quality of which was much improved.

Life was happy, but the initiates were not universally loved. Boy 666 avoided Mencken, who made it clear he was not a forgiving man. Mencken's contempt was not exclusive; he did not spare any member of the cohort his opinion, which was they were, without exception, stupid. Based on no evidence, he mocked them: "Every one of you thinks he'll be Chief Justice one day!" The insult had an unintended and contrary effect in Boy 666, if not the rest.

As far as the initiates were concerned, the Special Master was the boss man. The Chief Justice was a remote figure, glimpsed only at a distance, brooding and awful. In their memory, he was big and silent as a black blimp and passed through the halls with unvarying, inexorable momentum.

One day, a week after the group was complete, a boy was pulled away from his afternoon routine. When he came back, word was passed that the Chief Justice had interviewed him personally. More boys were pulled aside for the same reason, at a rate of three or four per day. Boy 666 was desperate for dope.

A dorm mate returned from his interview, dazed. Boy 666 led him down to a quiet place deep in the tunnels below the court to get the skinny.

"Well, what is the Chief like?"

"He doesn't wear his long black wig in his office. He looks older without it, and more ordinary."

Perfect. Somebody with an eye for detail.

"The thing that surprised me is, despite his age, his hair hasn't turned gray. If his peepers weren't so baggy, or his face so wrinkly, or his skin so yellow and blotchy, or his teeth so rotten, I wouldn't think he was very old."

"What did he want to talk about?"

"He asked me where I'm from."

"Where you're from or...where you're *from?*"

"*From.* He wanted my rescue story."

"Rescue?"

"That's what they call it, here in the capital. When a boy is taken."

"What did you tell him?"

"Not much. I was taken pretty young. I know some French, so I'm French. Or Quebecker.

"So, he was just trying to get to know you?"

"I think there was more to it than that. It made a big difference to him whether I came from Quebec."

"Why?"

"Dunno. He also wanted to know about the special– " Here, he lowered his voice and continued, "the Special Master. Wanted to know how he recruited me, what he said to me, that sort of thing."

"And you told him…?"

"Nothing. The Special Master never said anything to me. He just picked me out of a crowd, me and a few others. I didn't realize it at the time, but now that I'm here, it's clear—"

"We all look alike."

"Yeah, we all look alike. That was a big deal to him. It's…weird."

"Really weird. So what else did the Chief—?"

But Boy 666 was cut off, as this other boy had more to say. "He asked about my grades in school, what I did at the farm I was at, stuff like that. But, the thing is—"

"Yeah?"

"—he wasn't paying attention. I could tell he didn't really care about that stuff."

"So why did he ask?"

"How should I know? Maybe he's got to fill out some report."

This was nonsense, of course, and Boy 666 objected. "The Chief Justice doesn't—"

"Yeah, I know." The dorm mate tipped his head side to side, trying to shake out the right word. "The Chief Justice doesn't *report*."

Both boys thought about that for a moment.

The dorm mate spoke more quietly. "One more thing about the Chief."

"Yes."

"There was giggle water on his breath. Really strong."

"Oh?" Boy 666 was interested.

"Have you ever been around drinkers?"

"Not really."

"The bosses at my farm were drinkers. All of them. Some of the boys, too—they found the stash. You learn about drunks that way. There are three kinds."

"Three kinds?"

"Three kinds of drunks. Corny drunks, sad drunks, and angry drunks. The angry drunks are the dangerous ones. If you ever run into an angry drunk, watch him like a raven."

"So, what kind is the Chief?"

"Not sure. But I know what he ain't."

"What?"

"A corny drunk."

CHAPTER TWENTY-FIVE

The Interview

Boy 666 was the last to be summoned for an interview, and he knew it. Were he not the type to notice, the Chief Justice made sure he did know: "I've saved you for last. Time to find out what all the fuss is about."

Boy 666 had noticed no such fuss. It could have only come from the Special Master, who was inexplicably absent.

The Chief took him to the first robing room, a place off limits to the initiates. Boy 666 warmed to the privilege. He was no snob, but anybody likes a compliment.

"We'll go as browns. So much easier, where we're headed," said the Chief. One of the wardrobes held well-worn buckskins. "Find something your size and put it on." The Chief took a suit that fitted his girth. Boy 666 found a jacket and pants with fringe to fit his athletic dimensions. He hesitated, but the Chief disrobed to his underwear, heedless of the indignity.

When they were ready, they looked like two men right off the frontier, or more precisely, two city men pretending to be such. *Phony pony* was what the look was called, and it was never out of style in the capital. They would fit right in.

"Traveling surrounded by clerks gets to be a bore," said the Chief as they took a tunnel out the back, "and sometimes I like to be free of their listening ears."

Boy 666 silently inspected this and every sentence for meaning.

They decamped to an alley a couple of blocks east of the court building. Both were now free men in a free country: a rare treat for the Chief and an utter novelty for the boy. They walked with their elbows thrust out just a little farther than normal. They beamed. They were on the town.

A paddy wagon raced down the street, too fast, then halted abruptly in front of an apartment building. Clerks jumped out and burst through the door. The Chief held up his hand—indeed, everyone on the street stopped and watched with a wary eye. The clerks hauled valuables out—furniture, trunks, a few watches on chains—and tossed them into the vehicle. A brown stumbled out of the door, blood streaming down his face, and received another blow to the head that took him out of the action.

Boy 666 waited for a sign from the Chief. What could justify this kind of behavior? Nobody was being arrested. The clerks looked like nothing more than bandits on a looting spree.

The Chief needed to intervene. But all the while, he just stood there, his hand pressing against Boy 666's arm, until the paddy wagon, full to the gills, departed.

The Chief led them to a tavern called Peg-Leg Polly. The quaint wooden sign showed a pirate's parrot with a patch over one eye and a crutch under one wing. The wooden leg was thrust forward in a jaunty pose while the free wing held a frothy mug aloft in a drunken welcome. The effect would be twee were the sign and the whole establishment not clothed in the dignifying patina of centuries.

What some would call patina, others would call filth.

"I love this place," sighed the Chief as he settled into the most private booth in the back. "Knew the owner too, way back when. Still do, in a sense." Some memory made him smirk. He caught the eye of a server and ordered drinks with a barely perceptible nod of his head. "There's a story there."

For the next half hour, Boy 666 said not a word. If this was an interview, it was of a peculiar kind. The Chief's drinks came in a slow, steady stream—beers at first, then liquor—while Boy 666, never dropping his guard, nursed his original wooden mug with tiny sips, making it last.

The Chief's story was about John Patterson, a big man in the capital. While still a clerk, the Chief had cultivated friendships with the city's big fish, and Patterson was the biggest. His taverns, boarding houses and apartment buildings were the tip of his financial iceberg, but the Chief heard the rumors and confirmed, by means he did not elaborate, that Patterson had "interests" in opium dens, gambling, cock fighting, bear baiting—every imaginable illegality.

"There were other entertainments," said the Chief, and here he leaned his head in. Boy 666 imitated the pose and felt the *frisson* of shared secrecy. "Evil stuff; really evil. There were these hunts, only for the richest and most trusted customers. They used live humans as the game. Hunting *men*."

The Chief waited for the words to take effect, enjoying the moment. The man was quite a story teller, and Boy 666 noticed, even as the greater part of his mind reeled at the thought.

He played the part of the listener perfectly. It was hard not to. "Hunting men?" he said, with what he knew must be a dumbfounded expression.

"Patterson had ties with the people running the prisons. He had his hooks in everywhere. Whenever a prisoner proved impossible to handle—and they get a lot of those; guys go berserk behind bars—Patterson would take the prisoner off their hands. For a fee, of course. He'd turn the man loose on this island he had in the Chesapeake, and a paying customer would hunt him down. There ain't nothin' like *that* excitement, you can bet. The hunter would get a gun, and the prisoner a ball and chain—no reason to make it *too* fair—but there was real danger. Some of these prisoners were extremely cunning. Patterson got good at picking the ones that were nuts, but not too nuts. Yeah, finding the right nut—there's an art to that. Toward the end, it got so that every once in a while, the prisoner would win a round or two.

"By escaping?"

"By killing. There was no escaping."

The Chief looked away, thinking. In the big open room, some men with blackened fingers were playing a game involving an open light socket.

The Chief's brain was taking a while.

"There was this one hunt..."

The Chief was shy now. Boy 666 held his breath, not moving. This was something.

"The prey was wounded—a trail of blood. Should have been a piece of cake. But he got up in a tree, and the hunter was foolish. Young and cocky. The prey got up a tree—up a tree! The ball was supposed to make that impossible—and he dropped down on the hunter. He took the gun. Took the gun! Lucky he didn't get a shot off—he only had one shot left, and was afraid to blow it. No fool, really, counting the bullets as he dodged them. So the hunter had to keep on the run, always moving, for two full days. Two days! No sleep or food. Exhausting. But in the end, the wound did it. The prey collapsed. The hunter circled around, got the gun and shot him. But his hand was shaking and the prey wasn't dead. So he took care of him with a rock. Have you ever killed a man, or an animal, with a rock?"

"No," Boy 666 whispered. He had seen rats in traps. That was not even close.

"The skull is tough. It won't break on the first try."

The Chief drank deep of his beer and wiped his mouth.

"It wasn't wrong, you know. Only the nastiest prisoners were used. Guys should have been executed anyway. But still."

The Chief was still wiping his mouth.

"It...does something to you, bare hands like that."

This story meant something but Boy 666 did not want to know what.

"You said, 'toward the end.'"

"What?"

"The hunts came to an end?"

"Oh, well. Patterson got too powerful, and the old Chief Justice didn't like it. I decided to take Patterson out. That's what got me a bench on the seat. A seat on the bench. And the rest is history, as they say.

The Chief was drinking bourbon now. Beer for meditation, liquor for celebration. Boy 666 made a note of it.

A howl erupted in the next room. Some game involving beaver pelts and sharpened pool cues was getting out of hand.

"How did you 'take out' Patterson?"

"Patterson was one of those businessmen who doesn't get government. Odd really, for somebody in Burrsburg. I sold him a pig in a poke—and pig, now that I think of it, is the perfect word. I got him a seat in congress."

"Why on earth would he fall for that?"

"This was before the lock-down. You weren't even born then. Think how things were at the time. Running out of Natural Born Citizens. Anybody could see with a brain –with a *brain* could *see*–the Senate's days were numbered. The presidency was one of those, uh—revolvers?—revolving doors. Everybody expecting the House of Representatives to become the center. The power. A House seat was quite the lure.

"Blacks were terrified. By the House taking over. Had to defend ourselves. Stave off disaster."

"So, you pitched your plan—"

"Pitched, my ass. In this town, you take your chance and don't ask permission. That's a lesson for you, sonny boy."

The Chief winked. It took some effort. He had really drunk enough. Was there any way to halt the flow of alcohol?

"A seat opened sudden-like. That was my doing. Rival candidates, disqualified. Also my doing. Months ahead of time, when nobody suspected. Necessary sentences got inserted into court opinions. That was all me. Polls were manned by volunteers I picked. Myself. I lined pockets with money from Patterson. Moving parts, lots of moving parts, but I kept 'em oiled. Patterson got his seat in congress.

"That's the way you do it, sonny-boy. You build a trap, make the rat pay the bill!" These last words exploded in a wet, boozy guffaw.

Boy 666 wiped his face discretely.

"And then. In the fullness of time. I locked congress down. Nobody gets out. Let them scratch each other's eyes out in there—who cares? It's all for their 'protection'. I made it all happen, worked without a hitch. What country are you from?"

So, the interview was starting.

"Canada."

"Sure of that?"

"My earliest memory is this regiment of the Canadian—"

"No parents?"

"I don't remember them. Well, not very well."

Boy 666 could not have explained why he shaded that truth.

"That's...suggestive." The Chief was both suspicious and amused. "Really no earlier memories...of..."

"Not many."

"We'll see. What's your view of the Great Reformation?"

Be careful. The man is out of his mind.

"The Poe Presidency was a disaster, and it showed us, once and for all, that in order to return to the intent of our piratical founders we simply could not tolerate feminine influence—"

"Applesauce." The Chief's smile was patronizing.

"Your honor?"

"Pure applesauce. Why not tolerate feminine influence?"

Boy 666 was an experienced debater, but he had never treated this topic as debatable. Still, he found a point of attack.

"Our founders were pirates."

"Who had pirate wives."

"Well, some of them."

"Every other country in the world has women."

Now I've got you!

"*Those* God-fearers? What about American exceptionalism? We are the shining pyre on a hill."

"A country needs babies."

"We are a nation of immigrants."

"A cliche." He pronounced it to rhyme with *glitch*.

Boy 666 frowned. The Chief elaborated. "Save that kind of talk for the rubes."

"Well, I guess I'm one of the rubes. Besides, the Great Reformation put in motion a chain of events that resulted in the judiciocracy. You regret it?"

"Ha! Got me there. Got me good." Boy 666 basked the glow of victory. The Chief stared into his shot glass, as though it were a crystal ball. Something he saw in there terrified him.

"All those women. That bastard Buchanan. He *killed* them. Bodies of thousands. Millions."

The Chief was back to his beer mug and began to weep, quietly, into it.

Satan help us.

"Millions of women, shot without mercy, piled up everywhere. They built *bonfires*. Giant bonfires *on fire*. Have you seen the Mathew Brady photographs? Blood-soaked dresses, staining the snow! The *women!*"

The Chief was sobbing now, openly. The entire tavern was conspicuously not noticing.

No. Not a corny drunk.

CHAPTER TWENTY-SIX

A Walk in the Snow

The next few minutes saw quite a river of alcohol flow down the Chief's gullet. The Chief was getting really plastered. Getting him home was going to be difficult. What to do?

Boy 666 tried a gambit. "Best be going."

The Chief's answering grunt contained both acquiescence and resistance. Necessity cast the deciding vote. Boy 666 pulled the Chief out of the booth and leaned him against the wall.

Boy 666 caught the eye of the owner. The jaded look he got in reply suggested this was all typical, and that the bill would be settled later. Boy 666 got the Chief's momentum aimed toward the exit, and no one challenged them.

Well, of course no one would. That was well, as Boy 666 had no money. He never had. As a Canadian he was too young, as a mine slave too poor, and as a black too rich, to carry cash.

The freezing air of the street temporarily roused the Chief. They walked up Constitution Avenue, right in the middle of the empty street, according to the Chief's insistence. There was a path through the falling snow in the street.

They came to the alley of the secret entrance. The Chief trudged on, oblivious.

Boy 666 took the Chief by the elbow and steered him into a sweeping turn. The Chief growled, shook off his hand, and trudged on, straight for the rear wall of the court building, looming just like the fortress of heedless might that it was.

Decision time. The Chief's route was indiscreet. The Chief would be angry if his secret were exposed. When the powerful made mistakes, it was their prerogative to blame the weak. Boy 666 would be the fall guy if he stayed with the Chief.

He turned down the alley as the Chief wobbled on alone.

He went into the alley. His last sight of the Chief, swaying like the Burr Monument in a strong wind, stayed with him, rebuking him. The Chief needed him.

He ran back to the street. The Chief was nowhere in the near-empty street. He must have wandered into—

O Satan! There!

A brown mound lay atop a bigger, white mound. The Chief lay on his back in a snowdrift, snoring. The falling snow melted as it landed on him. One large flake perched high on his eyelash, intact and undisturbed.

Boy 666 pulled on the Chief's arm but knew before he did it he would not be able to raise the heavy man. He shook the Chief. He thought of slapping him, and dismissed it.

He took hold of the Chief's feet and spun his body around.

The new position gave him no advantage. The Chief had settled deeper into the drift.

Boy 666's heart was pounding. This was very bad.

His mind was forced into new avenues of thought. He could go get help, or he could drag the Chief through the street.

He dragged the Chief through the street. The frozen ground was a small mercy; its slippery surface made the job easier but more urgent.

No one gave help or issued challenge. Boy 666 was figuring out how this town worked: people kept their heads down and the government did what it wished.

Boy 666 dragged the Chief to a service entrance in the back of the court. Desperate, he pounded on the door. A watchman opened it and recognized the initiate. Boy 666 was careful to stand so as to block the view of the Chief. Improvising, he sent the brown on a ridiculous errand. (Eggnog. It was the only thing that came to mind.) The word of a black, even a snot-nosed twerp, was law.

Repairmen had built a fence around this side of the court building. Construction sites were everywhere in the capital; their ubiquity was a result of how little construction happened. Boy 666 broke down the rickety gate and took a wheel barrow from among the tools piled there. He tipped it over and knocked free the snow and ice.

The Chief's breathing was noisy and ragged. Fear of the man's imminent death drove the boy on. He rolled the Chief into the tilted wheelbarrow and levered it into an upright position. The old man's undignified sprawl made the barrow tipsy.

Boy 666 pushed his load with all haste through the wide open door. Although the frigid wind was blowing snow into the building, no one had come to investigate. He pushed the wheel barrow through the empty hallways to the nearest elevator.

The elevator operator was gone for the night. Good. Still unseen, they descended and Boy 666 wheeled the Chief all the way down to his apartment, easing past two guards who sat on the floor, asleep. He found the bedroom and flipped the Chief onto the canopied bed. The

Chief's weight pinned the blankets in place, but Boy 666 pulled the corners out from where they were tucked and covered the Chief as best he could.

He returned the wheelbarrow to where he found it. Still, no one appeared to challenge him. The pounding in his chest subsided. His right hand tightened into a fist of victory; disaster had threatened, and he had beat it.

Another worry loomed. The cold might have got in the Chief's bones. Boy 666 had shivered through plenty of sleepless winter nights when his body could not warm itself, and his was a young, healthy body not loaded with alcohol or dragged through snow.

Exhausted, Boy 666 returned to the Chief's apartment. The guards continued their slumbering vigil. Boy 666 found the Chief lying on the bed exactly where he had been put.

Build a fire? Warm the blankets on the steam radiator? Fetch some hot water bottles? What to do?

Find some blankets.

Boy 666 explored the many rooms of the apartment. One door had weather stripping. He opened it.

Steam rushed out to greet him like an over-eager host. Immediately he knew this was the place he needed. He fiddled with the unfamiliar light switch: it was a dimmer knob. Faint electric lights filled the room with an ultramarine glow that filtered up through waters of a heated pool. This was the Chief's personal grotto.

Back to the bedroom. No time to fetch the wheelbarrow. Boy 666 pulled the Chief into a sitting position. The old man's compressed gut released a profound belch that vibrated the room like a church bell. With the greatest physical effort of the evening, Boy 666 pulled the

Chief over his back, draping him like the world's most encumbering cape.

Keeping his balance was tricky, but Boy 666 exulted, figuring he had the situation licked. He staggered into the grotto. With extreme care, he walked down the wet steps right into the pool. The buoyancy from the water helped him lower the Chief safely into the water's hot embrace.

Boy 666 stripped down to his skivvies and hung his duds over a radiator. He sank into the pool. The soothing steam was paradisiacal after the cold and fear of the last hour.

Boy 666 had years of experience as an asbestos miner. Getting the Chief out of his sodden clothes was not nearly the most miserable work he had ever done—not by a long shot—but in a certain way, it was the most repugnant. As he did it—and it was quite a long time before it was done—Boy 666 had to worry about keeping the Chief upright. More than once the slippery white mass of flesh nearly toppled over.

In the end, the job was done. Still, Boy 666 dared not leave. There was no way he could haul the Chief out of the pool on his own, nor would he squander his hard-won secrecy by summoning help.

No, there was nothing to do but wait for the Chief to revive.

Drowsiness was his new enemy. He moved back and forth between the cool air and the hot water and thereby kept alert. He slapped himself. He hummed various work songs the teachers had taught. The Chief never stirred, and Boy 666 made bold to sing the irreverent versions the boys had invented.

He stayed awake and kept the Chief alive. Time passed, maybe an hour, maybe three. At last, with a convulsive inward snort, the Chief's head jerked up. His peepers opened wide and darted around the cave.

Boy 666 waited, unmoving. The Chief's bloodshot eyes looked at him in confusion, then recognition, then some other emotion Boy 666 could not interpret.

The Chief, who was nothing if not canny, said nothing. He simply stood up, walked out of the pool, and returned to his apartment.

Boy 666 gathered up his duds and followed the Chief. The old man did not turn back to look at him, but simply pointed to the door to the hallway. Boy 666 let himself out without a word. He found his bed but his racing mind never let him sleep.

The next day, late in the morning, while Boy 666 was at combat lessons, the Chief appeared up on the metal catwalk that overlooked the gym. Boy 666 and the Chief looked at each other for a moment, then the Chief simply nodded and left.

They understood each other. Nothing was ever said about the events of the previous night.

Boy 666 had done well. He expected the Chief would reward him. His expectation proved correct. But the adventure had replaced his awe with a new emotion: pity.

CHAPTER TWENTY-SEVEN

Cathedral

Sundays were church days. Unlike school, where Trotsky and Schuyler did not hide their contempt, in court, the church was afforded something resembling respect. For a black, church attendance was expected. The Special Master marched them to church in set ranks, and a missing black would be noted.

As they marched through the plaza, the initiates gasped. Something brilliantly gilded launched dramatically from out of an upper window of the court. It was the Chief in a magnificent gilded taxi, come to lead the procession. To Boy 666's eye, the ravens were unbelievably huge creatures, lordly and terrifying.

The blacks marched to the Shrine of the Unwholesome Miasma, the seat of the Master in Lunacy and the largest Satanist cathedral in the world outside of Manhattan Island.

The great cathedral bells began to ring. This was not the cheerful *bim bim bong* of Christian worship, but rather a clangorous clank that promised red hot pitchforks and brazen seas of fire.

The ranks of blacks swept aside the few disorganized church-going browns as they marched through the *porta inferni* and into pews reserved for them in the front. Last of all, the Chief processed with the Master in Lunacy, church and state in lockstep on their joint mission of raising Hell in every corner of the world.

The smoke of incense spread throughout the huge space. It was narcotic by design.

The Chief and the Master in Lunacy sat simultaneously on their thrones, and the congregation followed suit. Boy 666 looked up, like any tourist. At the top of the columns he saw raven's nest capitals (decorative stonework, not real ones) supporting Gothic arches almost invisible in the smoky gloom above. Grotesques were everywhere. (Angels and saints were reserved for downspouts, outside.) Thousands of baleful stone peepers stared back at Boy 666, disapproving of him. They were there to make demands, not offer succor.

Let the Christians nurse on milk. Grace was for sissies.

Red was the predominant color of the stained glass. Lots of swirling fire, lots of open-mouthed enemies falling into pits, lots of blood spurting from warriors fighting the ceaseless fight.

Patriotic themes were not absent. The red stripes of the flag emerged from waving flames in more than one window, and the midnight black of the upper-left field made the Jolly Roger stand out from it all the more brilliantly.

And shine the windows did, for the sun was blazing, streaming in from the east window. Blotches of low-angled red rays painted the backs of the blacks in macabre patterns of hate.

But great bass drums were pounding, and Boy 666 could observe no more. The great rumble blotted out all thought.

Mallet-wielding liturgists in red robes threw themselves at the vast sheets of stretched buffalo hide, beating the drums with a vengeance. The floor vibrated in sympathy with the violent din. The congregation murmured, then roared, then screamed in answer. Boy 666 did not know the phrase *culture shock,* but he felt it. This was weird.

Abruptly, the sound stopped. The novices, not seeing the signal, kept shouting. Embarrassment.

The choir of men and boys stood. The men sang the part of the music that one would call *music*, while the boys contributed an insanely high assault on the ears somewhere between a scrape and a screech. For the first time in his life, Boy 666 gave thanks for his one bad ear.

They sang:

> "The Devil from his thirsty fangs
> Some Bloody Drops has thrown,
> And solemn Oaths have bound his Hate
> To show'r Damnation down."

That was it for the choir. A young man with a well-trimmed beard came forward with a guitar. He sang a medley, but worse, the congregation was expected to sing along. "They will know we are Satan's by our hate, by our hate" made sense at least, but a few chord changes took them to "Fish and chips and vinegar" and "Don't Throw Your Junk in My Back Yard"—what in Heaven?—followed by a bumpy transition to "The more we get together the happier we'll be" with rhythmic clapping. Boy 666 wondered if the life of an asbestos miner was so terrible after all.

So much for the worship. The congregation shifted in their seats and coughed. With a ponderous theatricality, the Master in Lunacy mounted the pulpit. Sermon time.

"You. Are. All."

Each word was a sentence. A paragraph, really. The old man's tiny eyes darted about, attempting eye contact with each of the few hundred worshipers.

"I say again: You. Are. All."

The Master in Lunacy found a small cup in the pulpit and took a sip of water. Or was it hooch? Whatever it was, it disrupted the mood. Boy 666 judged the Master in Lunacy in his heart—judged him, and found him wanting.

"You. Are. All. Going. To. Hell!"

That got a few murmurs from the crowd.

"You are all going to Hell." The Master in Lunacy paused again, consulted his notes, and spat the next line in a spasmodic hiss:

"Satan willing!"

This attempt at melodrama only annoyed Boy 666 all the more.

The burden of the sermon had something to do with how the people of Satan were failing to meet their quota, were failing to pull up their socks and failing to put on their big boy pants and failing to put their shoulders to the wheel and failing to buckle down and failing to give a hundred and ten percent and failing to let go and let Satan and failing to put their hands to the plow and failing to crank the corn husker of life and failing to tell whatever gods there may be to go jump in the lake and take a hike—failing in pretty much every area of life that a Satanist could fail.

And by the way did you know the Master in Lunacy worked on a farm when he was young? He got up every day at 4:00 a.m. to milk the chickens—ha ha ha!—and he never complained.

The congregation's murmurs of assent waxed and waned but a stone of disapproval calcified in Boy 666's gizzard. What, he wondered, was all this *for*? Where was the practical program for change? What direction ought we go, leader? How should we then live?

That question was never answered. As the sermon ended, the bearded singer led the congregation in a final round of "Don't throw your junk in my backyard" in a muted *a cappella*. The Master in Lunacy ceremonially cursed the congregants and made the sign of the Penta-gram over them.

One final bang of a drum ended the service. The blacks filed out. The smells and bells, the music, and above all the words, had done their unintended work: Boy 666 departed as a confirmed Asatanist.

Sunday dinner was a disappointment. Since the sermon ran long, the roast was burned.

PART THE EIGHTH: 1930

CHAPTER TWENTY-EIGHT

In the Woods

The following evening, the Special Master took Boy 666 aside.

"You'll be taking a trip with me. There's something I need you for—an important meeting. And secret, too; tell no one where you're going."

Boy 666 could hardly squeal about something he knew so little about, but he nodded, happy to receive special attention.

He was still thinking about this at bedtime. His favorite time to think was while pissing into the drain in the floor of the bathroom. At the edge of his vision he noticed a great expanse of black. His stream veered off target, splattering the wall.

"I'm sorry, your honor!" Boy 666 picked a towel off the floor and made to wipe up the mess.

"Forget that. Come with me. Quietly!"

In the Chief's office, they joined a boy, one of the new cohort, one of the "twins." He was sobbing. Or at least he was making a noise like sobbing.

"What are we going to do with this worthless recruit?"

The Chief's question was too bizarre to be anything but rhetorical. The whole situation was bizarre. The sobbing was patently phony, as was the Chief's anger. Boy 666's inexperience could not quite identify a put-up job when he saw it, but he was not completely fooled. An adult would have been insulted, or wary. Boy 666 was flattered, and once again, moved to pity: the poor Chief, who cannot even lie well.

"What should we do? I've asked him to help me in a dangerous job. He's turned yellow, says I should find somebody else to help me—somebody who knows how to *obey*. What do you think of that?"

"I'm afraid," said the boy. Boy 666 felt his cheeks heat up with embarrassment. This situation was unbearable.

"I'll do the job, Your Honor."

The Chief pretended to weigh the offer. It was not so much that the Chief was a terrible actor; it was only that the ensemble had not rehearsed their scene sufficiently.

"Very well." The Chief put a fatherly hand on Boy 666's shoulder. "And you, Charlie"—apparently that was the other boy's name—"are going to be punished severely." The Chief's voice rose unnaturally, as though for the benefit of an inattentive audience. "That is what happens to boys who are afraid to follow orders."

Charlie slunk out, still sobbing.

Oh, brother. This drama could really use an acting coach.

"666: pack your warmest clothes and come with me. We'll be gone for two days."

"Yes, Your Honor. But I have combat trials tomorrow."

"You have more important business."

Boy 666 threw his sleeping flannels—even they were black—into his rucksack and got into a cassock and heavy cape. He matched the

Chief's impatient strides to the ravenery where the stink of bird droppings was mitigated by the wide open window of the launch. The Chief's magnificent taxi awaited them with an overstaffed conspiracy of ravens, set a-jitter by the command for a night flight. Their lord was that giant raven Boy 666 had seen the day before.

"This is my oldest friend," said the Chief, petting the freakish monster. "I call him Abaddon, Lord of Ravens. He is my greatest accomplishment—" Here the Chief looked Boy 666 up and down. "—so far. I trained him myself."

"Rok!" shouted Abaddon, as if he understood the Chief perfectly. The sound from his wicked beak perturbed the quiet of the night.

We each remember our first ride on a raven taxi, don't we? Boy 666 never forgot this one. He felt free as a bird. They went north into the night, leaving the sickly light and smoke and stench of the capital behind them.

The dense layers of wool about him were a needful comfort. He put up his hood and scrunched down against the wind. The thought of the tattered tunic he used to wear in the mine—but that memory was disintegrating to dust. The miner boy, that boy he used to be, was a different person, a person long dead. The clerk he was now—that boy was very much alive.

A light appeared behind them, tiny but noticeable against the black sky. The Chief watched it with interest, but it proved no threat. The Chief's taxi made excellent time, and the light fell back and disappeared.

The Chief relaxed. "Snuff is the best tobacco," he said, offering some to Boy 666. They sat there, sniffing their pinches, the nicotine and the brisk air making them alert without purpose.

On and on they went: one hour, two hours, three. The Chief's famous garrulousness did not accompany them on this trip. The birds could not go such distances non-stop, naturally, but special accommodations applied to the Chief's taxi. It did not make periodic stops, nor even land to swap out one conspiracy for another, like the mail. Instead, Abaddon escorted exhausted conspiracy members down to raveneries below and returned with fresh replacements. Otherwise, Abaddon sat on his spot at the top bar of the taxi with his wings tucked in, as any aristocrat would.

Boy 666's life in the court was devoted to learning the ways of a gentleman, a scholar, a ruler, and a bureaucrat. As a matter of course he had been taught astrology. The stars were no longer meaningless patterns of lights, rather, they were familiar stories written in pointillist pictures. In the mines, they were hidden from him by nearsightedness and layers of rock; at the capital they were revealed to him in textbooks; now, in the infinite velvet of this rural night, without street lamps or devotional bonfires to dim them, the stars blazed in arrogant glory. *Oh thou art the Morning Star, Son of the Morning.* And for the first time, that familiar scripture meant something, meant more than something. After just one day as an Asatanist, there he was, in danger of losing his irreligion. Well, cut him some slack: he was only 18.

This long sleepless trip was also the longest stretch of idleness he could ever remember. He had no idea what to do with his mind.

He looked down. At the edge of a meadow he saw a goateed man, thin and freakishly tall, wearing trousers with red stripes, a blue tail coat, and a star-spangled top hat. He was pointing at Boy 666 with a bloody butcher's knife.

Uncle Sam!

Boy 666 blinked and the man was gone, replaced by swaying tree branches that formed a human outline.

False alarm. Calm down. Best get some rest.

The Chief was slumped in a corner of the platform, snoring gently. Boy 666 closed his eyes.

He opened them a moment later, but it was no moment. The dawn lit half the sky and his bones were stiff with the cold.

The waking Chief gave him a taciturn look, as though an examination of the boy's face might answer a nagging question. Then the Chief opened a satchel and produced a breakfast of johnnycake and honey. Coffee from an insulated jar was still warm and Boy 666 slurped its unfamiliar bitterness greedily.

On and on they went. More ravens rotated in and out. Boy 666 admired the mastery of Abaddon over the birds, and the Chief over Abaddon. This was organization, and it was a wonderful thing. A man could get things done with it.

Noon came, and the Chief produced a lunch of chicken sandwiches. When nature demanded, they relieved themselves over the side, and all the while the Chief was far too distracted to feel embarrassment, or cause it. They stopped for nothing.

The afternoon progressed, and the shadows of bare oak trees below lengthened. The warmth of the day began to fade. The cold night and idle day left Boy 666 with aching muscles, and he dreaded the coming night.

"Chief?" It was the first word he had dared to say all day. "How much longer?"

"Do you see that lake?"

It was at the edge of vision but big enough to put a notch in the horizon.

"We land at the far shore."

And that completed their conversation.

Before the hour was up, the lake was spread out beneath them. It was long and thin, and gorgeous among its hills. At its end, the birds descended on Abaddon's command. In this wilderness, the raveneries were sparse, so the birds were exhausted. They landed with a bump.

Boy 666 looked around. The Chief was watching nothing but him.

The water lapped a meadow of tall grasses. At the forest's edge stood a rustic cabin.

Out of the cabin walked an old brown. He halted, as though expecting somebody, but not them.

The Chief grunted with grim satisfaction. The brown ran back to the doorway and waited.

The Chief took Boy 666 by the shoulders. They stood eye to eye. The Chief's smile was the opposite of kindly.

"You are a patriot?"

Something about the question made Boy 666 want to cry. "Yes, Your Honor!"

"As an American, your first loyalty is to whom?"

"My Lord Satan."

"And who is Satan's regent on earth?"

Since the death of Crowley, there could be only one answer: "The Chief Justice."

The Chief's smile became fiercer, and Boy 666 was not sure which one of them would start crying first.

"If I ask you to do something, you'll obey me, right? You'll obey without question? You'll do it and not think a thing about it, now or later?"

The questions were evolving such that the last was a hoarse, insistent declaration, but Boy 666 whispered, "Yes, sir."

When he spoke again, the address was so odd that it startled the youth more than anything.

"My boy, your final test is upon you. Pass it and your horizons are"—the Chief was looking up into the sky, his eyes sparkling but his face frozen in sorrow—"practically limitless."

"Yes sir."

"Take this."

The Chief pulled out of his robe a long, cruel knife.

"Use the knife upon the brown there."

The brown could not have heard the Chief's command, but they heard his moan when the knife came into view.

Boy 666 took the knife in hand, and only then discovered that by doing so he had committed himself to the vile deed. And vile it was: the brown was old, and even from a distance, had the posture of a pig awaiting sacrifice.

The Brown was dressed in a hunter's coat, ironically the color brown. As Boy 666 drew near, he saw the man was confused more than anything.

Boy 666—the Chief Justice's personal assassin, as he must now view himself—backed the brown through the door. There was no egress, even if the brown were the fleeing type, and as the youth waited for his eyes to adjust to the low light, the homey smells of a wood fire pierced his heart, for reasons he could not understand.

The man waved his arms around the room, indicating the rough-sawn table, stools, hearth, and loft above, as if they might tell the assassin to relent. In his own defense, the man never said a mumbling word.

The boy assassin held out the knife. The issue was already decided. He would not do it slow, nor fast. He would just do it.

He remembered, stupidly, his combat instructor showing how to aim the blade upwards, through the ribs. There was a craft to hone.

The thrust made his victim stand on his toes—for a moment. He killed the man but his own soul felt the stab.

He came out of the cabin and blinked. Another raven taxi was coming in low over the lake. The black rider was shouting, urging the birds on. They landed hard in the grass.

When the black had run half way across the meadow, the boy assassin saw it was the Special Master. They met in the middle where the Chief waited.

"Oh merciful God!" It was an old Haitian curse.

The Special Master was looking at the boy assassin's hand. It and the knife were, much to the boy's shock, coated in the dead man's blood. If ever there were a picture of guilt, it was that.

The Special Master made a sound Boy 666 had never heard before: it was a human shriek. The Master dropped to his knees, then all fours. The screaming went on.

What had he done?

The Chief roared with laughter, and the sound of it was worse than the Master's screams. The boy had killed all the sanity and now the world was mad.

CHAPTER TWENTY-NINE

Bomb the France

A fter that, the court was never the same.

The Special Master avoided everyone. He stopped supervising the trainers, and the neglect trickled down to the boys. The Master's time was consumed by personal projects decidedly odd. He made a painting of the Chief Justice. No one had ever accused him of being an artist, and with that opinion the painting concurred. A small ceremony accompanied the hanging of the painting in the Chief's empty niche in the Great Hall, but little importance was given to it and the Chief's only reaction was tolerant avoidance. Then, even more bizarrely, there was talk of a statue, one the Special Master would have made of himself, to be placed in the courtroom. How could somebody be simultaneously so depressed and so vain?

Before the statue could be installed, the work of the court came to a halt. Trainers stopped even pretending to hold classes for the initiates. The flow of opinions from the Chief Justice was clogged. Browns fled the building. Clerks formed tight-knit groups in the hallways and set to paranoid whispering. The distraction worked its way so thoroughly through the culture that even those with the least connection to sources of rumor heard the stories, the improbable guesses of what had gone wrong. Even Boy 666 heard.

None knew, however, of the strange doings of the cabin except the three who had been there, and none of them said anything. Indeed, the Special Master stayed out of sight.

Justice Learned Hand, long thought to be the Chief's closest friend on the court, took charge of the statue project. Its installation did not merit even the slipshod pomp the painting had been given. One morning, it simply appeared in the Great Hall. The feud between Justice Hand and the Chief dated from that day.

The gossipy idleness was like a fever. Inevitably, it broke. The busy word passed from mouth to mouth: the Special Master had disappeared, and the Chief Justice ordered that his name never be spoken again.

The clerk Mencken was appointed interim Special Master. He threw himself into the job and got the initiates back into their training regimen. Still, Boy 666 figured the Chief would never give him the permanent job. As the *interim* title lingered, Mencken drew the same conclusion. He lost the blacks' respect, relied on sarcasm and insults to impose his will, and a vicious circle ensued. Boy 666 watched this drama play itself out, and learned what not to do.

The horror of the cabin never left him. Time dulled it into a low ache.

Boy 666 sought escape in his studies. He imagined how his teachers would rank him: *A good spirit, earnest, and very cooperative, immensely popular with his peers, yet oddly aloof, and most critically, not strong in academics. Kind to those below; polarizing to those above. His eye-sight is poor. Prospect: a little above average. Likely career destiny: middle manager.*

He had to do something about that.

The Chief called Boy 666 for more interviews. Once again, the summons came in the evening, but the destination, if possible was stranger than that of the cabin visit. Boy 666 was ushered to the Chief's personal grotto.

The steam was suffocating. Boy 666 could only barely make out the Chief sitting in the far end of the pool. Boy 666 had to decide, based on the Chief's mumbled instructions and the uncertain evidence of his eyes, how much he was expected to undress. The embarrass-ment was complete, but in the end he sat in the near end with nothing but brackish water to clothe his nakedness.

"We could bomb the France."

Thank Hades. The Chief is drunk.

He was drinking Pellisipian bourbon. It was his happiest drink, but it did not loosen him up. He seemed cagey. Boy 666 responded in kind.

"We could."

And with that, the interview ended. The Chief drank and the boy stewed.

The next night, no summons came. An evening in the initiates' dorm was becoming dangerous; they all knew he was somehow the Chief's pet, as he had been the Master's pet. The other boys began to avoid him. How to turn them around?

He picked the most good-natured boy.

"Have you ever thought about what it would be like to bomb the France?"

The boy took it as a joke, and ran with it. Others joined in. Once the group's size satisfied him, he redirected it.

"We should petition the court. Get the justices on board. Get the Chief on board."

"What?"

"We're blacks. Our problem is, we don't think like blacks. We have the power to make policy."

"Not us. We're just initiates."

"We're initiates"—Boy 666 pointed at his brain—"in here. People treat us as kids because we think we're kids."

He had them. It was that easy.

"We start thinking like blacks, others will start treating us that way. All we need is a cause."

They debated the petition. They debated what the petition should say, not whether the petition should be. Let the others decide the exact wording; Boy 666 got poor grades in law anyway.

It was just then—just as he was enjoying the changing tide—he saw somebody watching him.

It was a place high on the wall, where the bricks were especially cockeyed. The light had shifted and he saw into a crack that went all the way through the wall. He saw eyes. Somebody was using the crack as a peep hole.

"You could get in trouble talking like that."

Uh-oh. Apparently the debaters were wandering onto thin ice. What were they saying? Oh, yes: somebody had said the U.S. "steals" its immigrants from France.

"I think," said Boy 666—all eyes were on him, and he loved it—"we should call a spade a spade."

The eyes liked what they heard.

"Exactly," said the boldest boy. "The normal rules don't apply."

"We have a manifest destiny."

"It's American exceptionalism. We steal our citizens, and we shouldn't be afraid to say it."

But others objected. The talk lasted well into the night. All of them had schoolwork to do, and that made the debate fascinating. Boy 666 intervened as needed to make progress on the text of the petition. He needed that thing written, and he was not going to write it himself.

At some point, the eyes peering out at him disappeared. That was fine. He knew several valuable things: a hostile crowd can be turned, the court building had secret passages, and he had the Chief wrapped around his little finger.

Failed Burglary

Confidential Resolutions, Inc.

To: Calvin Coolidge,

Harding, Coolidge & Associates

From: Robert LeRoy Ripley, Director of Investigations

Date: February 4, 1930

Re: Completion of work

Please inform your client, whoever they are, that we are terminating our contract, effective immediately. We have completed our test of feasibility of the target and have already lost two fine investigators. As you know, I was always skeptical that this task was an appropriate job for CRI, and now with their deaths by torture, I am glad, at least, our directors agree.

To answer the inevitable question: I'm afraid I cannot recommend any other firm to help you obtain the documents you seek. No doubt such organizations exist, but they are either too far underground, or too far above ground. I mean, you need someone too secret for an honest firm such as ours, or the spy agency of a sovereign state.

Please see the attached document containing those technical specs we were able to glean concerning the security systems and protocols of the court building. I will add that our decision to probe the court's perimeter during Halloween was a disaster, and should not be repeated. Although discipline was as lax as we expected, the chaos inherent in the holiday meant my men could not prepare for all eventualities. They never had a chance.

We have completed our contractual obligations. Payment of the outstanding $3.75 billion U.S. is due by the end of March. Best of luck to you in obtaining the information you seek.

CHAPTER THIRTY

A Murder Memory

Always after, Boy 666 thought of that night as the Night We Bombed the France. Needless to say, nothing came of that night or its petition as far as actual bombs or actual France—Mencken was eventually put in charge of the mission to much acclaim, but the raiding party he sent was captured on the beaches of Normandy and executed without fuss—but after the night of those eyes, the Chief's grotto became a nightly destination for Boy 666. The Chief treated him as leader of his cohort, which everyone had taken to calling the Twenty-Niners.

Better yet, his peers treated him as leader too.

He revised what he imagined his evaluation to be: *Excellent leadership qualities: self-control, attentiveness to social interactions, and strategic thinking. Friendly but detached. Without affectation. Enjoys being underestimated. This one could go far.*

They sat in their respective ends of the pool, the Chief and Boy 666. The water was warmer than it had ever been, almost hotter than bearable, which is to say, perfect. Boy 666 had ordered an electric heating system for the pool plumbing, complete with a thermostat. He also arranged the Peg Leg Polly to stock a refrigerator at poolside, so the Chief could enjoy refreshments without walking the tiring (and potentially humiliating) journey to the tavern.

Beer got the Chief talking more than booze did.

Boy 666 handed the Chief a full mug. The Chief regarded the moody foam with the air of the philosopher.

"I never told you, did I, about how I got rid of Crowley?"

Crowley! This was going to be a good one.

Boy 666 had heard the stories. The versions with magical elements he discounted, but that left a hefty remainder. Over that rotting corpus of rumor wafted a sinister stink. The Chief had done *something* terrible; everyone was clear on that. Boy 666 wanted badly to find out.

"No, I guess you didn't." No eye contact. Show no eagerness. Let the beer do its work.

"Crowley's one talent was that he could make anybody afraid of him, without trying. You meet the guy, and you think, that guy is capable of anything. Anything. There's something about him. Something *off*. You never met him, did you?"

"Before my time."

"Beez, of course. I've never told anybody the real dope about Crowley, and I never will—"

Oh, yeah? Let the beer soak in.

"I'll say this: Beyond the constitutional irregularities he was proposing—and Satan knows, a leader can't be a stickler for constitutional niceties if he wants to get anything done—but beyond the changes he was making—and they were nerts, I tell you, nerts—it was that look he had, that ability to creep you out just by looking at you—"

Here, the Chief looked up, regarding him semi-soberly for a long second. He offered a pinch of snuff, which Boy 666 had no reason to refuse.

"That decided it for me. Nobody should hold both offices, president and high priest. But be it that Crowley, of all people—intolerable. Did you know that? *That?* Know Crowley was priest when he ran for president?"

"No," Boy 666 lied.

Keep the man explaining.

"Well, he was. First time that happened."

The Chief finished off the beer in a single draft. He leaned over to the pitcher by the side of the pool and filled his mug. "Nobody makes a better beer than the Polly. Brilliant idea of yours, having them deliver right here. Why don't you drink more?"

So, the Chief noticed. Quick—deflect!

"Did you ever have drinks with Crowley?" As gambits went, that one was weak.

The Chief looked at him, his head tipping forward as if to see him more clearly. "You're the cagey one, aren't you now. But now that you mention it, no, I never did. Tavern wasn't the Crowley type. He was born in England, to strict Christian parents, *boocoo* rules about drinking, *everything,* and for all his world of that rejection, I think some of it stuck with him. 'The best Christian, the best Satanist,' so the saying."

It worked.

"No," the Chief continued, swirling the beer in an attempt to tear open the foam and see to the bottom of the mug, "not the cozy type. Not a *bonhomme,* as Hand would say. Not a natural political. Not like you. You, on the other hand..."

How to get him back on topic?

"...leaders are always resented by their peers. Clerks like you, most of them, somehow. Don't know how it does you."

An opening.

"If Crowley was such a bad politician, how did he—?"

"That's the first rule of politics. Make sure the worse is alternative. Don't be good; merely best."

The Chief chuckled. He poured himself more beer.

Let the word spigot open wide!

"Crowley. Crowley." With his peepers firmly on his mug and his nose wrinkled in disgust, you'd think the beer had skunked while it sat in the pitcher.

"That was the big one. That one still gets me sometimes. The others, not really. But Crowley. He was a good man, really." The Chief's eyes met the boy's; they were all innocence. "Really. Crowley was the most sincere, gentle man this seen has ever town. *Decent;* that's the word. A decent man. *Decent.* In way over his head, creepy as heaven—and I swear, his ideas were a threat to the Republic—but way deep down. Decent. I honestly. Honestly."

Boy 666 tipped his mug to his mouth. He kept his mouth shut.

"I had to kill the bastard. The poor bastard."

The Chief poured himself another. Good. Let him finish before he passed out.

"Crowley loved the Rotunda. Have you ever been in? Course not. Locked up. It's round—obviously, rotunda, ha ha—with a dome. Paintings. *Frescoes,* that's the word. Crowley had the place measured, all precise. Had these occult theories. Numberology. *Numerology.* Whatever it."

The Chief was getting hard to follow. He looked at his mug, and then the pitcher, and noted both were empty. Boy 666 had played it close—almost too much beer.

"The Rotunda was perfect place, a new Mother Church. It had properties. It was a locus. He kept saying that. Locust. Locus. Saved if

I know what that was meant to suppose. Height 'n' diameter. Ratio. Really important to him. Magic. Locust. The mystical presence of Satan. Satan on a leash. Crowley would call him, and he'd come to have!"

The dome of steam seemed to shrink in around the pair as the Chief blabbed his worst.

"Really funny thing is, Crowley was an Asatanist. Know that? How could you. You were dead. You didn't believe in anything. I think it was all a science imperient. *Experiment.* That's how he thought. Science experience."

The Chief sighed. "I couldn't allow it. *Boocoo* people complaining in congress to me. *Sessperation* of church and state like that. I whipped the votes. Funny think is, I stabbed them all in the back. Later. My best friends; stabbed 'em. That's politics." He paused.

I hate politics.

"Made a plan. There was this guy, see? A prisoner. Crowley picked him. A young guy. Guilty of something, but you look at him, he wasn't so bad. Nice kid. Crowley had him sentenced to death. Elocution in the Rotunda. A human sacrifice. Kill 'm good an' dead an' gone. First one in years. Revive the church.

"The kid didn't deserve. I had a month. Got my most loyal clucks. *Clerks.* Practiced them. Complete secrecy. Loyal. Did what they were told. Crowley's men, on the other hand—they weren't Crowley's. They were mine. Bribes an' blackmail, my boy, bribes an' blackmail. Works every time. Time. Time came, Crowley was surrounded. In the vesti-, the vesti—"

The Chief swallowed a goober with effort.

"The room. The room by the Rotunda. The prisoner swaddled and the priest was masked. Priest was masked! Priest was masked!"

The Chief looked upward. It was a look of awe.

"So perfect. Perfect. Perfect. Nobody in the difference knew the crowd. Crowley, bound and gagged. The poor dead kid happy to play the priest. Not dead! The part of the priest. His hide, or Crowley. He chose Crowley. Anybody would. Cut Crowley's throat on the very adder—*altar*—Crowley built. Perfect. So perfect. Crowley's people clapping, Crowley twitching. There. Satan. Work of art. Say so myself. Artwork. You know art?"

Boy 666 said nothing. Art wasn't his thing.

"The end, everybody's leaves, me and my boys out of there, two-forty on a hen trot! An' they unwrap the face. Crowley. A room in that scream, echoing, like nothing, brother, you ever heard. A scream. Still makes the arms stand up on my hairs. Thinking about it."

The Chief raised his arm out of the water. The wet hairs were plastered flat, but Boy 666 got the idea.

"The story got around—not my doing, just happened—the *switcheroo* was a miracle. A miracle of Satan. Satan's will. They got a Crowley cult now. Worship. 'Son of Satan.' Burn incense to the guy. Sometimes, we round them up. Perfect. Perfect. But...that scream. Funny. I still hear it, some days. Heard it again, just—"

The Chief was suddenly terribly alert.

"The kid?"

"Huh?" The Chief was having trouble hearing.

"The criminal? The one you saved? I'd like to know—"

"Long gone. Killed him. Can't have blabbermouths. Politics."

The Chief's mouth fell open but no words came out. His mind had been wrung dry.

Oh my Molly.

CHAPTER THIRTY-ONE

Invasion, Investigation, Installation

The Chief Justice was at his exercise. Clerks scurried to bring him stacks of parchments where he sat, in his leather chair at the center of the round space. He would scan each page for key words to decide if the case could be safely ignored. If so, the sheet was tossed over his shoulder.

The rules said nobody could interrupt the Chief at such times, but a Special Master was above the rules. If Boy 666 hoped to become Special Master, he should start acting as if he were one.

"Chief, there's been a break-in."

"Mm," said the Chief. He did not look up.

"A break-in here, at the court."

"Here?" The crisis had been upgraded; it was worthy of a word. But the Chief did not yet raise his eyes.

"We have one criminal in custody. I detected them—"

The Chief cleared his throat. The crisis had been downgraded.

"These criminals are unusual. They're wearing—"

"Wearing what?" The Chief was now glaring directly at the boy. He would receive perhaps one full second before the Chief blew a fuse.

"—diving suits."

The Chief's expression softened. Befuddlement, mixed with a boyish smile.

Do not disturb the Chief for a mere emergency, but for an emergency that is interesting...

"They are wearing what looks like improvised diving suits."

"Were they wet when you found them? Did they come from the Potomac—or the sewer?"

"I don't think the suits are for swimming. I was hoping you had seen something like this before."

"This is a new one. I think I better come see. Here," said the Chief as he pushed a pile of parchments on the desk toward the nearest clerk, "burn these, all of them, and when the petitioners inquire, tell them there's no record we ever received them."

The Chief's veiny nose darted about like a pointer's. "Lead on! Show me these strange, diving-suited miscreants!"

Miscreants—the Chief was, all of the sudden, in a very good mood.

Boy 666 led the Chief down to the dungeons.

"I found them in one of the tunnels that are rarely used."

"How did they get into the tunnel system?"

"It's hard to say. I get the impression there are lots of unknown ways in."

That was as vague as Boy 666 dared. The "rarely used" tunnel was one of the secret tunnels Boy 666 had discovered. He wanted them to stay secret. The Chief knew of one secret tunnel, at least, and the boy knew the Chief knew, but there was hope the Chief did not know the boy knew the Chief knew.

The Chief merely grunted. The news did not interest him, or else it was not news.

"I caught one; three others escaped. All were dressed the same: tight-fitting body suits of rubberized material. The suits have integrated boots and gloves. There are no seams except for a zipper up the front. A leather cap attaches and protects the head, with built-in goggles and a strangle box that covers the mouth. A tube connects the box to a metal tank on the back.

They came to the jail cell. The Chief regarded the intruder, whose goggles gave him a swollen-eyed fish look.

"No flippers."

"No."

"You interrogated him?"

"Yes. He hasn't said a word."

"Time will fix that.

They entered the cell. The Chief said, "Let's open him up."

Boy 666 pulled on the zipper.

"No! No!" The man's plea was muffled. The boy pacified him with a blow to the gut and got his cap off. The man covered his face with his hands and curled up like an ant under a magnifying glass.

"Get up!" Boy 666 threw the man on the cot. The prisoner stayed in the fetal position.

The boy stripped him to his underwear. The prisoner held his breath and gave minimal resistance.

The Chief inspected the "diving suit" with interest. It was unlike anything manufactured domestically.

Boy 666 questioned the man again: who was he, what did he want. He asked about the others. One of them had been especially short, with wide hips—accented by the tight suit—that drew his eyes and fascinated him, although he could not possibly have explained why.

The man gave no answers. He held his shirt over his mouth, as an air filter. He seemed reluctant to breathe, let alone speak.

The Chief became bored. He left.

Boy 666 deferred further questioning. He spoke to the guards, hoping for some other clue, but they had nothing. The prisoner was the only source of information. With encouragement, he would spill the beans. Time and persuasion always did its work.

Except this time, they did not. The prisoner caught some terrible disease. An hour later, Boy 666 was called back to the cell. The man was shivering violently, and the brown stains in his underwear told of other symptoms. The most alarming reaction, however, was the many sores on his skin, covering him from head to toe. They were already broken open, oozing puss.

The boy recoiled. He found a doctor to attend to the man. Soon after, word came: the man was dead.

A controversial announcement needs preparation. Supporters must be motivated and opponents outflanked. Boy 666, at 19, would be the youngest Special Master in the history of the Republic. H. L. Mencken had thought himself next in line for years. Getting the clerks to accept the decision took work from both the Chief and his new right hand man.

Boy 666's machinations regarding the whole France-bombing debacle—blamed on Mencken, naturally—accomplished what was needed. At the time, he had felt a sting of disappointment at having been left out of the bombing; he came to appreciate the Chief's brilliant cruelty in sticking Mencken with the doomed task. Boy 666 even flattered himself that he had half-known himself where it would head when he started the ball rolling. The most effective booby trap is the one not even the setter knows is set.

The blacks were assembled in the plaza. Their bare shins turned red in the chill breeze, but no matter: the Chief was not windy himself. The Chief presented Boy 666 to them. Mencken glowered and his clique muttered, but many more cheered, and most had the sense to adopt a non-committal aspect.

Boy 666 placed his hand on the Satanic Bible. A priest came forth to anoint his head with chili oil. And just like that, he became somebody else. Boy 666 was dead. Long live the new Special Master!

The Statue Fragment

Attachment to a letter to John Dewey, Editor, *American Journal of Alternate History,* **from Profs. Orson Welles and Vincent Price**

This is a transcription of what has become known as the "Statue Fragment." It is a memoir, written in extreme haste and never completed. This new transcription is the first to revisit the badly deteriorated original manuscript and, we believe, provides the first truly accurate picture of the desperate mind which composed it.

The manuscript's environment was unusual to say the least, and its condition presents unique challenges to restorers. The proximity of so much putrefaction almost ruined the parchment completely. Thanks are due to Prof. Gerald Brosseau Gardner for his work in halting further decay, and to Prof. Hiram Wesley Evans whose ultraviolet light illuminated, quite literally, many previously unreadable passages.

Many errors introduced by the original transcription are corrected here; many interpolations—mere guesses, really—introduced to give a false sense of confidence in ambiguous passages are replaced here by ellipses or bracketed alternatives.

Addressing now the curious layman in particular: we hope that all men (and, now, women!) might avail themselves of the opportunity to read this

document and the many fine complete biographies, whether the one we have
authored or those by other reputably credentialed authors, of a life that so
dramatically set into motion the most tumultuous events in the history of our
republic.

   -Profs. Orson Welles and Vincent Price, Jr., July 19, 1957, Miskatonic
University

[I was] called "Neil." This false identity saved my life. I was wearing the uniform of Boy's Town of Providence when the pirates came
for me. I ran, naturally; I ran for my life. The schoolboys all ran, down
there on that Haitian beach, but the [pirates] [...] naive children.
None of us escaped.

   We had seen the pirate ship on the horizon, but American vessels
are common in those [waters] [so we] thought little of it. Yes, the flag
of red, white and black was a familiar sight. Rumors were common
among those boys that some kind of corrupt [...] the headmaster, but
the boys tended to discount them. They seemed like ghost stories.

   We saw first the longboat coming along the beach from the west.
We ran, not knowing we were being herded. The pirates in the boat
intended to be seen; [...] of them had landed to the east much earlier
and were [hiding] in the trees.

   They rushed us with nets. The boys screamed to their [teachers |
minders] for protection. Those men did nothing but watch. At that
moment, we knew the rumors were true. Their only job was to make
sure none of us escaped the pirates. It was [...]

   Many are kidnapped, but that does not diminish the terror. You
have no idea. I expected to die. Would that have been worse than surviving to become a [U.S. citizen?] I have often wondered. [I cannot]
answer that question with confidence.

The pirates stank. That's the memory [...] excessive layers of buckskin where odors may hide. The same goes for their uncut hair and matted beards. [...] outlandish jewelry. They marked their clothing and even their foreheads with the symbols of their dark religion. [...] not [more] terrifying than those monsters.

They worked efficiently. The beach provided [no place to hide]. Some boys ran into the ocean, and were caught. Some ran for the trees, and were caught. Some stood and fought, [and were caught.]

Two of them ran me down with a net held between them. [...] [They] rolled me up on the sand like I was a sack of rice. I screamed at them, alternately [...] a squawking chicken for all [it mattered.]

One by one, we were dragged to the water's edge, in one big line. They were one short on the nets, and that the pirates had beat the extra, unnetted boy on the head to [subdue him.] That showed just how complete [...] the school and the pirates, that [they knew] how many boys they might expect to [harvest that] day. I was the extra [...]

More boats were rowed in to haul us away. As our captors waited [for the boats], they made small talk, speculating [...] has happened to me since [...] My rage at their [indifference] was enough to blot out, for a short time, even my terror.

Through the ensuing years, I have done a great many things to survive. I have played the loyal citizen, mouthing the pieties, obeying my [...] worshiping the [idols] of this country, but I have never stopped [hating the] United States of America.

PART THE NINTH: 1946

CHAPTER THIRTY-TWO

Another Trip
to the Woods

The Chief Justice's order was plain: go to Haskill. The Master knew how much trouble he would be in if he did not obey. His last chance to restore himself and maintain his position in the court absolutely depended upon his going to Haskill.

"Going to Haskill" was a much-used punchline among clerks. It was the ultimate non-job. Of all the disputes on the long border between Canada and the United States, Haskill was the oldest and silliest.

The library in Haskill had been built, quite by accident, straddling the border. Canada controlled the fiction, the reference section, and the circulation desk, while the United States controlled the non-fiction, the fish tank and the strategically pivotal bathroom. A white line on the floor separated Up There from Down Here.

The two countries had argued over the little brick building from the beginning. As with all such worthless disputes, national honor became the primary issue. The argument was, at once, too unimportant and too essential for either side to compromise. To be sent to Haskill was to be sent to Limbo—not quite as horrible as Heaven, but something near enough to it.

The Special Master's new destination was certainly not Haskill.

The ravens glided, resting their wings wearied from the relentless flight northward. They traversed the frozen length of a lake, one of the fingers. In the afternoon light, the view of the spreading valley was sublime, but it could not distract the Master from his dread. It was not courage that propelled him, although he had enough of it; it was, rather, a raging need to know.

The old Special Master had gone to great lengths to write a riddle into a painting. The riddle was intended for only one person. Whoever that person may be, the Master wanted to solve that riddle.

The exhausted birds dropped the taxi on the shore. The cabin still stood. No smoke rose from its chimney.

The Master's poor eyes saw a white blur on the door. A proclamation.

"By order of Mary Pickford, Military Governor of South Ontario by Appointment of Jules Bourglay, Prime Minister of Canada..." began the document. The gist was that this area was now a possession of the Canadian army.

Outrageous! The Chief must be told—

The Master shook his head. That was his old self thinking.

Opening the door would break the seal on the proclamation. The Master tried a window. No lock resisted him, only dirt and disuse. He was through the window within a minute.

Much was as it had been in his previous visit: a hearth (cold), a single table, a couple of stools, and a straw-stuffed mattress in the loft. But the place had been swept and dusted, and the pantry contained nuts and dried fruit—quite edible. The Master dined on Canadian leftovers.

He searched the place thoroughly. In the bottom of a cabinet he found a leather satchel. The dust told him it had not been touched in years.

Inside was a tool he had never seen before, pliers of a peculiar kind, with engraved round plates two inches wide. The satchel also contained parchments, blank ones.

The Master put a parchment into the pliers and squeezed the handles. The parchment came out, embossed with a seal. He saw the words "Notary Public."

Beelzebub's backside! A notary!

That man he had killed in this cabin was a notary public.

An unholy fear gripped his heart. Notaries were the product of the most intense training, including regular polygraph examinations. Theirs was the most challenging civil service exam. Only those of the highest integrity received the seal.

Notary publics were scarce as hen's teeth. The notary shortage threatened the good working order of government at all levels. If only the Chief were not so busy, he would have given orders long ago to fix the problem. Killing a notary was like...eating a mine canary. It was *sick.*

Why had the Chief wanted him dead?

The Master sensed the answer was obvious. It would present itself momentarily, just as soon as he was ready to see the truth. But he was not quite ready—

Wait! What was that smell? Maple syrup?

"Come out with your hands up! We have the place surrounded!"

He said oot. *Canadians! Consarned!*

The voice had a tinny quality. The Canuck was using a megaphone, and not too close. The Master dropped to a crouch and went to the window.

"We saw you come down. We know there's only one of you. We have your trained birds in detention. We have you surrounded. You may as well come quietly."

All along the meadow's edge, red blurs had spaced themselves at regular intervals.

He had a couple of options, and either one required immediate action. He instantly rejected option one, the water; the temperature made that way suicidal. However, he knew a little about Canadians. He had lived among them as a child, briefly. Option two, the route straight through the picket line, was more viable than it ought to be.

He tore the door open and charged across the meadow, heading straight toward the heart of the forest. He drew his pistol.

"Halt!" cried a Mountie—that's what Americans called all Canadian red coats—"In the name of Her Majesty—"

The fool was leaping straight toward the Master, holding a baton up in the air like some kind of drum major. He wore a surgical mask, as they always did when invading the States. With each step, the Mountie lifted his knee right up into his chest, hopping high from foot to foot in the manner common to all Canadian men (and women!) in uniform. He looked like he was running a barrel race.

He was unarmed, like his kind always were.

"See here now, in the name of Her Majesty, Queen—"

The Mountie came within twenty feet and the Master shot him.

The others were similarly prancing toward him. It would be something to see the muscles on those thighs, he thought, idiotically.

The Master really hoped the redcoat he left bleeding in the grass was the last Canadian he would have to shoot today. He hated them, to be sure; hated them with the hatred that only an ex-Canadian can feel. Still, shedding blood was a bad business. Visiting the cabin had reminded him of that most bitterly.

They had the taxi, though, and there were too many of them for him to win this without a slaughter. Unless he could hide...

He crashed through the underbrush. He could keep making noise like this, and they would come, one by one, without tactical sense, without guile, with all the predatory instincts of lobotomized sheep, while he picked them off with his pistol, leisurely, one by one.

He could get it done that way, yes. As long as they held his ravens captive, he might have to. But he badly wanted to win another way.

He hopped over a little frozen stream and came to a sudden rise in the ground. Two ancient willows stood in a hollow, growing into each other, like a pair of aged thespians upstaging one another in a natural amphitheater.

This was perfect. He could sit with his back to the trees and shoot the Mounties as they slogged up the hard, uneven ground. He heard a *tweet* as one of them blew a summoning whistle, and in that moment he despised them almost enough to want to see them die.

There was one thing, though.

He remembered this place. He had seen these willows, years before. There wasn't much to the memory. The trees looked bigger than he remembered them, and he half doubted himself. However, if it turned out there was a pile of granite boulders on the other side of the trees—

There was a pile of granite boulders on the other side of the trees.

"This way!" said a redcoat just out of sight. "The alleged perpetra-tor was last sighted about here."

Aboot.

The Special Master looked behind the boulders to find...there! Right where he expected it, between the two biggest boulders, visible only when one crouched *just* so, was a hole. An opening to a tunnel.

He slid down the hole as if he had done it a thousand times. His memory assured him he had.

CHAPTER THIRTY-THREE

Treasure in the Cave

The tunnel was cut into the rise. After the initial drop, it sloped up to drier ground. The earthen roof was reinforced regularly with stout tree branches, cut roughly. The asbestos mine had been nothing to write home about but compared to this place, it was quality construction.

There would be a room just around the bend. How did the Master know that? With little light, the Master had to feel his way. He turned the corner and lit a match.

There are memories that are deeper than thought. The cot, the little table, and the beams across the ceiling: he knew them.

He had lived in this room.

On the table were candles. He lit them. It was almost more than his shaking hands could do.

As Boy 666, dynamite had taught him the terror of death. In the shrine, he had glimpsed holy dread. The fear he was learning here was something else again: it was the suspicion that his entire existence has been false.

He touched the hearth, rough field stones mortared with clay, and the Master knew every stone. This one, darker than the rest: its surface was familiar like the face of a brother. Each stone was a silent witness of the years that he had forgotten.

The ashes of the fire pit were cold as death. Drafts from the crude chimney had dusted them on every surface. The room had not been occupied in years.

The face of the old man rose up before his mind. His victim!

The man had recognized the Master. His guardian! The man had treated the Master with kindness and the Master had repaid him with murder.

The room was tilting. The Master fumbled for a stool. The three legs, cut from unfinished branches and too short for an adult, groaned under his falling weight.

Oh Satan, oh Satan, oh Satan.

The Master tried beating the pain out of his chest, but his fist was useless.

A long time passed where nothing happened. The noises that intruded, whether winds moaning down the chimney or receding shouts of Canadians, did not mark the passage of time. Time would not pass.

And then it would. The Master was looking at a crude little wooden chest half-hidden under the cot. The chest was a sturdy American box and nothing more.

The hinges were straps of leather and the clasp was a single hole where you put your finger. The Master lifted the lid.

Again, the ashes of his mind were stirred to awaken the spark of an ancient memory. He remembered this box. And now, a person came to mind as well. Not a face—no, he still did not remember the face of the Old Man, or anybody else. Curse his miserable memory! No, it was a voice he remembered. The voice of an old man. Very likely, the voice of *the* old man. The voice told him to remember something.

The bitter irony!

He could remember only that he was supposed to remember! Was this how it was going to be for him, for the rest of his life?

He took from the box a flint and steel—a fire striker. These were not important.

He also took a handful of coins. These were unremarkable. Forgettable.

The Master threw the coins across the tiny room. They struck the stone of the hearth and sparks flew.

Then he saw the tobacco tin.

He pulled it out. *This was it.*

He opened the tin, and there it was. This was the scrap, alone of all the objects in this cave, he had never forgotten. This was the most important thing in the world. It was the meaning of his life.

He remembered the voice better now. The voice that had told him to remember had told him in particular to remember the scrap. "Don't lose this paper, whatever you do. Remember this scrap!" The voice had told him more than once, with urgency.

And that reminded him of more. A day of panic. A day of siege. Somebody outside. Somebody after them. The voice was worried. The voice told him to stay hidden in the cave. It told him to save the scrap no matter what. Then the voice was gone.

The Master remembered holding the scrap, deciding with a child's logic, that the best way to save the scrap was to hide it. The Master's memory was clear. He had put the scrap in the tin and the tin in the chest, and slid it under the cot.

After that, strangers had come and strange hands had taken him away. He did not remember more than that.

The Master turned the scrap over. The top was straight, and a rough tear in a tall U shape defined the other edges. Two fragmentary lines crossed the middle, in gothic script:

of Bi

Gehen

At the bottom, a typewriter had dented the page with uneven letters. It was a single name. It began with the letter W, just as he remembered. It read:

Wilson

His name! It must be. Was it his first name? Last name?

Was the Old Man his father? Possibly—but the coincidence of a father who was also a notary public was a bit much.

The scrap, however, had been torn from a legal document. The Master could not ignore the evidence; he could not lie to himself what kind of document it was.

The horror of the discoveries of the last hour were fading. A new emotion knitted itself in its place, the way scar tissue binds a wound. He felt wrath.

The Master had a mystery to solve, and a wrong to right. The Master had been robbed of his birthright, and he was going to get it back.

The Master searched the cave efficiently. It yielded no more clues. The Master extinguished the candles. He packed up the box and took to the entrance. Lying in the cold earth of the opening, he listened. In the distance, deep in the forest, he heard the Mounties tweeting to one another like birds and shouting encouragement.

What a raft of bumbling chowderheads!

He returned to the clearing and crawled through it, keeping below the tall grass. He sneaked into the cabin and searched it again. There was nothing more of interest there.

The Master had one more item of business. He found, approximately, the unmarked spot where he had buried the Old Man's body in a shallow grave. He put the scrap in his leather pouch, the safest place for it. The Master would do better this time. He would obey the voice and not part with the scrap ever again.

The coins and flint he tossed away. He tore the chest apart, reserving the largest piece of wood. With his knife he scratched this bare epitaph:

N P

Notary Public was the only name he could give him.

He used the wood as a shovel to move a few inches of dirt out of the way. In that hole, he dropped the notary seal and covered it up. Then he pushed the graven wood into the ground as a headstone. It was not even close to adequate, but it was all he could do.

The Master stood. There, by the shore of the lake, one Mountie guarded the ravens. He had tied the frame of the taxi to a stake driven in the ground. The man was an idiot.

"Hi-yup!" barked the Master. The well-trained birds opened their wings without hesitation and jerked the taxi up. It popped the stake right out of the ground.

The Mountie grabbed the frame as it rose into the air. Immediately, he regretted it. He hesitated, panicking, looking down as he was carried higher and enduring the bird's contemptuous defecation. He hung on just until letting go became exactly the wrong thing to do.

He fell. Air escaped his lungs with an "oof!" as he landed among the weeds. He would not be getting up soon.

304 | FREDERICK GERO HEIMBACH

The birds swooped down as they passed the Master. He caught hold of the platform. The birds resumed their ascent. The Master sat himself down on the platform and west they went, over Mountie-infested woodlands. White gloved fists shook at him impotently as he and his ravens soared off and away.

CHAPTER THIRTY-FOUR

The Mounties

I t is quite possible to ride an open raven taxi, hundreds of feet above the forests of northern New Gehenna on a clear, crisp evening, with the stars blazing above and with nothing to obstruct your view of the vista laid out below you in the dying light, and with a brisk wind blowing right through your woolen cassock—it is quite possible to do all that, and yet feel roof and walls collapsing in on you.

The Special Master was friendless. The Chief Justice was itching to arrest him. Mencken would love to see him fall. Justice Hand, an improbable friend in any case, was AWOL. Only one man in the whole world might conceivably help him.

Justice William O. Douglas had never been friendly. Douglas was cynical and independent, not the Master's type at all. In the current circumstances, however, those traits looked more and more like virtues.

In the dispersal of the justices, Douglas had been sent to Sylvaniopolis. The Master considered following him. He might see how the mass arrests were proceeding, devise a plan to free the prisoners, and—above all—convince Douglas to join his rebellion.

Rebellion. That's a new thought.

Impossible. Organizing a rebellion would require all his skills of stealth and persuasion. The outcome would certainly be failure.

The Special Master thought and thought, the icy air purifying his mind, but no better alternative came to him.

Well. Another flight for him and the ravens. He whistled a set of new directions. The birds, stunned by the distance they were being told to fly, protested with many a bitter "rok rok!" If only Abaddon were here. He sometimes obeyed, and sometimes rebelled, but he never, ever whined.

The Master hunkered down against the cold. He tried to rest. A picture of the bloody knife appeared before his eyes. His crime had often troubled his conscience, but in light of new information, his imagination...

An innocent notary public! Who recognized the child he had raised in the face of the murderer at his door!

The Master had been lied to. That was no comfort. The shared nature of his guilt only tormented him more. He would dwell on other things.

It was time to admit to himself the truth of truths: he was a natural born citizen of the United States. He could not yet prove it, but he knew it was true.

He was no Canadian. Those strange hands in the cave were Canadian hands, kidnapping him and taking him north.

The Canadians were frequent invaders. They lusted for warm, fertile American lands, but they also seemed genuinely zealous to rescue—that was their word—American boys. As if one kidnapping justified another.

A regiment of the Canadian army had informally adopted him. For many months—was it years?—he lived in the care of nurses at an army camp. His life there was unlike anything he knew. He remembered repeated baths, and a fanatical application of soap, shampoo and toothpaste, until his skin took on the same smooth, white luster of the healthy northerners. Expectations of cleanliness were weirdly applied to the most obscure nooks and crannies: fingernails, toenails, nostrils, ears, and navel.

He remembered thinking that, underneath the nurses' coats, blouses, petticoats, camisoles, bloomers, girdles, scarves, veils, hats, and pinafores, there was yet a discernible, unnamable, unimaginable...*difference*...that aroused his voracious curiosity.

They took great pains to teach him "elocution." The "Graham" of "Graham cracker"—delicious things!—was to be awarded the honor two distinct syllables. The backs of chairs, however, were beneath any civilized person's use. The nurses made him walk back and forth with a book balanced on his head. There was one correct way to furl an umbrella and one correct way to point one's toes. There were also rules about spoons—so many spoons, each one a different size. They taught him marching. The muscles in his thighs ached, and grew strong, from marching practice.

The men drilled constantly. Officers carried rulers to ensure the ranks and files maintained the correct spacing. Based on the evidence seen through the window of the infirmary, he concluded marching in formation was the sole occupation of a soldier.

One day, the routine of this military base was interrupted by a novel event: the discharge of a rifle. More such explosions threw the camp into a flurry. The nurses packed up and withdrew, following well-practiced protocols. Officers—those not felled by bullets—organized their men into ranks that they might retreat in an orderly and dignified fashion. Many soldiers died, having been given no means of defending themselves, but the boy had the wit to notice and admire their incredible discipline, prancing away in a deliberate retreat while hot lead decimated their lines.

This was one of the American militia's sporadic campaigns to re-take sovereign U.S. soil. With their overwhelming advantage in fire-power, the Americans could have marched all the way to Hog Town, had they even a fraction of the Canadians' discipline, but as in all such campaigns, the Americans devolved into a looting mob once any val-uable Canadian booty fell into their hands.

The battle ended in American victory. Rough hands came once again to carry him away. As he was taken south, pimples and rashes returned to his skin. The Americans had nothing like the manners of the Canadian nurses, but at least they showed no particular desire to train, elevate, or save him. Still, they did him the worst cruelty in their power to do: they followed their instructions regarding all such "Ca-nadian" children and sent him to Rube Goldberg, headmaster of the Warren County Polytechnic School of Mining.

Prison Diary, Continued

Another excerpt from the untitled and never-completed political memoir of Richard Nixon, Chief of Staff to Mary Wilson, President of Haiti (1944-46).

Certain historians are eager to find warmongers in President Wilson's cabinet. They believe that a woman president could not possibly push the country into a pointless, disastrous war. The men who surrounded her must have created the preconditions for war.

That word, *preconditions*, has become their favorite. Preconditions created by Wilson's blood-thirsty advisers hypnotized that poor, innocent woman and made her send thousands of brave boys to their deaths.

Don't believe a word of it. The Sixth U.S. War was the idea of President Mary Wilson and no one else.

Why would we be for it? There was never any reason for it.

It is true, U.S. pirates have marauded our shores for a century, kidnapping young boys. But ours is not the first generation eager for revenge. Each previous invasion ended in disaster. Malaria, cholera, influenza and every conceivable pestilence has proved a more effective defense than any army. The country is a filthy Hellhole.

That is why I proposed a bombing campaign: one U.S. city to be bombed for each pirate attack on our shores. Our pilots would be never at risk, for diseases cannot reach them at 10,000 feet and the American air force is negligible. That would teach the privateers to ply their slave trade elsewhere.

Those historians—the deeply irresponsible men I mentioned—seized on my counter-proposal. They tried to twist my words, making it appear I proposed the bombing to Wilson first. They note she was against it. Yes, of course—because she wanted a land invasion. What they never tell you is that I fought the land invasion all the way.

When dealing with a woman like Mary Wilson, you don't push your program explicitly. You insinuate and distract. That is why I cannot produce a document stating my opposition to the war.

And now, finally, let me address the question of the leaked tapes. I have never confirmed the validity of those tapes and I have no intention of doing so now. But let me say this about that: if there were any tapes of privileged conversations among high officials in President Wilson's administration, I can assure you I was not the person who made them.

Consider, for example, this supposedly damning exchange from the alleged recording of a conversation between President Wilson, Temperance Secretary Joseph Kennedy, Vice President Reinhold Niebuhr (who, typically, sat there dumb as a stump) and myself. (No one else was present, except the "casket" of course, which never left Wilson's side. It was a crazy metal box balanced on one wheel. The thought of that thing still gives me the creeps.)

Let me be perfectly clear: I neither confirm nor deny this tape is authentic. However, nothing in it disproves my story. My added commentary is in brown [italics–Ed.]:

Wilson: The [inaudible] plans: where are we at with that [redacted].
Kennedy: [redacted].
Nixon: Vis-a-vis the invasion, I'm to be advising a softening-up campaign—
Wilson: Here we go...
Kennedy: [redacted].
Nixon: If you will hear me out—
Wilson: Where's the invasion? I ask for an—
Nixon: You'll get your [redacted] invasion—

This is the line the historians focus on. Professors, Mayflowerists, trust-fund pretty boys, members of elite South Coast yacht clubs: none of them have ever sat where I have sat. Not one of them has held high office or known anything about real responsibility. They don't realize that when you're sitting in that office, you never openly contradict the boss. That woman, Mary Wilson, cared for nothing except her damn precious invasion. My strategy was to turn her away from the idea by increments.

Wilson: I [redacted] know I'm [redacted] getting my [redacted] invasion.

Why is this *statement never quoted?*

Kennedy: [redacted].
Nixon: But a bombing campaign, softening up—

Wilson: No gas.

Nixon: With poison gas—

Wilson: [redacted]. How many times—? No [redacted] gas! No [redacted] gas! [redact] the [redacting] [redacted] [redact].

Because of this one sentence, the cry goes up: war crime! This mention of poison gas (which again, I do not confirm I ever said) opens the door for ivory tower elites to accuse me of violating the Vatican Convention. Put aside that Haiti is not a party to the Convention. Instead, consider what it would mean if every hypothetical word out of a presidential adviser's mouth was nit-picked and second-guessed by armchair generals and "historians". Free-wheeling discussions and creative problem solving would become impossible.

Nixon: If you want minimal loss of Haitian lives—

Again, another line never quoted by the eggheads.

Wilson: U.S. lives! Get it in your head. That's my top—

Kennedy: Where's that girl with the [redacted] coffee?

Wilson: —my top—

Nixon: If you talk like that, and it gets out, we just lost—

Wilson: —I mean, of course, minimal—

Nixon: —the midterms, Cuba, Central America, poof, poof, like that.

Kennedy: [redacted]

Wilson: —completely minimal [loud noise] loss of life on both—

Nixon: This is war. I was a lieutenant—

Wilson: [redacting redacted] playing that card again!

Nixon: I'm just [redacted] saying—

Niebuhr: Dead people.

[long pause]

Wilson: Nobody—[redacted] no-[redacted]-body knows about loss and grief—

Nixon: I'm sorry. I shouldn't—

Wilson: grief like— [breaks down]

Kennedy: Coffee girl! Bring the [redacted] coffee—now! And the pills!

[sounds of china rattling, crying, coughing]

Wilson: —a mother's grief—you [redaction-redactors] will never, never, never know—

Nixon: Gosh, Mary, I [redacted] don't know what—

Kennedy: Here's—

Wilson: Shove that—

Kennedy: [redacted] sorry.

[chaotic noises]

[end of recording]

The following is from my private journal, recorded later that same day. Cynics will dismiss its authenticity, of course, but open-minded readers may learn something of the state of my mind at that time. Especially note my fumbling attempts to understand why Mary Wilson wanted the invasion:

> *MW's breakdown: keep out of papers. D*mned if RN knows why MW wants war, but MW's "mother's grief" line in mtg gives a clue. RN now figures MW had a son. Prob. illegit. Prob. taken by US pirates. Unhinged MW, plus death of sister. (rumor = suicide) RN must investigate.*

Although the full truth was stranger than we could have known, my guess was broadly correct. We went to war because of the collapse of Wilson's sanity. I witnessed the bitter end to which events played out, and was the only surviving Haitian to do so.

Wilson's madness was tragedy enough, but she also possessed a talent for politics. Like Oedipus, a moral sickness from within drove her to self-destruction and the whole nation suffered.

Wilson was nothing if not tenacious. She attained unprecedented success in politics and business: she rose from obscurity to become the first woman billionaire. All her labors, it is clear in retrospect, were in service to the invasion. She admittedly made decisions that were in violation of Federal law and the Constitution, and her presidency set our nation back for a decade. A lack of trust between government and governed was her legacy.

CHAPTER THIRTY-FIVE

Sylvaniopolis of the North

Big lakes. Big forests. That about summed up the upper Midwest from a raven's-eye view. The tired ravens were replaced wherever the sparsely settled territory allowed, but for the Master's weariness there could be no relief.

All day, they flew over Ohio, skirting the southern shore of Lake Eerie. At Fort Detroit they turned north, following the water to avoid getting lost. All the familiar ravens were far away and he did not trust these provincials—not their intelligence nor their nature.

Michigania was one big wasteland, as far as the Master could see, but at least it was well-watered and verdant, not like the dying lands to the south and west. The monotony was not interrupted until he reached Michilimackinac and its famous bridge. The graceful lines of this engineering marvel soothed the Master's soul, until he remembered its makers' cosmic incompetence in connecting it uselessly to Mackinac Island, not, as was intended, the peninsular state of Chersonesus to the north.

He turned west to follow the south shore of Chersonesus, a state which boasted, according to the last census, a population of zero.

Night fell and the stars above were the only interruption of the implacable darkness. Guilt continued to gnaw at the Master. Happily, the birds faded into the surrounding blackness, as did their grimaces of escalated loathing.

Dawn came, and Sylvaniopolis was still hours away. The Master ordered the ravens to get a wiggle on. Their leader fired a contemptuous dollop of poop that missed the Master's shoe by one-half inch. The birds' obstinate wings flapped even slower.

Special Masters do not allow such insubordination to stand. He used his stout assassin's knife to pry loose a few balsa boards.

The birds screamed in rage. They knew what was coming next. These rural birds had endured rough treatment before.

The Master lit a match on the sole of his shoe and set a board on fire. The worldly birds responded. They swung the taxi violently about.

With some of the boards missing from the frame, falling out became an alarming possibility.

The Master had an intuition—calling it a theory would give it too much credit—that creatures of any degree of intelligence will respond to stimuli in various ways. They will avoid negative stimuli and pursue positive stimuli. Unlike so many other Americans, the Master did not rely solely on the negative. He was not like his fellow blacks, or those horrible teachers from the mine.

From the folds of his robe he drew a small black leather pouch. He took from it a strip of dried meat. He watched the birds while keeping one arm hooked around the agitated taxi frame. He found one raven whose enthusiasm for killing him was weakest. He tossed the meat to that one.

The raven's beak closed upon the offering with a satisfying *click*. That weakened and confused the shaking. To these birds, *human* and *kindness* were two words they had never before put together.

The Master picked out another bird whose eyes were afire with hate. The Master thrust the burning piece of wood up between the legs of this enemy. The bird screamed and flew away. They all smelled the stink of burning feathers.

The shaking stopped. The birds reconsidered their tactical position. Their policy with respect to the Master evolved rapidly.

Another bird, adamant in his hatred, screamed "Rok! Rok!" as if to say, "en garde!" and attacked the Master with poop. The Master parried and riposted with a flaming lunge. That raven also fled.

The Master followed up with a quick reward of meat to all the others. The lesson was not lost on the birds.

The Master shouted a command to hurry. Despite their diminished numbers, the birds made the wise choice. With regular rewards of meat along the way to fortify them, the ravens carried the taxi to Sylvaniopolis posthaste.

The rising sun was detaching itself from the horizon. At this latitude, that meant the morning was well underway. On Main Street of Sylvaniopolis, businesses were opening and a few browns were out and about. They goggled at the Master landing in his black wraps.

He needed to dress down.

The Master found a dry goods store and picked out some dungarees, a flannel shirt and a parka. He was shocked to learn his black habit did not grant him the privilege of taking the clothes *gratis*. He offered snuff by way of currency—thank Satan its quality far exceeded the local brands—and changed into the new outfit right there in front of the embarrassed salesman.

The sidewalks of Main Street had the darnedest things the Master had ever seen: huge drums, bigger than the bass drums of the cathedral, spaced regularly along the sidewalks. Pedestrians used them as a mode of transport, bouncing along from one to the next. They called it the drumhead expressway.

Those on the drums made excellent time compared to ordinary pedestrians. The Master instantly saw how, in a region with few raven taxis, the drums would be useful—although, come to think of it, the streets were becoming crowded with a shocking number of big diesel trucks as well. Where did they all come from?

He needed to find the prisoners. He made what he thought were discrete inquiries. The people of Sylvaniopolis were generally friendly, hailing one another in the old style with cries of "eh, whatever," but they recoiled from his questions. He wondered if there were something about himself that marked him as a Burrsburger.

"Can anybody tell me if the government is rounding up men who look like me?" He was standing in a coffee shop and addressing the mid-morning crowd with a raised voice. He had given up on the subtle approach.

The patrons studiously failed to notice him. He was making a hash of this.

One older man stood and walked out on unsteady feet. He passed the Master so close, they brushed elbows. The man's horny hand grasped the Master's briefly—an odd handshake where the pinkies interlocked and a forefinger touched the Master's wrist.

It happened too fast for the Master to be properly revolted. When he looked over his shoulder, the man was already gone.

It took the Master several seconds to know what to do.

Outside, he made a guess and ran left. Immediately, he heard a hiss in an alley as he flew past.

The old man was there, waiting for him.

"What do you know about—" began the Master, sounding angry without intending to.

The man opened his mouth to speak, revealing teeth rotten to the roots. His morning coffee had not washed away the foul reek in his breath.

"You're a Vicer, ain't ya?"

"A...what?"

"Oh, for dumb." The old man shook his head. "If you ain't, you should be."

"Do you know where—" Again, the Master felt irrational anger.

Relax. Let the man speak.

The man took a pulpy flyer from his pocket. "Come tonight. Tell'm Tightwad Ted sent ya."

The page read: *We Seek the Vice President Who Is to Come!* The crude drawing below was more crudely rendered by a woodblock printer, but the heroic face might just have been the Master's own.

The Master tried to memorize the fine print at the bottom, the when and where of the meeting.

The man snatched back the flyer and made to walk away. The Master grabbed the arm of his filthy coat.

"The prisoners—where are they?"

"With the other livestock." He grinned at that cheery thought, pointed vaguely to the south, and bolted out of the alley.

The Master made chase, but was stopped by a breeze out of the south. It carried the ripe aromas of the farm, potent despite the freezing cold. A stockyard was somewhere close.

CHAPTER THIRTY-SIX

Hog Heaven

This was the barn of barns. The stockyard was a vast room filled with a confusion of rough lumber: the zig-zag of unpainted rafters, uprights exclaiming their support of the walls, high horizontals of catwalks hanging from vertical suspenders, and the maze of gates below. It was so big, the far wall was partly obscured by a moist, noisome cloud of body heat.

Using his belt, the Master roped a high peg and climbed to a place where he could survey the space. He prowled along the catwalk, exposed and alert. At one end was a rustic amphitheater with a sawdust floor. From its loudspeakers came the voice of an auctioneer that overpowered the lowing, crowing, bleating and grunting of the condemned animals below.

The floor was divided into a grid of numbered pens and passageways. Some of the pens had had to be modified with extra boards and wire fencing for the new arrivals; cattle, sheep and hogs cannot climb like humans can.

The Master looked down at them, and he hid among the rafters, ashamed. Every one of the prisoners had black hair, was in his mid-thirties, was taller than average and had an athletic, strikingly attractive build. By the confidence of their raised voices, the Master knew that, in less dreadful circumstances, they would have been all gregarious and likable. Every one of them was a close copy of himself in face, age, physique and personality.

The cattle, sheep, and even hogs were willing to squat in the sawdust and await their fate. The men were not so complacent. American citizens, used to their Satan-given freedom, now reduced to the level of chattel, they were not taking it lying down. One of them kicked savagely, over and over, at a rough board on the gate of his pen, and the Master silently rejoiced in his defiance. The livestock handlers, in the unsought role of jailers, took no notice.

Sylvaniopolis, Sylvania, up near the headwaters of the Mississippi, was a large city with a healthy supply of these black-haired victims. Justice Douglas and his clerks had found two dozen.

The Master lowered himself to the floor and retrieved his belt with a flick. He found a diner next to the amphitheater—the sign said "Hog Heaven"—and his hunger overpowered his caution. Even here, in this squalid place with its whimsical "Eat more possum!" posters and its red and yellow squeeze bottles at every table, the lingering stink of aged manure was ubiquitous.

He heard an obnoxious voice above the diners, one he recognized. There, past all the browns in their coarse denim work coats and their manure-splattered overalls and their high-topped rubber boots stuck out on long legs into the aisle—there in the back, in a vinyl-upholstered booth, very conspicuous in his black robe and black sheriff's hat, sat Associate Justice William O. Douglas.

His six-shooter sat among the plates of burgers and chili fries, ready for action.

The justice spotted the Master before he could even consider hiding. "Move!" he told the clerks jammed with him in the small booth.

When they did not instantly obey, he smacked them viciously across the face.

The clerks were equally out of place. Their austere loin cloths earned them many sideways glances from the outlanders. The entire back wall of booths was occupied with blacks. The Master sat down.

"Took you long enough." Justice Douglas took a bite from his hamburger. His wooden teeth reeked of rot at the best of times; the condiments oozing through their cracks failed to make them less unlovely. The Justice wiped ketchup from his chin. "The locals here are so charming. I think I'll retire and open an authentic Sylvaniopolisian hamburger joint."

"Well, that assumes His Honor the Chief allows you to retire."

"Haw, haw haw! That's exactly the point, isn't it? I don't like being here. I don't like doing clerk's work. I don't know what the Chief wants with all these men we're rounding up, but I'm not optimistic about their long-term chances and I don't like the whole, sordid beeswax. Yet, I do it."

"Because you fear the Chief."

"Exactly. And so do you, or you did until yesterday. As I see it, there're two novel things happening. First, the Chief's bizarre order, unconstitutional even by his expansive definition of the term, to nick vast numbers of so-called suspects against whom there is not a shred of evidence."

"I—"

"*Shut your pie-hole, I'm talking.* Second, a small but highly interesting act of insubordination by the Chief's formerly most dependable and effective lackey."

"I am not disloyal, and I've done nothing against the Chief's orders. After you left, he changed—"

"Don't insult my intelligence. I have ears and eyes and a brain. The Chief's special pet is peeing on the carpet. That's an unstable scenario. The Chief is an incompetent dictator and a loathsome old wart of a man—"

The Master had simply never heard such words spoken. He was barely able to follow what came next.

"—but you are a simp. I wouldn't place any clams on you surviving the week."

"That is…hogwash."

"Don't kid yourself. Instead of arguing, you should be asking why the Chief picked you in the first place. It wasn't because of your brains; that's for sure. Not your loyalty; this week put the lie—"

The Master stood. "I'm going to pretend this conversation never happened. If I hear one more word like this, I'm going—"

"You're going *nowhere.*" The justice reached across a platter and jerked the Master down. "You sit there and listen while I say whatever I like."

The justice pulled a limp, cold fry from the grease pile.

"Look, I like you, I really do. Have a spud. Let me order you a malt. Waiter!"

The waiter took the order. The justice leaned back, watching the Master chew his way through a few sullen fries. Never one to endure waiting with equanimity, Douglas pawed his face and tore at his gray hair, leaving it a boar's nest.

The waiter brought the malts. All the time, the clerks studiously looked elsewhere. The Master supposed the closest of them were, quite possibly, out of earshot.

"Don't worry about *them.* I've got something over on each one of those little turds. They wouldn't dare go tattling to the Chief. You, though—you're clean as a baby's bottom. Tell me, what's your racket? Who *are* you?"

Were babies' bottoms notable for their cleanliness? The Master had no idea. "I...don't know. I thought I was Canadian. Rescued from the mines for my leadership qualities."

"Look, kid. Fat and happy is something you can't afford. You've got a few days at the most to figure out what the Chief is up to, and then a whole lot of people are going to die."

The Master put down a fry. "Consarn it, I don't like—"

"It doesn't matter what you like. I'm telling you, the Chief is up to something. These men are going to disappear. I feel it in my bones. You want to be among them?"

The justice took a swig from his brown soda pop. Bits of french fry and dill pickle swirled and settled in the bottle.

"I like you. I mean it. Yeah, you're stupid and annoying—but you're not half the moron that everyone says you are, and you sure as shootin' don't deserve to die. So, if you know something, anything, that will sort this out, spill it now."

Bluntness is not trustworthiness but it usually feels like it.

"Human sacrifice."

"Human—*what?*"

"The Chief has a deal with the Master in Lunacy: offer the prisoners on the altar to Satan."

"Bull. Shit."

The Master could have thrown a "don't kid yourself" right back in the justice's face, but there was no point.

Justice Douglas picked up a greasy fry and held it up. His almond eyes regarded it as it twitched in his unsteady grasp. He grimaced and harrumphed. He shoved the fry into the frigid mound of his untouched malt.

"Oh, boy. This is bad. I knew it was bad. But this is just...*bad*."

CHAPTER THIRTY-SEVEN

Like Lightning
from Heaven

A ssociate Justice Douglas and the Special Master walked out into the cold, crisp night. The stars were white needles of light. The Master was back to wearing black, and feeling the temperature. It never really got this cold down in the capital, and the Master pitied the clerks, with their exposed arms and legs, as they waddled a respectful distance behind them.

One star wandered. Out from the southeast it came, weaving about. It approached and resolved itself into an array of lights, red and green and white. An airplane!

The lights wobbled and bobbed. Airplanes were a rare sight, but the Master could tell something was wrong. He had heard night flying was difficult. Were there even five pilots in the whole U.S. qualified to do it?

"Let's go see!" the justice commanded. Clerks whistled for their taxis and in moments they were aloft, headed toward the grassy strip where airplanes always landed in this city, which was never.

The plane made three abortive approaches. The pilot was either a rookie or a lush; the plane weaved and lurched. The last attempt should have been aborted as well. Maybe the plane did not have enough gas for another try.

The clumsy plane came in too slow and sank like a stone. The landing gear snapped off and it belly-flopped. The sod was torn open as first the left, and then the right wing plowed the ground. The plane rotated completely and the tail plunged into a line of trees. The wings were sheared off by two stout trunks.

The Master ran to the plane. The clerks walked.

Gasoline was in the Master's nose. So much for the out-of-gas theory. The plane was nothing but a tangle of metal and shivered wood.

The air erupted into a fireball that turned the world rosy. The Master turned his face away. The clerks fell back, throwing up their arms before their faces. The Master kept on.

The fire came from the fuel tanks in the broken wings. Most of the fuselage was among the trees. The pilot's cockpit was nearest, but already engulfed in flames.

Write him off.

The Master circled around the fire. The glare dazzled him but he picked his way over fallen trees. The door on the side of the fuselage was wrinkled and already too hot to touch. Nearer up, the fuselage was broken open, but the flames denied him that access point.

The Master kicked at a window. It shattered. It was too small for a man to pass through. The situation was dire. The Master felt the side of his face broil.

"Help! The door!" A clerk's face appeared in the broken window.

"You push! I'll pull!" shouted the Master. He pulled off his robe and wrapped his hands in it. With this improvised oven mitt, he yanked the handle.

Blows from the other side loosened the door. On the third try, it popped open. The Master fell backward onto a burning log.

The Master screamed and rolled. The clerk ran through the open door and fled.

Coward!

The Master entered the plane. He choked on smoke. By bending low, he could breathe and see in the clearer air. Without thinking, he pulled off his belt and flipped its end into a loop.

The Chief!

The old man sprawled unconscious among seats unmoored and scattered about.

What a disaster.

Boom! Another explosion. Something on fire flew straight for the Chief's head. All instinct, the Master watched himself lasso the flying wreckage and deflect it. He threw the Chief over his shoulder, not knowing if he were dead or alive. The older man's mass sent the Master staggering sideways, against the hot bulkhead. The air was too smoky to permit a good bellow of pain. The Master got his balance and faced the door. It was so tiny, he wondered how the Chief ever fit through it.

There was no time for despair, let alone analysis. Ignoring the risk of plugging the only egress, the Master pushed the Chief through the oval hole. The Master blinked as the vast expanse of black-clad flesh popped through easily. He caught himself to avoid falling on top of his Chief, then dived through as another explosion sent a hot shock through the tube of the fuselage.

If the Chief were not dead before, he might well be now. He lay awkwardly on his back, an inverted curve atop a log, motionless.

The Master got the Chief up over his shoulder again. Taking terrible risks, he skipped over shadows from log to log. The heat at his back receded, and he laid the Chief down on the grass. Clerks stood a ways off, watching. "Get over here and help!" he screamed.

He reentered the plane. He made several trips, saving anybody, black or brown, who was not obviously dead.

He laid the last survivor on the ground among the others. He dropped to his knees, panting. The worthless clerks had finally found a way to help, swaddling the wounded with improvised bandages. None had taken charge, however. Justice Douglas was still standing apart, shivering, with an unreadable and unattractive expression on his face.

The Master steadied his breath. If anything needed doing, it was on him to do it.

"Bring the taxis around, as close to the fire as the birds will dare. Load the survivors, with the Chief and the injured going first. Take them to the local hospital—or whatever passes as such in this town. The others walk to that farm over there"—he pointed to a house in the distance with a yellow, inviting glow in its windows—"to get warm."

The Master rode with the Chief. He laid out his own body as a blanket to keep the Chief from freezing. He ordered the birds to keep low, and for once this ill-bred conspiracy obeyed without grumbling. Some curious locals looking up from the ground shouted directions to the nearest hospital—really, a doctor's house. The Master roused the occupant.

Dr. Dinshah Ghadiali ordered everyone out of the examination room, but the Master hovered. He needed to be sure the doctor's skills were sufficient.

There was no serious bleeding, no broken bones; maybe a concussion at the worst. The Doctor disdained medicine but illuminated the Chief's body with strange colored lights. Who knew what they were for, but they were powerful enough to give the Chief some much-needed warmth.

The Master retreated to the lobby and collapsed before the hearth, shivering violently. He had lost his luxurious cape and all he had on was a cassock.

A youth, the doctor's apprentice, threw logs on the fire and heated a cup of broth for the Master. He drank the liquid with infinite gratitude and felt life return to his numb body. The youth brought a blanket and threw it over him, never speaking a word, and rubbed his hands until the Master assured him with a gesture that he was fine.

"What's your name, son?"

The boy's eyes widened, but he attempted an answer. The words that came out were a staccato of stutters that, in the presence of such an important visitor, a black no less, never resolved into coherent words.

The Master squeezed the poor boy's shoulder to silence him. "I've got this ear, see?" The Master pointed helpfully. "I worked the mines when I was your age, and an explosion burst my eardrum. I can't understand too good."

The boy nodded.

"You like to help people. You're studying to become a doctor?"

The boy started to speak again, got stuck, thought better of it, and nodded again.

"You're lucky. Doctoring's so much better than mining. You'll have a good life and help lots of people."

Never mind the kid was an apprentice to a manifest quack.

The boy nodded enthusiastically. The Master tousled his hair and sent him on his way.

He dozed.

The night was cold, but the morning was colder still. It was still dark when the Special Master rose to help the Chief onto the waiting taxi. He ordered the ravens to the governor's residence. The governor had heard of the arrival of the Chief and had fled to Canada. Unannounced visits by the Chief often provoked panic in local officials.

The Master assigned clerks to bathe the Chief and put him to bed. He chose those who had been with Justice Douglas. It was satisfying to put them to work after their worthless behavior at the crash.

When he had satisfied himself that the Chief's health and safety were assured, the Master found a bed for himself and collapsed into it.

As he was sinking into the embrace of Morpheus, he remembered: the poster. The Vicers were meeting, right now. With that thought, sleep was impossible.

CHAPTER THIRTY-EIGHT

Go to Meetin'

T he voice on the other side of the door was barely audible. "Password," was all it said.

"I…wasn't told—" said the Special Master.

A bit of light shined in the darkness as a peephole was opened from the inside. A single peeper peeped out through the triangular opening, and registered shock as it focused on the Master.

"Lucifer's futon! Get yer ass in here," said the masked doorman as he jerked the Master by his black velvet collar over the threshold. "A face like that, yer not safe on the street."

"I'm the special—" said the Master, by way of explanation.

"No names, ya fool. Keep yer eyes open an' yer mouth shut. An' wear one o' these," he said as he gave the Master a red bandana. The Master tied it over the lower half of his face and found the cozy meeting room at the other end of the entrance hall.

A dozen men were in attendance, their bandanas making them appear like vaudeville bandits. They showed no curiosity and he took a seat on one of the few remaining available folding chairs; they only had eyes for the faded photograph in the gilded frame that hung between two American flags on the rostrum.

The face on the wall was vaguely familiar.

333

Somebody was doing something odd with a jaw harp. Somebody else was rhythmically scraping a washboard. And that other thing: was it called a musical saw? The strange sounds—"music" might be the correct word—made it hard to think. The men were grunting to a beat. The heat of the enclosed space and the intoxicating miasma of sound reduced the Master's mental state to a series of disjointed auditory and visual impressions. The effect reminded him of the Electoral College, but more elemental and unnerving. The college was the domesticated species; this was the wild.

In the confusion, only one thing was clear. The face on the wall was terribly important.

"Ooga-boo!" was, apparently, what everyone was shouting. The word, as it emerged involuntarily from the Master's mouth, expressed a feeling he had never known he had.

"Ooga-boo! Mumba-lum!" Everyone was standing, had been standing for some time now, and swaying. The air was thick with a sickly perfume; how could the Master have not noticed it before? He felt nauseated.

"Mathers! Mathers! Mathers! Mathers!"

Hell's chowhounds! That's who it was: the man on the wall was Samuel Liddell MacGregor Mathers, the last living vice president. The last dead vice president too, for that matter.

Another wave of nausea hit the Master. He fought down the gag reflex. His stomach was empty, thank Satan.

Everyone was silent and seated. How long had that been? The Master took his seat.

An honor guard marched out and formed a line before the portrait. On their dark clothes were painted skeleton bones and their masks were skulls.

An old man took the stage. The old man's entire head was covered by a feathered hood, an effigy of an American raven. Only his eyes were visible through two slits, and his mouth through the wide-open beak. He bowed before Mathers, then began his talk.

Although the room was small, the preacher spoke through a battery-powered bullhorn. The volume and distortion only added to the macabre surrealism of the scene.

The Master understood little, and remembered less. He only felt a kind of holy terror as word after blasphemous, treasonous word spilled forth from the raven's beak. The narcotic incense, the occasional *twang twang* of the jaw harp and the murmurs of the crowd, the scowling visage of Mathers, and above all the incitement to sedition coming from the mouth of a *Hell-forsaken raven for Satan's sake*, shook the Master to his core.

The room was silent. The Master was on his feet, stumbling toward the stage, tears trickling down his cheeks.

Raven man put down the bullhorn. He whispered, "Do you seek the Vice President Who Is to Come?"

"I..." The Master was too choked up to speak. He pulled up the bandana to wipe his tears, exposing his lower face.

"My God!" gasped Raven man. He goggled through his eye-holes. "It's you!"

A bolt of electric excitement shot through the crowd. Was this the One? Was he the promised Vice President?

Dozens of masked enthusiasts pressed toward the rostrum. The honor guard was confused; some pushed back the crowd while others turned to join in the rush.

"No. This is *all wrong*," shrieked Raven man. He hit a switch on the wall and plunged the room into darkness.

The Master's environment was transformed into a blind writhing of crazed limbs. An arm struck him hard on the temple, dazing him.

An authoritative hand pulled him up and out of the milling, shouting crowd. "This way." The Master was dragged through a door.

He and his unknown savior were in a hallway. In that clear air, the Master felt rational thought returning to his brain.

"It's *too early*, you fool! We need *time* to *organize*. Get *out of here!*"

A door to the outside opened. In the starlight, the Master got just a glimpse of the raven's gap-beaked, wrathful face glaring at him before he was thrust outside.

Bang! The door slammed shut. The Master could hear shouts of the hysterical crowd, muffled yet terrifying in their intensity. Clearly, the raven spoke true; he spoke truer, in fact, than any raven ever had.

He pulled off his bandana as he ran through the empty streets, dodging drifts of moon-washed snow. He jumped onto the drumhead expressway and rejoiced in the distance it put between him and the Vicers.

He let himself into the governor's mansion silently. Merciful hell, but no one was up yet. He would check on the Chief, then go to bed.

He opened the door to the Chief's room. A shadowy figure in a black body stocking sat in a chair by the empty bed.

"Where have you been?" It was H. L. Mencken.

The Master was speechless.

"There has been an incident. Sometime in the night, Associate Justice William O. Douglas died in his sleep."

CHAPTER THIRTY-NINE

Dearly Departed

The Master insisted on performing an autopsy himself. One of Mencken's flunkies came to hover.

"Thank you, clerk. You can wait in the hall. I'll call if I need your help."

"I am very willing to stay and assist you."

"No, thanks, I prefer to be alone with the body."

"I am at your service."

This clerk, this very junior clerk, was not budging from Justice Douglas' room. The clerk had a fixed idea of "service". The Special Master stared at the clerk and the clerk stared back, dully, with all the solicitousness of a stone.

The man was going to wait the Master out. Interesting. Only one thing would make him dare defy the Master.

So, he was under the direct orders of the Chief. The Master intended to investigate the death, and this clerk intended to stymie the investigation.

That told the Master ninety percent of what he wanted to know.

The clerks had heard Justice Douglas' reckless talk. The clerks viewed Justice Douglas with no fondness. They reported him to the Chief. They feared the Chief more than they feared Justice Douglas. And the Chief feared Justice Douglas more than he feared the Master.

The Special Master was at a crossroads. From here on out, it might be war between the Chief and him, however covert, however contrived. For the Master to choose war, ninety percent was not good enough. The Master needed one hundred percent. He needed to be sure.

The Master opened one of the corpse's eyelids. The dead peeper regarded him contemptuously. He picked up an arm and dropped it. He touched a wrist, as if feeling for a pulse. He tapped the knees and elbows. He placed his hand on the dead man's forehead and counted off thirty seconds on his pocket watch.

All theatrics. This parody of a coroner's work gave the Master time to think. The clerk stood at attention throughout, deadpan. If he found the Master's behavior suspicious, or ridiculous, he gave no sign.

The Master moved so his body would momentarily block the clerk's view of his hands. He stuck his finger in an eye socket and the eyeball jumped out with a satisfying *pop!* It hung there by the optic nerve. He tugged the nerve and made fumbling, grasping movements after the eye as it flew, bounced against the wall, and fell under the bed.

"Oh, crap," he said. "Fetch that, will you?" The Master's smile was an embarrassed one. "I wouldn't want the Chief to find out I did that."

The clerk moved, hesitated, moved, and hesitated. The Master had check-mated him. Crawling in the dust under a bed for a missing eyeball was beneath the dignity of a robed black. It was clerk's work.

The clerk caved. He crawled and pushed his way past the Master's legs. He was going to get it over with as quickly as possible.

The Master did not move his feet. They were impeding the clerk and he liked them that way.

As the clerk's swaddled butt disappeared under the bed, the Master bent over Justice Douglas' face and peeled back his lips. There, in the discolored mucous membranes, the Master saw what he expected: bruises, plus the imprint of wooden dentures pressed into the inside of the lips. The justice had suffocated when a hand was pressed over his mouth.

The clerk emerged from under the bed, his black loincloth showing the dirt.

"Here's your eyeball," the sullen man said.

"Thanks." Like an amateur undertaker, the Master pressed the eye back into place. The eyelid did not fully close. The result was bulgy and cock-eyed, but no one would care.

"There. Now the justice can see. He can see just fine."

By 1:00 p.m. the sun offered feeble warmth. All the blacks stood in the dirt of the street before the executive mansion. His honor the Chief Justice hovered above them in a raven taxi. He was in a foul mood.

"The plane of the loss is an inconvenience." The Chief paused, almost noticing his words were garbled. His eyes were bloodshot and weirdly unfocused. "Fortunately, the economy out here in this iced-over pigpen is booming."

The Chief revived his spirits with a fat pinch of chewing tobacco.

"This place is wild. Look at those drums!" The Chief's accusing forefinger stabbed at the drumhead expressway. Citizens bounced along it self-importantly. "Nobody authorized those things. They are obviously unsafe. And where's the toll system? The state government is not implementing half of my opinions. There are too many of these trucks on the road." The street was presently empty of vehicles, but eh, whatever. "How businesses can operate without a decent industrial policy, I cannot fathom."

Another fistful of tobacco calmed the Chief. The Special Master watched from the fringe of the crowd. The clerks had closed ranks to keep him there.

"So, my point is, there's a robust network of smugglers. They've imported a surprising number of semi-trucks from That Country to the North." The Chief Justice, whose blackened lips would never be polluted by uttering the name "Canada", spat off the side of the raven taxi. The ravens honored the gesture with a few dollops of sympathy pooping.

"I've appropriated semis to transport us and the suspects back to Burrsburg."

"We could put them on trial here," the Master called out, abandoning all sense. "Give them over to local law enforcement."

The Chief's head rotated ponderously, like that of the automaton of Death that emerged once an hour from the great clock on the tower of Burrsburg Cathedral. (Not that it kept time.)

His head came to a stop. He seemed to notice the Special Master for the first time, as one would a disgusting, but tiny, insect.

"What's the use of that?"

"Well, I don't see—"

"You don't see! I'd 'sarnin' say you don't." A long pause. "Appointing you Special Master was a mistake."

Mencken, that contemptible fool, grinned openly at those words.

"If you're not satisfied with me, I'll resign immediately."

"Applesauce."

The Chief clapped once and whistled. His taxi spun away. The clerks followed him to the stockyard.

Among the livestock pens, the Chief took direct control, barking orders to the clerks and leaving the Master with nothing to do. This was beneath the dignity of the Chief, and completely unprecedented.

Three semi-trucks drove up. One was appointed with carpeting, furniture, and an ice box for the Chief and the senior clerks. Another was fitted with benches for the rest of the blacks. A third, stripped bare, was where they would herd the suspects.

Clerks bustled about, prepping and fetching. When the Chief, red-faced and slick with sweat, went so far as to help lift a loading chute, the Master rebelled and snatched it away from him.

The Chief struck him hard across the face with the back of his hand.

The Master touched the corner of his mouth and found blood. The Chief glared at him, then tottered. Clerks sprang to assist him. He allowed them to drag him away without a backwards glance.

Clerks forced the prisoners up the chute into the empty semi. They protested, but the clerks had taken electric prods from the livestock handlers—the Chief especially admired this bit of provincial technology—and the suspects were loaded in due course. Mencken padlocked the door of the semi.

"We're taking them all the way to the capital?"

"Chief's orders." Mencken answered the Master's question with an absurd degree of good cheer. The Master considered how Mencken's face might be improved if his mouth were swollen shut.

"We'll need to let them out to feed them, let them relieve themselves."

"Don't need food, and as for relief, nature'll take its course."

"Tell me the combination to the lock," the Master said, but Mencken was already walking away. It would have been better to stay silent. Now everyone knew of his mutinous intent.

He could not let the prisoners reach the capital. There they would be killed. Most likely he would be killed himself.

He had to stop the convoy. He would think of a way.

Haiti
and
Environs

Nixon Autobiography

Chapter 21, "Launch," of the unpublished *Memoirs of Richard Nixon*, Second Draft

[This "Second Draft" is more properly seen as a complete rewrite of Nixon's memoirs. Although incomplete, it is less fragmentary, and its Olympian tone is that of a manuscript intended for eventual publication. It was begun after the author was pardoned by President Reinhold Niebuhr. The only paper copy was moved to a locked underground vault after the author began his career as an itinerant evangelist. It was destroyed by water damage when the vault cracked 300 years later, having never been read by anyone.]

Of all those who embarked on the Sixth Haitio-American War, I alone returned, dead or alive. It is a dubious distinction, to say the least.

President Mary Wilson was the anti-Joan of Arc; virginal and otherworldly, yet selfish and destructive. Her downfall was complete, but at the same time, it was completely personal, and the country recovered quickly. Unlike many, I foresaw the Puritan Reform Party would experience no permanent setback. Quaker Renewal won a landslide in 1948, but equilibrium reasserted itself in 1952.

That's why I have said nothing about what happened. My silence during my trial helped the PRP, and it suited my personal wishes perfectly. Now, however, the time has come for me to give account.

[Marginalia] *My reasons for writing this memoir remain opaque to me. To be perfectly clear to myself, I want to fill a gap in history. And yet, prison taught me a profound weariness with all worldly pursuits. At times I have craved death; at other times, I have hoped to unlock the mystery of life.*

The end of the war may be a mystery, but the launching of the armada was well documented. The press was on hand to film the great day. Wilson stood on the end of the Long Pier with me and her other closest advisers. We reviewed the battleships, aircraft carriers and multitude of landing craft assembled in Port of Washington. Never has our naval superiority been so ostentatiously displayed. President Wilson's admirals told her so many craft were not needed, and that we were neglecting our responsibilities in the Pacific. Wilson overruled them.

I joined Wilson aboard her flagship, the Battleship *Yucatan.* We were joined by more ships from Havana, Santo Domingo, Maracaibo, Kingston—all the principal ports of our nation. The bulk of the Pacific fleet joined us via the canals at Panama, Nicaragua and Oaxaca. I confess that, seeing all those brave sailors in dress white, the carriers bristling with aircraft, the Seraphim bombers roaring overhead and our newest commissioned vessel, the solar-powered submarine *Nautilus,* I felt optimism for the outcome of the war. I may have been even so foolish as to declare, as I was quoted in the Plymouth Times, that our victory was "inevitable."

A note of poor taste marred the celebrations. The whole parade stopped to watch costumed dancing girls perform a routine while dressed as syringes, pills, bars of soap, and medical kits. This was meant to remind our boys of the true enemy—American disease—but the girls flaunted their bare ankles in a most lascivious manner and likely had an effect on discipline quite the opposite of that intended.

We departed at high tide and the coast of Florida appeared off the port bow the next day. The lessons of previous invasions told us to avoid the Everglades at all cost. The president's generals—those who, like me, were too loyal to resign—had selected a landing site at Jacksonville along Florida's north Atlantic coast. It allowed us to bypass some of the worst swamps and the radiation around Lake Orlando.

We found Jacksonville abandoned by the enemy. Our boys stormed the beach and not a life was lost. They say no war plan survives the first encounter with the enemy, but our plan was in robust health as the sun set that third day.

The fourth day, the navy set to the cumbersome business of disembarking the power suits and their power plants.

The power plants are massive, self-contained, self-propelled atomic piles with concrete walls 16 feet thick and cooling towers atop. Each arrived on a ship custom designed just for it. Getting the power plants ashore was a nightmare. The operation was expected to take a day, but took a week. It was a harbinger of things to come.

The boys of the infantry displayed admirable self-restraint. It is a tribute to their training and character that they did not loot the town. Since none of them live to speak for themselves, I feel it important to quash any speculation about that. To a man, like the 300 at Thermopylae, they served with honor. *Non sibi sed patriae.*

At last the power plants reached dry ground. Their mighty treads found purchase. The power suits were attached to the 12 plants by armored umbilici and their crews lit them up, four suits to a plant. Together, the 48 pilots raised their plasma guns and fired a gratuitous, but absolutely thrilling, bolt of blue electric death into the air in the pre-dawn darkness. The enemy would have fled in terror, had any lingered.

That was the last joyful moment of the travail. From the start of the long march north to the capital, moving the power suits and their power plants was a miserable slog. As we learned—no, as President Wilson learned; for the rest of us had seen and believed the aerial photographs of the swamps and estuaries all along the chosen route—the "mobile" power plants were not mobile at all on such terrain.

We could have chosen another route, but the president had built a navy for this invasion, and by God, she was going to use it. Our route ran along the coast so our carriers could provide air support. This was a poor priority, and we all knew it. The president would not change her mind.

By the time we skirted the Okefenokee Swamp—barbarous name!—Wilson learned of disease afflicting the infantry. The pattern of former invasions repeated itself. America is filthy, and a magnet for every communicable disease.

"We have penicillin," was Wilson's glib reply. As if the laws of nature did not apply to us.

They still applied well enough. We learned America has a kind of genius for incubating new strains of diseases. We listened, horrified, as grim-faced officers briefed us on the spreading epidemics. Desperate boys on the ground tore open their medic kits and gave themselves injections, repeatedly, as they saw their buddies sicken and die. They emptied syringes into themselves by the millions and ate pills like candy. No matter; the infantry was decimated, then decimated again.

The president, at last bowing to reality, ordered the army to detour inland. On my urging, Wilson moved her command center off ship and henceforth we traveled with the army, sharing their risks.

Wilson ordered flights of carrier planes extended and multiplied. We lost *Enterprise* when an exhausted pilot crashed into the flight deck and set off a fire among live ordnance. An entire carrier task force became disoriented, sailed into a fog off Bermuda, and were never heard from again. To top it off, the *Bogotá* snapped in two and sank with all hands for no particular reason except a *Vancouver*-class battle cruiser built in 4 months cannot be other than a shoddy piece of work.

We had got as far as the city of Augusta when the ground game turned dreadful.

CHAPTER FORTY

The Bobby-Q

Somebody announced they were in eastern Assenisipia. The congestion of the city of Shicago and the tangle of roads around the southern curve of Lake Michigania was behind them. The floor of the rocking, bouncing semi-trailer abused the Special Master's sore backside where he sat, as far away from the stinking piss pot as possible.

The Chief had called for petitions, and his clerks hovered around his inert form. The parchments lay on an unsteady table before him. The trailer swayed around the potholes the driver successfully avoided, and bounced over potholes he did not, and every two minutes or so the petitions would slide off the table and a clerk would pick them up and stack them neatly again. The Chief watched the whole repeating cycle—wobble; fall; stack—with a cold passivity from his leather chair, saying nothing, ruminating on a wad of tobacco and spitting in the Special Master's direction. The Chief was in a foul mood and he was blessed if he was going to lift a finger. Better to snuff one candle than curse the light, as the saying went.

Mencken whispered an order and a junior clerk approached the Master. "Your gun needs cleaning." Other clerks came and stood around the Master with hard looks on their faces. The Master gave the clerk his pistol and the clerk put it in his pocket. He made no pretense of cleaning it.

The Master asked if they were stopping for lunch. No one answered. He felt a stirring of nostalgia for the asbestos mines. There, if somebody didn't like you, they beat the crap out of you and left it at that.

The Chief remembered the electric prods he had seen in Sylvaniopolis. That roused him. He spent a long time talking to a clerk who was known to be clever with his hands, instructing him how to build a bigger, better prod. For a brief time, the Chief was happier than he had been in years.

The semi kept slowing down and speeding up. There was talk of finding a place to stop. From the murmurs, the Master gathered they had passed through several towns recently emptied of all people. That tended to happen in these western states. Sometimes it was an epidemic, sometimes it was a gold rush or other group hallucination, sometimes it was an Uncle Sam sighting, and sometimes it was an outbreak of heretical enthusiasm.

Somebody looked out the peephole and said something about a huge pile of charred bodies.

Yep; heretical enthusiasm.

The semi continued on. The semi slowed, then stopped. The big doors opened and the Master saw a provincial downtown covered with dirty snow. Signs next to the truck warned, "Goathorn 12 Miles" and "No Parking This Sided [sic] the Street". Even the ugliness of this place—somebody said it was called Elkhart—was cheering after the ride in the metal box.

The Master smelled the alluring greasiness of a diner, an all-nighter called The Bobby-Q. The clerks lifted the Chief out of his chair and the old man walked on stiff legs to the back. Clerks were needed to lower the heavy Chief down to the ground but a few were spared to block the Master's way out of the truck.

"Can't I eat lunch?"

Silence.

"I'm hungry."

"We'll toss you a bone." He wasn't sure which clerk said that. Just one day ago, nobody would have dared.

"I need to take a dump."

"Wipe yourself on that fancy robe." This roused a chuckle from them.

The Chief turned, looked at the Master's feet, and grunted. The clerks relented and the Master got out.

In the distance, a few locals could still be sighted, ducking into doorways or alleys. Shouts of "Make way for the Chief Justice!" were purely ceremonial on the empty sidewalk.

The blacks stepped over two puddles of vomit on their way in. A two-puker? Not bad.

The Chief took a seat at the diner's long Bakelite-tiled counter. Clerks took the stools on either side of him as patrons threw down their forks and gave up their seats. The wide-eyed waiter swept dirty dishes off the counter into a bin with great, rushed sweeps of his arm, not caring that some of the glasses shattered.

There were no stools left so the Master sat in a booth. Half-eaten meals sat before him on the table. He looked around and saw, among the locals huddled in the back, the two men who had been sitting there moments before. He waved them back to their lunch.

The men were too terrified to disobey.

The Master gave the men opposite him a kindly smile. "Come here much?"

"Oh, no sir, we wouldn't dare..."

The other just shook his head. He had no nose, just ragged holes. Probably the work of snuff cancer, not a knife. Probably.

"Looks like you took one on the beezer."

No one laughed at the Master's feeble joke.

"Well, I'm the Special Master to his honor the Chief Justice."

This only cowed them more.

"What's that you're eating there?"

"A sinker," the talkative one mumbled.

"Taste good?"

"Pert near." This last was almost inaudible. The man flung the donut onto the floor.

Never had the Master struggled so with small talk.

He asked the quiet one, "how's your soup?"

"It'll burn yer gozzle," the other answered in his stead.

"What's your name?"

"I..." He seemed to lose his train of thought.

The other began quietly to weep. "Please don't kill us," came the whisper.

The notion came upon the Master just then, with a sickening force, that everything he knew about his country and his place in it might be a vast lie.

"I need to use the toilet," the Master announced.

The bathroom was an outhouse in the back. Mencken followed him, too close for flight and too far away from a sucker punch.

The outhouse was the classic affair, with weathered wood, a slanting roof and a star-shaped cutout. The Master went in and disrobed.

It got dark; Mencken's head blocked the light as he peeked in. Apparently there was no shred of dignity the Master was going to be permitted.

He took his time, forming a plan. He gave his audience quite a performance, grunting and contorting his face.

He finished and took his robe in his hand. He burst out the door. Mencken leaped back, ready for that trick, but not ready for the vast expanse of thick black crushed velvet that parachuted over his head. The Master punched him hard in the gut, then threw him on the ground and put him out with a few efficient kicks.

The Master pulled his robe back on. He ran to the prison semi. It was unguarded but that would not last. He climbed up the back as quietly as he could, but he was in haste and the trailer creaked as he got on its roof.

Both cab doors opened. The suspicious drivers came out, guns drawn. The Master considered the situation. He could probably ambush one man, steal his gun, and win the resulting shoot out with the other, but he wanted neither to kill nor to alert the others.

He could wait for the drivers to discover Mencken lying in the dirt. This would lead to a man hunt, dispersing the clerks and improving his odds. He could then overpower the few remaining and hijack the semi and somehow elude his pursuers.

He could slide off the roof, with luck (much luck) avoid notice, and run. He might find a cooperative local to hide him, but that would eliminate any chance to save the prisoners.

He could get on the roof of the diner, then jump down when the Chief came out and hold a gun to his head, using him as a hostage to...to...

The screen door went *bang!* against the diner wall. The blacks spilled out. The drivers jumped back into their semi.

Mencken staggered around the corner. "The Master has escaped!"

The Chief Justice halted and looked at Mencken. His lip curled up.

"If you think I'm staying in this heavenhole one more second because of your screw-up, you've got another thing coming. Here! You and...you"—the Chief pointed at two junior clerks—"stay with this idiot and find the Master. Don't come back to the capital without him."

With many awkward handholds, clerks lifted the Chief into his semi. Most clerks were reluctant to leave their prisoner behind, but the Chief began shouting for the convoy to leave. Worse, the locals were making bold to gawk, and if there's one thing a black must always avoid, it is to appear indecisive before browns.

Doors of semis slammed shut. Engines fired up. The Master, uncertain, never left his position and a faceful of diesel exhaust made him cough and gag. Browns heard him and pointed, amazed, but the blacks were oblivious, mentally shaking the dust of this one-horse town from their feet. The convoy lurched from the curb with the Special Master clinging for dear life.

Nixon Autobiography

Chapter 22, "Disaster Strikes" of the unpublished *Memoirs* (Second Draft) of Richard Nixon

It was nearly December and by all accounts, hurricanes should not have been a risk. However, we received reports of a tropical storm of unusual strength forming in the Atlantic. Daily, the warnings became more alarming. The President's admirals requested that the navy return to its ports. The President refused. As the storm was upgraded to a hurricane, they stopped requesting and began insisting. Reluctantly, and to her mind, generously, she countered with a proposal that the army divert resources for capturing the American ports such as Savannah and Charleston. Squabbling over this idea consumed precious time. By this point, President Wilson's ability to command awe was gone. Her judgment was not trusted by anyone.

The admirals moved their ships as they pleased and Wilson was left with nothing to do but threaten and plead. It was too late: the hurricane came up the coast of the United States and simply destroyed our entire navy.

I remember well going to Myrtle Beach to inspect the damage. Offshore, we could see the hull of the *Unsinkable*, which had run aground and capsized. Even this close to land, the wreck had offered up not a single survivor. Its captain was Bebe Rebozo, a dear friend. His command had endured all of two weeks.

I was hardly the only one to experience loss. I witnessed John Mack, Secretary of Agriculture—why does a president bring the nation's top *farmer* to war? Madness!—weeping openly over the loss of his son.

The entire military apparatus, from private first class to secretary of war, came to an unspoken agreement. The mutiny was as total as a mutiny ever can be. The army gathered itself and turned back south.

Wilson threw one final tantrum. I would be very glad if I could forget that performance. Perhaps the devilment of the place we had invaded had possessed her. She screamed her vocal cords to a bloody pulp. I saw foam on her lips. She declared she would march to the capital if she had to go alone. She pulled her own hair, then turned on others, striking out impotently at top generals and lowly body guards alike. Those of us present said nothing. We restrained her when she was in danger of harming herself or others, but beyond that, we rode it out, much like our boys had waited for the hurricane to pass.

Exhaustion overtook her in the end and she collapsed. Her personal maid laid her on a bed. She lay like that, silent and unresponsive even when her eyes were open, for three days. In that time, only a few of us remained. From that moment, Vice President Niebuhr took the reins of government into his capable hands.

Of the Miami boat lift in which so many civilians died, I have nothing to add. Much has already been written and I did not witness it.

A few of us stayed with the president. I had burned many bridges to join her inner circle and I knew myself to be collateral damage in her self-destruction. My career was over.

Seeing President Wilson rise on the third day was horrifying. She was weirdly composed and steady of voice, and she showed no animosity toward anyone. In fact, she never again mentioned the deserters. However, her determination to continue north was harder than ever. The adamant was transformed, by extreme pressure, into the diamond.

She refreshed herself with food and drink, then called us to her war room. Standing over a huge map, she learned of the locations of stragglers. She issued quiet commands and dispatched aides who were too astonished to argue.

Over the next few days, a rump of her original invading horde was gathered together. Her generalship became even more personal and detail-obsessed. She requisitioned a horse and rode about, goading her army into lines of battle. The countryside was scoured for food, weapons and supplies.

An important discovery was brought to her attention. During the chaos, a corporal had befriended some crows in an abandoned "taxi station", as the Americans call them.

(He was one of those people with a natural charisma for animals. It is a quality I envy. Only one animal has ever loved me, and Checkers has been dead now for many years.)

This corporal learned how to fly a taxi, which is the consarnedest thing, a lightweight platform carried by the birds. The man convinced the crows to carry him to President Wilson's command center.

His stunt almost got him shot down. Were there not a general order to conserve ammunition, he would have died for it. As it was, President Wilson saw the advantage immediately. She ordered all taxis commandeered and brought to the command center.

This led to the second disaster.

CHAPTER FORTY-ONE

Cold Road

The convoy of semis bounced along Interstate 80, a "highway" whose builders took an improvisational approach. Asphalt appeared in places, and worse, an occasional patch of loose brick. The Special Master, clinging to his frigid perch on the last semi's roof, learned to dread the violent ride through asphalt and to prefer the simplicity and all-American straightforwardness of a good, dry, well-packed stretch of gravel.

Not all the gravel was dry and well-packed, however. As they entered Kiddsylvania, the tumbleweeds and sand dunes of Assenisippia and Ohio gave way to rolling hills and flowing rainwater cutting gullies right across the highway. A brutal freezing rain began pounded the convoy, lashing the Master at forty miles per hour.

Bam! Bam! Bam! Shock absorbers were a known technology to Americans but had not really caught on everywhere. As these trucks were appropriated (i.e., stolen) from Sylvaniopolis, they were built especially well. The bumps that should have broken an axle were merely bone-jarring.

The Master slid across the wet ice on the roof as it tipped left, then right. There was no place to get a grip.

"Low Bridge Clearance 13 ft 4 in" said a sign. Signs on this road only imperfectly correlated with reality. He had passed about a dozen

"Work Zone" signs since leaving Elkhart and not once had he seen work. Still, a clearance of 13' 4" was too low; he had better not be on the roof when—

They rounded a corner and there was the overpass, fifty feet away.

The Master rolled, terrified, to the back. The crumbly concrete bridge with its exposed rebar swooped upon him, sweeping him along like a cruel broom.

The Master rolled right off the end of the trailer. He flailed with all four appendages and his hand caught the handle of the door.

His weight on the handle bent it down and the rod that latched the door bent out in a U shape. The overpass flew past above him and choking dust swirled in the semi's wake. The door popped open and the Master rode it like a bucking bronco.

The door's rusty hinges groaned and the prisoners within the trailer shrieked. The Master saw fingers reach around the edge of the door. As the prisoners pulled the door shut, he swung himself around its edge. The prisoners shrieked a second time at the sight of his grim visage and frozen hair. One had the sense to grab the billowing sleeves of his robe and pull him in.

He fell on the floor in a heap. The latch on the door was ruined now, thanks to him, and the door banged rhythmically in the wind. He didn't see how it was done but somebody used an old sneaker wedged into the crack between the doors to keep the door still, mostly shut.

The air in that place was foul. One corner of the trailer had been designated a toilet. The open door let in the wind and wet, but it also relieved the stink.

"I can't believe it—we caught ourselves a Black!"

"Let's kill him!"

"No! We'll use him as a hostage!"

The Master held up a patient hand and waited for the arguing to die down. "Look at my face. I'm just like you. I'm a prisoner too."

"Scrap you; why have *we* been pinched?"

The Master could not see why they should not hear the real dope.

"The high priest is reinstating human sacrifice—"

The uproar consisted of a mix of terror and scoffing which resolved into arguing and took a while to settle down.

"—human sacrifice, I'm telling you, with the full support of the Chief Justice. You're the first victims."

More shouting. The back door worked loose from its shoe wedge and it flopped about. The blast elicited a round of curses and somebody was forced to volunteer another sneaker as a door stop. Then the prisoners resumed arguing among themselves.

"Human sacrifice? Nobody believes in that stuff anymore!"

"Then why were we pinched?"

"Yeah, tell us that, Mr. Black. Why were we—out of all people—singled out?"

"I don't know. But—"

Cries of contempt at his ignorance interrupted him.

"I don't know, *exactly*, but look at yourselves. Haven't you noticed—"

"Yeah, we all look alike."

"Same age, face, hair—"

"Yeah. So tell us, Mr. Black: why does the Chief Justice want everyone who looks like us?"

"Well, many of my fellow clerks look like me too, and the Chief intends to sacrifice them. But..."

"Yes?" A mob of identical faces leaned in, eager.

"...but...I don't know any more than that."

The prisoners' reaction was a kind of animal growl. Some moved and seconded a reconsideration of the previously tabled motion to kill the Master. A raucous debate ensued. It was not clear what the division of the house would be, were the question to be called.

"Hey, hey!" The Master shouted them down. "I opened the door for you, didn't I? We can crawl out the back and escape."

"Maybe you enjoy hanging off that door. I prefer to live."

"We're gonna die anyway."

"If you believe Blackie there. I *don't.*"

"Look," said the Master, "I'll volunteer for the most dangerous job. I'll crawl back out and up onto the roof. From there, I'll drop down onto the cab and distract the driver. When he stops, you all jump out and rush the cab. They've got guns, but the whole crowd of you can overpower—"

"Ah! See that? He's giving us the 'least' dangerous job."

They laughed their bitter heads off. The Master recalled that, even in an orphanage, there are degrees of loneliness.

"Okay, look. We can simply wait until the truck stops. It's got to stop eventually. When that happens, we run out the back and disperse. I'll figure out some meeting point. When they give up hunting us, you can join me and we'll go—"

"Wait a minute, Blackie. Who died and made you sheriff?"

"I have training in hand-to-hand combat. Who else here does?"

The one who was calling him "Blackie" made a rude gesture but no one said a word.

"Well, then. We'll look for a barn—no, that's not specific enough. We'll gather at the nearest town, around after midnight, at, um—"

The light got dimmer and the roar of the tires increased threefold.

"We're in a tunnel!" The Master had no clear idea what to do, but he smelled opportunity. He pushed open the door and leaped outward to swing on it. He jerked up and down, trying to tear the hinges off. It wasn't clear in his mind how he would survive if they broke free.

The tunnel was narrow. The door swung out and bricks scraped the Master's back, taking a bit of his robe with them. This was crazy.

The Master hung on the bent latching rod, hoping it would bend some more. It did, easily—a little too easily. The rod slid out of its top bracket and the whole blivet bent back. He flipped over and hung on with his head inches from the ground.

In the midst of the terror and confusion, in the murk of the tunnel, the Master thought he saw something impossible: a man on a motorized bicycle, racing up the tunnel, reaching out with a helping hand. The man's entire head was covered with a devilish, open-beaked raven mask.

The Master had lost his ever-loving mind.

"Help!"

Even a crowd as hostile as the prisoners could not ignore that scream. Hands pulled the door around and other hands pulled him up on his latching rod.

They dragged him inside. The semi emerged from the tunnel and everything was brighter again. He stood and looked out, but whatever he had seen—if it was even real—was gone. As his eyes scanned the barren landscape, his right hand gripped the cold, twisted latching rod.

Nixon Autobiography

Chapter 23, "Another Disaster" of the unpublished *Memoirs* (Second Draft) of Richard Nixon

Crows are not men. Perhaps, if months had been available, the president could have got what she wanted—a "crow corps", by which our forces could fly up the coast.

President Wilson would not spend months. She gave our boys mere hours to master the birds.

When the boys failed to do so, she punished them cruelly. And, as sure as night follows day, the boys passed that cruelty on to the birds.

The birds did not like it. Not one bit.

I have said the crows' reasoning power is limited, but when it comes to revenge, they are clever enough. The boys took to whacking the birds with sticks to make the taxis go, so the birds simply dropped the taxis. Seeing a few of their fellows killed that way, the boys wised up and attacked the birds on the ground. The birds flew away. They returned when offered food, however and the boys whacked them when they came close. When the birds flew away again, the boys threw rocks at them.

I am not known for my charm, but even I could see this approach would fail.

How they communicate, I do not know, but the crows came to a collective decision. In every location, the crows responded as one.

The crows dive-bombed the boys and pooped in their eyes, ears and mouths. Their accuracy was astonishing.

Wilson and I saw it happen from inside her headquarters, a hardware store in Chapel Hill. We were safe, but the rest were vulnerable. Every single soldier, from general to buck private, was defiled.

When they had completed the work, the crows retreated to high branches and waited. I made sure Wilson stayed safe inside her headquarters.

The next day, our boys woke up swollen, feverish, pockmarked, and blind.

If you wish to know the full measure of horror this world can offer, spend an hour watching a crowd of men mill about, far from home, newly blind and helpless. Panic, rage, and piteous cries for help—if you have any sense of fellow-feeling, try to imagine it. And over all, with silent and unblinking stares too heartless for gloating, presided the crows. The crows! If God grant me but one wish, let those devils burn in the fires of perdition forever.

What happened next is not my fault. If it were up to me, I would not have abandoned the army. I would have got those boys home, or died trying.

The boys turned on us. The army turned into a mob. When they found, with groping hands, the headquarters, they attacked us, shattering the windows and cutting themselves bloody as they crawled in.

I got Wilson out the back door. We avoided the men, ducking and dodging their waving arms until we got to a truck. All the time the crows watched us, their heads twitching about as crows' heads do. For some reason they did not attempt to poop-bomb us. Their bowels must have been empty.

Wilson ordered me to drive to where the power suits were parked. I had no counter-plan, so I obeyed.

The place was abandoned. The power suits stood in ranks, virile, yet stupidly inert. The undying fires of their atomic cores burned uselessly.

Wilson climbed the ladder on the side of the nearest power suit and popped the hatch open. The running lights lit in sequence, starting at the head and running down the limbs. I waited a few minutes more and saw the power suit's first movement: an awkward jerk of the head.

"So that's how..." boomed Wilson's voice. She had belted herself into the cockpit and put on the headset. Its microphone amplified her voice a thousand times.

She could speak, and likely see and hear too, via the machine. She was teaching herself the controls.

The power suit's right arm rose, under Wilson's command. The arm lowered, then rose again. After a few false starts involving the bending of fingers and even the wiggling of the machine's huge toes, Wilson put the right hand on the ground, palm up, right in front of me.

"Get on," boomed the order.

When thirty feet of atom-powered armor commands you, you obey.

Her hand lifted me in fits and starts to the top of the next power suit in line. Mimicking her, I popped open the hatch and got in the monster.

I really have to hand it to our Haitian engineers. The fit and finish on these suits is marvelous. The armor is hard and polished and practically invulnerable to any weapon the Americans possessed.

It was a testament to our advanced Haitian civilization, but also to the president's willpower. Unlike the *Vancouver*-class ships, these power suits were her pet project.

I sat in the cockpit, simply admiring the surfaces around me. The seat was upholstered with fine black calf's skin. Arm and leg wraps opened as I sat down and enveloped my limbs. Moments after arriving, the thing fit me like an old shoe. A headset lowered down upon my head and immediately my eyes, ears and even nose were flooded with information. I could smell the enemy, miles away. I could feel atom power pulsing in my loins. I could taste the terrain beneath my feet. I was born anew as a god. Nothing would gainsay me.

Nothing but myself. I moved my thumb and the arm of the power suit swung up wildly, smacking its own head with incredible violence. My headset communicated the event to me in the form of pain to my temple.

By trial and error Wilson and I gained control of our heads and arms, and practiced ever more fluid and precise movements. The hours flew by. We gave no thought to our bodily needs, but our suits did, forcing food and drink upon us like a hovering mother and carrying away our bodily wastes with efficiency. The boundary between body and suit dissolved. I was no longer Richard Nixon, a balding and pointy-nosed man; I was a thirty-foot titan of metal and atom energy.

I glanced at President Wilson, and I was astounded to see the face of her suit reshaping itself. It was becoming an idealized metal effigy, a beautiful golden mask, of Mary Wilson herself.

It was a surreal day, unlike any I have ever known. Wilson and I moved our arms, playing a game of mirror, then charades. We played patty cake, and the field echoed with the clang of heavy metal hands slapping together.

(Words fail. Only a Shakespeare or an Aeschylus could adequately describe the tragicomedy—two insane atom-powered robots reduced to childish games while our comrades wandered, helpless and dying.)

We got control of our legs and we danced. We waltzed, we did the foxtrot, and we did the eastern swing. I, the old backslider, taught an elderly Puritan the popular Quaker dances.

The reader must regard me with horror. I will not try to justify myself. I don't expect the reader to understand.

When night fell, we slept, side by side on the ground, and in the morning, we rose and resumed our training immediately. For me, there was nothing else to do.

Wilson discovered a hatch in her side that opened on a storage compartment. She was excessively pleased by it. She still had her "casket" with her, a strange, futuristic beveled box of polished metal that never left her side. I had thought she would have to leave it behind, but no—she gently slid it into the compartment and closed the hatch tight.

Late that second day, the president discovered how to control the movement of the atom power plant. The huge box rode on four gigantic metal treads, and the President set it rolling north.

That's when it became clear to me Wilson's new plan. She wanted the two of us to march to the capital in the suits. My heart sank.

We had to ditch the other two power suits, the empty ones attached to our plant. I had learned how to fire a blast of hot blue energy out of my head cannon with three quick blinks of the right eye. (The first time I tried it, a curious cow died an instant, incandescent death.) I used the "plasma", as it is called, to sever the umbilici. The heat cauterized the wound, so to speak, but a bit of glowing yellow-green atom ichor leaked out, killing the grass instantly wherever it fell. I am told the stuff is very dangerous, but the armor protected me.

We marched north. The suits were unstoppable, but not fast. We made only 20-25 miles per day.

I was glad at least that there was little fighting. Many of the Americans fled before us. Many more astonished us by bowing down and worshiping us like the filthy pagans they were. Those few who put up a fight were armed with shotguns and rifles and these were as toys against us. Occasionally the President would transform one of these farmer-militiamen into a patch of soot with a single plasma blast. These attacks seemed arbitrary.

We left North Cibinesis and entered Alexandria. Here, finally, our diligence faltered, and I learned that Wilson's policy was, if anything, too merciful.

We stopped at dusk and lay side by side. I could only guess at that point what I looked like, but her face and curvaceous armor was the most beautiful physical form I have ever beheld—a platonic ideal. I touched her face and contemplated its perfection, and she did the same to mine.

I felt for her every kind of love described by the sages of old: Dante's love for the girl Beatrice; Damon's love for his friend Pythias; David's love for his son Absalom.

I dared to ask the question tormenting me for ages. "Mary," I said, fumbling for words, "whatever revenge you want, it's not—I mean, are you sure this is *worth* it?"

She said, "Forgiveness, you mean?"

I nodded my great metal head.

Her reply astonished me: "If only such a thing existed in this world!"

We fell into an exhausted sleep. We set no watch.

Someone piled dynamite against a tread of the power plant. We awoke to an explosion and alarms ringing in our earphones.

When the air cleared, we saw the damaged tread. The dynamite could not break it, but it had bent enough that it would not turn. I thought we were stuck.

The president thought no such thing. She spent hours trying to bend the tread back with her mighty arms. Abandoning that idea, she used the plasma like a welder to cut the tread right off. That doomed the plant to turn in circles. Wilson kept it straight by pulling on her umbilicus, and so long as she did that, progress could be made.

We were on a death march. It was a *via dolorosa,* a Sisyphean nightmare with many lurching steps and halts as our umbilici jerked us back. We made one or two miles per day. It was Marsyas under Apollo's knife. It was crucifixion.

I did not suggest giving up. Small talk was unthinkable. Wilson never mentioned our purpose, or the odds, or our dead soldiers. The occasional terse command was her only speech.

The U.S. army never appeared. Opposition was disorganized. Most natives seemed happy to risk death for the chance to look reverently at our faces. I was living a bizarre nightmare.

We came to a small lake in Alexandria and stopped for the night. At sunrise, I awoke. It was one of those mornings where the air is dead still and the world feels small and enclosed, like a snow globe. My mind was clear and pure.

The surface of the lake reflected the light of the dawn like a perfect mirror. The universe was silent and placid, offering me neither condemnation nor forgiveness. I was Alone.

I bent over to look down into the water. I saw my face.

I have since learned the purpose behind these beautiful faces. Researchers in the Hexagon told me a dehumanized enemy is easier to kill. Faceless, monstrous robots would inspire hatred and blood lust. This suit assumes a beautiful, godlike face to soften the enemy. One does not harm what one adores.

The face I was looking at was a Richard Nixon I had never seen before. It transformed me into a golden Apollo with a flowing mane of silver. The eyes of RN looked out with childlike innocence and the wisdom of the Ancient of Days. I was a holy being.

It was love at first sight. I know it sounds ridiculous but it is true.

I began to weep. A horrible pity came over me, a pity for the man behind the mask, the man who would never be equal to the one into whose magnificent eyes I looked. I wept and wept and could not stop.

The suit, following its design, wept with me. Great shining drops fell from its eyes and rippled the perfect surface of the lake. The tears were diamonds. Literally diamonds. I caught a few in my great armored fingers and marveled at these flawless gems, each one worth a fortune. If someone reading these words went and found that lake, he could get rich.

President Wilson woke and I wiped my eyes. If she saw my tears, she showed no interest. She busied herself caring for her precious "casket", taking it out and brushing nonexistent dust off of it, and the awkward moment passed.

January came and went. February came and we limped to the bank of the Potomac River. On the far side, we saw the capital. I felt a strange disappointment.

There was a single bridge across the river, and I could not believe it. It was made of wood, a crooked and splintery thing. I wondered if it could hold up the weight of an ox cart, let alone our suits and their massive atom power plant. We simply stood there for a while, assessing the thing. Time was not on our side, though, as organized resistance was gathering at last. Wilson decided we had to risk the bridge.

CHAPTER FORTY-TWO

Trailer Door

"All right, here's the plan."

The prisoners were listening to the Master. Well, half-listening. The important lesson of the last few minutes was that the best way to obligate hostile men is to force *them* to help *you*.

"First, I'll pick for us some prominent landmark. When the plan succeeds—"

"*If* the plan succeeds."

"No, *Brownie*," said the Master, pointing with his metal rod, "I mean *when* the plan succeeds, we'll flee the scene of the accident and disperse. No later than midnight tonight, we'll gather at the meeting place, and I'll instruct you as to how we will get to the capital undetected—"

"See, there's so many problems right there, I hardly know where to begin." It was the man the Master had called "Brownie." "Your potty plan's not going to work. Even if it does, you're not going to lead us and we're not going to follow. We sure as Satan don't want to go to the capital. I'm saying, it's every man for hisself—"

"We've *got* to go to the capital. Other prisoners, men just like you, from every city in the country, are being taken to the capital as we speak. We are their only hope—"

"Then they got no hope."

"We have to *try*."

"Let's do it the democratic way. All in favor of every man for hisself, say aye!"

"Aye!"

The motion carried.

"See, Blackie? This is how it goes when the likes of you don't have the power. The people decide how they like it, and you just have to live with it."

The Master was finding his impotence singularly unpleasant.

"All right then," he said, his voice feeling tight and dry. "I'll save your sorry hides and if you're not grateful, that's your beeswax." He went to the doorway, saw a brazen pentagram atop the dome of a dilapidated rural Satanist temple set on a pretty round hill in the distance. "I'll stop this truck, and those who want can meet me at that temple, right there, at midnight tonight. The rest of you can go to Heaven!"

There was no reason to hesitate. The Master swung himself up onto the roof of the trailer. One man at least was helpful and handed the rod up to him.

The Master crawled forward on the roof, glad that it had stopped raining and a bit of sunshine had cleared the ice. He dropped down upon the roof of the cab. The drivers certainly heard the sound, but stealth was no longer an issue. He swung the rod down hard against the windshield.

The windshield shattered on the first blow and the jagged shards of glass flew into the faces of the screaming men.

The Master tossed the rod aside and slid through the opening, legs first. He was too much in a hurry to mind the sharp edges of glass.

He curled up like a ball of yarn between the two men. The passenger, half-blinded by glass, got his pistol out. The Master dispatched the man with one blow of his elbow. The driver was less incapacitated, but had his driving to mind, so the Master held him off with his left hand while he opened the passenger door with his other. He threw his shoulder and the passenger fell out of the cab with a shriek.

The Master now had both hands to work on the driver. He wondered if tossing the rod was a good idea.

He saw the sign: "Low Clearance 12 ft. 10 in." He looked at the overpass drawing near. It was crumbly and sagged in the middle—probably less than 12 feet. The Master had an inspiration.

The driver saw the overpass and tried to brake. The Master stamped his foot down on the accelerator. The speedo indicated a harrowing 55 miles per hour.

The Master grabbed the wheel and swerved the semi toward the lowest point of the overpass' inverted arch. The driver howled in fear.

There was no stopping the semi now. The Master howled too.

Baaaang!

The roof of the trailer caught the overpass. The Master hit the dash. He was vaguely aware of a cargo of live bodies shifting violently in the back.

The tractor, having a lower roof, missed the overpass completely. It's linkage to the trailer tore apart with a metallic scream. The tractor lumbered on at reduced speed, leaving behind a trailer wedged into place.

The Master and the driver, bruised and bloody, fought for consciousness and the steering wheel. The tractor weaved over the road even as the drivers of the semis ahead, finally aware that something was terribly amiss, braked to a halt. The driver and the Master drove their tractor into the ditch. They spilled from the cab as one being, a self-flagellating beast with four limbs.

Clerks came with guns drawn. The Master untangled himself and leaped to his feet. Out of the corner of his eye he saw Browns, injured but mobile, staggering from the trailer a quarter of a mile back and heading for the hills.

The Master was surrounded and outnumbered. As he stood there, eyes darting about for a means of escape, a man on a motorized bicycle and wearing a raven mask emerged from behind the wrecked trailer. He drove past the Master, quite slow, appraising the situation but not stopping. The wind had set the mask slightly askew and from out of one of the eye holes strung an impossibly long eyebrow hair. Almost before the Master could understand what he was seeing, the motorized bicycle was gone.

"Stick 'em up," ordered a gun-toting clerk.

The Master raised his hands. They were a bloody mess from the broken glass.

Nixon Autobiography

Chapter 24, "Final Disaster", of the unpublished *Memoirs* (Second Draft) of Richard Nixon

I was careless and fired at a platoon of men who stood at the far end of the bridge. I think, in retrospect, they were making a furtive attempt to set fire to the bridge. I made up for them in spades. I draped them in white hot plasma and sent them to their Lord in Hell. In the process, I started an inferno.

"Come on!" shouted the President. We pulled with all our skill. The bridge shook beneath us. We waded into the fire, unharmed. We raced against the flames, and lost. We broke through the burning wood and tumbled head over heels into the river.

We settled into the mud. I confess I panicked. Wilson and I could still communicate underwater. When she heard me ask how to eject from the cockpit, she addressed me with a cold contempt that calmed me.

"We have come this far. We will continue!"

Wilson fired her plasma weapon just to see what would happen. The water boiled furiously and the agitated water freed my legs. I crawled forward, then returned the favor, aiding her escape.

The umbilici were long enough so we could reach the retaining wall on the far bank. I climbed to the top and hauled myself out of the water. I gasped, only then noticing I had been pointlessly holding my breath.

President Wilson joined me. We set our heels on the stout concrete wall and pulled on our umbilici. The powerful motors in the arms and legs of our suits were driven to extremes. The suit's feedback systems tortured our muscles with pain as we exceeded the suits' design limits. Even so, the suits did what we asked them to do. We pulled the dead weight of the power plant right out of the water and onto the edge of the wall. The power plant tipped over the edge and crashed upon us.

Our suits did not escape unscathed. For a time it looked as though we might have survived our swim only to be trapped under our own equipment.

President Wilson's legs were broken beyond repair, but her arms were able to lift the power plant a few feet. My arms were useless, one being torn out of its socket and the other crushed, but I could kick with my legs and I got myself free. I knelt down and propped up the power plant with my head. President Wilson caught hold of my umbilicus and pulled herself out. I let the power plant fall back down with a resounding crash.

"Come here," Wilson said.

I bent over her and she put her arms around my neck. I stood up with her hanging on me, her useless legs dangling. The childlike quality of the gesture moved me almost to diamonds. We were face to face but I could not look at her.

"Carry me, my darling," she said to me, choked with an emotion I dared not acknowledge. "Just a few blocks. Set me down at the Supreme Court building, and your work will be done, good and faithful servant."

Step by ponderous step, I marched with my war bride about my neck and the plant dragging behind me. The motors rasped in protest and the feedback to my legs was a scream of pain, a punishment for the implacable will which compelled them forward.

The enemy had organized at last. These soldiers were wearing black, most of them in ridiculous body stockings fitting snug from armpit to calf. I had to look twice to assure myself they were men.

The attacks against us redoubled but their bullets could not have been more irrelevant. Warriors approached with visors pulled low. Their deaths would have sat easy on my conscience, but my plasma gun had been ripped off my head.

My on-board map directed me through the streets. It was a technology, like so much else around me, invented expressly for the suit. It displayed a map on a televisor with my present location at the center, updating as I moved. It was just one of the many examples of the great good that could have come about if Wilson's great gifts had been devoted toward wholesome ends.

The stink of burnt rubber filled the cockpit as my suit shuffled painfully down an avenue. On my left was the dome of the Capitol building, with an absurd statue at the top, that of a hand making an obscene gesture. I took it personally. On my right, clearly indicated on the televisor, was the columned portico of the Supreme Court.

I was beyond all sense or sanity. I trudged on, caring nothing of the ordnance that flew about me. To my right, some fools had pushed an old fashioned brass cannon into the street. I suppose they pulled it out of a museum.

An officer mouthed an inaudible command and the cannon fired. The cannonball flew by, missing my cockpit by inches. The ball smashed into their Capitol building, leaving a gaping hole in the wall. The cannon itself shattered, killing the crew that manned it. I was an indifferent observer to this little drama.

My suit was bent over into a crouch as it inched along. My enemies were more numerous, but mostly unarmed. Angry fists were the worst they could deploy against me.

My lack of offensive weaponry emboldened them. Like a pack of curs, they struck at my suit's metal legs with whatever was nifty: umbrellas, brooms, and the like. Again, the thought came to me that this was my *via dolorosa* but the comparison was too obscene even for an old reprobate like me.

"Just a little more. That's right, sister, you can do it," whispered the President. "I always knew you'd come back to me." The woman's madness had reached its full measure.

I crossed the plaza of the Supreme Court and paused before its steps. The crowd fell back as three impressive figures emerged from the court, each wearing a luxurious yet vaguely sinister robe—like something a vampire would wear to a graduation. The man on the left was a sour-faced elder sporting the most ghastly eyebrow I have ever seen. The man in the middle looked as sick and broken-down as I felt. The man on the right was about my age, but more athletic, his thick, glossy hair radiating vigor and his face displaying an appealing optimism despite his stern gaze.

They stood there, armed only with a flagpole, an electric cattle prod, and a rope. This last the younger man twirled, cowboy style, in a hypnotizing rhythm. To complete this tableau of insanity, there stood next to me a great scaffold with dozens of victims guarded by men in bright red.

I staggered halfway up the steps. President Wilson let go of my neck and slid down.

"Thank you, Dick," she said. "You may go now. I'll take it from here."

I stood there dumbly, unable to understand what I should do next.

A whole company of men came and stood at the edges of the plaza, in black or white or brown. A moment arrived where the whole company stood still. After all my struggle to arrive at this place, I had no idea what would happen next.

President Wilson's suit powered down and its running lights went dark. Its hatch popped open.

President Wilson, looking older than her 66 years, unbuckled herself and slid down to the pavement. She pulled a pistol out of her belt as she faced the enemy.

Obedient to the last, I turned my suit around. My long, horrible *Via Dolorosa Parte Seconda* back to Haiti is worthy of a separate volume. This account of the war, however, must end as it began: with Mary Wilson. I cannot say what her fate was, because I did not witness it. But let me be perfectly clear: when I left her, she was still very much alive.

Here the author put down his pen. Of the events inside the Supreme Court building, or his long, harrowing journey back to Haiti, he never wrote a word.

It is believed this writing was abandoned shortly before the start of the 19th Great Awakening during the administration of President Billy Graham.

The last surviving copy of this document was an audio recording, on a golden LP phonograph record. In a strange and deeply ironic gesture, the author, by then a famous evangelist, placed the record surreptitiously aboard the space probe Voyager in place of the one intended, a recorded greeting by President Graham to space aliens. As of this date (910372 Anno Domini) it remains undiscovered and unheard by any sentient being in the universe.

PART THE TENTH: 1946

CHAPTER FORTY-THREE

Back to the Capital

They tied him up, good and tight, and tossed him into the corner of the Chief's semi. For good measure, they stuffed his mouth with a strip of cloth torn from his own robe. What were they afraid he might possibly say?

He was laid directly on the metal bed with nothing to cushion his head. Every bump in the road was communicated like some esoteric telegraph code directly to his skull. The dull hours passed, with little conversation beyond the Chief Justice calling for whiskey. The Master nursed a headache that grew to blot out every thought of hope or fear.

He slept, and woke. A clerk gave him some water. The clerks whispered over their own petty disputes as the Chief Justice himself napped. The Master listened, hearing nothing, thinking nothing, caring nothing. He struggled, for the tenth time, against his inescapable bonds. The semi stopped for fuel and a change of drivers. The Master slept again.

Come early morning of the next day, the miserable journey ended. The door opened and the clerks got the Chief out. Hard drinking and a shortage of sleep had put the Chief into almost a comatose state. The

Master wondered what orders the clerks had been given regarding himself, and what liberties they might take with them. His old illusions were gone: they hated him. They had always hated him.

They unloaded the semi. The Master was the last of the baggage to be removed. Two clerks picked him up like a sack of lima beans and carried him out.

He gasped. Hundreds of manacled prisoners, all look-alikes, stood in a ragged line with heads bent down and feet hobbled as they waited to be herded into the dungeon of the court building. They alternately moaned and cried in fear. The clerks guarding them were understaffed, and testy for it. The Master remembered: so many clerks were missing—the entire Cohort of '29.

In the plaza, carpenters busied themselves nailing lumber into...what was it? Some kind of unholy framework which stark silhouette spelled out "execution" against the blue. It was all strangling ropes and decapitating blades—an instrument of mass death, with a bonfire to finish it all off. The Master's moans joined those of the prisoners.

He was not required to wait in line. Clerks walked him past his fellow prisoners through halls and down many steps to where the dungeons were. Others were crammed in at eight to a cell, but he was locked up alone, out of sight and sound of the others. He was flattered; they considered him dangerous.

At least he could relieve himself and eat like a human being again. In the quiet, his throbbing brain could think.

He was cut off from the bustle and business of the court and that was its own kind of torture. He could tell from faint vibrations of distant violence that something was up—something big. That knowledge comforted him not at all.

A jailer brought him food. That meant it was supper time. He said, "I want to talk to the Chief," but the man, a sullen old brown, not even a clerk, did not grant him the courtesy of a reply.

This cell could not hold a prisoner, not for any stretch of time, if the prisoner was the least bit resourceful. There was even a dirt floor! The Master could dig his way out, if they let him live that long.

The place was damp and not quite warm. The Master paced, maneuvering around the sink, piss bucket, and cot.

The light was low and never varied, but enough time passed that he was sure it was night. He sat. He knew sleep was the one useful accomplishment allowed him, and his head still throbbed, but he was reluctant to lie down. The sooner he slept, the sooner he would wake and have to decide how to spend his waking hours.

He started awake. Had he been sleeping?

A shape, blacker than the shadows, stood before him. It rotated to reveal a pale face.

CHAPTER FORTY-FOUR

Talk to the Hand

"**B**onsoir!"

"Ah!"

The Master's sphincter's already dodgy maintenance of its perimeter very nearly experienced catastrophic compromise at the sight of this foreign apparition—but it was only Learned Hand.

Justice Learned Hand! The old black was standing before him, regarding him with tenderness alloyed with contempt.

"What the Limbo akimbo are you doing here?"

"I came to see you."

The Master sat up. His head no longer throbbed; he could hear his own thoughts over the ache.

"Just like that: you came to see me."

"Oh yes. I come and go as I please."

"You were locked up—"

"Ineptly. The knots were grannies. The lid on my cage was never bolted down. I found out the first day they put me there. I've taken French leave many times."

"You're lying. That doesn't make... Why—?"

"Yes, I'm lying. I never left my cell once. I'm still there, locked up." Justice Hand's eyebrow slanted ironically.

"No, but you—" The Master's mind was not so clear after all. "Well...it's the whole...*dishonesty*—"

That tore it. Hand roared, slapping his knee.

He caught his breath as the echoes settled. "Did you ever consider that your precious Chief Justice is not very bright?"

Whatever pity was due Hand evaporated. But the old justice was still speaking, the old caginess gone.

"He's the type I hate most: never so certain of himself as when he's being a complete chucklehead. He fell into a regular schedule for our torture sessions. Once a week—like clockwork! You should have called him on that. I was able to take trips out of the capital. I've been to Canada—"

"Bull hockey! You always came back? Back to your cage? To your beatings?"

Hand was sneering now. "That was no cage and those were no beatings."

"Well, I'm glad for you." The Master pointed at the door. "Now, get the Heaven out of here."

Hand leaned against the wall. Bricks slid loose and crumbly mortar trickled onto the ground.

"I've started this all wrong." Hand dusted himself off self-consciously. "See, I know things. I'm pretty sure you know things. Let's be friends—put our heads together. *Pari passu.*"

"I'd rather stay ignorant, if it hurts you."

"Come on. We're natural allies. We have a common enemy."

Oh great. Logic.

"I've been prowling around, eavesdropping. I found these secret tunnels, all over this place—you know about them?"

The Master said nothing. Hand would have to do better.

"The latest news is not good. The Chief has terrible plans—"

"Human sacrifice. By the Church."

The Master had not planned on blurting that out.

"Ah!" Hand's eyebrow was elated, and the Master hated it all the more. "See, it works. We're swapping dope."

The Master stood, towering over Hand.

"Give me more, and we'll see how far this goes."

"That's the spirit! As I said, I've been to Canada, several times. Can you guess what I was looking for?"

"Well, I'm Canadian—"

"Bingo! I wanted to prove something, something about you—"

"If I was born there."

"Yes! Because—"

"Because the Chief suspected I was a Natural Born Citizen."

"You know! You know all about it! You're not as dumb as everyone says."

"Except—"

No. Slow down. Do not give away the most valuable prize. Sell it dearly.

"I already know about you and your Vicers."

Hand's eyebrow shook like a pom pom as a shock wave passed through it.

"Very clever. Yes, I'm building a movement. However, that tells me nothing new. Your turn: give me something *good*.

"I know...something about Natural Born Citizens. But!" He paused. "You're going to have to give me something first. Something big."

"What is this crap? Let's see..."

The hunt was on, and Hand was having a blast. The Master was in deep danger of liking the old rascal.

"You knew, didn't you, the Chief and I are old friends? Grew up on a farm together?"

That irrelevance did not deserve a reply.

"I was the raven breeder. He was the raven trainer. It was a hobby for me; for him it was all business. A stroke of genius it was, really; he *invented* raven taxis. But without my birds, the whole project would have never—" Hand giggled. "—got off the ground."

The Master was not amused. He wanted something *useful*.

"There's this: something that happened before you came to the Court, before Orlando even."

Hand's voice dropped to a whisper.

"The previous Special Master disappeared. Simply went AWOL. For four years. Did you know that?"

"You mean, before he disappeared for good?"

"Right."

Nope, didn't know that.

"The Chief was beside himself. Once he became Chief Justice, he made finding the Special Master the top priority of government. There were search parties. Anybody suspected of helping the Special Master was questioned. It got brutal—quite the production. They finally found him, hiding. There was this cabin in the woods—"

"By the Finger Lakes."

"The Devil—you know the place!"

"The Chief took me there, just before my promotion."

"Yes! What happened?"

"There was an old man living there. The old Special Master was there too, but arrived too late. Too late! The Chief was very interested in what I would do. Watching me like a hawk. I now think—"

"Yes?"

"I think he wanted to see if I recognized the place."

"And did you?"

Hand had the same look the Chief had, those years ago when he gave the order to kill. A predator's anticipation.

"No." Hand's eyebrow slumped, disappointed. "The Chief ordered me to kill the old man who lived there—"

"And you did it? You killed him."

"Yes."

"Ah."

"It was all a test. The Chief—and the old Master—both wanted to know if I had—"

"Been born there."

"Yes. Born there."

"And you passed the test. Or failed, depending on how you look at it."

"Yes."

"And combine what you said about the cabin with what I said about the Special Master's disappearance. It can only mean that—"

"The Special Master had a son."

"Bingo."

Hand shook his head, letting this new knowledge settle.

He continued. "I'm guessing the Master—the old Master—probably went to Canada. Wherever it was, he found a woman—maybe married her! That happens—but anyway, for sure they had a child. For some reason, that child was raised in New Gehenna, not Ontario. The mother didn't stick around. Did she die? Or leave him? We don't know. And the biggest question of all—"

"Which country was the child born in?"

"Bing. Go." Hand's eyebrow was twisting itself into knots. "If that kid was born in that cabin, on U.S. soil—"

"A natural born citizen."

"Yes! And a threat to the Chief."

"A mortal threat."

"Yes."

Hand picked at a spot in the wall, releasing a tiny avalanche of the powdery mortar. He spoke to himself, with a kind of grim amusement.

"And so, the Master, having been dragged back to the capital city, lost contact with his son. The kid was a toddler at the time, so years go by and the Master can't recognize the kid anymore. But, he has an idea what the kid would look like, so, having regained the trust of the Chief, gets permission to leave the capital and starts roaming the northern states. His excuse is, he's recruiting promising young men to clerkships."

His eyes flashed as he looked straight at the Master. "But his real motive is to find his lost son!"

"And that explains why all my cohort looks the same. And why the Chief's prisoners all look the same. The Chief is searching for the same person."

"But the Chief doesn't need to find him. He just wants him dead. He can afford to be indiscriminate."

"Kill them all, and let Satan sort them out."

Hand giggled. What was wrong with the old goat? This was not a joke. This was a *crime*.

"What I don't understand... Look at you: your face; your voice; even your mannerisms. You came from the mines of New Gehenna, right? You are the perfect candidate. You're him. You're *him*. Are you absolutely certain you did not recognize that cabin?"

"I didn't recognize the cabin, or the old man who lived there. But—"

Hand's eyebrow stood erect. "But? *But?*" Hand clapped a liver-spotted hand over his mouth. "Oh. My. Satan."

This was the Master's priceless coin; he was now committed to spending it.

"Based on what Congressman Flood said—"

"Flood!"

"—and clues in the painting—"

"The painting! Yes!"

"I returned to the cabin. I found a hidden cave there, nearby in the woods. I—"

"Yes?"

"I... I recognized it."

"Hells." A gasp. All amusement was gone now.

"I lived in that cave. And the old man was a notary—"

"A notary *public!* Bouncing boggarts o' Beelzebub! You're the one. You're the *lost son.*"

"Yes."

"The Natural Born Citizen, come to overthrow the Chief."

"We can't prove that."

"But we *know* it. Shanks o' Satan! There was no other reason for the old Master to keep you hidden in New Gehenna. You must have been born there!"

The Master threw up his hands. "Well, this has been a fascinating bedtime story, but what good does it do us? I can't prove I'm a natural born citizen, so I cannot overthrow the Chief. However—"

"There's a mass murder about to be committed."

"All for nothing. And I can stop it."

The eyebrow traced a slow arc on Hand's forehead as comprehension formed in his mind. "Great Satan... No!"

"I can save all these innocent men—"

"No. That's ridiculous. You're innocent—"

"I am *not* innocent." The Master took hold of Hand's robe. "I *murdered* that old man. The man who raised me and cared for me. I killed him without hesitation."

"No..."

"He died for his kindness, not knowing why. *Not knowing why!*"

"You didn't know either!"

"I should have! I should have recognized his face."

"You were a child. You were the *victim*. The Chief—even the old Master, your father!—put you on your path. They chose your fate for you."

"Oh Satan..."

The walls of the cell were crooked.

Just like everything in this country. The mortar was crumbling and, let's be honest, the walls had not been straight or strong even on the day their bricks were laid. Everything in this hell-vomited country was wrong. Wrong! Americans could not do anything right. The incompetence and sheer snot-nosed bass-ackward mule-headed stupidity—it was the saddest thing in the world. America was a shitpit country and the Master had made it worse. He had wanted to make it better but in the end he made it worse.

Better to have never been born.

The Master wept. He slipped off the cot, unaware. He lay on the floor, able to do nothing but smite his breast.

Hand—or at least Hand's former, ironic self—was gone. In this country without women, the men had do what mothering they could. Hand sat down by the Master on the ground, drew the weeping Master to himself, and cradled him there in the cold and dirt and filth. Nothing was said. The storm took its time.

The Master composed himself. "I know what I have to do."

"Shut up."

"No! I'm determined. I'll tell the Chief I am the child from the cabin. He'll release the other prisoners."

"It won't work. They've been promised to the Master in Lunacy."

"The Master in Lunacy is *nothing*. If the Chief has no reason to kill them, they won't die."

"The Chief isn't rational anymore. He's really slipping. We can't predict—"

"I'm tired of being the Chief's puppet. I'm going to do what I'm going to do. The Chief will react however he likes."

"Think of your country! You are the natural born citizen. You have a destiny!"

"Save that for your Vicers. I'm a mindless killing machine. *That's* my destiny, and *I defy it*."

"There's one more piece of information I have. It changes everything you've said."

"Well?"

"Haiti has invaded."

Those words did not...make sense.

"The Haitian army has *landed*. In Florida, back in November. In typical American efficiency"—the ironic Hand was back, with a vengeance—"the news didn't reach the capital until this week. Fortunately, the Haitians have experienced all their usual problems, plus some new disasters they've invented just for the occasion. Still, a remnant has reached northern Alexandria, led personally by their president, Mary Wilson."

Just barely the Master suppressed his flinch. He had felt a blaze of searing fire shoot between his ears at the mention of that name: *Wilson*.

"The Chief, that old, stupid, idiotic *fool*, is only now organizing a defense. It's possible the government will be overthrown without you needing to do a thing."

"I'm not making any assumptions about that."

"Nor should you. But promise me you'll do nothing until we see how this plays out."

"I'm not promising you anything."

"Very well. Life is made up of a series of judgments on insufficient data, and if we waited to run down all our doubts, it would flow past us. So be that way; promise me nothing. But I'm telling you: don't do anything stupid."

Hand stood up. "Oh, I almost forgot. It's your turn."

"My turn?" The Master stood up too and brushed the dust off his bottom.

"*Quid pro quo.* I tell you something, you tell me something. I told you about the Haitians. So, yeah: it's your turn."

Mary Wilson.

The Master put his hands in his pocket. He felt the scrap of parchment there. His thumb traced the name as if he could feel the ink.

"I don't have anything. I've told you everything I know."

The eyebrow scowled, all suspicion. The Master knew himself to be an unpracticed liar. He made a supreme effort to relax his face, as Hand pulled loose a brick that released a shower of friable mortar.

"Very well then. Sorry about this."

With more energy than the Master could have expected, Hand lifted the brick and belted him. The last things he saw were the justice's hands catching him, and stars.

CHAPTER FORTY-FIVE

Petition

Somebody was coming, methodically working his way through the locked doors at various stations down the tunnel. The Special Master rose from the dirt. He rinsed the foulness from his mouth with brackish water from the tiny, rust-stained sink.

There were two of them, two blacks emerging from the gloom. The jailer guiding them spun the key in the lock with a practiced flip of the wrist. Into the cell stepped the Chief Justice and the biggest, beefiest clerk.

The Chief inspected the cell. He took note of the sink, the piss bucket, the filthy cot, the stonework in the walls, the rat droppings in the corners. He sniffed at the dampness. He looked back at the sputtering torch on its sconce in the tunnel, casting shadows like accusing fingers through the barred door.

"Nice place." The Chief's eyes never stopped wandering. "You've really risen in the world."

Nothing.

The Chief offered the Master some snuff. He took it, gave it a perfunctory sniff and felt his dull mind sharpened by the acrid scent.

"When I found you, you were clawing through the mines like an animal."

The Chief Justice was playing the martyr. He was acting as if this conversation was an infinitely painful task which his fine sense of duty would not permit him to avoid.

"Like a mole or something. Lower than a dog or a cat, a...*thing.*

"Have you ever met one of them—the miners? The old ones, who count themselves lucky,—lucky!—because they didn't die in a rock slide or get their arms chewed off by some machinery? Have you watched them as they tried to speak and couldn't from the black sludge clogging their lungs?"

"Have *you?*"

"Shut your *yap*! I *saved* you from all that. Pulled you out—"

"*You?* No. It was the old Special Master."

"And why he picked you, I'll never know. Worthless, ungrateful little *shit*—"

"You know exactly why he picked me. Me, and all the others. We fit a certain physical description." The Master had nothing to lose, so he said it: "It was all about the cabin, wasn't it."

"The cabin! What do you know? You know doodly-squat. It was obvious you had never been there."

Say nothing. Let the old boob talk. Maybe he'll let something slip.

"Nothing happened at the cabin. Nothing that anybody can ever prove. The old Special Master took that secret to—" The Chief caught himself. Then, with care, he said: "—to his grave."

"I wonder. Is he really dead?"

"It's been twenty years! Where is he?"

The Chief did not know. Not for sure. Interesting.

And then it was clear, as evident as a lightning bolt: Justice Learned Hand knew. He knew! That little snake held it back!

But the Chief was talking.

"You disappointed me, but I didn't come here to complain. Eh, whatever: I'm used to dealing with ingrates. If I have suffered, if I have been lain on the altar of sacrifice daily for a nation of dullards, so what? I am the Chief Justice! The one man standing between the United States and disaster. Leadership is sacrifice; I never expected any different when I agreed to take this job."

How many rivals were murdered so he could "agree" to take the job?

"I have come for one reason only. The Republic is in danger. She faces her gravest crisis yet. I am willing to cast aside my pride and dignity if it means saving this country. The question is, do you feel the same? Are you a patriot? Your country needs you."

This was not what the Master had expected.

"The Haitians have attacked. Satan knows why, but they have. The Powers of Hell have risen to destroy America's enemies as they always do, yet a small force of Haitians remains. They're attacking us with a cruel new weapon our soldiers can't stop."

By that he meant the underfed, underpaid and undertrained U.S. army had fled. The Master had asked many times for funds to restore the military but the Chief always denied him. They had sown weakness and now they reaped—

"The soldiers are ignoring my orders. For some reason, they always respected you."

"They don't respect—"

"Believe me. If *you* rallied them, they would repel this invader."

The Chief looked up, almost meeting the Master eye to eye.

"I'm offering you your life. Will you come to your country's aid?"

"Will I save your sorry ass—that's the real question you are asking."

"This is bigger than you or me!"

"Drop dead."

"Spiteful to the last! You'd rather *die* than help me."

"And why should I want to help you? But that's not even the point."

The Master let the Chief hang, confused and wary, for a moment.

"Why shouldn't I welcome these Haitians? Why shouldn't every red-blooded, freedom-loving American want them to come in and kick your ass? How could they be any worse than you, with your incompetence, your pointless cruelty, your—"

"Aargh!"

Out of the Chief's mouth came a stream of gibberish, too inarticulate for words but too complex for mere screaming. It was, perhaps, the language of Hell itself, intuited by a mind marinated for years in evil. He waved his blue-veined hands in the air, tore at his own hair, and pawed at the Special Master's robe with a flaccid grip, finding no purchase.

The beefy clerk eased the Chief aside and delivered a fist to the Master's jaw.

The Master turned his head and the blow glanced aside. Without a pump he landed a blow in the man's exposed gut. As the clerk doubled over, the Master threw his other fist against the outward-thrusting jaw. The clerk whiplashed and fell.

The jailer, with shaky hands, struggled to push open the door, but the clerk's body blocked it where it lay.

Throughout the years of the Master's service, many men had tried to lay hands upon the Chief Justice. Browns with rejected petitions, Whites with crazy plots, even clerks with personal grudges—all had attacked the Chief at one time or another with fists, knives or guns. Always the Master had foiled the plot, beaten back the attacker, caught the knife blade between his palms, or stood in the way of a pointed gun.

"Enough!" The Special Master caught the Chief Justice by his robe, lifted him up and threw him against the rusticated brickwork.

"Oof!" The Chief Justice deflated like a spent, black dirigible amid a cloud of mortar dust.

"You're over! I will not help you. Your threats or offers mean nothing."

He threw the Chief onto the cot. He went to the opposite corner of the cell, a few feet away, and sat down Indian style, his arms and legs as crossed barricades.

"You're not going to kill me?" the Chief said, his voice rasping in amazement.

"Get out."

"Wait. Wait! I'll offer you half the States. We'll divide the country. Take whichever you want. You go your way, I'll go mine."

"'The King also offered his daughter's hand in marriage'—is that how the story goes?"

"What do *you* know about *that?*" All weakness had disappeared. The Chief was roaring now, on his feet, shaking with rage. "There is no daughter! *THERE IS NO DAUGHTER!*"

The Chief pulled his robe tight about himself, and slapped the moaning clerk into awareness. The jailer got the door open at last. The Chief looked the Master square in the eye for the first time.

"You don't know *bupkis* about me or what I've done. You never did. You never will. And those who do know—you will *never find them.*"

The Chief, with his entourage of one, paraded out and down the tunnel like the Lord of Millions that he was.

The jailer slammed the door shut and spun the key and left the Master there in the dirt, angry, pathetic, and alone.

The Special Master remembered that he had intended to offer himself as a sacrifice, the one for the many. That door was closed, latched and locked. He might surrender to a monster; he would never negotiate with a weasel.

CHAPTER FORTY-SIX

Who Will Bribe the Bribers?

Well, that went completely catawampus.

The Special Master should have played that little scene with the Chief Justice different. Go along. Cooperate. Then use his freedom for...for escape, or revenge, or something.

So complete was his abnegation, he could muster no regret. His execution was no longer something he could fear, or even imagine. The Chief's helplessness was obvious to him, a hard, bright thing like quartz exposed among blasted rock. The Chief was too dependent on him—too stupid, frankly—to survive the crisis without the Master's cooperation.

The Master was done cooperating.

Had not Justice Hand come and gone as he pleased? This cell had a way out. The jailer was bribable, or the walls hid a secret tunnel.

He rolled off his cot and examined the brickwork, touching, pushing, probing. The task drove away every thought of unhappiness. Loose bricks fell away to expose only more loose bricks.

From time to time there was distant shouting, a thing unheard of in the court building. Chaos reigned outside. A booming thud, soft but profound, vibrated the cell at regular intervals. The Master made haste. He was needed.

If the secret passageway existed, it was very secret indeed. Time to talk to the jailer.

In any security system, the point of vulnerability is the human element. The Master had known from the first that bribing the jailer was the thing to try. His only hesitation was...

"Hey! You, there! Jailer!" The Master rattled his cell door.

The brown came, but he took his time. He must show the high and mighty black who was in charge. He approached at an odd pace, asymmetrical without exactly being a limp, as though each step was fraught with risk.

He had a big ring of keys on his belt that weighed him down and threatened to pull the pants right off his scrawny hips. The man looked whacked. Was drink his weakness? Maybe Hand offered him no bribe at all, but got past him while he was passed out.

"Dry up!"

The Master had stopped banging on the bars when the jailer came into sight, but the Brown's mental inertia compelled him to shout. "Yer not goin' nowhere so you just shut yer yap or yer gonna find out why."

The Master hesitated, regretful. The jailer waited, imperious. He had hobbled this far and he was not going to waste it, whether he had a reason to stay or no. He made a show of inspecting, from a distance, the Master and his cell. He confirmed the Master had in his possession no explosives, picks, shovels, backhoes, giant pet moles, or any other excavation equipment.

Still, the jailer scowled, dissatisfied. Perhaps he wanted an excuse to punish the Master. The Master wondered what form the punishment would take. No chance the jailer would come into the cell and "teach him a lesson", as the scrawny brown would be no match for him in close quarters.

"So, been working here long?"

The Master's voice cracked. He knew this gambit would fail even as he began speaking it. The jailer regarded him with cold contempt, manifestly glad for the new opportunity to loathe him.

The Master had never thought about bribes from this side of the transaction. In his position, he had received many offers; indeed, in a country like the United States, bribes were a near-daily occurrence. The Master's disadvantage was that he had been incorruptible. His only experience with bribes were the failures.

He understood it now: bribing was a kind of dance, a courtship. The swain must charm, avoiding either indifference or over-eagerness. There was a vocabulary to be learned, a patois made of the syntax of honest discourse and the semantics of corruption.

The Master should have paid attention to those offers. The whole process disgusted him. He searched his memory for a useful example. Bribers always came with the inducement in hand. The Master's situation was awkward in that respect. If he regained power, he could reward the jailer without limit, but he could regain his power only through a revolution. Revolutions were notoriously tricky to predict.

How did the bribers always put it? Always asking for a "donation" to a cause. Always talking about "gifts" and "consideration". They were always deferential to a fault, even calling him "your lordship" sometimes. Flattery wouldn't work here; the jailer would see it as weakness.

"I guess they don't pay you much."

Man, this was awkward. The jailer gave him the fisheye, but how could he not be insulted? Still, nothing to do but plow on ahead. The booming noise, sounding like giant feet stomping on the plaza, was sending trickles of dust down from the ceiling. The situation outside was building to a crisis and the Master craved to be in the thick of it.

"If I were running this place, I'd treat you better."

The jailer's sudden lunging toward the Master with arms stretched out in an embrace was not, strictly speaking, a reaction to this latest sally, and it was definitely not an indication of sympathy. What had happened is that a hefty rock had struck him violently in the back of the head.

CHAPTER FORTY-SEVEN

Showdown

The jailer slumped against the cell door. The Master, always the opportunist, grabbed the ring of keys and pulled them close as the jailer twisted to the ground, unconscious. The Master heard the pounding of approaching feet but he stayed focused on getting the jailer's belt undone and slipping the ring off it.

He looked up.

"So, *Blackie*, this where you staying these days?"

It was "Brownie" and the other twins from the semi. Did *everyone* have to insult him with the same, stale joke?

The men did doodly-squat to help or hinder him as he got his cell door open. When the Master stepped into the tunnel, they turned away, their purpose being accomplished.

"Wait! You're here—you came—to break me out?"

"Look, Buddy-Roe, I guess you don't know what's going on," said Brownie, jerking his thumb toward the exit, "but it's a war zone out there. We can't afford to have you rotting in the calaboose while the country falls apart."

"But—you could have run in the opposite direction. You came—to rescue me?" The Master stuck out his hand.

Brownie slapped it away carelessly. "Touching—but we gotta go!"

The Master followed them through turns and branchings until they reached a particular side tunnel. He stopped and shouted:

"Thank you!"

Brownie and the others looked back but he darted away. He used a hidden entrance to the secret tunnels.

He climbed to the ground level. The sounds of war were everywhere up here: booming, crashing, small-arms fire, shouting and screaming. An explosion sounded like it came from an old-fashioned cannon.

He slipped into the robing room. He pulled a black robe over his head; he wanted its warmth, protection, and above all, its instant authority. He found his belt and even his knife, right where they should be.

He ran out into the Great Hall. The place was going bananas. Blacks and browns ran about with no discernible reason.

Outside was where the action was. He ran to the lobby. A fleeing clerk glanced at him, looked again hard, faltered, and then resumed running. Challenging the Master was not a priority. Good.

The front door of the court building was wide open, and a wide black silhouette filled it. The Chief Justice. The man was preparing to face the invader. That took courage. Or its identical twin, suicidal despair.

Behind him, somebody approached. Slowly, insouciantly, Associate Justice Learned Hand processed through the Great Hall. He had found a robe to wear and looked the part of the wise old judge like never before. He plucked a flag from the wall and joined the Master, with his eyebrow set at a knife's edge as the only sign he noticed the drama all around them.

They stepped out upon the portico. Three blacks lined up at the edge of the steps, Chief, Master, and Hand. The Chief gave them the barest of nods, as one would give to companions who were expected, but slightly tardy.

That was the Chief for you, enigmatic to the end. No, scratch that—not enigmatic; just plain nerts.

Hand tore the flag off the pole and tossed it away. No one rebuked him for his disrespect. He tested the heft of the pole. It was his weapon.

The Master was prepared to see a fearsome fighting force assaulting the plaza. Nothing from his whole life prepared him for what he saw.

Around the edge of the plaza was assembled a vast throng. Besides the curious browns in a great arc, there were bleachers set up for the entire Electoral College, a block of blazing white. Reds darted around a huge structure, a combination high altar and scaffolding, upon which browns and blacks, the Twenty-Niners, were bound, ready to be executed. Mencken, back in town, stood among the other clerks. Across the street, from the entrance of the Capitol, the crowd roiled as hundreds of gap-mouthed, crazed-eyed congressmen, blinking, with faces as pale as their attire, staggered to join the crowd. It was a startlingly diverse group, representing all of Burrsburg society in a way that had not been seen in the city for years. It was united in one emotion: rage.

But the crowd was not the most astonishing thing the Master saw.

Across the plaza, leaving footprints of shattered paving stones, stomped a giant war robot. Its armor gleamed where it was not blackened and dented by war. It was thirty feet tall and armless; sparking cables hung uselessly from its broad shoulders and its armpits were stained with hydraulic fluid. Around its neck hung the remains of another robot, this one legless, suspended there like a playful child. The robots were unhindered by the many bullets fired at them, not to mention the angry shouts of the crowd, but their forward progress proceeded ponderously, slowed by the power cable that dragged a concrete cube the size of a factory behind it. The cube and the robots were very much the worse for wear, and yet they came on, inexorable, terrifying, and tragically beautiful.

"My Satan. My Satan."

The Master waited for inevitable death, immobile. When death did not come, he wondered: had they no weapons? If so, they were invulnerable, yet nearly impotent. This was a tactical situation unique in his experience and never anticipated in any of his training.

The three blacks retreated to just inside the doorway.

"What of our assets?"

"What?" The Chief treated the Master's question like a foreign language.

"The *army*. Where is it deployed? Has it been routed? Can it regroup?"

"There isn't one."

It was the Master's turn to react stupidly. "The army? It's been...wiped—"

"There is no army!" The Chief quivered with rage. "There never was an army."

"We...don't—?"

"All those opinions I issued, all those appropriations I raised: nothing! The generals took the money and spent it on who knows what! All those reports—conscripts, barracks, guns, ammo—all lies! They lied! To me! To *me!*"

The Chief paused to catch his breath.

"I ordered an attack and nothing happened. So I sent clerks and they came back saying the generals were AWOL. We blew a week just sorting it all out. No infantry, no tanks, no airplanes—of *course*, no airplanes—no navy, no *nothing*. The...betrayal..."

The Chief closed his eyes and waved away the imaginary army like a mosquito.

There was nothing to do for it but wait and watch the drama play out.

The great robot with its companion walked around the great framework of gallows, now full of bound victims waiting helplessly to die.

The robot came to the marble steps of the Court and climbed them half way. It occurred to the Master than these robots were not quite impotent; if the one with legs could kick, it could do serious damage.

A voice spoke, booming from a speaker:

"Thank you, Dick. You may go now. I'll take it from here."

It was a high-pitched voice. The Master could make no sense of it; it was neither a man nor a boy.

Justice Hand provided the identification. "A woman."

CHAPTER FORTY-EIGHT

Chief v. President

The robot with legs bent down to release the robot with arms with a tenderness the Master was sure he was not imagining.

Hand giggled.

They heard a tapping noise coming from the robot lying before them. A seam appeared about the back of the head. With a burst of pressurized air, a hatch opened and a ladder, pointless in this position, unfolded with a precision unknown to American experience. The Master caught a whiff of something strange, an artificial yet clean smell.

The person inside, the "woman", crawled out. She was thin, and likely old, if her stiff-jointed movements were not the fault of strapping into a pilot's chair for who knew how long. She was wearing a kind of one-piece suit like the flight suits the air force pilots wore—or rather, like the suits that had been contracted to be manufactured, but did not exist, for pilots who had been drafted, but were AWOL, to fly airplanes that were purchased but never delivered.

She wore some kind of complicated headphones and her white hair was done up in a curious way, with lots of swirls that were too neat to be accidental. She removed an elaborate pair of goggles, pulled out wire-rimmed cheaters and, with all deliberateness, put them on.

In response to some kind of signal from her, another hatch opened in the belly of her robot and a strange metal box slid out. It was polished metal and it made the Master instantly think of a casket, except too small. It moved forward over the ground on a single wheel. The means by which it remained upright was completely mysterious.

The other robot, the standing one, likewise opened up, and a man with a five-o'clock shadow and receding hairline came down the ladder. As a precaution, he took hold of a jagged strip of armor hanging from his damaged robot, worrying it until it snapped clean off. He found a solid hold on it with both hands and advanced with it before him like an archangel's sword.

He stood to the left of the woman. The metal box positioned itself on the right. There was no question which of them was the leader.

"Who's in charge here?" she demanded.

"I am the Special Master to his honor the Chief Justice of the United States, and I'm placing you under—"

"You!" The woman stabbed a bony finger and the Chief. "Fatty! Are you the one running this two-bit operation?"

"I'm the Chief Justice!" Boomed the Chief. "Who in Sam Hill do you think you are, invading my country?"

"I'm President Mary Wilson of the Federal Republic of Haiti!"

Wilson!

"And I'm Richard Nixon," said the man, irrelevantly.

President Wilson elbowed him aside. "I've come for my sister! What have you done with her?"

Sister?

The word was so unexpected, so unfamiliar. The Master was dumbfounded. The clerks buzzed among themselves, confused.

The Chief showed no confusion; his mouth twisted in rage.

Hand clapped his hand to his mouth. "God in Heaven," he murmured.

"Arrest that woman!" screamed the Chief, purple with apoplexy. "No! Kill her!"

He charged at the woman, cattle prod outstretched. She slapped the prod out of his hand and raised a thing shaped vaguely like a gun. "You brought a blaster?" said Nixon idiotically, but the Master had already snapped his rope belt; the blaster went skipping down the steps.

Nixon responded by swinging his too-heavy sword. Hand blocked the blow easily with his flagpole, but the Master parried with his belt and the three weapons became an entangled mess. They wrestled with this conglomeration until it too went flying across the plaza.

The Chief punched the president. The glancing blow merely baited her, and she landed her palm across his cheek in a satisfying *slap*. Nixon turned to help her but Hand stuck out his foot and Nixon went down hard, pulling Hand with him. They rolled down the steps.

Wilson stuck a finger in the Chief's eye and the Master lowered his shoulder to tackle her, when some instinct, more primal than any training, made him hesitate. The president took the opening he gave, kicking him square in the crotch.

The Master fell to his knees. The Chief got a hold on the president's hair. At the periphery of his vision, the Master sensed Hand and Nixon's combat had devolved into a savage biting and scratching match. Despite the pain shooting through his legs, the Master stood. Wilson clawed herself free and slipped past Chief and Master. She ran right through the entrance, into the court building. The strange box, perfectly balanced on its one wheel, peeled out and followed her.

"Stop her! She's dangerous! She's a liar!" The Chief had lost all dignity.

"Where is she?" President Wilson's voice echoed from within. The Chief and the Master chased after her, with Hand and Nixon and a herd of waddling blacks right behind.

"What have you done with her?" The President's voice echoed among the columns and niches and pickled heads of the Great Hall.

Wilson turned to face her pursuers.

"You kidnapped her. 1897—do you remember? She wasn't supposed to be taken, but there was this boy—a good-for-nothing kid—she followed him, and was carried away.

"I spent a fortune. A lifetime! I came myself, more than once. All the clues pointed here, to this city, this court. Then the trail went cold.

"So now I'm asking you, Mr. Chief Justice. I won't take no for an answer. Either I leave with my sister, or none of us gets out of here alive!"

From her pocket Wilson pulled a dull gray sphere. It had a single red light that blinked on and off and it rested heavy in her hand.

"Oh shit! Oh shit!" shrieked Nixon.

The three blacks could think of no comment worthy of this bewildering turn of events.

"...or none of us gets out of here alive!" Wilson repeated, really screaming the words this time.

The Master, the Chief and the associate justice looked at one another, confused.

"I'm not bluffing!"

The Master caught the old woman by the arm.

"This is an *atomgranate*! It's armed! The red flashing—"

The Master tugged at the sphere in her hand.

"It's got the explosive force of ten—If I let go—"

The Master pried the sphere loose and tossed it aside. Whatever explosive force it had, it wasn't using it.

"You *morons* don't know an *atomgranate* when you see one? *Morons!*" screamed the president, then softer, "Lucky thing I *was* bluffing."

"*Damn* lucky," gasped Nixon.

"See? She's a liar," said the Chief. "Don't believe anything she says."

"Why not?" said Hand, the tips of his eyebrow turning up in a grin. "It's all making sense."

"So! You know!" said Wilson.

"There are no sisters here," said the Master, "no women anywhere—least of all in this court."

"I believe the president is right," said Hand. "There was one. Once upon a time. Wasn't there, Mr. Chief Justice?"

"I don't know what—Lies! It's all lies!"

Learned Hand waved the Chief's words aside. "I think there was one woman—a girl, really—who, having been mistaken for a boy, found it necessary to maintain the pretense. She was smart and disciplined—she takes after her relatives in that regard," and here the associate justice bowed slightly toward the president, "and you, Chief, promoted her to the clerkship. In time, you became Chief Justice and appointed her—"

Hand pointed histrionically to the statue towering over them on its plinth in the center of the Great Hall.

MEMO

Harding, Coolidge & Associates

To: Mary Ann Wilson
From: Calvin Coolidge
Date: June 9, 1899 Anno Domini

Re: Investigation into Disappearance of Nelle Wilson

First, let me express my sympathy for your plight. God's will is mysterious, and not always in accordance with our wishes. The results of our investigation has not yielded the breakthrough you hoped for. However, we have some information and a suggested future course of action.

My conclusion: your daughter was kidnapped by American pirates as you feared. There is some evidence she was not immediately murdered, and that she is still alive somewhere in the United States.

The details of the investigation are as follows:

Evidence from the Home

The police report found your daughter disappeared sometime in the early morning hours of April 17, 1897 as a probable runaway. Her bedroom window was open at a time of year when the air conditioning was on. There was no sign of forced entry. Most tellingly, you reported a suitcase and several changes of clothing were missing.

Thus far, we concur with the police report. Beyond this point, we find the police seriously deficient. The police interviewed Nelle's closest friends and concluded none of them knew of any plan for her to run away.

However, we detected a conspiracy of silence in the answers of Nelle's closest confidant, your daughter Mary LaVina Wilson. Among our investigative techniques are certain psychologically manipulative approaches which go beyond what the police use (but which are not necessarily outside the law) and which would give us more certainty. We could use these techniques on Mary if given your express, written consent.

Our suspicions center on a young man named Chester Gillette, based on the vehemence of Mary's denials. It may be Nelle was infatuated with him. Chester is described as attractive and charming, but also wild. His parents are an excellent couple but despite a devout upbringing he has gotten in trouble with the law through a predictable pattern of vandalism, smoking, loitering, absences from school, petty theft, and public drunkenness. He has stopped attending church. His mother describes him as "uncontrollable."

In the beginning of 1897, the Juvenile Court of Port of Washington assigned Chester to Boy's Town of Providence, a reform school on the north coast. This "school" has a notorious reputation for "pirate bait."

Mary told us Nelle became melancholy. This coincided with Chester's departure.

(Incidentally, we were never able to determine the nature of the relationship between Nelle and Chester. There may have been an element of wishful thinking on Nelle's part.)

Assuming our psychological tests have not led us astray, Mary lied to the police—a felony. When confronted about this, she hinted at a promise made to Nelle, which she may have regarded as morally more binding than telling the truth to you or the police.

Evidence of Travel to Providence

A clerk at the Adams St. bus station thought he remembered Nelle from a photograph. He could not say when she had come or what ticket she had bought. There was an express bus to Providence which left at 5:50 a.m. on the morning Nelle disappeared. No one from the local cab services or the airport remembered seeing Nelle. No record of her, or anyone matching her description, is on any airplane or helo passenger manifest. I conclude Nelle took the bus to Providence.

No one could identify Nelle from a photograph from any Providence hotel, restaurant, or church.

A suggestive bit of evidence is the disappearance of a student uniform from the Boy's Town repository. It was of the smallest size—i.e., approximately Nelle's size. Note the uniform disappeared while at the laundry, located outside the fenced perimeter.

Interview with Chester

We interviewed Chester extensively. His story was consistent and adamant, in spite of our psychological tricks as mentioned above. He denied having seen Nelle at Boy's Town. This I found plausible. He denied having a relationship with her, or even knowing she was "in love" with him. This I doubt; Chester is lying, but to what extent, I cannot say.

In any event, there is no evidence whatsoever that Chester is responsible for Nelle's disappearance. Had he murdered Nelle, he would not have had the means to dispose of the body. His whereabouts are accounted for at all times on the days in question. I am satisfied by the integrity of the school's security (though not its motives otherwise, obviously). Given the school's reputation, boys would escape if they could, yet escapes are unheard of. Chester never left the school during the time in question.

The final circumstantial evidence is the most telling. On the morning of April 23, a group of boys were taken to North Beach near Boy's Town for recreation. They were in uniform. The beach is public, unfenced, and avoided by others; the boys are restrained by electric collars and not closely watched (for obvious reasons). A young person in uniform could freely mix with the boys without attracting attention.

Information from Guard "X"

The following information comes from a guard at the school. In exchange for the information we offered a substantial payment and full anonymity. The payment contributes to the unusually high fee. You asked us to be thorough. (See the attached invoice.) His name has not been recorded anywhere by me, but I can vouch that he exists and that multiple tests confirm his credibility. I will refer to him in this report as X.

X was guarding the boys on the beach on the day in question. A group of pirates emerged from the jungle and captured some of the boys. (Chester was not among them, as it happens.) This was all observed by X. His job is to make sure that boys do not escape by other means.

According to X's tally, seven boys were taken to the beach but he counted eight put into the pirate's longboat. X was afraid he had made an error, but when he received no reprimand, he stopped worrying about it.

Conclusions

I feel confident in concluding your daughter was the thief of the uniform, that she mixed with the boys on the beach in an attempt to contact Chester, and that she was one of the "boys" captured in the pirate raid.

In rare cases that girls are captured by the pirates, their bodies are sometimes found washed up on the beach. It is widely believed the pirates have a policy of killing the women quite soon after capture. You can take some small solace in the knowledge that, if your daughter was killed, she did not suffer long.

However, her body was never found. Given her disguise and her age, it is plausible she was able to pass as a boy throughout the voyage and arrive in America alive.

Future Action

This is as far as this investigation takes us, given our current mandate from you. Continuing this investigation into America is feasible, however. We have associates with whom we work within the United States. Contact me if you want me to proceed. Expect the fees to be substantially higher.

Statue

"You appointed her your Special Master," said Justice Hand.

"You're lying!" said the Chief Justice, hunching like a man before a storm.

"Your anger betrays you," said Hand, "and if it is a lie, then why has *Madame Présidente* come so far—"

"I am certain my sister came here. My investigation—"

"Stop!" It was the Special Master, clamping his hands over his ears. "Stop talking!"

"I'm afraid you need to hear this," said Hand as he gently pulled the Master's arms down, "and we might as well state the obvious: the old Special Master was your mother. And your father—" Hand's eyebrow formed thousands of accusing points aimed at the Chief Justice.

The Chief said, "What you're implying is...disgusting! I wouldn't even know...how—"

"No, no, no!" The Master shook his head slowly, as if to loosen the terrible thought from his mind.

"One can only imagine the poor girl's panic," said Hand, "the first time she accompanied the Chief to his grotto."

"Shut up!" roared the Master.

"We never—I don't—it wasn't like that!" howled the Chief.

"You monster!" screamed President Wilson.

Hand shrugged. "I suppose it's possible you were ignorant—and maybe still are—about *la différence.* Yet, nature took its course, when you and she disrobed—"

Something was wrong with the Master's eyes. He blinked, but it was as if somebody had blown out the lights. He staggered, then threw a punch where he guessed Learned Hand was standing. His knuckles connected with the old man's ribs. The pain was terrible, although not nearly terrible enough.

He felt the old man collapse. His vision improved. He lunged at a shape darker than the surrounding gloom. His hands closed around pleats of rich velour. He beat the ponderous form with the backs of his clenched hands and the form, his Chief and father, wrestled with him weakly, slowly, as though they were under water. They lost their collective center of gravity and toppled into a heap.

"If I could, I'd kill you both, right where you lay," said President Wilson.

"I have been thoughtless," said Hand, rising and rubbing his sore chest, "but now I see the pity. Chief Justice: you must have convinced yourself that the odd goings on were not what they were. She hid her pregnancy from you and ran away. You were suspicious, but unsure."

From a niche, Hand took the pickled head that sat there, that of Chief Justice John Ruskin. He tested the heft of the hideous thing as one might appraise a cantaloupe in a market.

"You, *Madame Présidente,* are finally receiving the confirmation you have sought so long."

"Disgusting! You disgust me—all of you! Only one thing matters now: is my sister alive? Do you have her somewhere?"

"I'm very sorry. Your sister is dead."

He paused as the woman bowed her head, looking all of a sudden like she was 100 years old. The metal box balanced behind her edged forward.

"Mother," whispered Mary Wilson, "I'm sorry."

"But to answer your other question," continued Hand, "yes: I do have her somewhere. Right here."

Hand threw the pickled head with great force directly at the plaster statue of the old Special Master.

The plaster shattered. The statue collapsed. Everyone coughed as dust rose in clouds.

Scattered among the plaster lay a crumbly parchment, fragments of decayed cloth, and a set of bones.

"Just before her second disappearance, your sister came to me. She was sick—hemorrhaging badly. I saw the blood on her robe, and assumed it was a digestive problem. To the end, I never guessed it was a problem unique to *la femme.* She knew she was dying. She was in despair, believing her son was lost forever. Still, she kept her secrets, even from me, to the very end."

Hand took the painting of the Chief down from the wall as he kept talking.

"She made a painting—this ugly, *ugly* painting. She still hoped her son was among the Cohort of '29—she had given up on you, Master, as you know—and placed clues in it she thought he alone could decipher—*c'est tragique!* Then, she asked me to hide her body in plaster, and *voilà!* I made the statue. Those are her bones lying there."

"Oh, merciful Heavens!" President Wilson was on her knees now, pushing aside the plaster pieces. There are two bodies here!"

And so there were. One adult skeleton, and, among the dust and decay, the half-formed remains of the child in her womb when she died.

"Pregnant." Hand spoke the word with profound sadness. The last of his cynicism was used up.

"My brother...or *sister*," whispered the Special Master, in awe.

"Mother. Mother!" All sanity slipped from President Wilson's tenuous grasp. She was talking to the metal box now. She was weeping hysterically, and talking to a box.

"Mother! I'm so sorry. I'm *so sorry!*" She hugged the box, but the cold steel shrugged her off and rolled forward, pausing over the wreck of plaster and bones.

A little door, not previously visible, opened in the front of the box. A strange, narrow tube, fashioned by some complicated means far beyond the understanding of the Americans, emerged from the box on a telescoping rod. The device sucked up dust from among the bones with its pointy metal snout, and all present held their breaths as it performed some kind of trial.

The probe clicked, and a green light blinked.

Mary Wilson fell to her knees and wailed. The probe retracted into the box on its telescoping rod. The metal box pivoted. Something unexplainable about the way it behaved alarmed the Master.

Wilson raised her hands to embrace the box. The box seemed to nuzzle her. She cradled it to her bosom.

Something made a soft *slook!* sound.

The room fell dead silent as Wilson's sobs halted and her forehead went *clank* on the box's metal lid. Her hands fell limp to her sides. Ponderously, like a mighty oak, she tipped backwards.

"Aargh!" The animal roar came from Nixon. He saw before the others what the box had done to Mary LaVina Wilson, President of the Federal Republic of Haiti. It had telescoped its rod into her chest, piercing her heart.

CHAPTER FIFTY

Made Whole Again

Nixon fell on top of the box. It wobbled, but stayed upright by some miraculous means. He beat its metal top with his fists, bawling without shame or sense. The box pivoted once, then twice, trying to shake its rider, then lunged toward the entrance.

The Chief, the Master, and Hand, still holding the portrait, picked up their skirts and gave pursuit. Outside, they watched as the box thumped down the steps and zigzagged about the plaza. Nixon was jarred and shaken, but he clung to his perch and even got in a few more blows. He must have damaged the box's ability to see because its turns became erratic.

It collided violently with the standing robot and stopped. Even then, it stayed upright.

The three blacks stood dumbly. Even the crowd, swelled by the addition of manifestly insane escapees from congress, said nothing.

Nixon picked himself up from where he had fallen. He tugged at the damaged metal exterior until the top peeled right back in his hands. Everyone gasped. There in the box, exposed now to the world, lay a human brain floating in a glass orb. Bubbles trickled lazily upward in viscous fluid, and tubes and wires ran in complicated tangles in and out of the bottom of this medical abomination.

Nixon got his hands on his makeshift sword. With a primitive bellow, he struck the glass globe. Glass and brain matter flew everywhere, some a great distance. Those nearby screamed and fled. He continued with his labor, bellowing and striking, long after the glass and its gelatinous contents were scattered. The brain's lifespan, sustained through unnatural means by the most modern technology, ended in primitive violence.

The three blacks stood unmoving, awestruck.

Nixon dropped his sword and looked around in dawning awareness. He straightened himself and brushed some of the brain matter off his jumpsuit. He turned a full circle, but saw nowhere to go. He mounted the ladder on the back of his robot. At the top, he paused before the open hatch. His face cracked open in an unfathomable smile and he raised his right hand in a weird, two-fingered wave.

As the confused crowd did not respond, Nixon crawled into his robot. With much groaning of damaged armor, the hatch closed and the ladder folded itself up. Lights all around the robot's head lit up. The robot turned about by means of many tiny steps that would have been comical if the situation were not so threatening. Like an exhausted old man, the robot scooped up its cable and draped it over its shoulder. In this way, it shuffled out of the plaza and returned whence it came.

The Master's untiring tactical mind thought of ropes and lariats and places to position the clerks so as to topple the great gizmo, but he ordered no action. It is not always wise to interfere with the enemy when he is retreating. He watched the noisy thing disappear behind the library of congress. Only the power cable moved as its slack was taken up by the plodding *thud thud* of the robot.

Taking up the slack took time, and all the while, the Blacks simply stood and watched. Finally, inevitably, the power cable tightened. The *thud thud* rhythm slowed as the cable groaned under the strain. The battered cube, coated with mud, thrusting broken protrusions all about it and with long gashes where it had been dragged on its sides, began to pivot. Once aligned with the direction of the robot, with a violent "Screech!" it slid along the flagstones of the plaza. The other robot, still attached, was dragged along too. The last of the Sixth American Invasion withdrew.

Justice Learned Hand was the first to disturb the calm.

"This man here"—he took the Special Master's hand and raised it high—"is a natural born citizen!"

The crowd murmured dubiously.

"He is the Vice President Who Is to Come! Vicers! To me! To me! Guard your Vice President apparent!"

In all that vast throng—blacks and browns, condemned men on the gallows and lurid priests guarding them, congressmen and presidential electors in white—not one person stepped forward.

"Vicers! Come forth! I've called you here—thousands of you!"

Hand's eyes darted over the faces in the crowd.

"You there! Vincent Price!" Hand pointed at a brown in the crowd. "I know *you're* a Vicer! Come up here!"

The brown turned and fled.

"Vicers! Come *on!*" Hand was begging now.

The Chief's mocking laughter silenced the old justice.

"A natural born citizen? Really? *Really?* Where's your proof?"

Hand said nothing.

"Clerks! Arrest these two. They are traitors."

The Chief waved his hands to stir up his followers to action, but the weirdness quotient of the day had long since passed its saturation point and nobody in the crowd was prepared to act on the mere say-so of anybody.

"I think—" Hand was speaking to himself, but sucked in a lungful of air to address the assembly. "I think the clerks will be interested to learn their Chief has been engaging in conjugal—"

That got everyone's attention.

"I say," Hand shouted, "*conjugal relations*—"

"That's a *lie!*" roared the Chief.

"Shut *up!*" shouted the Master. "Shut *up* about *my mother!*"

The assembly mumbled. The Master's sincerity was obvious. A tide was turning.

"You *fathered* this man—the Special Master," shouted Hand with rising confidence.

"You *filthy, disgusting*—"

The crowd inched forward. They spoke among themselves. They were prepared to believe, if only somebody would help their unbelief.

The Chief struck a pose like an attorney before a jury. "Where's the *documentation?*" He shouted.

Hand spoke to the Master with an urgent *sotto voce*. "The painting!" Hand held it up so the Master could see. "Think! This is a message from your mother. Is there a clue you haven't solved?"

"Well, we know the fingers are lakes—the cabin I've *been* to—"

"Who are you going to believe—" the Chief was bawling.

"—I know; that other hand. Why are there so many forefingers?"

"More lakes?"

"Master in Lunacy: begin the executions!" shouted the Chief. Up on the scaffold, J. Edgar Hoover, swaddled in crimson, raised a staff.

"Satan!" gasped the Master, distracted. "Not lakes."

"The crooked frame, maybe?"

"Wait! Of course! Not *fingers*, but *finger*."

Hand looked down at the painting stupidly.

"One finger, in motion."

"Yes! And we didn't get that because, let's face it, the Special Master was a lousy—"

"A circular motion!"

The Master and the associate justice looked at each other, bug-eyed.

On the scaffold, other priests made busy. "Kill them all!" ordered the Chief.

The Master turned the painting around. The back was covered with paper. He ripped it away.

"There's writing here," said the Master. "It's a legal document."

"Legal document, my ass. It's a—"

Hand raised his voice to a full-on bellow. "It's a birth certificate!"

The crowd went dumb. The priests halted. The Chief pivoted.

"Applesauce. *Applesauce!* You'll never be able to link this certificate with the Master. Or anybody for that—"

"Look there," said the Master, speaking so everyone could hear, "the crooked frame was covering up the notary's seal down there, and up here—"

"—the name is torn away," said the Chief, suddenly very pleased.

"Part of the name is torn away," said Hand, "but you can read most of it."

"The middle name is completely missing! This document is invalid!"

"The name is mostly there. Any reasonable court would rule—"

"*This* court will rule it invalid! Without the full name—"

"I have it!" cried the Master.

From his pocket he fished a well-worn piece of parchment and placed it into the jagged, V-shaped gap at the top of the document. Everybody could see that, despite its age, it fit perfectly.

"This is the missing piece. This is the middle name. This is my birth certificate."

The Master read his birth name for the first time. He told it to himself in a whisper:

```
Ronald Wilson Reagan
```

CHAPTER FIFTY-ONE

"Rok! Rok!"

The birth certificate galvanized the fence-sitters. Vicers applauded. Scores of electors, led by their president, left their bleachers and pressed toward Special Master Reagan, wanting to see the parchment. It only hardened the priests' determination. The Chief, sensing how the crowd would divide, hissed to clerk Mencken, "follow me!" and backed his way to the foot of the scaffold.

Mencken and a small knot of clerks followed the Chief, but without his urgency. Were they yet persuadable? Their finely trained legal minds could not deny the certificate's authenticity but their depraved political minds could still go either way.

"Begin the executions!" shouted the Chief to the Master in Lunacy.

The senior priest clapped his hands and personally grasped a lever. It would release the trap door for the first bound victim.

"Master! These men will die, *one by one*, until you surrender to me!"

"Never!"

"Pull!"

"Thinks he's at a skeet shoot," muttered Justice Hand.

The Master in Lunacy pulled the lever.

The victim fell fast. The Master's hand moved faster.

435

Just as the rope grew taut, the Master's flying knife pierced its knot at the crossbeam above. With a little *pop* the rope parted. Victim, noose, and snaking rope all fell together in a clumsy pile on the ground.

"Confound you! Another!" shouted the Master in Lunacy.

The Master rushed the scaffold, followed by Hand and a gaggle of electors led by their president, Adam Clayton Powell.

The under-priests hesitated. Hoover screeched, "Satan commands you!"

Clerk Mencken eyed the Master in Lunacy through hooded slits. Which did he loathe more—Special Master Reagan, or the church?

Master Reagan was climbing a beam of the scaffold. Electors were swarming its steps.

Mencken made his decision. "Stop those red devils!"

The crowd broke for the scaffold. Somebody shouted "V.P.! V.P.!" and others took up the chant.

The under-priests lost their nerve. The men in red leaped off the scaffold and ran, but they were already surrounded by browns, and none escaped. Reagan apprehended Hoover, and just like that, the danger to the prisoners evaporated.

A shrill whistle ripped through the tumult. It came from the Chief Justice. He stood a little apart, his lost electric prod in his hand again, and surrounded by several fallen browns zapped into unconsciousness. He was looking up at a high window.

Lordly Abaddon and his winged conspiracy, the last of the Chief's loyal followers, swooped down. They knew doodly-squat of what had transpired, and were notoriously poor lawyers in any case. To gasps from the crowd, they lowered their taxi just until the Chief could catch hold of the lowest bar.

"Up, you yucks! Fly up!"

The taxi's momentum carried the birds forward as they struggled to rise. They would clear the scaffold, but not by much.

The Master climbed to the top beam of the scaffold. He teetered for the barest moment, then he leaped.

He caught the bar and hung next to the Chief. The birds redoubled their flapping to adjust to the extra weight.

The Chief lifted himself so as to grip a piece of balsa wood. He was using the wood for insulation, the Master saw. The Chief touched his rod to the metal frame of the taxi and a flash of energy flowed through it.

"Rooook!" screamed the ravens—but the taxi stayed in their grasp.

Master Reagan had already let go. As he fell he caught the Chief's foot.

The Chief went "oof!" as the air blew out of his lungs, but he held on. He looked down at the Master, but he dared not use his rod.

"I saved you from the mines! I gave you everything!"

The Master was long past arguing. He climbed, using his father's body as a rope.

"We could have invaded Canada together! We could have bombed the France!"

The taxi continued to rise. Master Reagan had never seen a taxi reach such insane heights.

The Chief shook. The Master hung on tenaciously. The entire taxi shook, and Abaddon's ravens croaked in protest.

Master Reagan grabbed the lowest bar of the taxi's metal frame. He hung on to the Chief's belt with his other hand. So long as they were in contact, the Chief could not use his rod.

The Chief twisted and kicked but the Master still would not let go.

This was not doing anybody any good.

Special Master Reagan yanked the Chief's belt hard. The old man lost his grip on his rod. As it fell, the Chief snatched at it with his hand and caught it, but to do so, he lost his grip on the taxi.

The Chief flipped over in Reagan's hand and slid out of his grasp. His arm crooked around the Chief's ankle and held on. He felt the full weight of the fat Chief stretch his shoulder joints.

The Master groaned, and hung on.

He could do no more than hang on.

"Help!"

Abaddon croaked out a "Rok! Rok!" and more than a score of the birds let go of the taxi. The whole thing—ravens, frame, and men—lurched, as raven wings smote the air desperately.

The sub-conspiracy flew down to the Chief, following Abaddon's orders. Their claws caught him by the shoulders, arms, legs and even hair, lifting him up until the Master felt safe to release him.

Relieved of some of its weight, the taxi rose. The sub-conspiracy lifted the Chief to the taxi platform and deposited him there.

The Chief clung to the balsa floor of the platform, paralyzed by terror. The Master hung from the low bar, his exhausted muscles not responding to his brain's command to climb.

"Help!" the Master called again. The sub-conspiracy came to him, lifting him up as they did the Chief.

"Keep that *monster* away from me!" roared the Chief. Finding fresh courage, he stood as the birds came to him and thrust his rod at the nearest bird.

Zap!

The electrocuted bird fell, leaving behind the reek of burnt feathers and flesh.

The surviving ravens raged, crying "Rok! Rok!" The sub-conspiracy swerved away from the rod. The Master was swung about as the ravens pitched and yawed, vying to put their human cargo on the platform without dooming him to electrocution.

Abaddon's tactical prowess was not exhausted, however.

"Rok! Rok! Rok!" he croaked verbosely.

"What?" shouted the Chief, looking up, disoriented. He sensed, without fully understanding, his vulnerability.

"Rok!" On Abaddon's final command, a rain of raven poop—nay, a torrent, a deluge, a Niagara Falls—poured down.

The Chief covered his face, but it was already slick with white. His eyes and nose were full of excrement. His magnificent robe was coated with it, and it dripped down his shoulders like white icing on a chocolate cake.

The Chief waved his arms around blindly, swatting at the out-of-reach ravens above him. The poop continued to rain down. The Master marveled at the birds' capacity. Their bowels were like piping tubes wielded by the world's most petty and vindictive pastry chefs.

The Chief spun around. The floor of the platform was slick with the whiteness. He slipped and, with an inarticulate scream, the Chief fell off the taxi and plummeted toward the Earth.

The sub-conspiracy set the Master on the platform. Without hesitation, the Master dove.

"Ro-o-o-ok!" complained Abaddon. This was not part of his plan.

The Master stretched out, head down, toward the Chief. In that streamlined position, and with the Chief's robe parachuting, the Master closed the gap.

Outmaneuvered and enraged, Abaddon croaked a "Rok! Rok!". His ravens dropped the taxi and, in tight formation, power dived toward the Master.

The Master caught the Chief. He squeezed the Chief's hand and forced the rod from it.

The Master was still falling head down. The ground was coming up fast. He pleaded:

"God, God,

Cod, cod..."

The claws of a great bird closed upon his ankles.

Many more claws found purchase all over his body. Others took hold of the Chief as well, and the terrible strain on his arms lessened.

With only a few feet to spare, the whole conspiracy—men and ravens—slowed to a hover. They settled with supreme grace onto the west porch of the Capitol building. There, they rested for a moment. A few dozen feet away they saw, without really comprehending, a taxi frame smashed upon the ground.

CHAPTER FIFTY-TWO

I Swear

From all sides, the crowd gathered: black clerks, knock-kneed and waddling, looking wary; white electors, exultant and teary-eyed, passing around shears and knives with which they cut off their beards; red priests, raging, faces the color of their robes; white congressmen, shambling escapees from the Capitol flinching at the brilliance of the sun; and browns of every description from the government buildings, restaurants, hotels, saloons, banks, race tracks, opium dens, and gambling halls clustered about the seat of power.

"Deliverance! Restitution!" These and other polysyllabic legalisms, some in Latin (some in backwards Latin! This was the world's only satanic republic, after all) filled the ears of the Chief. Everyone was shouting something, either in celebration, protest, or in the case of the squinting congressmen, simple physical pain.

J. Edgar Hoover was no exception.

"Sacrifice! We have promised Satan blood. He is not to be denied! Sacrifice!"

Reagan pointed. "Clerks: arrest the priests!"

In the new dispensation, the priests were impotent. The clerks made quick work of subduing them.

President Powell of the Electoral College pushed his way to the front of the crowd, where he could address the Master. "We have examined your birth certificate, Mr. Reagan. I have polled, in haste, the electors. The vote is unanimous: you—"

Powell dropped to one knee. Others near him followed suit, and the gesture passed through the throng in an ever-widening wave.

"You are—" The president's voice caught. "—the vice president-elect!"

The words were spoken in stentorian fashion, easily heard by all. Their extreme novelty stunned the crowd to momentary silence.

Somewhere in the back, somebody started clapping. From back to front, a cheer broke out and traversed the crowd in a second wave, a reflection of the first.

Master Reagan—Vice President-Elect Reagan—felt many hands taking hold of his. Men were pounding him on the back. The emotion of the crowd hit him as a tangible, radiant blast of love. It felt good—very good.

Justice Hand was at his side. Always one step ahead, he had procured a massive, leather-bound copy of the Satanic Bible.

Clerks helped them stand atop an empty plinth where everybody could see them. Clearly, the people were wanting a speech. Reagan vaguely considered that history was being made, that future generations would well note and long remember what was said here today. He felt utterly unprepared, yet calm and confident.

"My fellow Americans—"

A conventional beginning. Uninspired. Yet, the crowd murmured its encouragement. This was an easy group to please.

He smiled. The crowd applauded, even laughed, in joy, not mockery. The people and he were one.

"—our long national nightmare is over."

The crowd erupted in cheers. They were ecstatic. The Chief had inspired nobody, ruling instead through fear and bureaucratic inertia. The people hungered, nay, *starved,* for a rousing speech.

"We have been told, by our masters in Burrsburg, that the people are on the wrong track. Our problems have been blamed on a 'malaise', a rot that stems not from the leaders, but the led. Well, I'm here before you today to tell you: I do not agree."

A weak line, yet the crowd ate it up.

Reagan, inspired by the fresh wave of clapping, shouted:

"Government is not the solution to our problem; government is the problem!"

Yes! Now we're rolling.

"It's time we reformed the system. We need to return to the old ways, when all three branches of government were functional. We'll bring an end to one-man rule and return—"

Premature clapping. That sentence was misplayed. Of course the people wanted to express their loathing of the Chief.

"—and return to the orderly legislative process!"

Now the crowd had permission to cheer, and they let it loose.

Reagan looked across the sea of faces to where a group of whites stood. Among the crazed expressions, one pair of lucid eyes burned into his. Congressman Tip O'Neill was looking at him with vengeful loathing. That was a fence not easily mended. If only the congressmen had not escaped until Reagan himself could free them.

"Well, this administration's objective will be a healthy, vigorous, growing economy that provides equal opportunities for all Americans, with no barriers born of the color of a man's suit of clothes." Vigorous applause. "And we need to end the disgraceful practice of stealing our future from foreign shores. We need a native-born population—and to do that, we need women as partners in the American Experiment!"

The crowd started to applaud after the first sentence, but faltered at the word "women."

Give them time; women could not be all that bad.

"The Church needs to stop meddling in business not its own."

The newly-released prisoners, Reagan's twins, lead the crowd in throaty roars.

Whoa, the crowd really liked that one. Push that issue hard; maybe even get a constitutional amendment.

"As you have expressed your confidence in me," Reagan continued as he looked to the electors, "with great humility, and a hopeful prayer that—"

He faltered for a moment.

That who: Satan? God? Better use a neutral term. Ah! Found one.

"—that the *Supreme Judge* may smile upon our efforts as we work together for a brighter future, I accept the responsibility you have placed on my shoulders. I am ready to recite the oath of office of Vice President of the United States!"

The crowd went nuts. The cheering went on and on.

Wait—was the Master supposed to make the speech after the oath? Not a problem; this had not been done in years. Nobody present knew the difference.

The crowd settled down and Justice Hand stepped forward with the Satanic Bible, opened to II Beelzebub 14:7:

Beat your plowshares into swords, and your pruning hooks into spears.

Not the passage Reagan would have chosen. No time to quibble, however.

Hand made the sign of the pentagram and intoned, "Eh, whatever! Mr. Reagan, raise your right fist. Do you solemnly swear to faithfully execute the Office of Vice President of the United States, and with every fiber of your being, as Satan gives you strength, do battle with the forces of light, spit on the enemies of Hell, bomb the France, and endeavor ever to preserve, protect and defend the..."

Justice Learned Hand was at a loss for words.

"...the Constitution..." whispered Reagan.

"Scratch's matches! I almost forgot to check. How *old* are you?"

What on earth was he talking about?

"How old? Well, I don't know."

"A vice president must be 35."

"I'm *probably* 35—"

"Wait—I'm a chowderhead! We've got your birth certificate right here!"

Hand pulled the parchment from his robe. "Let's see...Birth Certificate State of New Gehenna blah blah Ronald Wilson Reagan blah blah...here's the date! It says you were born on February 12 in 1911. This is 1946. Today's date is..."

The Associate Justice's eyes rolled up as he did the math.

The old man's face exploded into a grin. Then he laughed out loud. He stuck out his hand.

"Happy birthday, Mr. Vice President!"

The Thirteenth Amendment

Amendment to the Constitution of the United States of America Article XIII

Final Draft

SECTION 1. The United States shall be no longer dedicated to the greater glory of Satan or the advancement of his will throughout the world.

SECTION 2. Congress shall make no law for the establishment of any religion, nor the free exercise thereof, with the following provisions:

A. Every Tuesday, Thursday and Saturday, the United States shall be dedicated to the greater glory of Satan and the advancement of his will throughout the world.

B. Every December, the United States shall be dedicated to the honor of Krampus and Frau Perchta, other religious obligations notwithstanding the free exercise of which this provision shall in nowise be construed to proscribe. Congress shall make laws to define and enforce this provision.

C. Congress may impose taxes and levies upon the churches, corporations, organizations and associations dedicated to the practice of the following religions: Christianity, Judaism, Mohammedanism, Hinduism, Buddhism, Clemensism, Conjuring and Yarb Work, and Powwowing. Nothing in this amendment shall be construed to permit any impediment to the free exercise of these or any religions.

D. Christianity may not be observed on Sunday, nor Judaism on Saturday, nor Mohammedanism on Friday.

E. No non-Satanic house of worship may be built within one half mile of any school, mine, factory, farm, hospital, government building, sports stadium, liquor store, hotel, or any retail establishment selling books, guns, or livestock.

F. The state of Massachusetts is exempt from any or all provisions of this amendment.

SECTION 3. The state of Chersonesus dedicates itself to the One True Holy and Apostolic Catholic Church and its head, the Pope and Vicar of Christ. Blessed be Jesus Christ! Blessed be his Mother! Long Live his Holiness Pope Pius XII!

SECTION 4. No non-Satanic religion may proselytize a minor child. Adult residents of the several states may not proselytize their minor children, domestic servants, or resident dependents.

SECTION 5. Religious displays on public lands shall be limited to those already in place at the time of the ratification of this amendment. Rivers, forests, mountains and other geological features which, according to popular legend, are imbued with magical power, or religious significance otherwise, shall be destroyed, re-engineered or defaced wherever practical. Congress shall appropriate funds as needed to enforce this provision.

SECTION 6. Nothing in this amendment shall be construed as an insult to Satan, his priests or his bishops. Nothing in this amendment shall be construed as an impediment to the free exercise, nor the primacy, of the one, true satanic religion.

SECTION 7. The month of January shall be dedicated to the worship of Hindu gods. The several states shall appropriate funds as appropriate and reasonable for the public acknowledgment of this fine religion and its many fine contributions to world culture.

SECTION 8. All houses of commerce and places of business shall be closed on Sundays out of respect to the god of the Christians, except in the states of Connecticut, Florida, Massachusetts, New Gehenna, Ohio, Polypotamia, and Rabisu.

SECTION 9. No saloons or liquor stores, nor any late night loud carousing or any loud noise of any kind between the hours of 10:00 p.m. and 7:00 a.m., will be permitted within a half mile radius of the address of 17 Beekman Place, New Gehenna, New Gehenna, upon penalty of flogging. Congressman Irving Berlin of 17 Beekman Place,

New Gehenna, New Gehenna, is hereby deputized with unlimited authority and immunity to enforce this provision.

SECTION 10. May Satan breathe the fire of a thousand hells, wherein brimstone floweth like liquid flame and the souls of his enemies writhe in agony FOREVER, upon any who gainsay his will! Death to the enemies of Satan! Die Puritans, DIE DIE DIE! All Hail Satan!

MEMO

Harding, Coolidge & Associates

Memo to: Mary Ann Wilson
From: Calvin Coolidge
Date: August 2, 1899 Anno Domini

Re: Nelle Wilson Disappearance and Questioning of Mary LaVina Wilson

We have completed our second round of questioning of your daughter, Mary LaVina. We employed the advanced psychological techniques you, as the sole custodial parent, have authorized in your letter of July 19. We have learned the following information.

Mary LaVina admits her statements to you and the police were not true.

Mary LaVina acknowledges her sister was infatuated with Chester Gillette and that she (Mary LaVina) knew of these feelings months before the disappearance. She agreed to help her sister join Chester and helped plan the disappearance.

Mary LaVina said Nelle required of her an oath of secrecy involving very strong curses on the oath-breaker. I will spare you the details. I have been in this business for years and have seen a lot, but the thought that such hair-raising language would be imagined by an adolescent girl, much less spoken in a blood oath, is unique in my experience. It seems your daughter Nelle is an exceptional girl, for good or ill, and exerted a powerful control over Mary LaVina despite being the younger.

The girls "collected" enough cash for Nelle to purchase a bus ticket. Mary LaVina helped gather information on the reform school. She said the idea to steal a school uniform was hers; she was insistent on that point.

This last point removes all reasonable doubt as to Nelle's whereabouts. She was on the beach as we suspected, mistaken for a boy, and kidnapped by pirates. No more profit may come from further sifting the information we have. Let us know if you want to continue the investigation within the borders of the United States.

Although it exceeds my professional role, I feel compelled to offer you some advice. Your daughter Nelle may still be alive, and you can best serve her by focusing all your energies on finding her, not apportioning blame. Beyond that, Mary LaVina, despite her youthful folly, is still your daughter. I urge you to consider the best interests of all your family, and avoid further strife and division. Forgive your daughter, as Christ has forgiven us all. She is mortified by what she has done. I beg you, lay not this sin to her charge.

Bill

Comprehensive Immigration Reform Act of 1946

The Comprehensive Immigration Act of 1946 (Act of August 15, 1946) [H. R. 758305248]

Preamble

Whereas that procreation being the primary means that by which nature has provided that the population might be maintained although the old may die and go to Hell, and that the feminine arts and preferences have been shown, by their absence these several years, to be of no little value:

Be it enacted by the Senate and House of Representatives of the United States of America in Congress assembled,

Title I

The Great Reform Act of 1851 is repealed.

The right of women to reside within the several states shall not be questioned.

452

Title II

Senator Oswald Mosley, members of his immediate family, and all blood descendants in perpetuity, shall forever be exempt from all taxes, whether federal, state or local, and each shall be due a stipend from the Federal government each year equal to 150 percent of the median personal income in the united states, except that Senator Mosley's stipend shall be 500 percent, no, make that 800 percent, and this provision shall be exempted from repeal by any future statute or constitutional amendment. Congress shall appropriate funds as necessary to fulfill this sacred obligation. Did you get that all down or will I have to repeat myself again you chowderhead?

Title III

Congress shall have the power to regulate female immigration and childbirth, with the following excepted:

1. Women may not exceed 20 percent of all persons entering the United States by immigration in any even-numbered year, nor 17 percent in any year divisible by 13, nor shall any pregnant woman immigrate, nor any woman exceeding 45 years of age, unless a fine no less than $5,000 be paid in compensation, or four years of labor indentured to the United States or its designated representatives, unless she demonstrate proficiency in the following skills: computational mathematics, metallurgy, avian husbandry, or chemical engineering.

2. No priestess of any unsatanic religion, nor any so-called satanic religion other than the true Church, may enter the United States unless she renounce her god for a period of no less than three years.

3. We are given to understand from the testimony of sources we consider reliable that Nordic women are "hot."

4. The number of women entering the United States in any year may not exceed the following:

From the Republic of Haiti: 87.7166 women

From the France: 4616.5 women

From other places within the French Empire: 1,846.6666 women

From the Kingdom of Great Britain: 13,849 women

From other places within the British Empire: 2,7792333 [sic] women

From all other places within the British Commonwealth excepting Canada: 369.3333 women

From Canada: 242.8366 women

From Mexico: 415.45 women

From any South American Nation: 369.3333 women

From the Russian Empire: 11,080 women

From German Empire: 3693.3333 women

From the Kingdom of Italy: 512.45 women

From Spain: 277 women

From any Nordic country: 33,240 women

From any African country: 821.7666 women

From China: 1,846.6666 women

From the Empire of Japan: 903.0197 women

From Antarctica: 32.3166 women

From any other nation: 92.3333 women

CHAPTER FIFTY-THREE

Eh, Whatever

"Nice view." Justice Learned Hand had not yet looked at his host, maybe because he wanted to prove himself the one person in the capital city not awed by a 99 percent approval rating, or maybe simply because, at 400 feet above the National Mall, the panorama truly commanded his attention.

Vice President Ronald Reagan said nothing.

"I hear you're working on a constitutional amendment: freedom of religion." Hand's eyebrow cocked impishly. "I hadn't realized you left the Church of Satan."

"I didn't leave the Church of Satan. The Church of Satan left me."

"No need to get prickly; I'm on your side. Coerced belief is no belief at all."

"I do hope we can disestablish the church."

"Good. I'm a skeptic myself. Obviously, a physical Hell doesn't exist. It's merely a beautiful metaphor."

With that, the wind kicked up with an angry howl. Windows rattled and the room swayed in nauseating oscillations.

"Have you heard the latest conspiracy theory?"

"What?"

"Ronald Wilson Reagan. Six letters in each name. 666. The Beast of the Christian Apocalypse."

"Oh. Do you think..."

Reagan's voice trailed off. Hand was laughing at him.

"If my Vicers had only known...oh boy!"

Vice President Reagan joined the Justice at one of the two huge, eye-shaped windows, his legs bent on the swaying deck. "They told me I could have any office I liked—short of the Oval Office, of course. They had no idea I would take them literally."

"Ha! The looks on their faces when you told them—the top the Burr Monument!"

"There's no better view in the capital."

"You've sent a clear signal regarding the new pecking order."

"That wasn't my intent. Settling in here gives me a pretext to do some extensive remodeling. The Burr Monument is going to look rather different when I'm done with it."

"The new scaffolding they just put up?"

Reagan sighed. "I know—now it's scaffolding on scaffolding on scaffolding. But that's an emergency measure. They told me the monument would collapse at any moment."

"The horn?"

"The horn, the fangs—the whole face will be redone. When I look out across the Mall—Capitol building, White House, Supreme Court, Buchanan Memorial—I want to see through the peepers of Aaron Burr the man, not some ghastly devil's head."

"Speaking of ghastly, did you hear? Those lunatics in the House elected a new speaker. Somebody named O'Neill. I forgot the first name."

"Not Tip O'Neill, I hope."

"That's it!"

Uh oh.

The men looked out. Lights came on, one by one, in the dusk.

Reagan said, "The old ways are passing. It's morning in America."

The eyebrow recoiled ironically. "Best of luck with that."

"Well, I've spoken to the president."

"That must have been an elevating conversation."

"President Hall has his lucid moments, believe it or not. I had some advice for him—advice about what to do with you."

"Don't even try it. I'll refuse. Find somebody else to replace your fath—"

Oops.

"My *father*. You can say it. I'm glad he fled the country, but still, he is my father."

"Very well. But in any case, I won't take the job. Find someone else to be the new Chief Justice."

"Gus Hall already did."

"What?"

The eyebrow's utter confusion amused Reagan. Hand had wanted to be asked.

"President Hall nominated Abaddon."

"Abaddon? *Abaddon?*"

From his perch by the wall, Abaddon protested with a "Rok!"

"Please tell me your Senate's not going to confirm a *bird* for the high court."

"It's not *my* Senate, but no, Abaddon doesn't have the votes. Don't worry, though. I've spoken to Hall. We have the perfect role for you."

"I can't imagine."

Reagan showed Hand a document. The associate justice's mouth fell open.

"Ambassador? No. No! Forget it. Like I said—"

"Too late. The President loved my idea, and signed it immediately. The Senate confirmed you. You're going to the France."

"You little...*chiseler!* That signature is as phony as—"

"I assure you, the president's hand held the pen."

"A *prima facie* admission of guilt! You *moved* his hand while he drooled into a cup."

"This document is as legal as anything else in this town. More to the point, my 99 percent approval rating *says* it's legal."

"How quickly power corrupts."

"Applesauce. I simply tailor my arguments to the particular judge."

"It doesn't matter. I won't accept."

The Vice President sat down at his desk and made a tent of his fingers.

"Tell me something. You were our ambassador to the France for—what was it?—eight years?"

"More like nine. What of it?"

"What did you do all that time?"

"What are you implying?"

"Only what the old Chief Justice was implying—that at some point, living abroad, living in the most romantic city in the world, surrounded by women, you might just have acquired some, uh, *hands on* experience in learning about—how did the Chief put it?—where babies come from."

"That's none of your goldarn beeswax." Hand's face was a carving in ice.

"But there's one thing I don't understand. When you were a *prisoner* in the Chief's cage, you came and went as you pleased. Criminy, you even made trips to Canada. You could have escaped back to the

France. You could have rejoined your, well, whoever you might have wanted to rejoin."

"My Vicers needed—I don't—you just stop right—"

"You chose to stay here. Burrsburg: the city you loathe. Why is that?"

"I'm done here. I'm resigning from the Court."

Hand made to go.

"Let me tell you a story."

Learned Hand would not face Reagan, but neither would he leave.

"You fell in love when you were in France. You got married. Hades, maybe you had children. Word got back to Burrsburg. You were pinched and put in jail. During the Orlando crisis, you were sent south to fight. You sneaked behind enemy lines, blew up the whole blessed Haitian army, and became a hero. The Chief, your old friend, put you on the court. Right there—you had your freedom; you could have arranged an escape. You could have gone back to the France. But by then, time had passed. Years."

Hand's defiant back was his only answer. Reagan pressed his attack.

"Too many years! A terrible fear gnawed at you. Your wife had not heard from you. Maybe she had given up. Maybe she had divorced you."

Hand bowed his head.

"I'm sorry." Vice President Reagan stood and placed a hand on the justice's shoulder. "I've never been in love. I have no idea."

Hand settled into a chair. The eyebrow had gone completely limp. Abaddon, the only witness, listened with detachment.

Hand laughed a bitter little laugh. "You can't keep a marriage secret when it's 800 guests in Notre Dame." His laughter stopped. "By the time I *could* get a message to her, I—*couldn't.*"

"But you don't know—"

"This is hopeless. What are the chances—?"

"Greater than nothing."

"No. I can't—"

"You can give up, and then it's all your fault. Or you can go back. There's a risk she'll slam the door in your face. Gehenna, there's a risk she's, well, that she's passed away. But at least—"

Hand's silence completed the sentence.

Reagan played the old man like a fiddle. Without one further word, he put the rolled up parchment in one of the associate justice's hands and a ticket to the France in the other. Ever so gently, Reagan led Hand into the lobby. Waiting clerks encircled Hand to herd him directly to his ship.

Reagan returned to his office. The sky was black. He watched lights from various raven taxis flit about; one of them must be Hand's.

He picked up a report and began to read.

The subject's full name is Elia Kazan. He survived his term at the Warren County Polytechnic School of Mining. Disciplinary records do not mention the specific incident you inquired about, but the record contains many gaps. Rumor suggests Kazan now lives in Manhattan as a leader in a secretive movement dedicated to radical politics and/or puppet theatrics. I hope to have him located by my next report.

So, the main question still went unanswered. Reagan half-hoped he would never hear it. There were so many reasons to expect the worst: Mencken's foot-dragging, Goldberg's vindictiveness, and above all, the lack of oversight on his own part. If Goldberg had not chopped Elia's nose off, then or later, it would have been a miracle. The thought had haunted him for years. He had to learn the truth, no matter what. He did not tolerate cowardice on Justice Hand's part and, by Heaven, he would not tolerate it on his own.

Reagan opened a drawer and pulled out a catalog. He flipped through the glossy pages, looking at the pictures. It had been smuggled in from Haiti. It was a catalog for women's underwear. Haiti being Haiti, very little was revealed—but a starving man will see a feast in another man's leftovers.

That delicate hand emerging from a sleeve! That hair falling gently upon a shoulder!

Reagan pushed the catalog to one side. On his desk lay the draft of an immigration bill presently before Congress.

Speaker O'Neil would not be forgiving. Reagan would have to go over his head and cut deals with individual Congressmen. It would be messy, but the Vice President was an optimist. He would see his reforms enacted. Females would take their place beside men as citizens of the United States of America.

Reagan looked at the catalog again. His finger traced the curve of a hip. Reagan thought maybe he would like to meet some of those females.

He had wanted to ask Learned Hand. The delicacy of their conversation had not allowed it, but now it felt urgent. He would send a coded letter by diplomatic pouch to Hand right away.

Where *do* babies come from?